TRAITORS
FROM INSIDE OUT

BOOKS BY MM JUSTINE

Traitors From Inside Out

Traitors Unleashed

Traitors Beyond Insanity

TRAITORS
FROM INSIDE OUT

BOOK 1: TRAITORS TRILOGY

MM Justine

Matchstick Literary
3000 Atrium Way
Mt. Laurel, NJ 08054
www.matchliterary.com
1-888-306-8885

This book is printed on crème 50lb paper.

Published by Matchstick Literary 01/21/2020

ISBN: 164-550-4530
ISBN: 978-1-6455-0453-5

www.mmjustine.com

For Mom, for all time.

PRAISES FOR TRAITORS FROM INSIDE OUT

'Traitors from Inside Out is a tale of fiction from fact. This story was so in touch with reality that I found it difficult to tell if this novel was a documented non-fiction, or not. If there was ever a fiction to educate the unknowing, this is one such book.' ~ Lou Ron

'This was an erudite, exciting well-written book. It's frightening because it could very well take place right now. A chillingly good read!' ~ R Tianna Lawrence

'A page-turner! I was hooked on the story. This is a great book with great characters and an intense thrilling plot, dealing with delicate issues like corruption, betrayal, cheating, murder, government discrepancies, and Martina's fight to save humanity from the actions of the traitors. I absolutely loved the character of Martina, a strong and independent female protagonist. The book discusses serious issues in a very well crafted manner. Congratulations to the author, MM. Justine.' ~ Shefali Banerji

'Great book, I was hooked. Dark, mysterious and very entertaining. Looking forward to the next book.' ~ James Lovesy

'This book changed my outlook on many things, it brought my attention to the cruelties of this world and also the remarkable work of the author, MM Justine, who created such characters that move people's hearts. Martina, the heroine, is a dauntless woman, who has flaws but her heart is pure. She wishes humanity well, and fearlessly fights for what she believes in, till the end.' ~ Shifa Sarguru

ACKNOWLEDGEMENTS

I owe my deepest gratitude to those who read and commented on the manuscript throughout its development, in particular, Kjell and Håkan, thank you for your constant support, and Elizabeth, you brighten my world. Micheal, Karin, Robert, and Christina, thank you for providing me with wisdom. Josephine, I will never forget the things you have done for me. My very special thanks to Brenda, Ann, and Nasser, you are the guiding light in my life. I acknowledge you for encouraging me to seek my dreams.

ABOUT THE AUTHOR

MM Justine, is a Swedish/Ugandan author. She was born in Uganda, the pearl of Africa, where she grew up on the shores of Lake Victoria, in Entebbe. She has traveled widely, lived, and worked on four continents. She long dreamed of writing stories relevant to our changing world. She finally plucked up the courage to write, The Traitors Trilogy. She is a corporate executive with long experience in both public and private sector. MM Justine lives in Sweden with her family

Chapter 1

Martina Strömstedt Edgren watched dreary clouds swell, hovering dankly above the doleful gathering. She then saw them, the focus of her dread: two black coffins, elegantly surfaced, and dabbed with fresh snowflakes that muffled their glimmer. The cross carefully impressed on the apex of each coffin in a deep, glossy golden colour. She closed her eyes, pushing back tears, striving to bear the grief that weighed heavily on her heart. Mamma and Pappa lay silent inside those two black coffins, no longer revivable.

The mid-March snow lay like a white blanket over the landscape of Woodland Cemetery in Enskededalen, south of Stockholm. The place lay deserted apart from a dozen people standing in a circle, freezing in winter attire. Their sombre gazes focused on two gaping holes in the ground. An owl hooted in the distance as a drizzle of snow whirled in the air. The priest read a verse from the Bible and then said, 'Let us pray.'

Prayer concluded in one echoed 'amen', and the mourners burst into a reverberating, sonorous hymn as if the resounding lyrics would rouse the dead.

Martina's black coat flapped in the wind, and her high heels hurt her frozen feet, magnifying terror in her mind for what was yet to come. Her mind flashed and she flinched recalling her father's words. 'Remember, Martina, to find the other half of the formula. If anything happens to me…find the missing half.'

'Oh, Pappa,' Martina silently moaned. The wind nudged her pink cheeks. She shivered, leaning her languid body against a gentleman in a black coat. He bore a close resemblance to her, almost as if they were twins.

One by one the Group said their sombre farewells and with bowed heads departed to the chapel at the far end of the burial grounds. She regarded relatives and friends who had turned up to share in her grief and was overcome by a surge of tears. She cast a last agonized look at the coffins in the graves as she walked away, supported by the gentleman.

Among the trees lurked a shadow of a man in grey coat and matching hat. He stood at a distance, observing the procession. His facial expression betrayed no reaction to what he saw.

Ambling on, following the trail of mourners, Martina glimpsed the shadowy man in the trees and started. 'Who is there?' she said in a weak voice.

'Where?' responded Sebastian Strömstedt.

'I thought I saw a figure lurking behind the trees,' she said, pointing to the cluster of pine trees to her left. Sebastian turned and surveyed the trees without locating the object of concern. 'There is nothing there,' he said, steering her forward.

The chapel was built in a simple dome, well illuminated by lamps hanging on the walls and from high along the ceiling. There were candles in brass candlesticks on the altar table and several more glowing in sconces. There were twelve rows of fine wooden benches accessible by aisles. The pulpit was raised on an unenclosed stage. Thousands of colourful flowers, from the mourners and well-wishers, adorned the altar.

To the left was a door leading to the reception area and a miniature kitchen. People mingled in the reception room exchanging words of grief, musing on the tragedy that had taken two wonderful lives. Maybe it was just as well they had vacated this planet in the same blow. The mourners held their coffee cups, taking it in small sips.

The church attendant approached Martina and asked if there was anything more he could do for her.

'Ask my cousin Lisa, over there holding a tray of sandwiches,' said Martina.

The solitary stranger, in grey suit with a grave expression on his face, stood observing the mourners. His lack of interest in the occasion was apparent, but his reason for being there was something he kept to himself. Holding his hat in hand, he picked up a sandwich from Lisa's tray, nibbled at it, and asked to speak to Martina. Lisa pointed to the lady in a black skirt suit standing with an elderly man near the coffee table. The man sauntered on, his mind focused on the newly appointed

CEO of Althonat. As he approached her, he thrust his half-eaten sandwich in the trash can in a corner. He rubbed his freezing hands together to warm them up. He approached the elderly man first.

'Good afternoon,' he said as he offered his hand in greeting. 'Quite a funeral; well attended by the elite.'

'What are you doing here?' asked the elderly man without taking his hand, avoiding his gaze as if he wished to dissociate himself from the man. Before the stranger could reply, the elderly man stalked off to the other side of the room to talk to the press.

Martina noted Uncle Stellan's unenthusiastic interaction with the stranger and wondered whether he knew him. She took a sip of her tea as she observed the stranger – his sleek dark hair, chiselled jaw, and grey designer suit. She knew it was the man who had lurked behind the trees. Funeral invitations did not specify attire, which meant black was desired. But his grey suit was in bad taste. He must have been fifty or more. She watched him as he moved towards her.

'Dr Martina Strömstedt?' asked the stranger tentatively.

'Dr Martina Strömstedt Edgren,' said Martina, a stern look on her face mingled with anguish.

'I'm sorry for your loss.'

'Are we acquainted?'

The man did not answer. Instead he stared at her, noticing her pale complexion, sorrowful eyes, and grief-stricken face. She looked younger than her thirty-three years.

'I'm Dr Steven Rangor,' murmured the stranger, and then without warning he added, 'The death of Dr Peter Strömstedt has robbed the international community of a brilliant scientist. Sad his company is without a natural successor. It's bound to fade into obscurity.'

'That's enough,' Martina said in a pitched, firm tone. 'I think you should leave.' Her sharp voice cut through the air like a knife. Whatever signs of softness she had mustered were gone. A hushed silence spread through the room as heads and faces turned, seeking the source of outrage.

Steven Rangor stared back at her icy blue eyes, thinking, what a volatile reaction. She is going to be quite a bundle to deal with.

An urgent voice called her name. Turning towards the voice, Martina saw her brother, Sebastian. He came over and whispered something in her ear as he held her coat open for her to put on.

'It's the hospital,' said Sebastian. 'We must leave.' Martina's face cringed, and they left the room abruptly.

Traffic throbbed in central Stockholm under the afternoon rush hour. The Mercedes accelerated rapidly as it left Ring Road, turned left, and taxied up the driveway to Stockholm South General Hospital. Sebastian parked the car with a jolt. They sprinted out across the parking lot and through the entrance to the elevators. The elevator doors burst open. They entered, and it whisked them to the third floor. They were still panting and gasping when they arrived at the reception desk.

The Nurse, in white top and pants, looked up at Martina from her computer screen. 'Dr Martina Strömstedt Edgren?' she inquired.

'Yes,' said Martina, still panting.

'If you'd like to wait, I'll let the doctor know you're here. The waiting room is through there,' she said, pointing to a white door, a smile on her red painted lips.

'Is he all right?' asked Martina.

'The attending doctor will soon be with you, if you'll please wait.'

'Thank you,' muttered Martina politely, but inside she wanted to scream.

Sebastian opened the door to the waiting room. It was familiar, the same room they'd been coming to for the last three weeks. In a daze, Martina entered the room, confused and exhausted, a silent prayer on her lips: Please, Lord, let him live. Let him live. She sat next to Sebastian, thinking for the first time, what happened?

'What did the Nurse say when she called?'

'Joachim suffered another cardiac arrest,' said Sebastian. 'She called your phone first, but you weren't answering, so she called me.'

A tall man with dark brown hair strolled into the waiting room. He was wearing a black leather jacket and jeans. His hair was ruffled, probably from the wind. He wore a worried look on his face. 'Thomas,' Martina cried as she sprang towards him, and they hugged.

Thomas shook Sebastian's hand and returned his focus to Martina. He noticed her ashen grey face and puffed eyes and knew she had been crying. His heart was bleeding for Joachim, and yet he wanted to be strong for her. He guided her to the chairs, and they sat down.

'Is Joachim all right?' asked Thomas.

'He suffered another cardiac arrest,' murmured Martina. 'We're waiting for the doctor.'

A slender man emerged into the waiting room and gazed around.

'Joachim Edgren,' he called out. Martina's heart flipped as she leaped to her feet, her heart in her mouth. She wanted to know, but then again, she didn't want to know.

'I'm Dr Lennart Lantz,' said the slender man.

'Doctor, we're the Strömstedt Edgren family,' said Sebastian grasping the doctor's hand.

The doctor smiled as he shook Sebastian's hand and then, hesitated briefly as he recognized Martina. 'Martina, it's your son, is it?' he said as he shook her hand and smiled again. 'It has been a while.'

'Yes, Lennart, it is my son,' said Martina forcing a smile.

'I'm Joachim's father,' said Thomas, stretching his hand to greet the doctor.

'Come this way,' said the doctor.

They walked down the corridor to a small patient's room with a single bed and four chairs. They took seats.

'My apologies,' said the doctor as he cleared his voice. 'Joachim suffered another cardiac arrest. We managed to revive his heart. He is stable but in critical condition. However, our greatest concern is that he suffered severe contusions to the head, in the accident, and the MRI shows he still has swelling in his brain. We continue to keep him in induced coma while we mindfully watch and monitor brain swelling.'

'What about internal bleeding?' asked Martina.

'He suffered severe internal bleeding, principally to his rib cage and diaphragm, but we've managed to repair them, and we were able to save his spleen.'

'What is the prognosis?' asked Martina.

'It's difficult to say at the moment. It's possible he could make a complete recovery, but we just have to wait and see.'

'How long is he going to be in a coma?' asked Thomas.

'That depends on how his brain responds. Usually three to four days.'

'Can we see him?' asked Sebastian.

'Yes, you should be able to see him in about thirty minutes. He's been taken to the ICU, on the sixth floor.'

'Thank you, Doctor,' said Sebastian.

Sebastian and Thomas returned to the waiting room while Martina stayed talking to Dr Lantz on an informal level, colleague to colleague.

The ICU on the sixth floor was a stiff, sterile, functional ward with beeping machinery. Joachim was the only patient in the room. Needles and tubes probed his body, while screens and monitors brought second-to-second updates about the status of his condition.

Thomas grabbed a chair, bringing it near the bed. He sat down, watching Joachim's chest wall rise and fall, each time with a shudder that racked his body. He took his son's hand and squeezed it gently.

'Joachim, you're strong, you'll beat this,' he whispered. Sebastian stood at the foot of the bed, his lips moving silently in prayer.

Martina entered the room and Thomas stood up, offering her his chair.

'How is he?' she whispered as she sat, tears pooling in her eyes. Her little boy, fragile and weak, was fighting for his life. He looked pale and lifeless, eyes closed, face blank, with machines puffing to keep him alive. He looked smaller in bed than his five years of age. His hand felt cold to her touch as she kissed it.

'He's a fighter,' said Thomas, gazing at Martina.

'He's cold,' cried Martina. 'Thomas, can you check the closet in the corridor and get an extra blanket?'

Thomas left the room and returned with a blue blanket. He draped it over Joachim. Martina caressed Joachim's hands gently, warming them with hers. She prayed a mute prayer, willing him to live. I love you, Joachim. Please, live. My baby boy, live. She watched machines rising and falling, hissing like a train rolling out of station. She quivered at the sight of her son lying lifeless, so different from the lively boy he used to be.

'Take my jacket,' said Thomas as he took off his leather jacket and wrapped it around Martina's shoulders.

Sebastian went out and returned minutes later with a cup of tea. 'Here, drink this,' he said to her. Martina cradled the cup of tea in her hands, letting the warmth soothe her nerves. She took a sip and felt it begin to thaw her icy desperation.

Nurse Anneli came in and hovered over Joachim, checking his vital signs. 'All his vital signs are good,' she said with a smile.

*****

Thomas and Martina partly lived in the hospital keeping vigil over Joachim. Sebastian came and went on a daily basis.

Two days later Dr Lantz appeared with two nursing assistants.

'It's time to take Joachim to radiology. We're giving him a CT scan to see how his brain is doing.'

'I'll come along,' said Martina. The assistants wheeled Joachim's bed out of the room, and she followed in their wake. It gave Sebastian and Thomas a chance to interact.

'I'm glad you came,' said Sebastian. 'It means a lot to Martina.'

'He's my son too,' said Thomas. 'I couldn't let her go through this alone.'

'I'm glad you're still friends.'

'Oh… Martina and I will always be friends,' said Thomas, smiling.

'I wasn't happy about the divorce. You know that. But then, my sister has a mind of her own. I couldn't tell her what to do.'

'Don't mention it. I appreciate your vote of confidence.'

Sebastian told him about the chaotic time of their parents' death and how Martina was coping – sometimes calm and collected, other times breaking out in an emotional meltdown for days.

'She was very close to her father,' said Thomas.

'It has been tough on her. She was devastated. The first days she was a wreck and went about in a daze, sobbing inconsolably, anguish on her face, saying nothing. She was Father's little girl. I had to call Dr Eneroth to give her something to calm her down.'

'It must have been heartbreaking to lose both of them at the same time.'

The double doors to the ICU opened, and Nurse Anneli wheeled Joachim back. Standing outside were Martina, Dr Lantz, and another woman, deep in discussion. Thomas' eyes locked with hers, and she beckoned him and Sebastian to come forward.

'Renu, this is Mr Thomas Edgren, Joachim's father, and Mr Sebastian Strömstedt is his uncle,' said Dr Lantz. 'Gentlemen, this is Dr Renu Desai, the expert in the field.'

'Thomas, how are you holding up?' asked Dr Desai as she grasped Thomas' hand and then Sebastian's.

'I'm fine,' said Thomas. 'It's my son I'm worried about.'

'He's in good hands,' said Dr Desai.

Dr Desai was a short-haired, elfish woman with a shy smile; she spoke with a soft, fluent Swedish accent.

'As the lead physician for your son,' said Dr Desai, 'I'm pleased to tell you that all is on the right track. His vital signs are stable and strong. We have every confidence he'll make a complete recovery. The brain swelling has stopped and shows signs of decreasing. This is very encouraging, in view of what he's been through.'

'That's good news,' said Thomas.

'Renu, let's leave Martina's family to visit with Joachim,' said Dr Lantz as he turned and left with Dr Desai.

'Great seeing you, Martina,' said Dr Desai.

'Thank you, Renu,' said Martina.

In the ICU, Martina glanced at Joachim in bed, and for the first time since the accident she felt hopeful.

Sebastian's smartphone buzzed and he stepped out of the room.

Martina turned to Thomas. 'I wanted to move him to Althonat Hospital, but Dr Desai wouldn't hear of it.'

'She's right. Joachim is still fragile.'

'He'd be better off at Althonat hospital.'

'Give them a chance, Martina,' said Thomas. 'Let them do their job.'

'How did you know?' she said, changing the subject.

'Sebastian called. I took the next flight out,' said Thomas. 'Look, I'm so sorry about your parents. You and Sebastian have been so busy; we haven't had a chance to talk.'

'It was unexpected,' said Martina. 'They arrived from the States end of February. Mid-winter school holidays had just started. They took Joachim to Idre on a skiing holiday. On their way back, the Volvo plunged down the mountainside. I don't know the details, but Pappa and Mamma died instantly. Joachim was thrown miraculously on snow through the rear windscreen. I don't know how, but I guess he forgot to fasten his seat belt.'

'I thought he was dead when Sebastian called,' said Thomas. 'He said it was bad and I should come immediately.'

Sebastian returned to the room. 'Henrietta sends her love,' he said. 'She wanted to know how Joachim was doing.'

'That's sweet of her,' said Martina.

The next day Martina read to Joachim. The sound of machines puffing and fizzing dominated the room. She held his limp hand in hers as she read to him, squeezing it occasionally, encouraging him to get well. His fingers felt soft and warmer beneath her touch than yesterday. However, she worried about tomorrow, about returning to Althonat after being away for three weeks. This time she would be alone, without Pappa's backing.

Chapter 2

Althonat Towers, a huge twenty-storeyed office building in massive curved steel, concrete, and glass, dominated the skyline in central Stockholm. The legend ALTHONAT TOWERS gleamed discreetly in steel over the glass front doors. Inside, floors sparkled, emulating glistening glass walls.

At a quarter to ten Martina walked through the revolving entrance doors into the enormous white stone lobby. Behind the solid stony desk, two front desk supervisors in immaculate black suit jackets and white shirts smiled pleasantly at her. She smiled as she walked past and headed for the elevators. She smiled again at two passing security men smartly dressed in well-cut black suits. The elevator whisked her to the tenth floor. The elevator doors slid open, and she was in another lobby – again with a white stone desk. A young woman behind the reception desk rose to greet her.

Olof Olausson, Chairman of Althonat Board, stood at the front desk waiting for her. 'Nice to have you back, Martina,' he said as he grasped her hand.

'Thank you, Olof,' said Martina. 'Shall we?'

'Yes, this way, please,' said Olausson, waving his hand to a door to their immediate right.

Martina emerged in the atrium and took her place at the podium. Her natural charisma commanded respect and total silence fell upon the hall. Althonat staff rose to greet the new CEO and remained standing. Dim shafts of light from lamps on walls illuminated the hall, mirroring the gloom of the occasion. It would have been a pleasurable time if it wasn't in honour of the fallen CEO, Dr Peter Strömstedt, and his wife, Helena.

Dressed in charcoal skirt suit, light grey satin blouse, and striking heels, Martina looked fit for her new role. But the burden of stepping into her father's shoes daunted her. She wished she were somewhere else. Standing up there alone, with thousands of faces looking up to her, expectant and anticipating a future at Althonat, made her realize the magnitude of the task she was taking on. Her time had come prematurely; she felt unprepared for the task. Did she have vision enough to lead these people?

'Let's take a minute's silence,' said Martina. Her voice rolled and echoed in the large hall, ushering in a new unpredictable era. Heads bowed. Silence prevailed. When the audience looked up again, the gloom lifted, and the room burst into animated talk.

After the commemoration, Martina rode the elevator to her father's room on the twentieth floor – a room her father rarely used but which nevertheless existed as a symbol of his position in the organization. At the landing, she ran into Leila Eklund, senior researcher at Althonat.

'Martina,' said Leila, batting her heavily mascaraed eyelashes like butterfly wings.

Martina looked at Leila's glossy green mini-skirt, matching tight jacket, and skyscraper heels. Clearly, she understood that Leila needed a course in company dress code. 'Leila,' she said simply.

'I'm so sorry for your loss,' said Leila warmly.

'Thank you.'

'If there's anything you need…anything at all, please don't hesitate to ask.'

'I'll remember that,' said Martina as she moved on, thinking, if not for her brains – and Pappa – she would have fired Leila long ago.

Martina jingled a key in the lock and opened what had been her father's office. A trace of his aftershave lingered in the air, reminding her that he'd been there the day after they'd arrived from the States. The room was bright, spacious, and bedecked in warm colours. A maroon leather sofa set framed half of the room. Books in red leather bindings lined the bookcase along the left-hand wall. Through the window, the sun disappeared behind dark clouds. Martina sat in her father's chair, touching his black Omas Marte fountain pen. A photo of her and Sebastian hung on the opposite wall, reminiscent of better times in Hässelved farm. She must have been ten and Sebastian, thirteen. Despair filled her mind, and that crippling sensation of loss gripped her heart again. Tears flooded her eyes.

The summers spent with family at Hässelved farm, in southern Sweden, held special moments for her. The vast stretches of farmland and forest owned by her grandparents had started Pappa on a curious journey in alternative medicine: natural herbs with beneficial effects on long-term health that could effectively treat human illness. He focused on plants strengthening the immune system, propelling the body into self-healing – miracle healing – without hooking patients on drugs for life.

He set out on continuing research into the efficacy and possible adaptation of herbal therapies to treat and heal illnesses written off as incurable. His interest was to treat the whole person, body, soul, and spirit. He studied energetic medicine and researched chiropractic, acupuncture, homeopathy, and other therapies he knew would combine well with orthodox medicine to cure illness. His work paid off; he engineered a new natural herbal wonder drug, Rensblad, a miracle cure which he planned to integrate with orthodox treatment to provide optimum healthcare to patients.

Martina remembered her grandmother, Eleanor, once boasting, 'We rarely get sick, but if we do, our medicine cabinet is in our backyard.'

Times had turned against her father; no pharmaceutical company could put Rensblad into production. Disappointed, Pappa held on to his new natural medical formula looking for ways to protect it. One day he came home and announced he had resigned from his job at Radium Institute. Mamma was horrified. She knew Pappa was unhappy at work, disillusioned by more medicine in the medical profession than patients getting cured, and by the constant wear and tear on humans. Scooping up patients as if you were repairing dilapidated machines didn't appeal to him.

The publication of his findings on complementing orthodox medicine with alternative medicine as a cure for illness, in *Wonders Medical Journal*, sparked major inquiries into his study. He was discredited for his claims and witch-hunted by the media. His findings were declared false and publicly withdrawn from the journal. He migrated to the States with whatever professional integrity he had left.

A knock on the door startled Martina out of her reverie. She walked across the room and opened the door. It was her personal secretary,

Pia Palm. Pia apologized for intruding and asked if she was ready to meet a visitor.

'Who is it?' asked Martina.

'A Dr Steven Rangor.'

Martina frowned, vaguely recalling the stranger at the funeral. *The man is a piece of work. What does he want?* 'I can't see him today,' she said. 'I'm going to the hospital.'

'He's been coming every day asking for you. He says it is important.'

Martina paused a minute and then changed her mind. 'Okay, I'll see him.' Then she added, 'And, Pia, please see that the research department is updated on the dress code.'

'You ran into Leila?'

'I did. She needs to keep the focus on her job, not her attire.'

'I will take care of it.'

'Thank you. Please, show Dr Rangor to my office.'

Pia nodded and walked to the reception area where the visitor waited.

Martina locked her father's room and headed across the hall to her room.

Rangor walked right in and stopped, arms akimbo. He moved farther into the room, leaving the door ajar, surveying the room: the great red wooden desk before Martina, the elaborate oxblood leather chair she sat on making her look like a queen on a pedestal. The leather sofa set, in off-white colour, adorned half the space, giving an air of importance to the room. He noted the tantalizing view over Stockholm, through the large windows, and breathed a silent sigh. Works of art adorned the right-hand wall; they were still-life paintings of blossoms at different times of the year; peonies, roses, poppies, and cyclamen, all reflecting wonders of nature. The dark background intensified their colours. It was an opulent display of style and exquisite taste, much like the lady sitting on the throne.

Martina moved to meet him. As she grasped his hand, she noticed his glossy black hair and impeccable black suit. He looked as if he had just walked off a magazine page.

'Good afternoon, Mr...'

'Dr Steven Rangor,' said the man as he shook her hand. A firm grasp, she thought.

'Please sit down,' she said, waving to a chair in front of her desk as she returned to her seat.

With a smug smile on his face, Rangor ignored her offer to sit and remained standing, staring down at her. His dark eyes took in her silky blonde hair and flawless complexion. *Such striking beauty*, he thought. Then he shifted his gaze to the works of art.

'Exquisite features of art,' he said. 'This must have been a brilliant artist. He captured the essence of each subject.'

'It was a local artist in southern Sweden,' said Martina as she leaned back in her chair and crossed her legs. She glared at him, noting that he hadn't changed a bit since he had lurked in the woods. His blatant attitude and crude manner infuriated her to the core but nonetheless, her graceful manner prevailed; she wanly smiled at him.

Leaning forward, Martina pinned him with a steady gaze. 'What can I do for you, Mister …?'

'Doctor, Doctor Steven Rangor.'

Hearing his name only elevated her blood pressure. 'What can I do for you?' she asked again.

Finally, Rangor took a seat and stared at her as if he hadn't heard what she asked.

'Dr Rangor, are you in the habit of barging into people's places uninvited?'

Rangor glared at her, surprised by the richness of her tone and her poise; such precision was uncanny in a woman who had just buried her parents.

'Is that your opinion of me?' asked Rangor.

'Get to the point,' said Martina. 'I don't have all day.' In a rage she sprang up, walked across the room, her high heels rapping on the marble floor, and closed the door with a click. In another second she stood hovering over him, her burning gaze fixed on his dark darting eyes, gauging his reaction.

Rangor fidgeted in his chair as the intensity of her scorching gaze translated into a silent power struggle, suffocating him and menacing him in an oppressive manner. He cowered, answering rapidly to divert her attention. 'I…I worked for your father in New York,' he stammered. 'Before he passed on, he appointed me to assist with engineering the new natural booster, *Botanik Herbier.*'

A frown creased Martina's forehead, and a formidable silence fell over the room as she considered the unlikeliness of what he said. She turned and strolled to the window, her heels again echoing on the marble. She stood observing the dull grey sky; dry leafless trees stood like ghosts across the park. The *Botanik Herbier* project was confidential, and only a limited circle of people knew about it. Pappa couldn't have hired Rangor again after what he had done to him. She stood contemplating the hidden motive of the mysterious creature sitting in her office. She heard as Dr Rangor pushed back his chair and walked up to her.

'You seem angry,' said Rangor. 'Did I offend you in any way?'

Martina turned her piercing gaze on him and asked, 'Why did you attend the funeral?'

Rangor was stupefied by the question. 'Why…I…I came to pay my last respects to a friend, a man of vision. Was that wrong?'

Friend? Pappa was not his friend. 'You were not welcome.'

'Well, being American, maybe I erred in some code of conduct. But that doesn't mean I need to apologize for honouring a man in death.'

His overbearing tone, his hooded inquisitive eyes, and his rude manner depressed her soul. She glanced at Joachim's framed photograph on her desk, and images of Joachim lying limp in the hospital bed flashed before her eyes. She took a deep breath. The stranger must leave.

'Your son?' said Rangor, after following her wandering gaze.

'Tell me, are you saying you seek employment at Althonat?' she said, ignoring his remark.

Rangor gave her a vague smile.

'Just answer the question,' said Martina, spurning his inquiry.

'No, I work on a consultant basis,' he abruptly said, emphasising the last two words.

Consultant basis, my foot! The man is a steaming vehicle of concealment personified.

'Dr Rangor, I don't know who you are,' she said, 'and I doubt if my father made any such offer to you. But if he did, I'm not obliged to honour it.' Her face flared up and she made no attempt to disguise her anger.

The truth made Rangor tongue-tied. Martina stood gazing at him, not bothered by his muteness. After what seemed a long time, she stalked to the door, snatched it open, and, in a calm, composed voice, said, 'Get out.'

The doctor began to protest, but she cut him short, raising her voice, but only in volume. Her tone remained calm and impersonal. 'Don't argue with me. I've nothing to discuss with you. Not now, and not in the future.' She stood by the door waiting for him to move. 'Please, leave. I've nothing further to say to you.'

Rangor gazed at her in disbelief. He had heard of her authoritarian leadership style, but that she was stubborn, strong-willed, and unbending was new to him. He yielded and sauntered out of the room like a dismissed dog.

Martina still could not make out the stranger's motive for ingratiating himself upon her family. She couldn't understand why he had turned up at the funeral uninvited, and now this. She moved to her desk, scribbled a note, and left the room. She went downstairs and walked to the end of the corridor, to a door with sign reading, *Security Director, Torsten Widstam.* Torsten was on the phone. He saw her through the glass door and waved her in. She opened the door and entered just as he hung up.

He motioned her to a seat in front of his desk. She sat and crossed her long legs.

'Martina, how're you doing?' asked Torsten, compassion in his voice.

'I don't know. It hasn't sunk in yet. I can't believe they're gone.'

'Give it time,' said Torsten. 'How is Joachim?'

'He's still in a coma.'

'What do the doctors say?'

'That his vital signs are good, but only time will tell.'

'Hang in there,' said Torsten. 'Joachim is young. He's strong. He'll beat this.' Emotionally fragile, Martina blinked rapidly, pushing back the threatening tears.

'Now, what can I do for you?' asked Torsten.

She composed herself, cleared her voice, and said, 'I need a background check on this man.' She handed him a scribbled note and added, 'He's American. You may have to use our resources in the States.'

'I'll see what I can do,' said Torsten.

Soon she was back at the hospital, where she went directly to her son's bed. She focused on Joachim, who lay motionless, his breathing raspy and laboured, the ventilator pushing and sucking as usual. Touching his forehead, she established he was fever free. She stroked his cheek gently and whispered, 'Keep on fighting, baby boy.'

For the first time she noticed Sebastian who sat in a chair, in a corner, watching her. Thomas stood by the window with a cup of coffee in his hands. 'How is he?' she said.

Sebastian's sombre gaze fell on Thomas, who barely whispered, 'They're going to bring him out of his coma today.'

'Good,' said Martina. 'I'm sure he'll be fine. His fever is gone.'

'I know,' said Thomas. 'That's what Nurse Anneli said.'

Through the window the sun sat on the horizon like a big ball of red fire, reviving Martina's spirit and sense of well-being. She closed her eyes and shook her head, slowly clearing her mind of the confusion from babbling with that man Rangor. She joined Thomas at the window. The twilight transported her in memory to when she and Thomas had enjoyed watching sunsets from the balcony of their first apartment. They had just wedded.

'It's beautiful, isn't it?' said Thomas, recalling that she loved sunsets.

'Yes, it is,' she said with a warm smile.

The first time she'd seen him was when she'd graduated from Medical School, at Uppsala University. She'd graduated in the same class as his cousin, Allan. At the graduation ball, Martina noticed that Thomas had eyes on her all evening.

It was the last dance. With a swift foot, he stepped in and asked her to dance. She obliged. His eyes locked on her dazzling gaze. Her striking blue eyes emitted warmth, a benign sensation that shot through his body.

In the weeks that followed, he learned where she lived and quickly started courting her. Soon it was common knowledge that they were dating. They took long walks on Sunday evenings. Those who were outdoors on Sunday heard them talk in silent undertones, though they were too far to discern the words in discussion. They noted his masculine arm around her waist as she leaned on his chest, and they heard the occasional giggle of a woman in the company of her lover. At times they sat at the local café outside campus, sipping copious cups of cappuccinos and gazing deep into each other's eyes. Theirs was a relationship cemented in the sweet powers of compatibility, true affection, and emotions that grew and matured with their ever-changing lives.

Thomas had completed his MBA at Stockholm School of Economics a year earlier, and he was working as a business analyst at an Investment Bank. He procured a decent apartment in Bromma, north of Stockholm.

After graduation Martina travelled to the States to study a Master's degree in paediatrics, as well as specialized certification in alternative medicine and natural therapies. At that time her father founded Althonat in New York, a company dealing in medical research, Complementary medicine and the manufacture of alternative natural boosters.

Dr Peter Strömstedt realized his dream of opening the first Clinic for complementary medicine where medication, tests, and surgical operations were kept at a minimum in preference to alternative natural boosters, chiropractic, acupuncture, naturopathy, homeopathy and psychotherapy. Orthodox medicine and drugs were only used in emergencies of trauma and acute illness, for a limited time. Nothing should disrupt nature. The patient, doctor and therapist partnership was the right approach to adopt.

Martina worked with her father, helping him build the company, and understood that alternative medicine was individualized for each patient because causes and symptoms differed from patient to patient. And yet it was much cheaper and more effective since it treated the problem in depth, not just symptoms.

Martina's relationship with Thomas continued to mature. He visited her regularly, and they travelled on holidays around the States and the Caribbean. Soon, they were married in a simple ceremony at New York's City Hall.

Martina witnessed the devastating effects of autism, ADHD, and ADD in her friends' children and started researching natural alternative therapies for a cure. The results proved successful in the States, and she wanted to bring the same benefits to her home country. She knew of her father's lack of interest in his homeland, but nevertheless she presented the idea to him.

'You'll have to do that on your own,' said Peter Strömstedt. 'And of course, you have my blessings.'

Two years later Althonat qualified through the rigorous red tape of the Swedish medical regulators and opened a branch in Stockholm. Martina spearheaded the operation, making Stockholm the second branch to New York. Althonat's success was based on people's increased awareness about managing health and seeking both alternative boosters and orthodox medicine that delivered cures and resolved illness.

She smiled to herself, realizing the benefits Althonat delivered to people's health. Althonat would continue to grow, and her father's legacy would impact the world. A hooting owl from a nearby tree awoke her from daydreaming. Turning from the window, her gaze settled on Joachim in bed. His sluggish body lying inert jolted her back to reality. Her smile faded.

'Why were you smiling?' asked Thomas.

'Just thinking about life – the clock coursing, propelling us forward; yesterday turning into the past, creating memories; and yet today is a gift, and tomorrow is mysterious.'

'And that made you smile?'

'Yes. I've beautiful memories of the past, though the future is uncertain.'

'You don't have to fret about the future,' said Thomas. 'With your positive attitude, you'll be fine.'

Sebastian left, promising to return the next day. With Nurse Anneli's vigilant watch over Joachim, Martina and Thomas stepped out to get something to eat. They settled for a nearby restaurant across the street.

When they returned, Joachim looked different. It took Martina a moment to realize the suction and push of ventilator had vanished. Joachim was breathing on his own. Relief flooded through her body. She rushed to him, stroked his face, and kissed his forehead. His eyes were closed. Thomas took off to find Dr Lantz for an update, while Martina resumed her familiar seat beside Joachim's bed to maintain her watchful vigil. She took a tissue and gently wiped the spittle from her son's mouth.

She picked up *Otto och flugskräcken*, opened a page, and conscientiously started reading aloud about Otto standing in the glaring sun, gazing at Joppa in her pale pink dress. "'There you are,' said Joppa. 'It's good you came. I have the field hospital today, and I'm Nurse Thérèse. The dolls are the patients who have been hurt in an accident.' 'No,' says Otto, 'I want to be the helicopter pilot who flies the patients to hospital.'" Martina took Joachim's hand in hers as she read to the end. "'And finally, Otto saw a big fly on Joppa's head. Now everything is spoiled. It's rubbing its back tentacles against each other. It's about to attack.'"

'No, Mamma, it was a big black van that attacked,' Joachim rasped. He squeezed his mother's hand and opened his eyes.

Martina started, surprised by Joachim's outburst. But what big black van was he talking about? Her wonderment lasted only a moment. Instantly, she was engulfed by the joy of her son awakening.

Exhilarated sensations ran through her body. Her baby boy was back. He was all right. She looked deep in his sleepy blue eyes and kissed him on the cheek. Joachim smiled wearily at her.

'Oh, Joachim, you're back!' she cried. 'He's back. Joachim is back!' she said aloud, tears spilling down her cheeks. She wrapped her arms around him, and kissed his forehead, her tears moistening his face.

'Mamma, why are you crying?' asked Joachim, his voice hoarse. 'Where are we?'

Martina cradled his face in her hands, gazed in his face, and said, 'You're in hospital.' Joachim frowned, and Martina wondered if it was because he couldn't remember the accident or because he was touched by her display of affection.

'I love you, Joachim. It's a blessing you're back,' said Martina, as hope spread like an elixir through her veins.

She pressed the red bedside button, and Nurse Anneli appeared at once, followed by Thomas with Dr Lantz.

'He's awake,' said Martina. Thomas smiled, and the tension around his eyes vanished. Wow! Martina hadn't noticed Thomas was tense all the time. Thomas hugged her briefly as he moved near the bed, gazing at Joachim.

'Oh, dear boy, you're back,' said Thomas, a broad smile on his face. He bent over, touching the boy's forehead, caressing his hair. 'You gave us a scare.'

Joachim looked at his father with an impassive face, registering nothing. 'Pappa, I'm thirsty.' Thomas looked around and rested his gaze on Nurse Anneli.

'I'll get water,' said Anneli as she hurried from the room. When Thomas looked again at Joachim, the boy's eyes were closed and he had a blank look on his face. Thomas panicked and his face darkened with worry, afraid he had slipped into a coma again.

'Joachim?' said Thomas.

'I'm here, Pappa,' Joachim muttered as his eyes fluttered open. Nurse Anneli appeared with a jug of ice water and a glass. She filled the glass with water and offered it to Joachim. Thomas raised him up a little higher on his pillows. Joachim took the glass and drank to his fill.

'More,' said Joachim. Nurse Anneli refilled his glass. He sipped it slowly this time, till the glass emptied.

Dr Lantz moved close to Joachim's bed with a warm smile on his face. 'Feeling better, Joachim?' he said.

Joachim looked at him impassively.

'I'm Dr Lantz, I've been in charge of you since you came to hospital. How are you feeling?'

'I'm okay,' muttered Joachim shyly.

'Nurse Anneli will check your vital signs, then I'll do a thorough examination. If all is well, you may go home tomorrow.' The doctor turned and smiled at Martina and Thomas. 'He's such an adorable child,' he said.

'Thank you, doctor,' said Thomas, grasping the doctor's hand. Martina walked Dr Lantz to the door, seeking reassurance that Joachim would be fine at home. They stood talking for a while, and then Dr Lantz smiled again and left.

*****

The next morning Martina sat in the office, reading paperwork and answering e-mails. The IT department had transferred her father's correspondence to her inbox mail, which was brimming. Some people didn't even know he had died. Working quickly, she went through the lot, answering all of them. A tough exercise, imparting sorrowful news to people. Some business mail needed a detailed response. She moved those items to a special folder to tackle later.

A white envelope emblazoned with the word *Confidential* lay on her desk. She promptly opened it. It was from Torsten – results of the background check on Dr Steven Rangor. It stated that he was born on the twenty-fifth March 1968. Business owner: Medical Solutions Consultancy, New York. One of the best neurologists and researchers in the USA. Dr Peter Strömstedt hired him in the founding phases of Althonat to assist with analysis of the first natural boosters before they hit the market. He was married to wife number one, Suzanna Hathaway. They had two sons. Six years later they went through a bitter divorce. Shortly after, Suzanna died under mysterious circumstances. Dr Steven Rangor remarried, and divorced. Details of his second marriage are scant and unsubstantiated. Martina read on.

She paused. The second wife, also divorced…who could that be? And what about the three missing years before he surfaced in Stockholm? Where had he been? Was that the clue to his sudden arrival in Stockholm? She hurriedly stashed the papers back in the envelope and put it away in the desk drawer. Further investigation must be done on this man.

Out of the blue she drifted, remembering Joachim's first words when he awoke from the coma: 'Mamma, it was a big black van that attacked.' What did he mean?

Her phone buzzed. She answered, 'Martina.'

'It's Thomas.'

'How is Joachim?'

'He's fine. Dr Lantz said he can go home today.'

'That's wonderful news,' said Martina with a wide smile on her face.

'Listen, a police detective called. He wanted to speak to Joachim about the accident.'

Martina stopped to think, *what is wrong with law enforcement officers? My son just woke from a coma. For God's sake, let them back off.*

'Martina?'

'I'm here, Thomas. We can't allow it. I don't want him traumatized.'

Thomas deferred, not wanting to engage in a heated discussion with Martina. Maybe she was right; she was the doctor, and a paediatrician at that.

'I'll speak to the detective,' said Thomas. 'Are you coming soon?'

'I'm coming to pick you up, in an hour. It will be great to have Joachim home.'

'Yes, it will be terrific,' said Thomas. 'See you then.'

Arriving at Slottsville house, Martina's home in Lidingö, north of Stockholm, Thomas helped Joachim out of the car, noticing the place he'd once called home hadn't changed much even though everything was under snow, including the sea that gleamed in shards of ice. The home had been their wedding gift from Martina's parents, but when they divorced, she'd bought him out.

Astrid, the housekeeper, opened the door, and Joachim jumped into her arms. 'Welcome home, Joachim,' she said. 'Good afternoon, Mr Edgren.'

'Good afternoon,' said Thomas as he hung his leather jacket in the hallway railing. The white walls in the hallway were adorned with still life oil paintings. He moved down the hallway towards the opening into the great room. A set of new chestnut chesterfield armchairs encircled a contemporary stone mantel fireplace. An enormous set of ceiling-to-floor glass doors opened onto the outdoor room, overlooking the shimmering sea. To the right, as ever, stood the sweeping staircase with its elegant polished wooden balustrade. He noticed family photos on the wall, above the walnut chest. Photos of Joachim stood where the wedding portraits had been. A kind of mocking symbolism tore at his heart as he realized the future he would never have with the woman he loved, as it had been withdrawn from his life.

'Pappa, I want to go see Leo,' said Joachim, startling him out of his reverie.

'Ask your mother, boy.'

'You may go, Joachim, if you feel up to it,' said Martina, 'but only for a short while.'

Joachim ran to the neighbours' to play with Leo. Astrid came in with herbal tea for Martina and coffee for Thomas. She announced dinner would be ready at six. Martina and Thomas sat in the great room talking, eating blueberry muffins. They tasted good. Martina realized this was the first time since the accident she had eaten without being tormented by nausea.

'I want Joachim to come stay with me in London,' said Thomas.

Shocked, Martina lowered her cup of tea, and put it down on the table wondering what had brought this on. 'Is this about custody?' She knew the custody battle was long settled, but it flared up whenever Joachim's safety came into question.

'He will be safer with me.' Thomas recognised he was treading on delicate ground. But he didn't care; it was now or never. He was hurt that Martina had initiated the divorce for reasons he thought trivial. For his part, he had never really understood her reason for divorcing him. His son growing up without a proper family disturbed him, and now this exposure to risk unsettled him.

Martina closed her eyes momentarily, and took a deep breath. If only she could regain her peace of mind and her equilibrium, she would be all right. After her parents' death, Joachim's ordeal, and Rangor's deliberate deception, she didn't need Thomas hacking at her.

'No, Joachim stays here with me.'

'Martina, you can't protect him. We almost lost him.'

'And it's my fault?' she queried.

'I didn't say that.'

Rays of light from the window danced on her golden hair, cascading to her shoulders. Thomas drank in the sight of her fine long legs and longed for the sweet sound of her voice – tender when she wasn't angry. He knew he was still in love with her.

'Move Althonat Headquarters to London; come live there with Joachim.'

'You've already figured it out, haven't you? Trying to run my life again,' she said. 'That is exactly why I divorced you.'

'Martina, re-marry me,' blurted Thomas.

Where did that come from? He must be joking. But his face was without the tiniest smile. 'Is that what this is all about…marriage?' asked Martina, her voice stern and unimpressed.

Thomas said nothing but gauged her curt reaction. He was half disappointed, half hurt. He wanted to ask her if she no longer felt anything for him but dared not, sensing it wasn't her favourite subject. He remembered they had connected well at the hospital. The strong bond between them persisted. He hoped Martina tapped into those feelings too.

The circumstances contributing to their unexpected rendezvous were unpleasant but rekindled an old flame familiar to both of them. He understood Martina's rejecting a reunion, in view of her unfortunate circumstances; the unexpected responsibilities placed on her shoulders. He relented, comforting himself that the timing was wrong.

'Thomas, you're out of line. You may see Joachim whenever you like, and he can come visit you. That's what we agreed on.' She changed the subject: 'Are you hungry?'

'No, I think I'll pass on dinner,' said Thomas. 'I'd better get going. Where is Joachim?'

'In the kitchen with Astrid,' said Martina. 'Astrid cooked, you know. She will be disappointed if you don't dine with us.'

They supped in the dining room, keeping their differences at bay and making civilized conversation.

After dinner, Thomas said goodbye to Joachim and left to prepare for his early morning flight to London.

In her bedroom, Martina switched on the art deco table lamp, a charming figure of a young girl in bronze resting on a marble base. She gazed at the figure, looking so serene and unaffected. Where had her serenity gone? Why was everything chaotic, sad, clouded, and dark? She remembered causing havoc when she had announced her divorce; her mother wouldn't hear it; her father was disappointed but respected her decision; Sebastian told her right out that it was improper and that she should work it out with Thomas. She wondered if she had divorced him in haste. How could it be that he wanted to tie the knot with her again – that he was still in love with her? She shook her head, not comprehending what he'd said.

She wandered to Joachim's room, opened the door slightly, and peered inside. He was asleep. Punctilious Astrid must have read bedtime stories to him and tucked him in.

As she returned to bed, her mind flashed back to Rangor. Why was he engaging in deceitful pretence? And how did he know about Botanik Herbier? Pappa couldn't have told him about it, after what he had done to him. Somebody at Althonat must be leaking information to him.

Chapter 3

On Friday afternoon white fields sparkled with snow, but the sun braced the clear blue sky with a promise of spring. At Norrtälje, the red Mercedes Coupé thrust forward on the gravel road towards Väddö. Martina drove another ten minutes. In the distance, the red storied mansion lay concealed behind trees. She turned in the driveway and wheeled the car round a left bend, taking in the snow-capped gardens against a fall in sterling. She continued uphill at a slower speed. The Strömstedt family country home, Landegrind house, was in full view. She parked the Mercedes beside Sebastian's Lexus LS and stepped from the car. She paused and took a deep breath of the cold country air. Sebastian had arrived, from Stockholm, with Joachim and Astrid earlier in the day.

In the hallway, she heard Joachim playing with the neighbour's son upstairs.

Astrid came downstairs. 'Did you have a pleasant drive?' she said kindly.

'Yes, traffic was light and the weather mild and sunny.'

'The weather is supposed to be fine all weekend, though I'm not sure.' Her eyes gazed at the darkening sky through the window as she picked up the bags and scurried upstairs. Halfway up, she turned and said, 'Dinner will be ready when you want.'

The hallway opened up into a large living area where three off-white shell-back armchairs surrounded a stone fireplace. The soft cushions scattered on chairs were steeped in varied colours: brown, orange and maroon. The décor blended with white walls, mirroring the Slottsville house in Stockholm. A mixture of dark and light wood and contemporary abstract art gave a rich ambience to the room.

Logs blazed heartily in the fireplace, casting a glow over the stone masonry and a reassuring flicker into the darkest corner, her father's rocking chair stood near the fireplace, reminding her of his absence.

Her mother's baking books lay on the centrepiece glass table, just as they had on the day they had left for Idre. She missed her father's robust voice and her mother's chattering about unimportant things. Her eyes wandered through the large windows beyond the front porch and into a birch tree. Two blue tits hopped and played; a mother and its baby. She smiled, happy Joachim was home.

'There you are,' said Sebastian as he walked in through the sliding French doors. He came forward, and kissed her on the cheek. 'I didn't expect you so soon.'

'I finished what I was doing early,' said Martina. 'I wrote thank-you notes.'

'A small gesture but very important,' said Sebastian. 'What about the flowers? There were too many flowers.'

'I sent them, as charity, to patients at Althonat Hospital.'

'That was a lovely gesture.'

'Sit down. We need to talk,' said Martina as she settled in her father's rocking chair.

'What?' asked Sebastian as he sank in the shell armchair.

'Are you familiar with the name Steven Rangor?'

A frown came over Sebastian's brow, and then his face clouded. 'A Dr Steven Rangor, you mean?'

'Yes, the American?'

'Why? He briefly worked for Pappa, in New York, as a consultant.'

'He was at the funeral, and he came to the office to see me the other day.'

'What is he doing in Stockholm?' asked Sebastian. 'It can't be that he came for the funeral. What did he want?'

'He said Pappa assigned him to work on Botanik Herbier.'

Sebastian sat upright, and paled with fear. 'You didn't believe him, did you?'

'No, of course not.'

Sebastian eased back in the chair and exhaled but his eyes were still furious at his sister. 'He's an imposter,' said Sebastian, his voice deep and dark. 'Don't go near him.'

'I didn't go near him. He came to me.'

'Don't allow him anywhere near you,' thundered Sebastian. 'You're CEO; you need to be vigilant.'

'Why are you so angry? I haven't done anything.'

'You asked if I was familiar with the name,' said Sebastian. 'As if you don't know what he did to Pappa!'

'Pappa never talked much about it. Besides, I just wanted to be sure he was the man in question.'

'Now you know, be careful.'

'Back off, Sebastian. It was just a question.'

Astrid came in and announced dinner was ready.

They gathered around the dark wood table in the kitchen and ate in silence. Martina was watching Joachim. She was a bit worried about his poor appetite. He hardly touched his potatoes au gratin and beef steak.

'Drink your milk, Joachim,' said Martina.

'Mamma, I can't.'

'Can I bring you some nypon soup instead?' asked Martina.

'Yes, mamma.'

Martina walked to the kitchen and returned with a bowl of nypon soup. She sat next to him and fed him with a spoon. Joachim ate to his fill, and asked if he can go to bed.

'Yes, sweetheart, said Martina as she kissed his hair. 'I'll come and tuck you in.'

'Goodnight, Uncle Sebastian,' said Joachin as he rose from the table.

'Sleep well, Joachim,' said Sebastian.

After putting Joachim to bed, Martina retired to the study while Sebastian sat in the TV room catching up on news.

An urgent buzz disturbed the evening silence – the doorbell. Sebastian glanced at his watch. It was past eight. He rose and walked to the hallway, peered through the viewport, and saw a woman and a boy. It was the neighbour, Ebba Strand, and her son. He opened the door.

'Come in, Ebba,' said Sebastian.

'Good evening, Sebastian,' said Ebba. 'I'm sorry to intrude upon you but I had to come.'

Ebba walked in, guiding the boy by the arm. The boy, about eight years old, seemed oblivious, drooling and grinning at empty space.

'What is it?' asked Martina as she came into the room and motioned Ebba to a seat. Sebastian excused himself, returning to the TV room.

Ebba sat cuddling her son who constantly rocked himself, a stunned look on his face. The boy, handsome with grey-green eyes, the image of his mother, was wearing grey gym pants and a black T-shirt.

'It's my son, Nicholas. He's taken a turn for the worse; he keeps chewing his toes. Look, they are all bloody.' At a glance, Martina saw he wore just socks with no shoes. The socks were soaked, oozing blood. 'He has severe mood swings; he kicked holes in his bedroom door, broke the car windshield, and is up all night giggling, moving furniture. He even spat on a woman in the street.'

'How long has this been going on?' asked Martina.

'It's two weeks now. It seems something flares up in him, triggering a chain reaction of bizarre behaviour.'

Martina knew Nicholas had been normal till he got a vaccine shot at three years of age. He had suffered an immediate high fever, lost eye contact, communication capabilities, and developed behaviour problems.

Observing the boy, Martina suspected the vaccine had caused a toxic internal environment in his system, bringing about his condition.

'We need to do an evaluation. Bring him to Althonat Hospital on Monday,' said Martina.

A desperate look flickered in Ebba's eyes, and she drew her son closer. Martina read her mind.

'I'll give him something to calm him down so he can sleep. And I will bandage up his feet. But you must bring him to the Clinic f—'

In mid-sentence, Martina heard an aggressive pounding on the door. It was a pounding, not a buzz on the doorbell. Sebastian returned and opened the door, anger evident on his face. A man in jeans and T-shirt stormed in. His face steamed as red as a crayfish. It was Patrick Strand, Ebba's husband. Without greeting or acknowledging his neighbours, he strode to the living room, grabbed his wife by the arm, and swept her and Nicholas towards the door. He stumbled against the centrepiece table, knocking over an Orrefors crystal bowl. He ignored it as it teetered and toppled to the floor, shattering to shards. Martina uttered a quack. A stink of alcohol permeated the room as Patrick led his family out.

'Hey, watch it,' said Sebastian, gauging the man's move, ready to take him on.

Patrick pretended nothing had happened. Ebba did as she was told and guided her son out in step with her husband, head bowed, avoiding eye contact with Martina.

'Patrick, please, let me take care of Nicholas,' cried Martina. 'Ebba is right.'

'My son is no guinea pig; to hell with unscientific medicine,' growled Patrick as he exited.

Crushed, Martina crouched on the sofa, frustration deep in her heart. Patrick Strand was a headless clone, a stupid, rigid man. He constantly rejected natural alternative therapies as treatment for his son, yet as she had explained countless times, it was the best cure for Nicholas' condition.

Martina dragged her limp body up from the sofa and headed for the study to do some work. She had barely sat down when she heard a tormented wail from Joachim's bedroom. In a moment, she was up the stairs and in his room. She flipped on the light switch. Kneeling on his bedside, she touched his shoulder, shaking him gently, dragging him from the depth of his nightmare.

Joachim kicked, wailed and writhed in bed, eyes closed.

'Joachim, Joachim,' said Martina. 'I'm here. Mamma's here.' She sat on the bed and cuddled him in her lap.

He started, opened his yes, and gazed around erratically. 'What, Mamma?' he said, wide-eyed, fear on his face.

'You had a nightmare,' said Martina.

'Mamma, I'm scared. Sleep here with me.'

'Oh sweetheart, yes, yes.' She stretched out on the bed beside him. 'What're you scared of?'

'The big black van.'

'The van?' said Martina, compassion, and concern in her voice.

'Like the one in the accident. I see it in my sleep.'

Like the one in the accident? Martina silently marvelled. *A van was involved in the accident, and no one from the police investigation mentioned this? How come?*

'What do you remember about the van?'

'Not much, just that it was big and black,' said Joachim as he yawned.

'What did the van do?' asked Martina.

Joachim did not answer, but turned in bed and faced the wall. When she looked, he was asleep.

'I love you, Joachim,' she whispered and got off the bed, flipped the light switch and tiptoed out of the room, leaving the door open a crack.

Martina and Sebastian attended the reading of the will the next day. The thousands of acres of commercial land, plantations and forestland in South Carolina, USA, were to continue under Althonat management. The plantations and forest were to continue supplying raw materials for manufacture of natural alternative boosters. Their parents' home on the property was to be leased out to an institution furthering awareness of natural alternative health therapies. The Strömstedt family home in New York and Landegrind house in Stockholm were to be jointly owned by Martina and Sebastian. Althonat remained a family business.

Sebastian returned to his duties as military attaché at the Swedish embassy in Washington, D.C shortly after the reading of the will. His wife, Henrietta, and two daughters had stayed in Washington. The girls didn't want to miss school.

Chapter 4

Stellan Strömstedt glared a little harder at the flickering flames in the log fire. The firelight glinted in the glass of amber liquid clutched in his hand. He couldn't believe his brother was gone – dead and buried. His mood shifted between sorrow and the anger that seemed to pierce his heart over and over. His mouth curled in a grim thin line, seeking to quell his dejected mind, his fathomless gloom.

Thoughts of grief transported him to the graveyard, standing before the oblong boxes in which lay corpses. At first, he had betrayed no emotion, but when the priest started reading from the Bible, a spark of remorse had fluttered his heart and a tear dropped from his eye. His younger brother was gone – Peter, the man he'd learnt to contend with. They had scrapped over a dispute that lingered dark and deep, unresolved till the time of his departing. Peter Strömstedt was a man of many shades. Unlike him, distant and at times a discourteous figure; he had a flare for throwing himself at the wind, flying and tasting the unknown.

Stellan took a swig of the amber liquid in his glass, savouring the burning sensation as it glided down his throat. He winced and swallowed hard; then he put down the glass and started twiddling his fingers, as though unnerved by a past he could not change.

Growing up in Hässelved farm, in southern Sweden, they had been close; Peter studied medicine, he studied biology. In their leisure time they worked farmland with their parents and revelled in the fascinating discovery of alternative plant therapies. Even with their parents gone, they long continued to work side by side till unforeseeable winds turned the wheel of destiny, plunging them into a paralyzing feud. He retracted his thoughts, winding the clock back, unsure whether, given another chance, he would have acted differently under similar circumstances.

He blinked, searching for solace for his wretchedness. Things had just got bad; fate played a dirty game in his hand, causing him to lose his foothold and slip into the claws of temptation. Yet even as he sat there, guilt wrapped tightly around his heart like barbed wire around a piece of flesh. He felt his actions were well motivated. He needed to survive to get rid of his problems. Flames flared and flickered, dancing in the heat, and his anguished face twisted before the current of his thoughts.

He uttered a disconcerted yelp, almost a sob of regret at the tides that characterized their stormy relationships. He knew that, though his brother was dead and buried, his shadow loomed large in his life like a trapped spirit in a haunted house.

Chapter 5

Dalernesund, a picturesque small community in Haninge, stood on the shores of the Baltic Sea surrounded by variegated landscapes. Small villas and summer cottages dotted the shoreline, making Dalernesund a popular harbour for further travel to the southern archipelago. The tourist industry and water sports were popular in summer. Its strategic location had been important in the past as a meeting point for naval operations on the Baltic Sea.

Among the tranquil coverts lay a majestic villa well hidden from wandering eyes. Only a chosen few had seen the inside walls of Vittaby Villa.

In a sterile room Nurse Birgit Halonen held a new born baby in her arms. She set the baby on a table and pricked its finger for a drop of blood. This she put it in a vial, which she dropped in a machine which returned information on a computer monitor: cell mutation ninety per cent, permanent disability ninety-nine per cent, weakened body ninety-eight per cent, and life expectance thirty per cent.

A short stocky man with reptilian eyes entered the room and peered at the strange-looking little creature – its skin pale and heavily wrinkled, webbed tiny feet kicking at the ends of its emaciated little legs. The irises of its eyes were green, with tiny black pupils.

Dr Fritz Grenzken glared at the baby, and his cold eyes turned charcoal black. He examined it, poking its ribs, joints, stomach, and head with his hand and fingers. He held it by the legs with one hand and poked its spine and bottom with his knuckles. The baby shrieked like a mouse in a mousetrap.

Nurse Birgit winced, aghast at his cruelty. 'Enough,' she snapped, grasping the doctor's arm, and snatched the baby out of his grip.

The old doctor walked out of the room to the adjoining room. His he-goat beard and sagging jowls made him look older than his sixty-four years. He peered at the lifeless body of a young woman, who lay naked on a bed, and images of his father flooded his mind. The old man had spent long hours telling him about the genetic experiments he'd conducted on children in Nazi Germany. In Dachau concentration camp, he had infected subjects by injecting disease into their bodies and then treated them with drugs to test their relative efficiency; these were experiments conducted without the subjects' consent, and a thousand had died as a result. Gustav Grenzken was a loving father.

In 1947 German doctors were captured and put on trial in the USA. However, some managed to get away. The Red Cross mistakenly issued travel documents to many Nazis in the post-war chaos. This gave many mass murderers, like Gustav, an opportunity to evade capture. He escaped to Sweden with his son, Fritz, and was granted political asylum. He bought Vittaby Villa in Dalernesund, with Nazi money he'd smuggled out of Germany. He was a widower and raised his son alone, encouraging him to study medicine. When Gustav Grenzken died, Fritz took over his medical business, establishing a research facility and building extension wings including Devilund lab, a covert Clinic in the basement. He lived and worked in Vittaby Villa. He offered Nurse Birgit the west wing, self-contained with a living room, bedroom, bathroom, and kitchenette.

The baby's shrieking drew Fritz back from his daydreaming. He threw a white sheet over the woman's dead body and sauntered back to Birgit. The baby writhed and wriggled like a worm in Birgit's hands, crying till it was blue.

'Prepare her for post mortem,' said Grenzken.

'Who, the baby?' asked Birgit, irritation in her voice.

'No, the woman.'

'Now?'

'When you're finished,' said Grenzken as he walked out of the room.

In World War II, Hitler invaded Finland. Birgit's father was a navy officer. He was killed in the Lapland war between Finland and Nazi Germany. As war intensified, Birgit was transferred with other Finnish 'war children' to Sweden. She joined the Red Cross, taking courses in nursing and the German language. She found it difficult to get employment, but one day as she scanned the ads, she found that a

German-speaking Nurse was needed at Devilund Clinic. She jumped at the opportunity and got the job. The pay was generous.

The young woman who had died in childbirth had been brought in under mysterious circumstances. Dr Grenzken prescribed daily doses of injections administered by Nurse Birgit. Usually after the onset of injections the young woman groaned and moaned in pain. She complained of a creeping sensation under her skin, as if insects were moving under the surface. Grenzken prescribed more injections to alleviate the problem, but the problem was never resolved. It became a vicious circle of drug addiction till she went into labour prematurely.

Nurse Birgit took care of the motherless infant, feeding it powdered milk in a bottle. It showed no great appetite and never gained weight. The constant whining and whimpering was one thing Nurse Birgit could put up with, but when it started shedding skin like a snake, she freaked out. She summoned Dr Grenzken to the Nursery and poured out her emotional frustration on him.

She flipped the sheet off the baby's body. 'Look. Look at its skin. It's moulting like a snake,' she roared.

Grenzken glared at the infant's raw, slimy multi-coloured new skin and flinched, but maintained a normal demeanour. He was thinking the medicine given to the mother must have been too strong. He observed the infant's unnatural transparent skin, webbed feet, and signs of early aging in its face, understanding it was no longer human.

'Cover it up,' he said. Even he was repulsed by the tiny creature.

The infant lasted three weeks and passed away. For four days after the baby's death, Dr Grenzken remained confined to his basement laboratory, carrying out experiments and analysing post-mortem results of mother and child. Nurse Birgit observed him, keeping tabs on him. She noted that he only came down for meals, and each time she saw him, he seemed less at ease. She asked if there was anything he needed help with. He eyed her, said nothing, and went about his business.

A week later, four men in designer suits, well-groomed, and a woman with short hair landed at Vittaby Villa. Dr Grenzken closed the door and presented results of the experiment on mother and infant.

'It's a ground breaking new vaccine, targeting the DNA in a baby's somatic cells,' said Dr Grenzken, spitting out each syllable as if it were poison on his tongue.

'What does that mean?' asked the man in horn-rimmed glasses.

'It means Life-Vaccine injected in mother, incorporated in baby's genetic structure causing genetic malformations.' He paused for effect as he glared at the gathering. 'A change in DNA sequence within the baby's genes resulted in a new character, a trait unlike the parental type.'

A tremulous sigh swept through the room, heads turned, and faces glanced at each other revealing sentiments of unspoken words. Grenzken eyed his guests suspiciously, pondering if their moral barometer was high enough to reverse the course of their sin.

The man with silver-grey hair cleared his voice and said, 'We know this is a controversial illicit vaccine trial in mother and child. Highly sensitive too, since the mother was a minor, but how come she got pregnant?'

'That's the big question,' thundered the horn-rimmed glassed man. 'Offspring, normal or abnormal, was never the desired result. Remember, Fritz, our goal is population control.'

'That's true, but we're still in development stages of Life-Vaccine,' said Grenzken. 'We intend to perfect it soon. Our goal is to crimp the uterus to the size of a pea. That will eliminate chances of pregnancy.'

'Are effects of Life-Vaccine detectable in the body?' asked the woman.

'No, not detectable,' said Grenzken, firmly shaking his head. 'By the time effects of the vaccine are felt, the organs are damaged by Life-Vaccine. Organ failure is the main cause of death. That way the real cause of death is disguised.'

'May I ask the contents of this Life-Vaccine?' asked the man with a nose like a beak.

Grenzken shot him a fitful glare and evasively lowered his gaze to a pile of paper on table.

'Fritz, answer the question,' said the beak nose.

Grenzken raised his cold eyes, trying to maintain a professional attitude, though he believed details were a thing best kept to himself. Divulging them undermined confidentiality.

'Well, it contains a portion of Rensblad, the wonder drug, spiced with monkey kidney, brain-eating amoeba, pesticide, DNA of cancer virus, caterpillar eggs, mercury, and aluminium,' said Grenzken with a quaver in his voice. These were only some of the ingredients.

'Jesus Christ!' Uninhibited whispers rustled through the room.

'Wait a minute – Rensblad? What the hell are you people doi…?' said the elderly man, who until now had quietly sat twiddling his fingers with a kind of nervous tic. Suddenly animated, his icy blue eyes turned darker.

'Hold it and calm down,' said Grenzken, standing up to make his point. 'This is just in the development stages. In the end we might not use the Rensblad portion.'

The finger-twiddling man swallowed hard and relented, hoping it would come to that.

'Once Life-Vaccine is perfected,' said the woman with short hair, 'our target is to inoculate all females above age nine. The marketing division, at Citaraph pharmaceutical, should start plans to execute accordingly.' Her voice sounded rapid and frosty as she added, 'Over population is wearing down world resources. We are committed to bringing a balance between humanity and resources.'

'You confirm you'll use it when perfected?' asked the man with horn-rimmed glasses, his stern gaze directed towards the woman.

'Yes, we'll use it,' said the woman. 'That's what we ordered.'

Silence fell upon the room as everyone eyed each other, at first tentatively, and then heads nodded in unison. A faint smile crossed Grenzken's face as he raised his glass of mineral water in a dubious toast.

'That won't be necessary, doctor,' smirked the silver-haired man, revolted by Grenzken's gesture. 'I guess that's it.' He quickly took up his briefcase and vacated the room without any social graces of thank-you or goodbye. The others followed in his wake.

Dr Grenzken retired upstairs to his living quarters. The meticulously furnished rooms made lavish living but appeared dampened by the contrasting sombre serpentine-striped wallpaper. He hated that wallpaper, and one of these days he would change it. It reminded him of the numbing sensation gnawing at his limbs; a global depopulation vaccine to save resources for the rich.

Perfecting the study would not be an easy task. Test trials required ample numbers of female participants. Where was he going to find them?

He walked to the living room, crossing straight to the liquor cabinet. After studying the well-stocked bar, he took a glass and filled it with whisky. He gulped it down in one shot, flinched, enduring the bitter sting in his throat for the relief that would follow.

Chapter 6

Arriving at Althonat Towers, Martina saw a press photographer lurking outside. Although she hated the press, she flashed a smile and waved her hand as he took her photograph. She had long learnt to be friendly with the press. She went through the revolving doors and smiled at the desk supervisors as she headed for the elevators. She revelled in Joachim's recovery. He had stayed home with Astrid, still sick listed on doctor's orders. In a few weeks he should be able to return to day care.

Her encrypted private smartphone buzzed as she stepped out of the elevator. She dug for it in her bag and pressed the button. 'Martina,' she answered.

She tensed, listened, and then suddenly she stood still.

'Thank you, I'll check my email,' she said through gritted teeth and hung up. The change in mood was instant. Gone was the happy face, replaced by a long one. She opened her office door engrossed in thought. With a deliberate stride she walked to her desk and sat down, dumbfounded. Then she fired up her computer. Her hands flew over the keyboard as she logged in. She opened her encrypted mailbox. Intently, she gazed at the monitor, reading one item.

From: *Scorpio*
Subject: *Confidential: Illicit Life-Vaccine*
To: *CEO, Althonat*

Life-Vaccine is ready. It contains portion of Rensblad. Highly controversial but patented, and ready to roll on market. See effects in attachment.

Sincerely,
Scorpio.

Martina murmured, 'They're using Rensblad component? That is insane!'

She clicked on the attachment, and an image popped up on screen: a photo of a crinkled, skinny new born baby with ribs and spine sticking out, her arms like string beans and legs like toothpicks. No fat roll anywhere. Its eyes were dark green with minute pupils. A chilling sensation jolted through Martina's body like an electric current and settled in her spine. The image jarred her mind like an unexpected violent blow. She took a deep breath, regaining temporal equilibrium, and gazed out of the window in disbelief.

'What the hell is wrong with these lunatics?' she cried out loud. The words carried a sense of sorrow. She fell silent and once again stared out of the window. Rain started falling, and the skies lamented, as a thunderstorm roared like someone in the heavens was angry. A knock on the door startled her out of her horror. She quickly clicked away from the image on the monitor. 'Come in,' she hollered, her voice close to a whimper.

A well-groomed man in a dark suit and dark spectacles entered the room. Chief of Research department at Althonat, Sten Lindholm, stood before her desk, studying her pale ashen face. 'Are you all right?'

'You have the test results of the cell antidote?' asked Martina, disregarding his concern.

'We are in the final stages of testing. It looks good. The cell antidote is an excellent natural plant substance that protects the immune system, regardless of toxin levels in the blood. It contains no chemicals, no additives, no preservatives, but purely green foliage.'

'When is production due?' asked Martina.

'In six months I would say.'

'Make it three.'

'With the paperwork involved, licenses and all…I don't know.'

'You have ample resources; use them,' said Martina without looking at him, her gaze back on the computer monitor as she skimmed through another report.

'I'll see what I can do,' said Sten. He remained standing, waiting for her full attention.

'Yes, Sten?' asked Martina, raising her gaze with a quizzical frown.

'The preliminary analyses of samples from surveillance are ready.'

'Analysis of Life-Vaccine?' asked Martina.

'Yes.'

A deep fear mixed with anticipation steeled her for this news.

'Sit down,' said Martina. 'What did you find?'

Sten had her full attention. He sat and blinked rapidly, striving to ease the strange churn of dark undercurrents in the windows to his soul. Martina observed him, noticing an unfamiliar glaze over his eyes.

'It's odd they call it Life-Vaccine,' said Sten as he handed her the analysis report.

'What's odd?' she said, snatching the report from his hand.

'The Life-Vaccine. Its contents are macabre. It's true there are traces of Rensblad as anticipated, but also caterpillar eggs, green monkey kidney, antifreeze, heavy metals, brain-eating amoeba, DNA of cancer virus, even ground human tissue.' He slowly rubbed his forehead with his fingers, vexation growing in his eyes.

Flushes of shock smouldered in Martina's face. Her throat felt raw and sore. 'That doesn't meet legal criteria for valid science,' she inferred, her voice hoarse and pained. 'This is Nazi science, condemning people to death. How can they license it?'

'It's already on the market, in schools and hospitals, even on foreign seas going global.'

'Speed up work on the cell antidote. Make the three months one.'

Sten raised his fatigued eyes to meet her unwavering gaze. 'No, it's impossible.'

'Put in overtime, night shifts!' she said. 'Hire extra personnel, whatever you need to complete the task in a month!'

The pain that had settled in her spine earlier on became unbearable. She sprang up and paced the floor as she read the report. Then she stopped abruptly in her tracks and regarded Sten, who was slouched over in the chair, head buried in hands.

'What did you say? Ground human tissue?'

'Yes. It's insane, isn't it?' said Sten, turning his face to look at her, resignation in his voice.

'That is cannibalism,' retorted Martina. 'This is the most obnoxious, evil thing I've ever seen.'

The mood in the room turned thick and sultry. She was breathing deep and quickly, trying to ward off a hideous nausea that welled in her throat.

Sten straightened up in his chair, unnerved and visibly weary at heart. He noticed her complexion had paled like the white sheet of paper in her hand. Understanding the circumstances, he said nothing, hoping she would be all right.

'I've never seen anything like it,' said Sten. 'It's a devil's brew under the guise of a vaccine. These medical wizards care nothing about how much disease they inflict on people as long they have a Ferrari in their driveway.'

Martina glanced at her watch, remembering they must not be late. 'Let's go,' she said as she picked up a white folder and pen from her desk.

'I'd better get my papers,' said Sten, up and on his way to the door.

Althonat Board directors had gathered as Martina and Sten entered the boardroom. The royal blue carpet, matching chairs, and curtains gave an uncertain chill to the oval space. Crystal chandeliers hung high, dimly lighting the dusky room, marginally dispelling a certain gloom that radiated from light blue walls. In the middle was a large pear-shaped glass table with twelve chairs encircling it.

Board members sat with long doleful faces engaging in stilted talk. The chairman of Althonat Board, Olof Olausson, sat at the narrow end of the table in full view of all members. He had called the emergency meeting, and clearly everyone's mood was tense. Martina took her seat beside him. She whispered something in his ear. Olausson frowned and grew still. She lifted her gaze and found Jonas Eneroth's warm eyes, the Chief Medical officer at Althonat hospital. She allowed herself a soft smile which he returned.

There was only one point on the agenda: 'Life-Vaccine,' announced Olausson. He went on to present the facts: 'It has been confirmed that a controversial Life-Vaccine is on the market. Tests trials were conducted on live, unknowing humans.'

A subdued sigh was heard and the mood shifted to a vicious silence. Chief of Biology department, David Falk, choked on his coffee falling into a fit of coughing. He wobbled across to the door and hurriedly left the room, gasping for air.

'Is he all right?' asked Martina as she bolted up and hastened out in a panicked step to save David. Seconds translated into minutes of nothingness.

Abruptly, the doors opened, and Martina and David returned. David looked rattled, his face flushed but calm and collected.

The meeting resumed. Olausson continued, 'These findings are gravely disturbing in nature. Martina, please update us on the status of events.'

Martina cleared her voice. 'It's an unfortunate development. Life-Vaccine is a toxic mixture being passed off as a vaccine that protects from disease. It destroys the immune system and the intestines' ability to absorb nutrients as well causing defects in unborn children.'

'But the good news is that the cell antidote is on schedule. In a month, we shall have an antidote to counteract this menace.' The room heated up and her mouth went dry. She paused, picked up her glass, and took a sip of sparkling water. She continued, 'A clandestine group of people working under a firm called Citaraph is responsible for making the Life-Vaccine. According to information I received they simply call themselves The Group.'

'David,' asked Olausson, 'what's the worst case scenario?'

'Life-Vaccine is nothing like its name suggests,' said David. 'Its genetically modified DNA is a biohazard. If incorporated into human DNA, it will lead to actual genetic changes that can be devastating to humanity.'

The silence grew deeper in the room as everyone's mind twirled around the disturbing question of what kind of perfidious creatures would invent such a brew. This was the sort of treachery, only merciless perpetrators concealed in dark places could produce.

'They call it a life-prolonging drug that will protect from all diseases,' said Sten Lindholm, 'but that is a sham. Life-Vaccine is the most toxic chemical ever invented by the drug industry. These covert scientists are the fiercest and most dangerous foes against humanity.'

'Life-Vaccine has nothing to do with medicine, science, or disease,' said Martina. 'Money, yes, could be a motive but is that all? That's the question we need to ask.'

'Communities have to be informed and warned against Life-Vaccine,' said the Communications director, Sophie Silverblad.

'What about our lobbying organs?' asked Olausson.

Nils Tidholm, the Corporate attorney, lifted his gaze. 'We are lobbying the government to relax policies on natural alternative therapies and be more restrictive on patents for genetic research.'

'Genetic research has continued in fits and starts,' said Torsten Widstam, the security director. 'The government takes marginal interest, with no controls or safeguards in place.'

Olausson focused his gaze on Jonas, the chief medical officer at Althonat hospital. 'How are facilities at the hospital?'

'We're prepared for an epidemic of Life-Vaccine-induced illnesses, especially in the children's ward,' said Jonas. He spoke with the authority of a man who knew his work like the back of his hand.

'Martina?' asked Olausson.

'All departments need to pool resources in a concerted effort to combat this evil,' said Martina. 'We must avert the greatest danger for the greatest majority.'

'Diana, financial report?' asked Olausson.

A poised African woman with dark curly hair and a flawless brown complexion leaned forward in her chair. She was the Financial director at Althonat.

'Finances are in balance,' said Diana. 'Resources are readily available to carry out this task. Besides, we need to invest more in projects this year, to reduce our tax burden.'

After the meeting broke up, Martina stayed behind to discuss figures and logistics with Olausson.

Chapter 7

In her bathrobe, Martina left the basement gym and went upstairs to her bedroom. Exercise and a sauna bath had rejuvenated her body, giving her a sense of elevated energy levels. She opened the ceiling to floor glass doors and walked onto the balcony with its panoramic view over the sparkling sea. In the distance a Baltic Sea Ferry, Finland boat, cruised to Helsinki. A cool breeze washed over her, twirling her fluffy hair around her neck and shoulders. The grounds were wet from last night's rain, but the sun was peeping through the mist, promising a warm day. She dressed and wandered to the kitchen area. Astrid was emptying the dishwasher.

'Morning, Astrid.'

'Good morning, Martina.'

'Did my security guard take Joachim to day care?'

'You mean Simon?'

'Yes.'

'Leo's mother next door wanted to take him with Leo but Simon insisted he had specific instructions from you that he should take him,' said Astrid. 'Joachim was excited. It was his first day to go to day care since the accident.'

'He's been talking about it all the time.'

'What would you like for breakfast?'

'I'll have cereal, and carrot juice,' said Martina. 'In fact, I'll get it myself. Carry on with whatever you're doing.'

'No tea?'

'No, thanks.'

Järna, a small town in south-east Stockholm, was scantly populated, mainly a farming community with small businesses. On the outskirts were an elaborate, complex group of Althonat buildings: Althonat Hospital, the research centre, laboratories, offices, and a manufacturing plant simply known as The Plant. It was an imposing edifice in annexes, wings, and extensions - people also called it the Elephant. The grounds were expansive and surrounded by green areas.

Dr Jonas Eneroth, the Chief Medical officer, sat working in his office when he heard a knock on the door. He got up, and when he opened the door, there stood the woman who was now his boss, yet his interests in her were more than professional. In a black pencil skirt, delicate lace tank top and blazer, she looked gorgeous. There was a special glow to her porcelain skin, set off by her golden wavy hair. And the bright smile on her face made his heart stop. He had seen her only once since the funeral – at the emergency board meeting.

'What a pleasant surprise,' said Jonas. 'Why didn't you call?'

Martina stood beaming at him, drinking him in: tall and strongly built with finely chiselled features, his manner exquisite, his appearance distinguished. His well-tailored dark suit with red tie emphasized his good looks. He was the figure of a man well on his way to maturity, despite his brief thirty-eight years.

'Just as you said, I wanted to surprise you.'

He closed the door behind them, laid one hand on her waist and walked her into the room. He then clasped her and kissed her. She gazed at him, her blue eyes probing his face for signs of secret desires embedded in his striking greenish-brown eyes. Their lips locked again in a long, passionate kiss.

'You look lovely,' said Jonas as he released her. 'Come, sit here with me.'

He took her hand and led her to a sofa set to the left of the room. They sank to the sofa and sat side by side. A shaft of sunlight through the white curtains bathed the room in a lustrous, agreeable sheen. The office was sparely furnished – besides the sofa and a standing lamp next to it, only an overflowing bookcase, a large dark desk with a black leather chair, and a desktop computer standing amid stacks of papers occupied the room.

'How're you holding out?' he asked her when they were settled.

'Some days are good, some days I struggle to get out of bed.'

'It's a good sign you have some better days,' said Jonas. 'When Sebastian called, I knew I had to come right away.'

'I was numb. I couldn't get a grip on myself. I'm glad you came.'

'You were in shock. It was understandable,' said Jonas, caressing her knuckles, gauging her emotion.

'My heart was grieving but I kept thinking of the strangest things: Father's books, Joachim's socks Mother knitted for him, and Hässelved farm,' said Martina, her voice sounding pained and confused.

'What about Hässelved farm?'

'I'm not sure, but thoughts kept trailing in fragments…the wrangle between Pappa and Carlsson in particular nagged at me constantly. Sebastian and I were young; I can't remember what it was about. But after that row, Pappa and Stellan sold Hässelved farm.'

'Who was Carlsson?'

'He was our neighbour at Hässelved farm, a small farmer, an herbalist. He had a common interest in natural alternative medicine like Pappa.'

'Maybe it was a falling out of some sort,' said Jonas. 'Where's Carlsson now?'

'He died shortly after my parents moved to the States.'

'You think Carlsson's death is connected to your parents' accident?'

'There could be a clue,' said Martina. 'Father told Sebastian that he was coming to Stockholm to take care of something that had happened in Hässelved a long time ego, among other things.'

'He never gave Sebastian details?'

'No.'

'Did Carlsson die in a car accident too?'

'I don't know, said Martina. 'I know he had a son. I keep wondering if whatever the wrangle was about inspired the son to come after my parents.'

'Don't overthink things. Try to focus on the positive: on Joachim,' said Jonas, a serious look on his face.

'It's easier said than done. Thinking about Hässelved is compulsive behaviour with me these days.'

'Snap out of it, Martina,' said Jonas, his voice solemn but kind. 'There's nothing compulsive about remembering one's past.'

'You don't understand!'

'Tell me, how's Joachim?' asked Jonas, determined to change the subject.

'He's fine, apart from his nightmares,' said Martina as she rose from the sofa, smoothed her skirt, and walked gracefully over to the window, her stiletto heels clacking on the marble floor. The eerie sensation around her spine returned. She stood there watching a willow warbler jump from branch to branch and fly up and down as if confused by something invisible, something lurking. Finally, it settled on the treetop and broke into a song of high whistles merging in one trill which gradually quieted down, answered with a sudden shudder in Martina's body.

'Nightmares?' asked Jonas as he furrowed his brow.

'Since he woke from the coma, he's been having nightmares. He says he sees a big black van in his sleep. But he doesn't remember anything about the accident.'

'It could be trauma. He may need professional help to come to terms with what happened.'

'I'll wait and see how he is coping.'

Jonas gazed at Martina intently as she turned to face him. He noticed an air of mystery about her. It sparked an aura over his flesh and a soft breeze to his nerves, just like the day he had first seen her.

He had just completed his internship at Karoliska Institute, in Stockholm, and travelled to the United States for further studies in natural alternative therapies in New York. In his spare time, he took to the arts and enrolled in salsa class. By a stroke of luck, or by sheer coincidence, he met this charming Swedish girl with whom he shared the same profession and the same interests in alternative therapies and the arts. He was mesmerized and captivated by her energy and commanding intelligence – and a beauty unparalleled by any woman he had ever met. They were both Swedes, in a foreign country, circumstances that breathed vigour into their friendship, encouraging it to blossom like orchids in early spring.

But she told him her heart was taken; she could only be his friend. He was well aware her fiancé, Thomas Edgren, waited for her in Sweden, but that did not deter him from pursuing her. When he heard of her marriage to Thomas his heart broke, and it took years to swallow the disappointment. However, luck played into his hand again when he heard of Martina's divorce from Thomas.

'Where are the results of Nicholas' evaluation?' asked Martina, jolting him out of his reverie.

'Yes, of course,' said Jonas as he got up and moved towards the desk. He picked up papers and handed them to her. 'This way, please,' he said in a business-like tone and led the way to another room down the corridor. In the room was a single bed with a bedside table and two chairs. Crouched up in a foetal position was Nicholas, deep in sleep, propped up by two pillows. He looked peaceful.

'He's been sedated,' said Jonas. 'He hadn't slept for days.'

They stood observing the seemingly lifeless boy, speaking in low undertones.

'The tests revealed high toxic levels in his blood, contaminants of heavy metal, bird-cancer viruses and brain-eating amoeba.'

'That confirms my suspicions,' said Martina as she observed Nicholas' limp body rising and falling in rhythm with his breathing. 'It must be a poisonous vaccine they injected him with. That stuff cannot get into the body unless it is injected or ingested.'

'Brain-eating amoeba causes mental retardation and even brain cancer,' said Jonas. 'He also has bowel problems and eczema all over the body.'

'It's immune malfunction. Have you reviewed his history of toxin exposure?'

'Yes, Dr George Nasiro, the specialist in the field, prepared his nutritional protocol and immune builders based on that history.'

'Tell the doctor to use the natural remedy cocktail for detoxification, and then follow up with leaf and herbal protocol. That should flush toxins out and strengthen his immune system. Once that's done we shall investigate his disordered behavioural condition. Has the homoeopathist been to see him?'

'No, she's scheduled for tomorrow, but I doubt if we have time for that,' said Jonas, a worried look on his face as he studied the sleeping boy.

'Why?'

'His father threatened to sue us if we continued treating him. His mother is cooperative, but the father is adamant against our therapies.'

'We can't treat Nicholas against his father's will,' said Martina. 'Patrick Strand is a difficult man. I've tried to bring him around, but he's a hard nut to crack.'

'I'm expecting his mother anytime now. Perhaps you can speak to her to find a solution to the problem?'

'Ebba needs to stand up to her husband,' said Martina. 'Nicholas' life depends on it.'

'She managed to bring Nicholas here on her own,' said Jonas. 'I don't know how, but she did it. And I don't think her husband knows the boy is here.'

As they left Nicholas' room, a woman emerged from the far end of the corridor, running and howling. They couldn't hear what she was saying.

'What is it?' hollered Jonas.

'It's my husband. He's coming to take Nicholas away!' cried the woman. 'Please, stop him. Don't let him take my child away!'

As she came close, Jonas saw it was Ebba Strand. She was panting like a hard-run horse. The desperation in her eyes was palpable.

Behind her appeared the figure of a man in hot pursuit. His running was wobbly and uncoordinated. He wore a black trench coat. As he came into focus, Jonas noticed his flushed face. It was Patrick Strand. Martina quickly stepped back through a door into an empty room, thinking, *no need to speak to the Strands under a volatile situation.* She could hear the scuffle in the corridor, as man and wife tore at each other. Blows flew, and Ebba was shrieking. Jonas tried to contain the situation, but to no avail. Martina picked up the landline telephone in the room and called hospital security. Two uniformed officers soon arrived and restrained Patrick. He bellowed, threatening to sue the hospital. His speech was sluggard and lethargic.

Martina heard Jonas, irate, say, 'In here.' A door slammed with a loud bang, and silence prevailed. Martina opened the door to check if the coast was clear, but a foul stench of alcohol drifted up her nostrils. She reeled back, revolted. She knew Patrick was a heavy drinker, but stinking like that in the middle of the day indicated that his drinking was out of control.

She closed the door and wandered back into the room, gazing outside through the window. In the sky hovered dark clouds predicting an oncoming drizzle. Her gaze fell on the parking lot; a black Dodge van caught her attention. She recalled Joachim's nightmares, and an idea formed in her mind. She left the room, rushed out to the parking lot, and sat waiting in her Saab, watching the van.

Suddenly she saw Patrick and Ebba appear in the distance. Patrick pushed a slumped Nicholas in a wheelchair. Ebba followed a few steps behind, her head bowed and her gaze on the ground. They came into the parking lot and to her disbelief headed to the Dodge van. A huge man in black bomber jacket and black pants got out of the van and opened the door. He carried Nicholas into the van. Ebba and Patrick got in the rear seat on either side of Nicholas. The van pulled out of its parking space and hauled out of the driveway, speeding south.

Martina edged her old Saab, a 1960 model, out of the lot to follow. It had belonged to her father – one of his collector's items. Martina changed cars as one changes clothes: not as a show-off but as a security precaution. The Saab eased onto the main road and followed the van. The van continued on Interstate 57, emerging on European Highway to Sodertalje. At traffic place Moraberg, it turned right to interstate 225. Martina kept on the trail, avoiding detection. It started raining.

As it approached Västerhaninge, the van accelerated to pass a bus. Martina stayed behind the bus till it turned left and then sped up, catching the van as it rounded a bend, still at a safe distance. The van took a gravel road into open country, passing the Årsta seaside area.

The area was largely agriculture landscape. A few homes and farms were scattered at a distance from each other. She passed a local shopping centre. It was familiar territory; she had been here before. The van slowed down and turned right into a narrow road at the sign for Ribbyburg Clinic. She recognized the red-tiled double-storeyed building – Stellan's country home. When had it become a Clinic?

The van swerved right and then left into the driveway. Martina's foot hit the brakes. She reversed the Saab and drove back, looking for a shady place to park the car. She found a forest pocket with overgrown bushes on one side and piles of red bricks stacked up high on the other. It looked as if someone had abandoned a building project. She parked the Saab and rushed back to the driveway on foot. Leaving the driveway, she took a side path behind the hedges, coming into full view of the building. There were two other buildings in the compound, one alongside and the other opposite the big house which Stellan had once used as accommodation for stable employees and equipment storage. In a distance was the old stable.

Sheltered by the hedges, Martina saw the huge man helping Nicholas out of the van. A woman in white top and pants emerged from the house with a wheelchair. She must be a Nurse. The Strand family followed her into the house.

In the doorway appeared a dark-haired man in a dark suit. Another man in a camel-coloured suit joined the dark-haired man in the doorway. He seemed older and taller than the other man. They both moved outside into the compound.

A man in dark uniform with a black dog passed by the two men, paused to talk to them and then walked the dog away, disappearing behind the house.

Martina dashed forward, parting the hedges to get a better view. Her heels kept getting stuck in soft ground. She kicked them off and quivered as her silk-stockinged feet touched frozen ground. Nevertheless, she ran round the hedge and came to the rear of the house. A final squeeze through hedges brought her to the house. She tiptoed the full length of the wall to the front corner of the house, where she got a glimpse of the men. Her hand fell upon her mouth, suppressing a squeak. It was Rangor and her Uncle Stellan.

The sun lost its lustre, and the sky grew darker. Focusing, she sharpened her ears, her face contorted in anxiety and her shoulders slumped.

'What're you going to do with the boy?' asked Stellan.

'What kind of question is that?' asked Rangor. 'Treat him, of course.'

'Like a guinea pig?'

Martina almost yelped. *Guinea pigs!*

'You know you must not use those words,' Rangor replied. 'We research in modern medicine. We need to test and perfect the drugs we put on the market.'

'Such a noble cause for humanity,' said Stellan, sarcasm in his voice.

'You are well paid for this, aren't you?' retorted Rangor with some irritation.

'Yes, I'm so well paid, but I need to protect my integrity too, you know.'

'You gave up your integrity long ago,' said Rangor.

Stellan glared at him.

'You worry too much,' said Rangor, gazing at him intently, wondering why he was such a gutless wimp. 'You should be more like your brother, carefree and daring to step out and soar with the wind.'

'Don't you dare talk about my dead brother!' said Stellan, pain in his face. 'And don't change the subject. What kind of tests are you going to do on the boy?'

'Tests to make him comfortable, prepare him for rigorous testing at Devilund Clinic.'

'Devilund?'

'Yes, Devilund,' said Rangor. 'Dr Grenzken knows how to further our cause.'

'You know all this will come to haunt you,' said Stellan. He shrugged and began pacing slowly towards the corner where Martina was hiding.

Back to the hedges Martina tiptoed and quickly ducked out of sight as Stellan appeared round the corner. The darkness and her black attire provided perfect camouflage.

She scrambled up and back to the Saab. Her feet were raw and sore. She didn't know where her shoes were. Abruptly, she stopped, startled. A monstrous, hideous man stood on raised ground above the piles of bricks, behind the Saab, ogling her. Her heart pounded as if to rupture her chest. She wondered how long he had been standing there. It was the man who had driven the van.

Grabbing the car door, she jerked it open and jumped in. She started the engine, her eyes on the mirrors, gauging the beast. She eased the Saab out of its space, changed gears, and glided to the junction just before the turning into the road. In the mirrors she saw the man clomp from the raised ground, brick in hand, coming after her, sprinting like a racing robot in outer space. Panic-stricken, she accelerated fast. The man hurled the brick, striking the rear windscreen of the Saab.

The impact rocked the Saab, and the windscreen exploded into flying shards. Martina shrieked, and cringed, taking cover where there was no cover to take. Glass showered over her, leaving lacerations on her body. The Saab swerved and wavered, missing a squirrel that dashed across the road. She hit the brake pedal to no avail. The car thundered on, uninhibited, going at rocket speed. With her eyes on the rough terrain of the winding country road, she tightened her grip on the steering wheel. She floored the brake pedal again; nothing. She knew she was in trouble. Wide-eyed, with a silent prayer on her lips, she desperately searched for a safe place to plunge the car.

The highway was in view. Unable to stop, she aimed the Saab towards the strawberry field across the highway, praying no car would come in her way. Thrown up and down, shaking and twirling, she held her breath and hung on as the Saab roared unimpeded across the highway into the field. The tyres bounced and bumped on strawberry beds in a bumpy ride to the end of the strawberry field. Her body reverberated with every jolt. A tree stood in her way and she smashed helplessly into it, bringing the Saab to a sudden stop. Her body jerked forwards, her head and hands flumped lifelessly on the steering wheel. Streaks of blood ran down her head, smudging her face. Agony shot through her right leg and radiated to her upper hip.

In darkness, the silence was broken by an ominous rumble, and lightning bolted from the blue. The skies opened, rain drenched the earth and wind howled across the sleeping countryside, frosting the earth. The cold chilled her bones, making her body shiver as if taking on a fever.

Chapter 8

Few people danced around the maypole at midsummer celebrations. The skies remained dull and grey. Showers and icy breezes kept a tight grip on the land.

Grenzken woke to the spatter of rain on the windowpane. Helmut, his henchman, and Birgit had gone to pick up supplies. He spent the morning in the study with his laptop. Eventually, he went down to Devilund Clinic. The dimly lit corridor smelled of sanitized air. He walked along the corridor, peering through glass viewports in doors at inmates in bed. He stopped at room number six, noticing Anna, one of the inmates, sitting on the bare mattress, her face buried in her hands.

She was wearing a long white tunic. The bedding lay loose around her, drooping in a heap on the floor. Her thinning hair fluttered in the cool air from the ventilation system. Shafts of morning sunlight streamed through a small window near the ceiling, lighting up her pale neck, slouched shoulders reflecting her misery. Her face looked rugged and marred by severe nodular acne. From the way she sat lopsidedly, he could tell her intense headaches persisted.

He jingled a key in the lock and reached for the brass doorknob. It turned loosely in his hand. He pressed his palm against the door to open it. He could hear the sniffing and sobbing. His jaw tightened. He noticed wallpaper hung torn to pieces, as if she had been climbing the walls to still her pain.

The room had a single bed, a sideboard table and chair. Temperatures were kept low to avert virus and bacterial growth.

He closed the door behind him, walked up to her and bent to touch her chin, lifting her face up to gaze in her dark, weary eyes. She cringed and turned away. Her body quivered as she clutched her stomach and twisted her face in pain.

'I'm dying,' she whimpered between sobs, tears rolling down her cheeks. The white tunic she wore hung loosely on her body, revealing emaciated shoulders and a thin, elongated neck. Grenzken's heart clenched in horror. She was all bones. His apprehension was not in concern for her but rather a fear that her aggravated condition would prove detrimental to the research project. She was not eating enough, always throwing up everything they gave her. Something must be done about it.

'Calm down,' said Grenzken. 'The pain is just a side effect of the vaccine. It will cease in a few days. But you must eat. You need strength to get better.'

Anna gazed in his small probing eyes, which were a dirty green like the laminate floor he stood on. Her eyes locked with his in a battle of visual strength – the tormenter and subjugated. The rage in her eyes was like venom sprayed in his serpentine eyes. He blinked and quickly shifted his gaze away, as if the scene was getting rather oppressive for him. He sauntered over to the hanging torn wallpaper, grabbed it and ripped it off the wall.

'Stop damaging things,' he said, anger in his voice. 'Repairs cost.'

'Let me go,' whimpered Anna, nearly crying in despair. 'Plea… please, let me go.'

'Go where? I haven't even started with you,' said Grenzken, without turning to face her. 'I've great plans for you. Don't you understand? Besides, I told you to stop talking like that. You disappoint me.'

When he finally turned and dared to look at her, he saw a glaring mixture of animosity, hurt and desperation in her eyes. He blinked his gaze away again. He knew he could break her physical body but her psyche, if not tamed, would blow the project out of the water. Her constant hunger strikes and refusal to take medicine worried him.

His small leering eyes studied her. He had seen rebellion in her eyes from day one. When she had arrived at Devilund Clinic– heavily intoxicated with alcohol and street drugs – she was incapacitated for three days. When she finally woke, she didn't know where she was. Mute like a mouse, overly suspicious, she refused to answer questions. After much persuasion and convincing, she agreed to be examined, screened for risk factors and illnesses. He wasn't surprised to find her infested with sexually transmitted disease. She had been too long on the streets. She accepted treatment readily. Her pregnancy test came out negative.

The norm was to treat inmates, get them clean, and then initiate research trial programs. He really didn't know her background, but then he didn't care. Inmates were merchandise, products or instruments to work with just like a scalpel. Some of the merchandise came in fresh and juicy; some was hard and broken, in need of fixing before it was good for work.

The day she asked about going home, he feigned deafness. Unabated, she kept asking him. He told her he wanted to do more tests. That was when she exploded, smashing everything in her path in search of an exit route. That same day, he decided to move fast.

'You've to kill me first before you spike more needles under my skin,' she told him. That night Grenzken sedated and injected her with Life-Vaccine.

In days, a rash erupted on her skin like mushrooms on an anthill. Antibiotics cleared it, but it returned stronger than before, soon becoming chronic.

On one occasion she articulated her suspicions: 'You're poisoning me.'

The dizziness, nausea, vomiting and diarrhoea set in. She refused to eat. After the third injection, she complained of headaches, stomach cramping, and severe fatigue. Her hair started falling out. Putting her on fluids was no use; she kept removing the catheter from her arm. Her shrieking and squealing were of no consequence to Grenzken. The research trial must continue. When she started arching her back, he knew her immune system was loaded with toxins. It was time to move to the next procedure.

The phone rang, drawing Grenzken from his trance. He answered. It was Birgit, the Nurse, reminding him dinner was ready. He still had a lot of work to do. He declined dinner and instead asked her to send Helmut down with a sandwich and coffee.

At midnight Grenzken tiptoed downstairs, crossing the living room, deep in gloom, into the long hallway leading to Birgit's west wing. He grabbed the doorknob, slowly but firmly, and unfastened it like one whose hand was familiar with the latches. He glided past her sitting room, nudged the bedroom door and crossed the threshold into her sleeping chamber. Birgit lay asleep in her pearly queen bed. The window-shades were half drawn and the moonlight shimmered on her mature skin, giving it an ivory glow.

Grenzken stripped naked, his clothes falling into a mixed bundle on the floor. He crept under the soft bedclothes, his body revelling in her warmth. The sensual tang of oriental sandalwood musk, with a hint of lemon spice, tickled his nose. Birgit groaned, awakened by his touch, and turned to him, arching into him, tipping her hips. His blood roared through his veins like a wildfire, burning, stinging. They accelerated pace. She screamed in agony. He muffled a savage shout as he exploded in her untamed joy.

Helmut stood outside Birgit's outer door, pondering on the wild cries and sounds of euphoria coming from inside. His face contorted in painful disapproval.

*****

Anna turned and tossed in bed, drifting in and out of consciousness. Shadows of grey interspersed with flashes of pale blue light flickered in smoky fog deep in the forest. In dirty mud lay the lifeless body of a girl, short, thin and pregnant. Her long white tunic turned muddy. The girl's pale face she had once seen in the Devilund Clinic. The whistling wind whipped up a whirlwind of dead leaves, lifting and twirling them in the air. They rustled and flapped like butterflies in distress.

Then in a sudden spin, the leaves cascaded over the girl as if in a ceremonial burial. Dubious figures emerged from alleys of the dark forest. Her eyes widened as she saw a silhouette of men in lab gowns encircling her, armed with hypodermic needles. She narrowed her gaze, trying to get a glimpse of their faces. The men were faceless with spider webs over their faces. Anna bolted upright in bed. Her ear-splitting shriek tore through Devilund Clinic.

Bo, Grenzken's Registered Nurse, held her down, restraining her. He was preparing to draw blood from her arm. She looked around the room trying to get her bearings, a sense of place and time.

'Nightmares again?' asked Bo. Then she saw the needle in his hand.

'What are you doing?' she screamed. In a rage she threw off the bedding and kicked him in the crotch.

Bo reeled backwards, grabbing his crotch, and cringed in pain. 'Don't ever do that again!'

Before she could utter another word, Bo stuck her with a needle in her upper arm. She wavered back in the bed, wailing from shock. In minutes she'd drifted into unconsciousness. Bo left the room, closing the door behind him.

*****

Skimming through the morning *Daily News* at breakfast, Grenzken read, 'Althonat CEO in minor accident.' It didn't say how badly hurt she was. He had read about her work on Complementary medicine from medical journals. It was impressive, brilliant, but nothing like orthodox medicine. People needed treatment, quick fixes that suppressed and subdued symptoms of disease, not herbal cures. He cast aside the newspaper and switched to *Frangipani*, Althonat's newspaper – Martina's propaganda mouthpiece, as he called it. His mouth twisted into a grimace when he read she had sustained a broken leg and had left hospital.

*****

In the examination room Anna lay slouched back in the gynaecological chair with her legs spread out under a white sheet. Grenzken put on his surgical gloves and examined her inside; then he palpated her stomach, lifted her eyelids, and gazed in her pupils.

Bo the Nurse, and Richard, the lab assistant, alighted into the room closing the door behind them. Bo held a Petri dish, delicately balanced in his hands. Nestled in it was a zygote. He handed it to Grenzken, who took it without further ado and transferred it to Anna's fallopian tubes with the skill of a master breeder.

'Now hopefully our intentions of a successful pregnancy will be fulfilled,' said Grenzken as he pulled off surgical gloves, discarding them in a trash bin. He rubbed his hands together, a smirk on his face.

'Successful?' asked Richard, thinking, *how ironic*. 'The environment is toxic. The embryo will never survive.'

'It'll be interesting to see what happens,' said Grenzken, his glittering small eyes darting from Richard to Bo. 'Life-Vaccine is already incorporated into Anna's DNA. The process of genetic mutation is in motion.'

'Do you have to spell it out like that?' asked Richard.

Grenzken stared at him, sensing doubt and disloyalty in his statement.

'Her last Pap smear revealed high-grade precancerous lesions,' said Richard.

'Life-Vaccine doesn't cause disease,' said Grenzken, irritation in his voice. 'In the initial stages there may be side effects, but in the long run it protects against disease.'

'Her Pap smear was clear when she came in,' said Bo persistently. 'She must have contracted the lesions here, from Life-Vaccine.'

'Keep in mind, even undesired results are useful in research,' said Grenzken. 'They may lead to new discoveries.'

Richard and Bo glanced at each other with a foreboding expression on their faces.

'Whichever way we go, we can't lose,' continued Grenzken, with a sinister undertone. 'Plus, think about the rare opportunity we have here at Devilund. We experience a three-dimensional score on results: the physical, emotional and environmental reactions of inmates to treatment. That way, we develop a broader category of drugs rapidly and effectively ensure quick profit margins.'

'Quick profits?' asked Richard.

'I think we need to speak to the Group,' said Bo.

'The Group – yes, we can speak to the Group, but are they knowledgeable?'

The question hung in the air, for neither Bo nor Richard wanted to engage in absurdities, devoid of good sense and judgement. With a bleak expression on his face, Grenzken strode out of the room.

Richard remained behind to help Anna back to her room. Her body felt limp, and her breathing was regular. He lifted her onto the movable bed and wheeled her back to her room. He laid her in the bed and locked the door behind him.

After he left, Anna blinked and opened her eyes. Darkness gripped her soul. She cried, wringing her hands as if her heart would rupture. Quivering and shaking, she lay resigned to her fate, knowing she was a caged animal without hope of ever leaving Devilund alive. Disgusted by whatever Grenzken had inserted in her womb and what she had heard of their discussion, she wanted to die. The cramping in her stomach returned. She curled up in a tight ball, sobbing helplessly. She prepared to die.

Chapter 9

At Slottsville house, Astrid and Lisa busied themselves in the kitchen tidying up after lunch. Mona Stein, Martina's neighbour, sat in the great room, talking with Martina. She was not smiling. Martina sat with her right leg stretched out on the large chestnut chesterfield sofa, enclosed in a white cast. Every now and then she erupted into a dreadful cough which had lingered since her minor accident.

'What were you doing in Västerhaninge?' asked Mona.

Martina heard what she said but directed her gaze towards the window, watching white clouds merge into dark clouds building into pale grey skies. Strangely enough, she had asked herself the same question.

'The weatherman said these are the last days of summer,' said Martina.

'I asked you a question. Your son was worried sick about you when you didn't come home. He came to my place at eight wondering if you were at my house.'

'It was an emergency,' said Martina. 'I was going to call Joachim.'

'But you didn't,' remarked Mona. 'You've a demanding job, but you have a son too – a five-year-old, Martina.'

'I know. It's just that certain things can't be delegated.'

'You could have been killed.'

'Mona, please,' said Martina.

The conversation between the two women was familiar. Martina understood Mona meant well, but they had different value systems. Mona, a mother of three, worked part-time as a social worker to be able to take care of her children when they came home from school. She did not think it worthwhile for any mother to shackle herself to a corporate career, especially when her children were still small.

The strawberry farmer had found Martina unconscious, freezing in the cramped Saab. He had called an ambulance, which drove her to the nearest local hospital, but on arrival Lisa, her cousin, insisted she be transferred to Althonat Hospital. Dr Jonas Eneroth was waiting when they arrived. He said she had been lucky to come in when she did. She had a compound fracture of the right tibia and fibula. The seat belt had torn skin off her upper-left chest and left an ugly bruise. The lacerations from glass splinters were mild and would heal well, but the bacterial pneumonia she had contracted from the car's toxic air conditioner nearly did her in. Her fever peaked so high that one might have thought the internal sizzling could have executed any bacteria. Her shortness of breath required a dose of oxygen therapy. Her chest pains and coughing were mitigated by a hotchpotch of natural herbs. The doctor recommended plenty of rest and ordered her not to put weight on her right leg for six weeks.

Lisa emerged from the kitchen and sat on the sofa beside Mona.

'Your cousin is a stubborn woman,' said Mona as she shifted her gaze to Lisa.

Lisa smiled and said, 'I know. She works herself to the bone and seems to forget she has a son to take care of.'

'You two stop ganging up on me,' said Martina, struggling to reach for her crutches on the floor.

Mona and Lisa sneaked surreptitious glances at each other, sharing an amused smile. 'Where are you going?' asked Lisa.

'I'm going to visit Auntie Ingrid,' said Martina. 'Will you drive me?'

'Not in your condition. The doctor advised plenty of rest,' said Lisa. 'Besides, my mother may not want to see you.'

'Ingrid will see me,' said Martina, breaking into a cracking cough.

'Even if she sees you, she may be unresponsive.'

'You can't change my mind. Will you drive me?' asked Martina again as she fumbled to hoist herself onto the crutches. She winced from the pain and slumped back onto the sofa. Her upper body was regularly sore from hauling herself around on crutches.

'You aren't supposed to be putting weight on that leg,' said Mona as she rose to leave.

'Give my love to Roland and the children,' said Martina.

'I will,' said Mona, as she walked out leaving the two relatives to quibble with each other.

Lisa recalled that, when they were young, her family had been close with Martina's family, but things had changed when Martina's family moved to America. Lisa knew her mother was fond of Martina but feared her visit might irritate old wounds.

'What is it that is so urgent, you must see her today?' asked Lisa.

'I'll drive myself then,' said Martina as she hobbled past her on crutches.

'Okay, I'll drive you.'

In the reception area at Beckomburg Mental Hospital, Martina and Lisa sat in the waiting room. A Nurse came and said, 'Ingrid will see you now.' They followed her down a long corridor. As they walked, the Nurse said, 'She has been very depressed these last few days. It's normal for elderly people to suffer with melancholic depression. Perhaps your visit will cheer her up.' In the middle of the corridor, she opened a door and called out as they entered, 'Ingrid, you have visitors.'

The room stood in semi-darkness with faint rays of sunset casting gloomy shadows of odd figures against the walls, as if emphasizing a life marred by a difficult past. In a bedside sofa sat a woman with grey hair. She wore a white hospital shirt, slippers, and a black woollen shawl draped over her shoulders. Her high cheekbones emphasized the gauntness of her face. From her soft facial features, one could tell she had once been beautiful. Her eyes had lost their youthful glimmer and were passive, giving nothing away, devoid of joy or anger – empty.

Martina and Lisa approached, bent, and kissed her on the cheek. They sat in the two empty chairs across from her. She showed neither vigour nor vitality. Her mood was languid, unaffected, bordering on indifference.

'Mamma, how are you feeling today?' asked Lisa.

Ingrid sat silent, glowering at Lisa as if she didn't recognize her.

'Ingrid, it's us – Lisa and Martina,' said Martina.

Ingrid said nothing, just glared at her.

Martina leaned forward and took her fragile hand. 'I was in Ribbyburg the other day.'

'Ribbyburg!' she said, animated by the mentioning of her former country home. For a moment there was a flicker of joy in her eyes. 'Are…are we going to Ribbyburg?'

'No, not today,' said Martina in a firm voice. 'Today I want you to help me.'

'Help you?'

'Who bought Ribbyburg after you and Stellan divorced?'

'Sold? We never sold Ribbyburg,' said Ingrid. She then fell silent, watching Martina with narrowed eyes. She bit her lower lip and gazed up the ceiling as if trying to remember something.

'It was those troubled years, when Stellan's biochemical company was sued for leaking hazardous waste in surrounding land areas. The company was fined millions of kroner in damages by the court and ordered to clean up the waste. It destroyed us financially. We lost our town-house and put all the money into saving the company. That is when Stellan came to America to ask your father for financial help. For some reason, they had a big falling out.' Ingrid paused, took a deep breath, and asked for a glass of water.

Lisa pressed a button on the bedside. A Nurse appeared, and she asked her to bring water. In minutes she returned with a jug of icy water and a glass. Lisa poured some in a glass and handed it to her mother. Ingrid took a few sips and, with shaking hands, set the glass on the side table. For the first time, she noticed the cast on Martina's leg. 'Who did you fight this time?'

'I fell down,' lied Martina, not wanting to bog her down in unnecessary details. 'What about Ribbyburg?' Martina asked, coaxing Ingrid to continue. Ingrid looked at her, swallowed and shifted her gaze to her fingers, entwining them, playing with them, saying nothing.

'Ingrid?' said Martina.

Ingrid ignored her, picked the glass of water and took a long slow sip. Martina sighed softly and looked at Lisa, who rolled her eyes.

'To save Ribbyburg we transferred the title deed to Lisa,' said Ingrid finally in a slow monotone voice. 'Lisa was still a minor.'

Gazing at mother and daughter, Martina realized they were unaware Ribbyburg had been turned into a private Clinic.

'When Stellan returned from America, he was very angry with your father for refusing him financial help. By then it was too late… to…to salvage the company. He was deeply in debt. He talked about your father having a dossier on him and his friends. He said your father threatened to hand the dossier over to the police, should anything happen to him.'

'Should anything happen to him?' asked Martina, raising her brow in a wide-eyed glare. 'What was in the dossier?'

'I don't know,' said Ingrid. 'On the other hand, Stellan was happy to have met a businessman in America who offered to help him recover financially.'

'Who?' asked Martina as she abruptly rattled into another snappy cough.

'I don't remember his name,' said Ingrid. 'Lisa told me he attended your father's funeral.'

'Dr Steven Rangor,' said Lisa. 'When Father returned from the States, he made me sign legal papers. He said it was an insurance policy for the property. I didn't understand much at the time, so I signed. It turned out I had transferred legal ownership of Ribbyburg back to him. To think that he had to lie to get it back made me angry.'

'Ingrid, do you remember a man called Carlsson, in Hässelved?'

'Carlsson, the farmer,' said Ingrid in a thin voice.

'Yes. He had a row with Pappa and Stellan. Do you remember what it was about?'

Ingrid stared at her, and her eyes glazed over as if she was shocked. She pressed her lips in a thin line and remained silent.

'What was the brawl about?' prompted Martina.

Ingrid remained tight lipped.

'She's tired,' said Lisa. 'Leave her alone.'

Martina studied Lisa and made another attempt at the question. 'Didn't Carls—' In mid-sentence Lisa, shaking her head, laid a hand on Martina's arm to stop her.

The Nurse came in with Ingrid's dinner on a wheeled tray. As Martina and Lisa got up to leave, Ingrid surveyed their faces, and then out of the blue said, 'Carlsson was the best local herbalist in southern Sweden.'

Intrigued by her sudden liveliness, Martina sat down again. 'Herbalist?'

'Yes, one of the best there was,' said Ingrid.

'Was?'

'He died of alcoholism shortly after your parents moved to the States.'

'And the row…what was it about?'

A clink was heard as Ingrid forked a morsel of potato from her plate and put it in her mouth in slow motion. Her gaze remained on the plate as she chewed with slow deliberation. 'Such tasty food they have here,' she said.

A flash of anger flirted on Martina's face. She couldn't escape the thought that Ingrid was teasing her patience.

'Let's go, Martina,' said Lisa. Martina relented, rising to her feet, understanding it was a time-consuming task to draw information out of Ingrid.

'Shame on you two for taking so long to visit me,' said Ingrid with an innocent smile.

The ladies were surprised by her sudden remark. Martina turned a sympathetic gaze on her, acknowledged her complaint, and kissed both her cheeks. They promised to visit more often.

They drove away in silence. Martina was preoccupied with weaving pieces of information together like a jigsaw puzzle trying to get the big picture. The dossier was an interesting twist, but finding it was sure to be a challenge. Family disagreements were something Pappa had protected them against like keeping dirty linen under carpet. She knew Pappa had spent hours discussing medicinal herbs with Carlsson, but why did they have a row?

She remembered Carlsson had a son who taunted and hollered insults at her and Sebastian whenever he found them playing in the woods at Hässelved farm. He always broke out in spasms of hiccups whenever he was enraged. It was their only saving grace. When he did, he was embarrassed, so he left.

Martina stared out of the window, watching buildings and trees fly by, deep in thought.

'Did you know Ribbyburg was turned into a Clinic?' asked Martina.

'You mean Father turned our country home into a Clinic?' asked Lisa.

'Yes, I happened to be driving by on the day of the accident. Suddenly I saw a sign for Ribbyburg Clinic.'

'Since he grabbed Ribbyburg from me, we've never spoken,' said Lisa. 'And I've never been there since then.'

'I didn't want to upset your mother by bringing it up. How are court proceedings?'

'The lawyer is working on it. But it's difficult to prove I didn't know what I was doing when I signed the title deed,' said Lisa. 'I doubt if I'll ever recover Ribbyburg.'

'Don't give up,' said Martina. 'One day it will be yours.'

At Slottsville house the sweet smell of fresh-made pancakes filled the air. Lisa left immediately after dropping Martina off. Thomas and Joachim had just returned from the Zoo and sat at the dining table eating pancakes with whipped cream and cranberry jam.

'Mamma, mother bear got two small baby bears,' said Joachim.

'At Skansen Zoo?'

'Yes. Look, Mamma. I took a photo of the baby bears with Pappa's smartphone.'

Martina leaned in to gaze at the brown cubs on the monitor. 'Ooh, they are cute,' said Martina.

'I'll upload them on my laptop,' said Joachim as he scooted away to his room.

'You came anyway?' asked Martina, turning to Thomas. 'I told you I was fine. It was a minor accident.'

'I wanted to be there for you and Joachim.'

'That wasn't necessary.'

'I have to be there for my son when his mother is not well.'

'You're a good father, Thomas,' she said as she joined him at the table. Astrid brought her a plate of pancakes and toppings. As she ate, she told him about Ingrid.

He told her about his job and that he had asked for transfer back to Stockholm.

'Is that what you really want?' asked Martina.

'I miss my son,' said Thomas, a sad look on his face.

'But you wanted to move to London in the first place.'

'I know, but that was when I thought we would be moving as a family,' said Thomas. 'When you and Joachim didn't join me, and after the divorce, it was never the same.'

'You knew I didn't want to move to London, but you insisted.'

'Bad decision made in haste,' said Thomas. 'I hate to say it, but I regret that decision.'

'What about Wendy? Is she moving to Stockholm too?'

'It didn't work out. She married someone else.'

'I'm sorry.'

Thomas picked up the *Frangipani* from the table and paged through it. Martina sat reflecting on what Thomas had just said. *He regrets that decision.* She felt sad for him. But why was he transferring to Stockholm before his five-year contract ended? Was Joachim the only reason?

'Thomas, are you doing this because you hope…expect things will be like they were between us before the divorce?'

He put down the paper and looked at her.

'Martina, I can't hide the fact that I'm still in love with you. Any hope for a reunion with you would make me a happy man.'

'It would be wrong of me to raise your hopes in regard to a reunion, but for Joachim's sake I'm glad you're moving back to Stockholm.'

His heart died a little at these words from her, but he decided he wasn't giving up on her yet. He'd made his position clear, and that was what mattered for the moment.

'You've done a good job with *Frangipani*. It's enlightening,' said Thomas, moving to a more neutral topic.

'Yes, people have embraced it. When time comes they will recognize the truth and move against anyone trying to grab their natural heritage.'

'There're those who lobby for banning alternative natural medicine and therapies.'

'Those are the ones with a secret agenda,' said Martina. 'They shouldn't be trusted.'

'A secret agenda? What's that?'

'It's business; nothing to bother yourself with.'

'You look tired.'

'You're right. I think I'd better turn in.' She steadied her hands on the table trying to get up.

'You shouldn't be using that leg,' said Thomas.

'And how do you know that?'

'Joachim told me.'

'My son, revealing my secrets,' said Martina, a smile on her face.

'Only when it concerns your best interests,' said Thomas.

Standing up, Thomas offered her his hand. She grasped it, and he helped her up. She staggered, almost losing her balance. Thomas grabbed her waist, holding her tight against him longer than necessary, gazing into her striking blue eyes.

'It's okay. I'm stable now.'

He let her go, picked up her clutches, and handed them to her. As she wobbled to the stairway, Thomas said, 'I'll be leaving for London tomorrow.'

Martina turned to look at him, taking him in – her ex-husband. He still looked hot in those stretch gabardine pants and shirt.

'It was nice of you to come. Joachim and I appreciate that,' said Martina. 'Astrid will see you out.' She wobbled on upstairs. Thomas stood gazing at her till she disappeared.

Chapter 10

Landegrind house, with its well-tended gardens and hedges mixed with colourful summer flowers, on sunny summer days was transformed into a natural picture card. This Saturday morning, Martina sat in the study working at her laptop. Her thoughts drifted to Ingrid; she seemed reluctant to talk about Carlsson. Surely, she knew more than she was letting on. Relationships are built, cemented, tested and shattered by life's experiences. Some relationships last a lifetime; others cool off to remain inactive, while others die a permanent death like Pappa's with Uncle Stellan. At the funeral Rangor had turned up uninvited, and Stellan feigned unfamiliarity with him, yet what she had seen in Ribbyburg spoke volumes. They were still friends – in business and going strong. Did they have a hand in her parents' accident? She shook her head and discarded the scenario at once, not wishing to venture into speculation.

She remembered that Police Chief Inspector Tord Stenbeck had promised to call her if there was a breakthrough in the investigation. She hadn't heard from him. She picked up the landline phone and dialled a number. 'Inspector Tord Stenbeck,' a voice answered.

'Inspector, it's Martina Strömstedt Edgren.'

'Dr Edgren, what can I do for you?'

'How is the investigation coming along?'

'The technical evidence is due for analysis.'

'Due for analysis?' asked Martina. 'I thought it was completed?'

'We're working on it.'

'Do you think it was an accident or homicide?'

'It's too early in the investigation to tell.'

'Is it possible another car was involved in the accident?'

'Who told you that?'

'I thought maybe…just by—'

'Dr Edgren, no other car was involved, and you'd do well to discard any such ideas.'

There was a brief silence as Martina mentally counted to ten, reining in her anger, a technique she had learned at a leadership course. It gave her time to reflect and refrain from saying anything that she might regret later. Even over the phone she perceived Stenbeck's displeasure, his unwillingness to be of service to her. He was a man who expected his word to go unchallenged. There was something unsettling about his voice. It sounded mechanical and soulless. She couldn't pinpoint it, but it awakened something within her, something that remained elusive and difficult to define.

'Dr Edgren, are you there?'

'Yes, I'm here. What's taking so long?'

'We requested to interview with your son some time back,' said Stenbeck, 'but his father declined. Is it possible to do it now?'

'No, I don't think so.'

'Perhaps there's something you can do to help move the investigation forward.'

'And what is that?'

'Allow us to hypnotize your son.'

'Hypnotize? That's out of question. I can't allow it.'

'It might help open up his amnesia.'

'I say no, and that's my final say on this matter,' said Martina. 'I would rather you stopped focusing on my son and find the cause of the accident.'

'Dr Edgren, we need your cooperation here.'

'Thank you, Inspector,' said Martina. 'I'll leave you to get on with your work.' She hung up and sat gazing at Joachim's photo on the wall, fuming about the Inspector's bizarre suggestion to hypnotize a five-year-old boy. That aside, she did not want to dwell on Stenbeck today.

The August sun smiled down, and the sky beamed in a clear blue that seemed to heighten the anticipation of what was to come. Preparations were underway for the Althonat yearly grill. On the lawn, in front of the house, stood the red-hot smouldering grill, ready to set the mood of the evening. The fire blazed, sending sparks in the air. The torrential rains that had tormented them in July were a thing of the past. However, thanks to the rains, Martina's gardens were in full bloom. The surrounding vegetation flourished in deep shades of green. The main flower garden was a cottage-style garden with a chaotic blend of colours and heights, and yet it felt harmonious. It was anchored by cascading carpet roses, clusters of tulips, daffodils, and climbers, and old-fashioned hollyhocks in shades of peach and yellow. A sea of purple coneflowers gleamed, beckoning butterflies and dragonflies to stop for a while.

Next to it a sizeable vegetable garden abounded with juicy red and yellow tomatoes, pole beans, pumpkins, peas, lettuce, sweetcorn, and paprika in red, yellow, and green. Everything on this vast yet snug property was bright, thriving and well kept. Everything looked and breathed money – like a queen's ransom in the bank.

The guests started arriving. First Jonas and then Torsten. Sophie arrived with packages of her own contribution to the feast, though Martina had specified not to bring anything.

Jonas and Torsten remained outside, admiring Martina's garden, while Sophie went inside to help Martina.

'It's said when your plants thrive, your life thrives too,' said Jonas.

'That may be true,' said Torsten. 'But it's her landscaping gardener I'm interested in.'

'That's a secret,' hollered Martina, standing on the veranda doing last minute touches.

'Oh yeah!' said Torsten.

'It's the vegetables that appeal to me most,' said Jonas. 'What's your secret for success?'

'I told you, I'm not telling,' said Martina, with a smile as she stood back assessing the dinner table.

Four wooden rectangular tables were pushed together to form a large table with sixteen chairs encircling it. In the middle of the table were a cluster of candelabra, creating a festive mood full of mystery, romance, and downright spookiness. Perfect, she thought; a vase of flowers from her garden would do magic.

'Gentlemen, there are drinks at the bar,' she called to Jonas and Torsten. 'Please, help yourselves.' She went to the side table, in the middle of the veranda, to check on porcelain. A dozen white pearl Villeroy Boch dinner plates, cutlery, and glass sets stood intricately positioned. Glasses glinted in the fading sunlight. She picked up one of the glasses and removed a speck of dirt with a kitchen towel.

In one corner of the veranda, a set of white sofas with a low wood table in the middle completed the perfect picture of relaxation.

Nils, David and Olausson arrived. They quickly climbed the staircase to the veranda, and their faces, as they rose into the shade above the last stairs, met the gazes of all the party assembled. They were welcomed with glances and nods by the sitting assembly. The empty seats quickly filled around the table. Torsten, the self-appointed bartender, took command, serving drinks with meticulous attention to detail. The conversation was light, sociable, and reminiscent of recent summer holidays. Sophie talked on, rather for attention than for the pleasure of utterance.

Those who had brought swimming costumes plunged into the pool, and took a swim. Then they sat relaxing around the pool, soaking in the last sun, sipping drinks.

Others sat in a half-attentive mood, observing cheering birds as they huddled for shelter under fences, or watching a rabbit skip away into the bushes. A few guests stood on the lawn, sipping chilled drinks and engaging in small talk. Finally, Diana and Sten arrived.

The host emerged with marinades of beef, chicken, and vegetables, which she handed over to Lasse, the attending barbeque chef. Martina had hired him from a trendy restaurant in town; he was a long-time friend who catered all her summer barbeques. Lasse, a pompous forty-year-old man in his regalia of white apron and toque, juggled utensils and set to work.

Martina, the vivacious host, ascended the stairs to greet her guests. A roll of laughter and enthusiasm rang high and loud as they marvelled at how well she looked; her cast was gone, and she had regained something of her old bounding step. Their chatter, their good-humoured innuendoes, their warm hugs and handshakes, revived her sprits. As the evening wore on, she caught the infection of their excitement and grew joyful.

'Why, your glasses are empty,' said Martina. 'Torsten, please, bring some more wine.'

She found her way to an empty seat beside Nils. 'Hi, Nils, how were your holidays in South America? You haven't had a chance to tell me about it.'

'It was wonderful. My wife says we should do it again.'

'I can imagine,' said Martina. 'And you spoke Spanish?'

'A little; my wife is better than I. She's from Argentina.'

'Oh, I see.'

'You look well,' said Nils. 'That accident almost did you in.'

'No...no one does me in, Nils.'

'I understand someone disabled your brakes.'

'It's true, and quite spooky knowing someone wanted me in harm's way.'

'Do you know who did it?'

'No clue. We might never know.'

'Why do you say that?'

'The investigation was closed.'

A moment's silence elapsed as if surprised minds needed minutes to grasp what had transpired. Then spontaneous mumbling erupted among those who were alert and astonished by what she had just said.

'Such audacity that they closed a case without investigating,' said Sophie, pounding her fist on the table.

'Smashing your windscreen was a gross criminal act,' interjected Diana. 'That was an intentional, malicious attack. It should have been investigated.'

'God knows the detectives did their best,' said Martina. 'But the Chief Inspector's orders stopped the investigation.'

'What? You mean Tord Stenbeck closed the investigation?' said Torsten.

'Yes, he did,' said Martina.

'That seems out of normal police procedure,' said Torsten.

'Sounds like a cover-up,' remarked Sophie.

That aside, Martina got to her feet, not wanting to quarrel about Tord Stenbeck. She clicked a fork against her wineglass, calling for attention. Instant silence fell upon the assembly.

'I would like to propose a toast,' said Martina. Everyone lifted their glasses and she said, 'To good health, and to working relationships.'

'We drink to that,' reciprocated everyone. Wineglasses clinked around the table, and as one they took a sip.

The chatter, confusion and giggles erupted once more. The news of closing down the investigation seemed to dampen the ambience of the evening as bright minds wondered in silence where the country was heading with such a police force.

The sweet scent of sizzling food permeated the air, sharpening taste buds. The juicy bits of chicken and beef, served on beds of fresh natural herbs, arrived at table. Lasse slowly but pointedly laid out the sumptuous meal in the middle of the table, making sure guests feasted their eyes before appeasing their palates. Vegetables came in a spectrum of colours, an edible rainbow: red and orange paprika, brown mushrooms, green sizzled zucchini and asparagus, red onions, and purple eggplant. The guests ate as they talked. Their unconscious munching was accompanied by brief moments of silence. The drinking elevated the alcoholic vapours floating in the darkening atmosphere. Jazz music played from a stereo in the background, soothing unsettled senses.

The shimmering candles on the table, amid plates of food and glinting glassware, illuminated the veranda like a lighthouse. The cloudless grey sky stayed calm, alluring the guests into a night of indulgence. The breeze cooled sweaty temples as the birds retired to warm their nests.

'Martina, you've outdone yourself again,' said Jonas as he refilled his glass.

'Wait till you see dessert!' she replied, as she pushed her chair back and crossed her long shapely legs for more comfort and took a sip at her wine. She was in exuberant spirits as she sat watching the guests swinging to a salsa beat from the stereo. The large ceiling-to-floor glass doors to the living room had been opened wide. Living room furniture had been moved against the walls, setting up an impromptu dance floor. Martina and the guests sat on the veranda in full view of the dancing area.

She sat talking to Olausson in an animated manner, her hands flying, her sensual lips moving fast. Jonas sat watching her from across the table, thinking how beautiful she looked tonight. He blinked twice, blinded by the diamond pendant dangling above her cleavage, suspended on a chain that sparkled whenever she turned her neck. An electrifying sensation ran down his spine; the mood was right, the music enticing. He longed to take her in his arms. He hated breaking up their talk, but he couldn't help it. He moved slowly around the table and asked her to dance. She obliged and excused herself, letting him lead her to the dance floor.

The boom-boom opening tones of salsa music sounded, vibrating in her chest. Only the beams of ceiling-mounted spotlights cut the darkness in the room. They had the floor to themselves and stood waiting for their eyes to adjust to the dim lighting. The scent of burning candles, alcohol, and food filled the air while the audience waited with bated breath for the unexpected performance.

He placed his hand on her back; she placed hers on his shoulder. Then they started moving, gazing in each other's eyes, dancing lightly on their toes, breaking momentum rocking to the syncopated ubiquitous beat. He gave her the claves – twisting, tugging, pushing, and checking. They turned, paused, dipped and cross-bodied, wiggled hips to the staccato horns. He stepped in and out, taking her with him, exploding in a swirling twist of hips, deep dipping, and unbridled chemistry. Her green print flare dress accentuated her waist, floating with the motion, turning and twirling in the air. Their bodies radiated sensuality, vibrating to the rhythm, throbbing to climax and timing.

As the music died down, they turned to the crowd, flung their arms out, and bowed. The watchers applauded loudly, sensationally amused and entertained. 'More, more,' cried the gathering.

Jonas eyed Martina, and they both broke out in laughter. 'I didn't think my leg would hold, but it did,' said Martina, gasping for breath.

'You're sensational,' said Jonas, taking her hand and leading her off the dance floor.

The music changed to an African beat, speeding up the pace and flipping the vibe. Diana and Sten took to the floor and started grinding simultaneously to the robust haunting sound of 'Valu, Valu' by José Chameleon. Torsten and Sophie joined them.

The dancing had worked magic on Martina; she became light-footed and lifted herself with a sudden grace and elegance she hadn't felt in months. For the first time since her parents died she realized she had been in an endless spiral of conundrums that threatened her happiness. The realization appealed to her willingness to recapture her old fervour and zest for life.

She alighted in the kitchen. Sophie was already there standing by the stove making custard sauce while Diana stood by the kitchen table preparing whipped cream to serve with dessert. Martina peered into the opened secret packages they had brought with them, feasting her eyes on rhubarb crumble and bittersweet chocolate tart.

'Wow, that looks enticing. I'll make coffee to match a bombastic barbecue and rich dessert,' said Martina as she set to work with the coffee brewer.

Sophie and Diana left to serve the dessert. Martina fumbled with the coffee brewer, not sure how to fit the sill, but when she spilled ground coffee all over the floor, she chuckled at herself and set to work cleaning up. She could hear wild bursts of laughter mixed with music and lively talk. The wine had gone to everyone's head, and Martina laughed along, even though she didn't know what was funny. She had given Astrid a day off, and here she was with everything under control.

Outside, a dark figure emerged from the shadows and mounted the veranda stairs. The figure stood before the guests – a frail woman, dressed in a floral print maxi dress over which she had draped a black shawl. She gazed around frantically, searching for a familiar face, and then said something, but it fell on deaf ears. Ignored, she sauntered across the living room towards the kitchen door. Standing at the threshold, Martina was in full view standing at the kitchen sink with her back towards the figure. Hesitantly, the woman stepped into the kitchen but changed her mind, retreating fast. Instinctively, Martina turned and saw her silhouette disappearing farther into the living room. She went after her.

'Ebba.'

Ebba turned hesitantly, renegotiating her tentative step. Martina sensed something was wrong. She walked up to her, took her by the arm, and brought her to the kitchen area. She offered her a seat at the table. Ebba sat silent, a grim expression on her face. Under her shawl, Martina noticed, she clutched something.

'Ebba, what is it?' Ebba maintained her stance, saying nothing, gazing into space, her eyes puffed and fatigued. 'What is under your shawl?'

Martina hadn't seen her since the day Nicholas was taken from the hospital by her husband. At a loss about what was bothering Ebba, Martina made a cup of herbal tea and gave it to her, hoping it would help her to relax and open up.

'Here, drink some tea.'

Ebba lifted the cup and took a few sips. Martina sat down and regarded her, wondering what had befallen the poor woman. Ebba drank her tea in silence till the cup was empty. The music went on in the living room, echoing in the kitchen. Jessica Anderson was singing 'Wake Up.'

Suddenly Jonas appeared in the doorway. He was surprised to see Ebba, but his face remained impassive. Ebba gazed at him with a weary smile. 'Mrs Strand,' he said.

'Dr Eneroth,' said Ebba as she rose from her seat and shook his hand. In an awkward gesture or rather embarrassed move, she said, 'I'm sorry about the last time we met at the hospital.'

'No, please, don't apologize,' said Jonas. 'It was not your fault. How's Nicholas?'

'It's very complicated,' said Ebba. 'That's why I'm here to speak to Martina.'

'Please, continue,' said Jonas as he turned to Martina.

'Martina, I'll take the coffee if it is ready.'

Martina turned to a side table, took a tray of cups and thermos, and handed it to him.

'Will you manage?' she said. 'You can make two trips perhaps.'

'I'll manage all right,' said Jonas.

He left, and Martina closed the kitchen door behind him and returned to Ebba. She sat down and took her hand. 'Ebba, you obviously came here to tell me something. What is it?'

Colour returned to Ebba's face. She cleared her throat, leaned forward in her seat, and retrieved a brown envelope from under her shawl. On the front was written *Confidential* in red letters. She pulled out a bundle of papers from the envelope, held together by a rubber band.

Ebba's phone sounded and she snatched it from her dress pocket. She gazed at the monitor, stilled; realizing who it was she pressed the off button without answering.

'It's my husband, Patrick, I don't want to speak to him,' she said. She put her phone on the table and went right on to say, 'I want you to have these,' she said as she pushed the bundle of papers towards Martina.

'What is it?'

'I apologize for barging in on your party.'

'Ebba, what is this?' asked Martina, her eyes shifting to the papers.

'There are agreements, photos, names, places, receipts to a bank account.'

'For what?' asked Martina.

'I divorced Patrick. We're selling the house. You know wha—' She stammered and choked on her words. 'The Ju…Judge granted full custody of our boys to Patrick.'

'What?' cried Martina. 'That is preposterous, senseless. What happened?'

'And that's not all.'

What more could be worse than a drunkard being granted custody of two small boys?

'He…sol…sold our son, Nicholas,' she stuttered, tears trailing her cheeks. 'But I didn't tell that to the Judge. I was afraid he wouldn't believe me.'

Martina shuddered and silently wondered what was she talking about. She was right about not telling that to a Judge. It was hard enough for her to believe what Ebba was saying. *Selling Nicholas…no, it can't be true.* Ebba must have misunderstood it all. It must be a mistake. In Ribbyburg, when she had seen Nicholas, he had been taken in for treatment, not to be sold. It couldn't be that Stellan and Rangor were… *No, it can't be.*

Martina shook her head and glared at Ebba in disbelief. 'What do mean he sold your son?'

'Patrick sold Nicholas to a medical research program in Ribbyburg.'

Martina's jaw dropped. The name Ribbyburg had a dreadful clang to it, but the word 'sold' sounded foreign under the circumstances.

'Sold? Are you out of your mind?' said Martina. 'No one sells a child for any reason.'

'You don't believe me? Look, it's all in there,' said Ebba, her face flaring up in anger. Grabbing the paper bundle, she tore at the rubber band, scattered papers over the table, and pointed a finger at a blue document.

'Read that. It's all here,' she repeated. 'I can't reach my son. He's been transferred to a secret private facility. They won't tell where he is. They won't let me see him.' Tears obscured her face.

'Ebba, calm down,' said Martina. 'When did this happen?'

'Things have been bad, very bad, since we left the hospital. I wanted to bring Nicholas back, but I was served with a court order,' she sobbed. Martina handed her a Kleenex tissue paper. Ebba took it and dabbed at her eyes.

'What court order?'

'The police and social welfare people charged me with neglecting my son, denying him proper medical attention,' wailed Ebba. 'I know it is Patrick…he reported me…him and his friends at Ribbyburg, insinuations, lies. He denies it, but I don't trust him. He's strange – such a pathetic excuse for a husband and father, always soaking in drink. He scares the hell out of me, Martina.'

The charge was so outrageous that Martina, lost for words, dropped her head in bafflement.

'He's not the man I married. He's changed,' cried Ebba.

On recovering from her initial shock, Martina looked through the papers slowly, numbed by the evil of mankind, thinking about Nicholas and where he might be. Poor little boy, he must be frightened out of his wits. The blue document was a copy of a bank wire transfer slip, in Patrick's name, to a foreign bank account. Such an amount! She had always believed children were invaluable, priceless gifts. No amount of money could pay for a child. Her mind shifted to Joachim and what she had gone through with him in hospital – the paralyzing fear, nerve-racking night vigils, and the stress of the ringing phone. No mother should ever have to go through such heart-breaking agony. Ebba must be devastated.

'This is what I salvaged before he cleaned out the house,' said Ebba, picking at the papers on the table, shuffling them back and forth angrily. The signs of anxiety in her face and voice, about all that had upset her mind in the situation, made a scene which Martina could not look away from, even though she was touched by the horror.

'Where's Patrick?'

'He keeps calling me, threatening me, but he doesn't tell me where he is,' cried Ebba. 'He took Felix, and they're gone.'

'Ebba, calm down,' said Martina. 'There must be a way to resolve this.'

The background music reminded Martina of the party in progress. She must have been missed by now. She must wrap it up with Ebba and get back.

'Keep these,' said Ebba as she pushed the papers across the table towards Martina.

'I can't take it,' said Martina. 'It's a matter for the police.'

'Just for safekeeping till I sort myself out. I've got to find a place to live. I'm going to Malmö tomorrow, to my parents. When I return, I'll know what to do. I must fight to get my children back.'

'How long will you be gone?'

'Three days. I've got to appear in court next week,' said Ebba. 'Martina, I might go to prison.'

'Oh, Ebba, I hope not,' said Martina, knowing she had not concealed the fear in her eyes. Leaning in, she hugged her friend long and hard. A knock on the door tore them apart.

'Come in,' said Martina.

It was Diana with thermos in hand. Noticing the tension in Martina's face, she hesitated. 'I hope I'm not interrupting anything, am I?' asked Diana.

'No, come in,' said Martina.

'We need more coffee,' said Diana. 'Don't pay me any attention. I'll get it.' She moved into the kitchen and set about working the coffee brewer.

'Ebba was just leaving,' said Martina as she picked up the papers from the table and stashed them back in the brown envelope. She put the envelope under her arm.

Ebba got to her feet, and they moved towards the living room. On the threshold they ran into Jonas. 'What's taking so long?' asked Jonas. 'Everybody's asking for you.' He cast a glare at Ebba.

'Ebba is leaving,' said Martina. 'I'll be there in a moment.'

Halfway through the living room, Martina changed her mind, steering Ebba back into the kitchen and out through the kitchen door. It was best to be discreet, in case Patrick turned up looking for her.

Outside, under the pale gaze of a waning moon, fear, sorrow, and ambiguous dread seemed to congeal in the night air.

'You'll need a good lawyer,' said Martina. 'If you don't have one, let me know.'

'I'll call you when I return and let you know,' said Ebba, a profound sadness in her moist eyes.

'I'll keep these,' said Martina indicating the brown envelope. 'But I'll expect you to contact the police when you return.'

'Thank you, Martina. I'll never forget this.'

'Where're you staying?'

'With my sister Eva, in Stockholm, but she has a family.'

'That's a long drive.'

'I'll be all right.'

'Take care, and call me,' said Martina as she hugged her.

Ebba walked towards the road where she had parked her car. Standing in awe, Martina watched as darkness engulfed Ebba, her heart aching for her, tears filling her eyes. She entered the kitchen and dried her eyes with a tissue. She noticed Ebba's phone laying on table. She picked it up and bolted to the driveway onto the road but saw only the tail lamps of her car disappearing in the distance. She came into the house and headed upstairs to her parents' bedroom. She removed the wall painting revealing a safe in the wall. She entered a combination in the keypad. The safe lock clicked open. She shifted papers and packages, making space. Suddenly a small brown leather wallet with a rubber band around it fell out onto the floor. She picked it up, opened it, and found a single key on a ring. On the ring was an oval metal piece engraved with the words Nordea Bank. It looked like a key to Bank safety deposit box. When she looked further in the wallet, she found a folded bank paper with her father's name and address. She opened it and read through, finding the box number. What could possibly be in the bank box?

She returned the key and paper to the wallet and dropped it in a bedside table drawer. She deposited Ebba's brown envelope and phone inside the wall safe, closed it, and hung the painting back on the wall. Then she headed downstairs and out into the enlivened gathering.

On seeing her, the gathering erupted in one vigorous chorus, 'Where have you been?' She fell into her good-humoured self with a flow of animated spirit which brightened every conversation she engaged in, charming the assembly with funny stories and jokes from everywhere under the sun. The giggles and laughter filled the night air, transporting the festivities to a climax. The stereo struck up 'Smiling Brown Eyes' by Lars Berglund.

Torsten came and asked her for a dance. He took her in his arms and swirled her across the floor. Torsten belonged to a generation of men that danced well. Her celebrative mood was back. The music ended with a clapping of hands from the assembly.

'Martina, here is your dessert,' said Diana, handing her a plate full of sweet things.

'Do I have to eat all this?'

'Oh, it's good. Just savour it.'

'You make it sound tempting.' Without warning she spotted Jonas, sitting in a corner on a white sofa.

'Watch me,' whispered Martina. 'I know who will help savour it.'

Martina arched her brow, nodding towards Jonas. Diana smiled. Martina wandered off, her movements so graceful they seemed effortless, like a soft breeze.

The cool night air washed over Jonas as he sat watching the moon, whose orb shone like a meteor streaming down, lighting a hazy atmosphere with a passive sheen. Activity slowed down, but it would be hours before the assembly retired.

Martina sank into the sofa beside Jonas. Jonas turned and smiled at her.

'I can see you're bored,' said Martina as she placed the dessert plate on the low table.

'Ah, ah, I'm not bored, just enjoying the beautiful moonlight, and of course your stories.'

'Which story did you enjoy most?' asked Martina.

'The one about a man who married many wives and started a wife farm,' chuckled Jonas.

'It sounded like Animal Farm,' Martina said with a giggle.

'It's such a splendid idea,' said Jonas. 'Maybe I should try it sometime.'

'But some wives will be more equal than others. How will you choose?'

'I'll play them like a game of chess,' said Jonas. 'And choose the winner.'

Martina slapped him hard on the thigh. Jonas winced and laughed out loud.

'Mr Polygamist, let me entice you with a candied dessert,' said Martina.

'Not unless you feed me,' said Jonas.

'Darling, I'd feed you anytime, but not in front of staff.'

'It's nice and shadowy here; no one will notice,' whispered Jonas in her ear. 'Besides, they're all intoxicated.' Martina laughed.

In the background stereo music died down. Instead, groggy, lethargic tongues set about singing party songs. Woolly-headed as they were, it was a potpourri of full, loud and deep sonorous sounds mixed with disordered talk and loud laughs.

The mood shifted advantageously for Martina to engage in a private session with her lover. Theirs was a hush-hush relationship, to be sipped in secrecy. They conversed in undertones, murmuring romantic poetry in each other's ear. His voice was silken and husky in her ear, hers gloriously velvet and soft to his cheek.

The soft feel of his voice slackened her muscles, making her lean softly on him, taking advantage of the assembly's drunken state. She reached up and kissed him. Their lips touched briefly, but he pulled her back and deepened the kiss. Their tongues entwined, tasting each other, satisfying their craving for one other. It was the noblest reward of the day.

All day she'd traversed landscapes of emotions – frustration, anger, uncertainty and dread – but now at last, love beckoned her to his bosom. They relished in each other as they devoured dessert. She fed him anyway but in a discreet manner, keeping confidences, avoiding social embarrassment.

'Want more?'

'No, thank you. I'm done,' said Jonas as he leaned and kissed a crumb off the corner of her mouth.

The assembly sang louder, their senses muffled and brains benumbed by alcohol.

'What did Mrs Strand want?' asked Jonas.

'She and her husband are divorcing. They're selling the house.'

'She seemed rattled, all right,' said Jonas. 'But she's better off without that bully.'

'Patrick Strand used to be a good man, but somewhere he changed and started drinking.'

'If security hadn't come quickly that day at the hospital, I'd have taken him on myself. He mishandled her. I reported the matter to the police, but she withdrew charges against him. It beats me why she did that.'

'It was me who called security from the next room.'

'So you did,' said Jonas. 'That reminds me. Where did you disappear that day? The next thing I heard, you were in an accident. Where did you go?'

A moment of silence passed. Jonas leaned in to gaze at her, wondering why she was quiet.

'I went for a drive to clear my mind.'

'I called your phone, but it was off all day.'

'Darling, it's such a beautiful night. Do we have to talk about this now?'

'Of course not, but just one question that's been bothering me. Where did they take Nicholas?'

'To a private Clinic in Ribbyburg.'

'Your Uncle's Clinic?'

'It's not his Clinic,' said Martina. 'He leases out the premises to Citaraph. It was his country home.'

'Is it a good Clinic?'

'I don't know, but I intend to find out.'

Jonas raised his brows, a worried look on his face. 'You don't have to do that yourself. Ask Torsten to check it out for you.'

In the distance at the top of the stairs, Martina saw two figures emerge onto the veranda. She was still leaning on Jonas' chest with his arm around her waist. The figures first gazed around, and then started moving towards her and Jonas. It was Olausson and Torsten. She pulled away from Jonas, sat upright, and squared her shoulders making herself decent. Jonas shifted on the sofa, putting space between them. In a second, the gentlemen had joined them.

'Martina, such a marvellous place you've here,' said Olausson. 'We've been around the grounds, all the way to the meadow.'

'Join us, please, sit down,' said Martina, a warm smile on her face. Jonas got to his feet and said, 'I'll get drinks.'

'I'll have red wine,' said Olausson.

'Falcon,' said Torsten.

'Red wine,' said Martina.

Olausson and Torsten sat in the two empty single sofas opposite Martina. 'It's beautiful out here this time of year,' said Torsten.

'Yes, it is,' said Martina. 'That's why I spend weekends here.'

'I remember when your father built this house. He put his craftsmanship into it,' said Olausson as he examined the floor tiles. 'Even the stones in this floor came from Hässelved farm.'

'He was still working at Radium Institute then,' said Martina.

Jonas returned with a tray of drinks and served. He took his seat beside Martina.

'But when it was completed,' said Torsten, 'he wanted to sell it and move to Hässelved farm.'

'To sell this house?' asked Jonas.

'Yes,' said Torsten.

Martina took a sip of her wine. It tasted delicious – cool and crisp. Pappa had wanted to move to Hässelved farm. That was news to her.

'He always talked about Hässelved farm,' said Olausson. 'He loved the natural flora and fauna, in southern Sweden. By then he was shifting to alternative medicine, and he was disillusioned about his work at the Institute.'

'We were surprised when he and Stellan instead sold Hässelved farm,' said Torsten.

'Hässelved farm…you mean the forestland and property in southern Sweden?' asked Jonas.

'Yes,' said Olausson. 'That is where he felt at home most.'

'And it was abrupt,' said Torsten. 'It was as if they had to get rid of it immediately.'

'Did he say why they sold?' asked Martina, surprised by things she was learning from her father's peers.

'After that he never talked about it,' said Torsten. 'Even Stellan never talks about it.'

Of course, Martina could ask Stellan, but that was out of the question. They hadn't spoken for years. It would seem awkward.

'Maybe something happened, forcing them to sell,' said Jonas.

'You're right, Jonas. It doesn't add up,' said Martina. 'Something must have happened.' Her mind drifted to Carlsson and the brawl he'd had with Pappa – and Ingrid's unwillingness to talk about it.

'I'm glad he didn't sell this house though,' said Jonas. 'It's lovely.'

Her past held mysteries she'd never known existed. Mysteries she must uncover to get to the truth of what had happened and what was happening. Pappa's long-time friends, Torsten and Olausson, were part of that link to the truth. Pappa had brought them aboard Althonat, trusting they would add to his dreams and vision for the business.

Martina thought she heard something. She straightened and looked around. The hedges rustled, shaking as if a storm was in the making. In the dim moonlight, she thought it was a dog, but instead a figure of a man emerged from under the bushes. His red training pants stood out in the shady night. Instead of walking, he wobbled, swayed, and tottered like a seesaw.

Martina sprang to her feet. 'Hey, who's there?' she hollered. The assembly was instantly alert; faces and heads turned in search of what aggravated her. Torsten, with the security reflex ingrained in him, flew down the stairs to confront a greasy-haired man, sweating like a drunken Irishman in a sauna. His crimson eyes were blinking brighter than his red pants. The stench of alcohol coming off him sent Torsten reeling backwards; clearly here was a man with an unbalanced mind. The sharp blade of an axe flickered in the moonlight as he dangled it in his hand.

'It's Patrick Strand,' said Martina as she glimpsed him approaching the veranda. Where had he been lurking? Jonas saw what she was about to do. Surprised by her lack of fear in the face of danger, he grabbed her hand, but Martina jerked him away. In a second she flew down the stairs.

'Martina, come back here,' cautioned Jonas. 'He's got an axe! Let Torsten take care of it!'

Martina grabbed a steel crowbar and moved towards Patrick, her blue eyes turned to ice. The assembly, aroused by the commotion, stood on the veranda watching the unfortunate turn of events unfold, fear gripping every heart.

'Turn around, and go back where you came from,' said Torsten.

'Where's Maar…M… Maaartina?' stuttered Patrick. 'Stuupid, stupid, silly woman.'

'I say go back, Strand,' said Martina, brandishing the crowbar.

Patrick stilled when he saw her, as if he'd never expected to. He widened his strained eyes trying to focus. 'Yoou, yuuu destrooy my family,' he stammered. 'Yuuu, missled my wi…wi…wife.'

'Leave, go back,' Martina said through clenched teeth.

Patrick mustered his energies for a final effort and walked a crooked line towards Martina. He lunged at her with the axe. She stepped easily aside and blocked the blow with the crowbar. The clash of metal struck sparks in the air. The smell of smoke mixed with burning metal filled the atmosphere. Somebody screamed, 'Violence, violence! Stop him!'

Jonas rushed and grabbed Martina from behind, pulling her out of danger. Patrick staggered backwards, almost landing on the smouldering grill. Then he regained his balance and charged like a lunatic at Martina. His eyes squinted to focus, his body tilted and swayed as he zig-zagged forwards. He hacked at her. Martina tumbled backwards in Jonas' grip, landing in a bundle on top of him, dodging the axe by millimetres.

'Stop him, stop him,' someone howled. 'He's crazy!'

Torsten restrained Patrick from behind, but not before a chaotic tumult erupted and complete pandemonium broke out as the assembly charged at the attacker like an angry mob after a common thief. The mob wrestled the culprit to the ground and pinned him down, where he moaned and yowled like a wounded pig. Someone made a call. In five minutes the police had arrived on the scene. The culprit was bundled into a police car and taken to sleep it off in jail.

*****

A scintillating velvet horizon announced the crack of dawn. A misty morning, the world caught between autumn and winter. The warm shades of autumn seemed to float in the fog as the early morning chirps of songbirds echoed through the valley.

Martina and Jonas lay silent in bed, flesh to flesh, listening to the drumming of their heartbeats. The walls of the universe seemed to fade away; all they knew was each other. A tantalizing scent of Martina's favourite perfume lingered in the unlit room. They touched, cuddled, and engaged in a rhythmic and synchronized battle of passion. The air around them was charged with their storm of frenzied writhing; he was straddling her; she arched upwards to take all of him, moving with him, feeling his hot thrust shoot through her like a tidal wave. Ripples of ecstasy overtook her, and seized by a rush of sensation so intense, she shuddered in a wild rapture. He groaned in blissful agony as he exploded in her. He buried his head in her shoulder and called out her name.

Chapter 11

In a tiny bar on the outskirts of Stockholm, two girls sat having drinks. One of the girls, the Bottle Blonde with dark eyes, chattered on about her big plans in the world's oldest profession. Her heavy eyelids drooped with neon blue mascara, and her cerise collagen-augmented lips pouted like the mouth of a clay pot. Her friend, breast implants proudly on display, sat gazing at her, the flowers and glitter in her brunette hair blinking like the red light district. They might have been in their late teens.

A man with a weather-beaten face sat across the table, his gaze darting to and fro as if he expected somebody. He looked like a weasel, and when he spoke, his voice sounded weak and small. 'Listen, girls, behave now, and make a good impression. You understand?' he said as he pointed a finger at the girls. The girls batted eyelids and nodded wide-eyed. A mixture of sweat and alcohol filled the air. Roxy Music blared in the background.

Then he saw the two men as they appeared at the door. Weasel pushed back his chair, got up, and crossed the room to meet them. They stood talking for a while at the door and then came in and sat with the girls. One of them, a tall, tight-faced man with a beak-like nose, looked like he had never learnt to smile. He did most of the talking. He wore a sportsman's cap that hid half his face. His companion, a rather reserved, overgrown man, sat with a lopsided grin on his face. He looked well-trained; muscles bulged in his taut-fitting black leather jacket. His face was scarred and seemed to be healing from scabs and blisters. His brownish yellow eyes shone like cheap jewellery in the semi-dark room. The beak nose ordered more drinks. After the waiter disappeared, he spoke in a low deliberate voice.

'You ladies ready for the night?'

'Anything you say, consider it done,' said the Bottle Blonde as she rolled her eyes, and Miss Breast Implants nodded her head in childish enthusiasm.

They sat talking about preferences, whims, price tags and working hours. All the while, more liquor flowed. The girls' spontaneous talk turned into uncoordinated giggles. The wine had gotten to them. The beak-nose raised his chin and signalled the Weasel with a look. They left the table and retired to a private room to conclude business; there, merchandise was approved and an envelope changed hands. The Weasel checked in the envelope, making a quick calculation as he ran his forefinger over the green notes. He looked up at the beak-nosed man and smiled in satisfaction. With a clasp of hands they sealed the deal and returned to join the girls.

At three in the morning, the party emerged from the bar. The girls half wobbled to the car, supported by the men. As they clambered into the back seat, suddenly the Bottle Blonde bolted off, hooking herself onto the arm of a passer-by. The stranger seemed surprised but played along until the Weasel caught up with her, grabbed her by the arm, and pulled her away.

'Get back in here,' he said as he dragged her to the car.

She climbed into the rear seat of the car and collapsed in giggles, covering her face with her hands. The bulky man got behind the wheel, and beside him sat the beak-nosed man. The car sped off towards south Stockholm. It arrived at Vittaby Villa, in Dalernesund, and parked behind the villa, near a hidden entrance to Devilund Clinic. Dr Fritz Grenzken opened the rear gate as if expecting them. He came to the car as the beak-nosed man jumped out. They shook hands and talked while the bulky man helped the tanked-up girls into Devilund Clinic.

The girls swayed and tottered forwards through the door, under the stern eye of the bulky man. Grenzken licked his lips and grinned at the beak-nosed man. The girls were dressed in miniskirts and short tank tops, revealing slender tummies.

'Good hunting,' said Grenzken. 'They look luscious.'

'They're good – young and fresh,' said the beak nose. 'I hope they're healthy too.'

'We'll soon find out.'

With their shady undertakings camouflaged by darkness, the men signed and exchanged documents. Again a handshake concluded business.

Dawn announced a new day and the two men proceeded into the villa to the dining area, where Ella, the housekeeper at Vittaby Villa, served an early breakfast buffet. Birgit sat engrossed in the *Frangipani* newspaper. She managed a brisk 'Good morning' without lifting her gaze from her reading.

It had been a long night, and the smell of fresh-brewed coffee awakened inhibited appetites. The beak-nosed man grabbed a side plate and made a sandwich of brown bread, cold cuts, and vegetables. He took a bite, savouring the crunchy taste filling his mouth. He munched on in silence.

Grenzken opted for crisp bread, topped up with sliced boiled eggs and caviar. 'You seemed enthralled by the *Frangipani*, Birgit,' he said.

'You won't believe this. Listen.' She cleared her throat. *'Life-Vaccine causes genetic mutations in people and their offspring thereafter. This idiotic practice by mad scientists will lead to serious consequences for humanity.'*

Birgit raised her eyes in a frown and glared at Grenzken. 'Fritz, is this true?'

'What rubbish. Life…Life-Vaccine, indeed…' Grenzken stuttered, a formidable expression spreading over his face, anger heating up his blood. Birgit, anxious to learn more, did not wait for Grenzken's answer.

'Wait, wait till you hear this. *Life-Vaccine is made from mixing various components: pest virus, heavy metals, animal tissues, antifreeze, and pesticide. The biggest danger is that it weakens the immune system.'* She read it with a horrified note in her voice and then continued, *'The population is advised to reject Life-Vaccine, and if anyone has already received shots, they should turn to Althonat Hospital for immediate evaluation.'*

'You don't really believe in tabloid gossip, Birgit,' said the beak-nosed man. 'It's all about money. *Frangipani*, and Althonat for that matter, exploits people by misleading them and brainwashing them.' He returned to munching his sausage and washed it down with a glass of orange juice.

'I doubt that. The woman behind *Frangipani* is a reputable doctor by medical standards,' said Birgit, staring at the beak nose. 'I don't believe her newspaper would print anything untrue. Besides, she's even launched a natural cell antidote against Life-Vaccine–induced illnesses.'

Grenzken took another sip at his coffee, put his cup down, and gave Birgit a look of undisguised rage.

'Birgit, don't ever read anything to me from *Frangipani* if you want to keep working for me,' said Grenzken. 'And as from today, I'm cancelling the *Frangipani* subscription.'

'But Fritz…'

'No, I mean it.'

Birgit soured, folded up the *Frangipani* under her arm, and stormed out of the room.

Grenzken got up and pressed a remote to activate the TV monitor. The news anchor blabbered on about Althonat's successes and then went on reporting 'demonstrations downtown against Life-Vaccine; people are rampaging against Citaraph, wanting to know the real health benefits of Life-Vaccine, angry their tax money is wasted on a vaccine that is damaging lives.' He changed to another news channel, and the same gabble was going on.

'What crap,' said Grenzken. 'Ludicrous, Althonat is all over the media.'

He jabbed the remote to silence the monitor and returned to the breakfast table, but his appetite was gone.

'You know she's right,' said the beak-nosed man, his voice metallic and cold. '*Frangipani* is a reputable newspaper, and well read by the masses.'

'Such negative publicity digs deep in our pockets,' said Grenzken. 'We can't afford it. We need to find a permanent solution to the problem.'

'This Althonat woman – I didn't think much of her,' said the beak-nosed man, 'but now she's more of a threat than her father. She's trumping up a pharmaceutical war, churning thunderclouds and flexing her muscles.'

'I suspected she was good but not to this ominous level. She has more guts than her father,' said Grenzken. 'What's this natural cell antidote I hear she's launching to counteract Life-Vaccine–induced illnesses?' He said it rather thinking aloud than asking a question. The beak-nosed man perceptibly said nothing, lost in his own struggle with the implications of what was happening and how its unravelling would impact him if left unabated.

It was like a game of football: you had to read your situation not just like a textbook but as your opponents understood it. Where was her strength, what were her vulnerabilities, what would she do next? With the Althonat woman, the moment she stepped into her father's shoes, even with her youth and inexperience, there was no way of knowing which way she would go. But now she had shown her hand, and the time had come to decide on a course of action.

Grenzken pushed his chair back, upsetting his coffee cup with the sudden motion. He reached for his laptop on the side table and logged in. He opened his mailbox and wrote an email. His cold fingers hovered over a button and then stabbed down.

Chapter 12

At breakfast, Joachim told his mother about the football tournament he'd attended on Saturday, in Gothenburg. The ride in the bus with his team was exciting, and he had enjoyed it.

'Mamma, we got a direct free kick, and I scored straight away. That's why we won.'

'You little strong buster,' said Martina. 'I knew you'd win.'

'We won the Junior National Championship, beating Gothenburg 3–2, and it was yeah, yeah, yeah!'

'Was it important for you to win?'

'Yes, we had to win,' said Joachim. 'Some boys cry if we lose.'

'But you don't cry, do you?'

'Only when I miss Greatpa and Greatma,' said Joachim with a shrug.

Martina's smiling face froze and turned sad. She reached out and put her hand over his little hand, caressed it, and kissed his forehead. 'I miss them too, sweetheart. I'll tell you what: we pack our backpacks and drive to Väddö. We'll do some work and then go eat pizza, at Pizzeria Salads Bar.'

Joachim's eyes lit up. 'Yes, Mamma, I love pizza.'

Neon colours of autumn foliage touched the senses of taste and smell. The scents tied into the season; chimney smoke, apples and plums filled the atmosphere. The gentle autumn breeze caused trees to shed leaves, leaving them bare as ghost trunks of wood.

Martina returned to the Strömstedt family country home, Landegrind house, with Joachim, to clean and put things in order for the winter season. They raked the lawn, planted fruit trees, and repaired broken summer furniture and put it away. She was skilled when it came to fixing things around the house. The joy came more from putting her mark on work well done, as one may say, than just mending stuff.

She remembered how, when she was a teenager, her father had put her and Sebastian to the task of mending and maintaining farm fixtures and fittings during summer holidays at Hässelved farm, in southern Sweden. She looked back at that time with deep gratitude. It had taught her a lot of things she could draw from to affect her life and her work, even as CEO. They had been the best years of her life.

On returning from Pizzeria Salads Bar, Joachim busied himself with Lego in his playroom. Martina went up to the attic – something she'd wanted to do since the funeral but hadn't got round to. She went up the stairs, opened the attic door with a key, and looked round at boxes stacked as high as the roof. She didn't know where to begin, but she planned to go through everything, establishing what to throw out and what to save.

She rummaged through the first box and sorted papers. In the stack of bank statements, electric bills, old life insurance policies, old files of income tax filings, she found a fair sampling of her past: drawings and paintings, school photographs, ballet class programs, swimming certificates. It was like rewinding the clock. Slipped among them was a postcard from the USA. She had forgotten that her grandparents had travelled to visit her parents. She and Sebastian were at boarding school at the time, in Sigtuna, outside Stockholm. *The weather is glorious. We've seen plenty of lovely things. We love you, Granny.* She shredded documents in an electric shredder in a corner.

One bundle of papers left in the box she'd been working on caught her interest. On top and under the bundle were business reports, but tucked in between was an old album. She retrieved it and paged through. They were photos from Hässelved farm. One picture stopped her in place. It was a photo of Pappa, Stellan, and a thin, tall man with a withered face and shrunken cheek bones. He seemed to have aged before his time. It was Carlsson. Beside him was a young man gazing up at the trio: Carlsson's son, the man who used to harass her and Sebastian. In the background of the photograph was a small red cottage in the middle of the woods. On the table before them were a display of plants, wildflowers, mushrooms, and other forest vegetation. Dislodging the photo from the album, Martina put it in her pants pocket. She cleared out the last box and left the attic.

On Monday morning Martina rushed to Nordea bank. Speaking to the service desk attendant, the lady asked for her ID. Martina handed it to her. The attendant turned to her computer and clicked away at the keyboard. She confirmed that the key belonged to her father's bank safety deposit box. Taking a form from her, Martina filled it in, signed it, and handed it back.

The attendant fed codes into the computer, opening the bank vault. Martina descended the stairs to the vault. Inside, with key in hand, she opened the bank box. There she found share certificates, property title deeds, small gold bars and coins in a leather bag. The items had been included in her father's will but she had forgotten about them.

At the bottom of the box was a large, thick white envelope addressed to her father. As she pulled it out, she noticed that the red seal was broken. She peered inside the envelope and found documents, photographs, reports, and videotapes. Enclosed was a scribbled note: *According to specification, yours, Scorpio.* Her heart pounded, and her mouth dried up. Could this be the dossier Ingrid had talked about? She pulled out the contents and scanned swiftly through the text in a report. She frowned at the photographs, exhilarated but frightened at the same time. It must be the dossier on Stellan.

She glanced at her watch; it was past eleven – time to catch up on lunch and get back to the office. She stuffed the white envelope into her brief case, locked the safety deposit box, closed the vault door, and ascended the stairs. She thanked the desk attendant with a nod and emerged into the chilled autumn breeze.

Financial director Diana Were and Chief accountant Kent Stenzon appeared in Martina's office. Diana, leaned forward in her chair, pulling papers out of a folder. She spoke with expertise about the positive indicators in the financial report, with guaranteed steady growth. In fact, Althonat had capacity for further expansion. Kent presented quarterly results, confirming accounts in balance.

Martina nodded in approval, a serious expression on her face.

'We must put funds to use,' added Diana. 'Otherwise Skatteverket will raise our tax bracket.

Martina wondered why Pappa had never stressed making necessary investments. So much capital lying around doing nothing was not her style.

'I'm glad the board sanctioned expansion,' said Martina. 'We're going global – opening up in Berlin, Paris, Tokyo, Kuala Lumpur, Kampala, Lagos, Beijing, Moscow, Mexico and Rio de Janeiro. And from now on, the corporate name will be Althonat Global with headquarters in Stockholm.'

'So, you're moving the headquaters from New York,' asked Kent.

'New York will always be our strong hold, but we need the European market too,' said Martina.

Her gaze shifted to Diana. 'Diana, could you spearhead operations in Beijing and Moscow? You speak Chinese and Russian. These are major emerging markets for us.'

'I'll be honoured,' reciprocated Diana with enthusiasm.

'What about the donation received last month?' asked Martina. 'Have you identified the donor?'

'You mean the hundred million Swedish kroner?' asked Kent.

'Yes.'

'It's Barbara Von Essen Nsamizi,' said Kent. 'However, there is a condition attached. Funds are specified for operations in Africa.'

'Good old Barbara,' said Martina. 'How generous of her. Put the funds on the Africa account. Also allocate funds for the construction of Althonat hospitals in the new markets. There's a backlog of patients as more people suffer adverse effects of Life-Vaccine. We must diversify services.'

As an afterthought she turned to Kent. 'What about Althonat yearly donations to the Nobel Foundation? Have they been allocated?'

'Yes, last week,' said Kent.

'Good. Will that be all?' asked Martina.

'One more thing,' said Diana. 'Installation of a new global accounting system is under way, and accounts are being overhauled. But there is a discrepancy.'

'What kind of discrepancy?' said Martina.

'Kent,' said Diana as she turned her gaze to Kent.

'Internal audit revealed a recurring transfer of funds from the New York account to a Shell Company,' said Kent.

'Shell Company?' said Martina.

'Yes, in the Caribbean,' said Kent.

'Authorized by whom?' asked Martina.

'Dr Peter Strömstedt was signatory, but the detail is missing.'

'The figure?' asked Martina.

'Five million dollars a year,' said Kent.

'That's substantial,' said Martina, shock evident in her voice.

What was Pappa doing with a Shell Company? Was it for purposes of cloaked identities, fictitious service schemes, fraud, or tax evasion?

'Stop all payments immediately,' said Martina. 'Diana, could you investigate this, take it up with Torsten. Ask him to look for red flag indicators.'

'Right,' said Diana.

'Will that be all?'

'Yes, that is all,' said Diana.

'Thank you,' said Martina, ending the meeting.

At last a moment on her own. Martina retreated to her father's office with the white envelope under her arm. Locking the door behind her, she emptied the contents of the envelope on the desk, sat down, and examined each item. An old newspaper clipping from a few years back, with three men standing, dressed in well-fitted suits, and a woman with a short haircut in an ill-fitted trouser suit. The man with the silly grin was Rangor. Stellan stood with his face half turned away from the camera. The third man was the CEO of Citaraph Pharmaceuticals, Jacob Mattsson. The woman, Lillian Linsjö, was chair of the Board at Citaraph and Permanent Secretary in the Ministry of Health and Welfare. The article mentioned 'bright brains joining Citaraph power Board team.' What a strange formulation, and what a cynical toxic combination: Citaraph, government, and two men of dubious moral fibre. Poor old Stellan also counted as a bright brain. Martina chuckled in amusement.

She picked up the video tape and gazed at it, realizing it was an old-fashioned gadget before DVDs had come. She switched on the TV monitor and slid the tape into the VCR. She activated the remote and the tape rustled and rolled into action; she was looking at activities in Devilund Clinic. She recognized Rangor, Stellan, Citaraph's CEO, and another stocky man with protruding eyes. He must be the unhinged scientist in charge of Devilund Clinic, Fritz Grenzken. His name had been in the report. The men haggled over the price for a piece of paper, which Rangor brandished in his hand. Stellan appeared agitated, clasped his arms above his head, threw them about, and then turned to Rangor in furious turmoil. Rangor, with open hands, pleaded with Stellan to accept the deal. But Stellan hesitated, shaking his head, saying that was not what they had agreed on.

Rangor took him aside. When they returned, Stellan's face screamed treachery. Rangor motioned the CEO with his eyes as he handed the paper to the stocky man. The CEO opened his briefcase, retrieved a document and pen, signed, and passed it on to Stellan. Stellan took the papers with hesitancy and glared at Rangor. Rangor prompted him with a wave of his hand to sign the dotted line. With his eyes tarred by guilt, Stellan capitulated and signed. Then he stood motionless, vexation growing on his face. Rangor sealed the deal with his signature. From their expressions, there was no spark, no celebration, only the sombre formality of a business transaction to acquire half the Rensblad formula. When all was done, the men seemed in a hurry to leave the room.

Martina switched off the player and monitor. Talk about Judas Iscariot and thirty pieces of silver. Poor Pappa, what he'd had to endure from Stellan. She recalled with sadness that her father had not been able to bring the formula to production due to the hostile environment from the medical establishment and the media. Yet, still, he did not know what to expect when he arrived in America. For safe keeping, he had given half the formula to Stellan just before he moved to the States. Martina sighed and turned back to the items on the table: copies of bank statements, wire transfer slips with millions of dollars to Stellan's secret foreign bank account. Martina understood the big picture. Surveillance reports from Scorpio depicted Stellan's day-to-day movements before his final act of betrayal.

As she surveyed the material on the table, a disturbing impulse possessed her – to shred it all, walk away, and forget about it. But what would that make her? What about her parents' death, the dossier before her, compiled by her father? What about Althonat Global? Would it survive if she ignored the information before her? And would humanity survive without Althonat Global? Hardly, she surmised. Her father's words rang in her head: 'Martina, remember the formula. If anything happens to me, try to recover the formula.' There was only one way to go: fight for her father's legacy; uproot the evil threatening humanity.

What that might entail, she didn't know, but she decided to dig deeper for the truth. The realization made her shudder, and then a horrible question forcibly came to her. *Why is this nefarious group injecting poison and disease into people? Who are they, and why are they doing this?*

That night she read to Joachim and put him to bed. She went to her bedroom, thinking to make it an early night. Her head throbbed. She kept being drawn back to that video tape of Stellan and those men in Devilund. *How could he do that to Pappa?* The phone alert sound made her jump. She picked it up and answered. 'Martina.'

'This is Greta Larsson, Ebba Strand's mother.'

'Yes, Mrs Larsson, how are you?'

'I'm sorry to inform you that Ebba died in a car accident.'

'Oh Lord…dear Lord no…please, no,' stuttered Martina. Thunderstruck and upset, she fell speechless. The wave of shock in her body numbed her senses. She saw Ebba's life flash before her eyes in slow motion: her struggles and tribulations, the last time she had seen her, broken and confused, in her kitchen. Yet her unbending will to stand for what was right and just had remained intact.

'Martina, are you there?'

Her mouth was dry. She swallowed. 'I'm here. What a tragedy. How did it happen?' she managed to say, tears moistening her cheeks.

'She was returning to Stockholm to appear in court. You know she divorced her husband, and had a court case pending?'

'Yes, I do.'

'Her car was hit by a van. The Audi was crushed beyond recognition.'

'I'm so sorry for your loss.'

'She gave me your number before she left, in case I couldn't reach her.'

'I don't know what to say. I'm sorry.'

'I wanted to let you know.'

'Thank you. Let me know when the funeral will be. I'll send flowers.' Martina hung up.

Her knees buckled, and she slumped on the bed. She gazed around the room, thinking how unfamiliar her large bed looked. And that radiant shade of gold on the lampshade, it seemed, had now turned sordid brown and looked alien. Everything looked peculiar, as if someone had squeezed the universe into a ball and rolled it towards some overwhelming disaster. To say her mind had been stretched, challenged and strained to the limit was an understatement. Her body quivered like a rag hanging in the wind. Flipping the light switch, she plunged the room into darkness and crawled into bed, still in jeans and T-shirt. She lay absolutely motionless and sobbed herself breathless.

Chapter 13

At Devilund Clinic, extraction of blood from inmates was under way. For Grenzken, the daily follow-up on inmates' body responses to medication and vaccine effectiveness on organ functions was vital. The effect of Life-Vaccines on human reproduction and development of the fetus were central to his research.

Bo checked on the two new inmates in isolation cells to see if their intoxication had worn off and if medical evaluations could begin. The girls were still drowsy. Another inmate had arrived during the week, a young boy. His constant chewing on his bloody toes, throwing things, and repetitive behaviour of rearranging furniture were challenges. The constant rasping and squeaking of metallic chair legs on the floor irritated everyone's nerves. To effect a sense of calm, Bo drugged the boy, restrained him on a chair, and left him in a zombie state, head thrown back and mouth drooling.

Richard came to a young woman who had recently undergone multiple procedures to perfect the effects of Life-Vaccine. Recent tests on hormone levels and organ functions revealed signs of premature ovarian failure and DNA contamination. Even Richard was shocked at the efficiency of the vaccine, making an eighteen-year-old slip into menopause. She lay crumpled up in bed, motionless, eyes closed. He lit a bedside lamp and bent towards her. He touched her arm and recoiled from her cold skin. He called her name, but she didn't answer. He cast her bedding to the floor, grabbed her by the shoulders, and shook her. Her body was limp, no response. He felt for her pulse. It wasn't there.

She was the fourth victim lost this week to Grenzken's insane research for a covert human sterilizing agent. Richard wondered briefly what he was doing in this despicable place. His dilemma took him back to his time in the military, when he had researched biological weapons for national security, for the good of a nation and citizens. The work aimed to protect citizens, but here citizens were the enemy. His reasons for working at Devilund were dictated by circumstances similar to what had got him into the military but mixed partly with friendship and partly with loyalty to his country. It might sound ridiculous and irrational, but yes, it was for his country and a higher purpose close to his heart that he was working in Devilund. He draped a sheet over the girl's cold body and left the room.

In Anna's room, she lay awake as usual, tormented by chronic pain. She looked weary and frail. He wondered why she had lasted so long. She had undergone another in-vitro fertilization procedure; the last had ended in miscarriage. The toxic cocktails of biological materials and hormones in Life-Vaccine produced antibodies that shut down the life and growth of the embryo.

Anna turned her head and gave Richard a feeble smile. She knew by instinct Richard was a good man but suspected circumstances or destiny must have led him to such a desolate place.

'How're you feeling today?' asked Richard.

'The same…cripp…crippling pain all the time,' stuttered Anna, panting in pain.

'I'm sorry. One day you'll be free from this place.' Anna gazed at him not understanding what he meant. Richard sat on a chair by her bedside and prepared his gadget for blood extraction. He realized how frail and weak she was. She could hardly speak. She stretched her arm for the procedure, but he changed his mind and did not take any blood. He sat for a while, gazing at her pale, bony face and shrunken eyes. He did not think she would last the night. He got up and left the room.

In the morning the doorbell buzzed. Richard went to his office, and on the security monitor he saw a man standing in the backyard beside a white van. It was the laundryman. He paused a second, thinking, then he pressed the intercom button and hollered, 'Coming!' He rushed to his room, sat down, and logged into his desktop computer. With encrypted codes he accessed the surveillance system; he clicked around, deactivated the system and then, logged out.

In the backyard, the cold breeze chilled his nerves, and dark grey clouds predicted a grim, gloomy day. The driver, an amicable man, offered a hand in greeting. They stood talking for a while. Richard went back inside and collected laundry sacks, making sure to secure doors behind him each time. After the laundryman left, Richard returned to his computer and re-activated the surveillance security system. He did his routine security checks, making sure everything was where it was supposed to be. He heard doors bang and close. It was Bo arriving for the morning shift.

The following day Grenzken returned from an international conference in Berlin. He came bearing gifts for Birgit – perfumes and chocolate – and for Helmut a new laptop. The threesome ate dinner together. He told them about his trip, about the bustling city of Berlin and how it had changed since the fall of the Berlin Wall. Beer there tasted better than Spendrups beer. He talked about his counterparts, and how impressed they were he still spoke fluent German. Helmut laughed, gazing at Grenzken with admiration.

After dinner Helmut retired to his evening errands, but first, Grenzken took him into Birgit's office and gave him an injection. Just like everything in Grenzken's life, these rituals happened on a daily basis. 'The double dose I gave you before I left lasted three days as expected,' said Grenzken. 'Now let's try something else. A triple dose should last longer. You know you need this to function.' Helmut groaned as the needle spiked his skin. He glared at Grenzken, and his eyes turned from grisly brownish green to a flaring yellow shade.

The mood was set for the night. Grenzken and Birgit retired to bed, where they lay cuddling in bed and eating chocolate. They fed each other, revelling in each other's fervour, and washed it down with a cocktail of icy cognac cut with lime juice. It added sparkle to the night. He touched her thigh, and that carnal sensation began claiming her. She brought her knee up. Grenzken suddenly retreated out of her grasp and pulled away.

'What is it, Fritz?'

'Hold it there. Don't move. I'm coming back,' said Grenzken as he bolted out of bed and left the room. He returned, flushing a syringe; he sat down and reached for Birgit's upper arm.

Birgit cringed away from him. 'What is that?'

'It's a gift for you, Birgit,' said Grenzken, a sinister grin on his face. 'Something I brought from Berlin.'

'No, noo…not that poison,' cried Birgit.

'Where did you get that notion from? This is a super drug. It'll make you feel great.'

'Not that poison again,' said Birgit. 'It lights a fire in me.'

'That's the purpose – to spice up your libido.'

'I prefer natural drive,' said Birgit, buttoning her negligee and moving away from the bed.

Grenzken edged in towards her, needle in hand. Before she could escape, he tore at her negligee, grabbed her upper arm, and injected her. Birgit screeched and reeled back on the bed, sobbing like a frightened child.

'Easy, easy now. It isn't that bad,' said Grenzken as he dropped the syringe and scrambled on top of her, one hand over her mouth and the other groping under her negligee.

Helmut heard the turmoil and came running. He stopped and listened outside the door, his hand on the brass knob, deciding whether to go in. As he listened, the sobbing subsided, turning into familiar sighs and moaning of gratification. He knew she was with him again.

Helmut reflected on how it had been between him and Grenzken before Birgit came. They had been close, and Grenzken paid attention to him in another way. He was kinder to him than his real parents. His father was a drug addict who beat and abused him and his mother on a regular basis. His mother was different – warm-hearted and caring, but a spineless coward when it came to standing up for herself and protecting him.

At times his father was gone for long periods, and out of nowhere he would return demanding money from his mother. His mother would give him everything she earned as a cleaner at the Vittaby Villa, leaving them without food for weeks on end. Those times, Grenzken was generous. He fed them and provided whatever they needed to survive.

One day his father had returned as usual, demanding money from his mother. Mother had no money. He beat her and left her for dead. He then turned on Helmut and landed a heavy blow on his jaw, cracking it into pieces. Grenzken had come to their rescue, taken them in, and nursed him and his mother to recovery. Ever since then, his jaw had been lopsided. When he was ten, his father returned as usual, asking for money. His mother had no money. He harassed her day and night, beat her up, and locked Helmut in a cupboard for a day. The next day Helmut was angry and determined to put a stop to it. He waited till his parents went to bed and then lit a fire that engulfed their bedroom, killing them.

Social Services came and took Helmut for placement in foster care. But he was an errant and wayward child. He never fitted in anywhere. Grenzken offered to adopt him. From that time, he had lived with Grenzken, who was like a father to him. He took Helmut to school, but he was a slow learner and unmotivated. He left school after ninth grade and started performing diverse jobs at the villa. They developed a strong bond of loyalty, and there wasn't anything he couldn't do for Grenzken. Then came Birgit and everything changed, especially when Grenzken began sleeping in her room. He felt Birgit had become more special to Grenzken than he was. At times Helmut hated Birgit.

Chapter 14

On arrival at Althonat Hospital, Martina noticed the chaotic overcrowded emergency room, mainly mothers and children. Glum faces in spiritless dispositions. Children throwing temper tantrums. A girl spun out of control, hitting and biting her mother, screaming at the top of her voice. A boy ran and threw a glass bottle across the room, where it exploded against a wall. Fascinated by the broken pieces of glass, he started picking them up with his hands before his mother grabbed him and lifted him away. We can't have it like this, thought Martina. It is getting dangerous for patients and staff.

She came to the patient room where Jonas waited for her, with seventeen-year-old Emilia and her mother, Vendela. The girl half sat in bed, while Vendela perched on the bedside holding her hand.

The air tensed as Jonas narrated the results of her evaluation. 'Loss of periods is highly unusual in a young girl like Emilia,' said Jonas. 'We know you were in perfect health before being vaccinated with Life-Vaccine.'

'Doctor, what did you find?' asked Vendela, her voice shaky and impatient.

Jonas swallowed, and looked gingerly at Martina.

Martina took over. As gentle and sensitively as she could, she broke the news. 'After testing numerous hormonal levels and organ functions, the results show that Emilia has what we call premature ovarian failure.'

'What does that mean?' asked Vendela.

'Further tests confirmed Emilia's ovaries have shut down, and she's totally and irrevocably infertile,' continued Martina. 'I'm sorry.'

'What? What are you saying?' asked Vendela. 'You mean she will never have children?' The desperation in Vendela's voice brought tears to Emilia's eyes. Vendela scowled at Martina as if hoping for a retraction, but there was no hope, no mistake.

'No,' said Martina kindly, 'She will never have children. I'm so sorry.'

Emilia cried hysterically as her mother cuddled and comforted her.

'It's my fault…all my fault,' cried Vendela. 'I encouraged her to take that Life-Vaccine. I pushed her into this misery. They said it would protect her from disease.'

'It's heartbreaking news,' said Martina kindly. 'but Emilia is still young, and medical science is advancing. I'm optimistic there will be solutions for her, in future, to help her get children.'

'Are you sure Life-Vaccine made her infertile?' asked Vendela.

'We could not confirm Life-Vaccine caused the destruction of her reproductive system,' said Jonas, 'but we've ruled out all other possible causes. The circumstantial evidence implicating Life-Vaccine is strong.'

Martina assured them the detoxification process would continue until all traces of poison were neutralized and eradicated from Emilia's system. 'When all organs are cleansed, the headaches, stomach aches and vomiting will cease.'

Vendela nodded and patted Emilia on the shoulder.

'The therapist will come in later today to re-establish her energy flow,' Martina went on. 'And we would like to offer psychological help, if that's all right with you, Emilia.'

'I'll think about it,' said Emilia.

'Do you have any questions?' asked Martina.

Vendela looked at Emilia, who lay back in bed and gazed at the ceiling without saying a word.

'No questions,' said Vendela. 'Thank you, Doctors.'

'Emilia, you'll be all right,' said Martina, gently touching Emilia's hand.

Back in Jonas' office, Martina stood by the window observing the forest outside, riotous autumn colours mixed with natural fading green. She was without vigour or energy, just like the fading scenery.

'What is it with you today?' asked Jonas. 'You're not your usual self.'

'How can I be, when young girls are becoming sterile?' said Martina. 'It's just that sometimes our best isn't enough. It's frustrating.'

'Your best is always enough,' said Jonas. 'You have to believe that.'

'It's highly unusual for a healthy young girl to go into early menopause.'

'It's a personal tragedy, one that will grow in magnitude as she marries, and yearns to start a family.'

'Millions of young girls were inoculated with Life-Vaccine. It's anyone's guess how many are already infertile,' said Martina. 'Some of them are maimed for life, with chronic pain, and many face an uncertain future with a high risk of getting cancer.'

A quick glance at her watch told her she was running late. She planted a quick kiss on Jonas' lips, picked up her bag and coat from a chair, and headed for the door. 'I have to go.'

'Where are you going?' asked Jonas. 'I thought we're on tonight for dinner, dancing, and maybe a little love.'

'I'm sorry, I can't. I've got to take Joachim to a football match. Then I have a meeting at the Nobel Foundation.'

'Well then, can I entice you into a secret getaway over the weekend?'

'Not possible,' said Martina. 'Thomas is coming to fetch Joachim. I have to be there. Besides, I've a backlog of work.'

'Really, so what does that mean for our relationship?' asked Jonas, trying to mask the pain in his voice but failing.

'It means nothing. Get it? Nothing,' said Martina as she flung her coat over her shoulders and left him open-mouthed with unspoken angry words.

Jonas stalked across the room, slammed the door shut, and banged his fist on it. He knew Thomas was back in town and wondered about the motives of his return. To him it defied logic for a man to quit a position as global director of finance, in London, for a branch directorship in Stockholm. He reckoned the only motive for such illogical behaviour most often involved a woman or money.

He suspected Thomas still held an old flame for Martina. He had seen them together, in the States, when Thomas and she were dating. Their bond of affection was solid on all levels – socially, intellectually, and maybe even physically. Everyone talked about them as the perfect couple. Besides, Martina was a sensual woman, so attractive that any man would fall twice over in love with her. The prospects of Thomas rekindling his love for Martina bothered him. He knew his love for Martina was unwavering, and no matter what, he would fight for her, if it came to that.

Chapter 15

Anticipation ran high as the macabre Halloween celebrations approached. Planning children's activities was high on the agenda. Darkness dominated the day as hours of sunshine diminished, and the sun migrated to the southern hemisphere. Warm autumn evenings were replaced by driving rains, raw winds, and snowstorms.

Thomas arrived at the Slottsville house, in Lidingö on Saturday morning. Astrid let him in and called out for Joachim. Joachim came pounding down the stairs and jumped into his father's arms. Thomas snatched him up in the air, bounced him up and down, swung him around, and then put him down. Joachim chuckled and then started talking about Halloween plans.

'Pappa, ten friends are coming to the Halloween party.'

'Ten friends?'

'Yes, and we're going to set up a mini-haunted house on your porch. We shall decorate it like a haunted house. Did you buy a pumpkin for a jack-o-lantern?'

Thomas smiled, listened, and dragged a hand through Joachim's already-rumpled hair.

'And the sodas, M&Ms, and scary movies,' said Thomas. 'Yes, yes, it's all in the car.'

'What about the ghosts, hobgoblins and scary faces?'

'You and your friends have to fix that,' said Thomas, placing a finger on Joachim's nose. He then tickled him in the stomach. Joachim slumped to the floor, rolling with laughter, begging him to stop.

Martina came to the bottom of the stairs, watching father and son. It warmed her heart to see Thomas and Joachim have a good time. He might have been a hard-headed husband, but his role as a father was unparalleled. Even with his playful manner, he instilled a sense of discipline and character in Joachim so admirable that she wished they saw more of each other. She knew sons emulate fathers, and fathers are an important role model in the formative years of a young boy. She wanted Joachim to have that.

'Joachim, go get your stuff,' said Martina.

Joachim scrambled upstairs. Martina regarded Thomas; his handsome-featured face gave him an exquisite appearance. His denim jeans and trucker jacket made him look like an American icon.

'You're looking cool today,' said Martina.

'If you mean relaxed, I'm not.'

'Feeling the pressure of entertaining ten wild boys?'

'Ha, that's an understatement. I'm breaking out in a sweat just thinking about it,' said Thomas, with a wide smile.

'You'll be all right,' said Martina. 'Just pretend you're five. It should be fun.'

'I'll play,' said Thomas. 'It sounds easy when you put it that way.'

Joachim scooted downstairs with his backpack.

As soon as the door closed behind them, Martina grabbed her phone and made a call.

'Hi, Lisa.'

'Martina,' answered Lisa on the other end of the line.

'Meet me at Landegrind house, now.' Pause. 'It's important.'

'What now?'

'Lisa, please, I'm counting on you.' Martina hung up.

She took the Mercedes. The backlog of work would have to wait. When she arrived in Väddö, a crowd stood outside gazing at Landegrind house. The main plate glass doors were gone, shattered to pieces. Shards of glass glistened like cheap jewels on the veranda. An elderly man standing in the crowd came forward. It was her neighbour, William. He lived across the street.

'William, thanks for calling. Did you see anything?' asked Martina, her voice hoarse and shaky.

'It was just before dawn when I heard the security alarm and a deafening sound. I ran from my house, and as I crossed the street, I saw two masked men disappear in the bushes heading towards the road. I ran after them, but as I got to the road, I heard a speeding car take off.'

'Did you see the car?'

'No, it was gone by the time I got there.'

The crowd closed in on her and William, most of them neighbours along the road, expressing shock, all talking at the same time. No one had seen anything, but the sound of the alarm and breaking glass had woken the whole neighbourhood.

The kitchen door was untouched. Martina opened it and let herself in. The kitchen was intact. She advanced to the living area; sofas and furniture had been thrown around as if a hurricane had swept through the house. Things lay strewn all over the room. The stairway was blocked by the mess. She stretched to navigate among the ruins, looking for a way to get to the bedroom area.

Things lay in shambles upstairs; mattresses had been cut open and thrown to the floor, drawers emptied and flung across the room. In the dressing area, closets had been turned out and clothes scattered everywhere. She continued to the attic and gasped when she came to the landing. The lock was broken and the door stood ajar; opened boxes, with contents welling out, cascaded down the stairs.

'My, my, who did this?' she asked herself aloud over and over again. It was either a senseless maniac or a person intent on looking for something. Her emotions felt as if they had been frozen in: she couldn't cry; she couldn't shout. Shock paralyzed her.

Stupefied she acted on impulse, taking a mental inventory of missing items. The Benjamin Petersen painting *Hawk and Black* was missing, but she saw it had been thrown outside on the grass. The Karl Larsson painting *Dinner under the Old Birch Tree* had been slashed in half, still hanging on the wall. Mamma's Orrefors 'Night and Day' crystal glass set and Kosta Boda 'Mingle' crystal bowls lay smashed to pieces. Her silverware lay trashed on the floor.

A sudden sound in the doorway startled her. It was Lisa.

'Oh God, what happened here?' said Lisa, half in tears. She looked as though someone doused her with cold water. Her horrified look jolted Martina's subdued emotions into a bombshell of outrage. She clambered up, and tore the slashed painting off the wall, flinging it across the floor. She grabbed a broken lamp shade and threw it across the room, where it landed on a broken table leg. The crashing sound aroused her senses, and her rising despair and trauma pained her heart. She picked up a metal statue, a souvenir of some kind, and hurled it across the room, almost hitting Lisa.

Lisa caught it in mid-air and frowned at her. 'What're you doing?' she said.

That did not stop Martina; she wobbled on through the clutter of books and furniture, grabbed a white antique chair, and smashed it into the fireplace, causing a cloud of ashes to fill the room.

The ear-splitting crash of the chair on the marble hearth jolted Lisa into action. 'Stop it, now!' she said. She seized Martina's arms, glared into her eyes and said, 'Stop it. Stop it!'

'Why me?' wailed Martina. 'Such lily-livered despicable, cowardly dogs! Spineless reptiles… Tails between legs like rabbits. Numbskulls, carnivorous, bloodsucking worms, and good-for-nothing beasts. What do they want, anyway?'

Lisa held her till she went limp in her arms, and they both slumped to the floor. They remained sitting there, Martina whimpering, at last shedding tears. Erratic spasms jerked through her body.

Then they heard a car outside. Martina's sobbing ceased instantly, and she bolted upright, wiping away tears. She saw a police car park outside and she gazed at Lisa. 'Did you call the police?'

'No. It must be the neighbours.'

Neighbours gathered again around two police officers, volunteering information about what they saw but really didn't see, or what they heard, and remarking on how terrible a thing it was to happen in such a crimeless area. Not in a hundred years had anything like this happened in Väddö. And what had Dr Edgren been up to, throwing late-night parties with loud music, plaguing the neighbourhood with restless nights? *She's changed since her parents died. She's wild, and it's disturbing.*

'And this is how kids behave when parents die,' lamented an elderly woman, in a blue night gown and white head gear. 'It's outrageous. Peter Strömstedt and his wife were orderly people, but the daughter is something else.' The woman scowled at Martina as she talked to the officer.

It was like a nightmare film on auto-play. Martina watched her neighbours turn on her one by one, judging her, even talking rubbish about her dead parents.

'Okay, everyone leave, go away,' said Martina in a firm, controlled voice. 'Get off my property.'

The crowd glared at her as if she were a misfit, a goddess of the underworld from Pluto. Nonetheless, they were gone in about five minutes.

Leaving the police to their investigation, Martina wandered around aimlessly, touching damaged things, feeling violated like a rape victim. She ended up in her parents' master bedroom. Her mother's designer gowns lay scattered on the floor; Father's valuable suits were crumpled and flung everywhere. She touched the painting hanging obliquely on the wall and suddenly remembered Ebba and the brown envelope she had given her. Her heart sank further in disarray, confronted with the sad reality of a dark, grey world, a world crushed in grief.

She took the painting down, revealing the wall safe. It was intact. She breathed a sigh of relief. She punched the combination in the keypad, and the lock clicked open. She took out the brown envelope, sat on the windowsill, the only place available, and took out document after document, reading, pondering at the evil of human nature. She stared at a sales contract, where Nicholas became merchandise, an item listed on paper, with no name, no gender, no uniqueness – just merchandise. The price was exorbitant, considering the nature of the merchandise. She, who had once thought humanity was priceless, was learning differently.

On a bank transfer slip, remuneration was whisked off furtively through cyberspace to a secret jurisdiction. No questions asked, no care, no conscience, but a little boy vanished from the surface of the earth. It was too simple to be true, unbelievable but sadly true. There was a photo of Rangor and Stellan watching a man in green scrubs bending over Nicholas in bed. Standing beside them were Grenzken and a heavily built man with a hawkish or beak nose. Who was he? On the back of the photo was scribbled Ribbyburg Clinic. Ebba must have taken it with her smartphone camera.

To think Stellan was involved in a conspiracy to sell a child made her disgusted. Whatever had happened to her kind, loving uncle was beyond her grasp. They say money corrupts. Was that what had happened to Stellan? And where was Nicholas? She asked herself dolefully, recalling his mother's sudden death. Ebba said they had moved him to a covert place.

Martina returned the documents to the wall safe. Her thoughts returned to the break in. The rooms, once filled with laughter and cheer, now stood in loneliness, in clouds of black that cast a shade over the sun. A place where everything used to be absolutely right, where she looked forward to the next day, was now like a silent disease, sucking energy and joy out of her life. She was in a cage, stuck in the middle of nowhere.

Her nerves ached, tied in knots, her breathing fitful as she turned to look through the large window, reacting to the drizzle spattering on glass. Her parents' room, living room, and attic had been the most heavily ransacked. It must be the other half of the Rensblad formula that they were looking for, or the dossier.

Her phone vibrated in her jeans pocket. She took it out and gazed at the monitor. It was Jonas. 'Hi, darling.'

'Just checking on you,' said Jonas. 'Your workload must be done by now.'

'Plans were upset,' said Martina. 'I'm in Väddö.'

'What's happened?'

'They broke into the house. The place is a mess.'

'Oh, that's a terrible, terrible thing, darling,' said Jonas. 'I thought I might entice you into going dancing, but that seems impossible now.'

'Maybe another time.'

'I can come over and help with whatever needs to be done.'

'It's late, Jonas. Thanks anyway,' said Martina. 'Lisa is here. We're cleaning up.'

'Take care, then. I love you.'

'I love you too.' She hung up.

Darkness gradually gathered. Martina descended the stairs. The cold metal on the banister sent shivers through her veins. Emotions came back as she regained control, breaking the bars of temporary insanity that had gripped her mind. Silence echoed through the walls, and emptiness consumed her as she longed to be somewhere else. She was not one to court controversy, but neither would she balk from voicing discrepancies even if she drew fire from it. There was a significant shift in her energy field, putting more space around her unhappiness, making whatever had happened here matter less. By the time she got to the ground floor, repair workers had replaced the plate glass doors and broken windows. Lisa was sorting and stacking things and sweeping away shards of glass, restoring a living space.

'You don't have to do that, Lisa. A cleaning company is coming tomorrow.'

'Some things can be saved,' said Lisa. 'We don't have to throw away everything.'

Reaching up the wall, Martina tore down a skewed painting that hung with a damaged canvas. She stood it against the wall. It could be sent for repair. She furrowed her brows, suddenly aware of the painting cast outside in the grass. It could be repaired too. She went and collected it.

Lisa worked systematically, with total focus. Martina regarded her as she worked, wondering whether she knew the man with a hawkish nose.

'Lisa, do you know a man with a hawkish nose or a beak nose? I saw a photo, and he seemed familiar, but I can't place him.'

'Big, tall man with a hard face as if it was chiselled out of stone?' asked Lisa.

'I guess so. I only saw him in a photo.'

'You mean Tord Stenbeck, the man who dated Mother after she divorced Father?' asked Lisa. 'Why, he's the Chief Inspector of police.'

'That's the name, Tord Stenbeck,' said Martina, trying to sound casual. Wait a minute…she startled in her track of thoughts. What was he doing in Ribbyburg with Stellan and Rangor? Did Ebba change her mind and tell the Judge her husband had sold Nicholas? Was the hawkish nose in Ribbyburg to investigate?

'I remember they were engaged to get married. Not that I recall his looks, though he seemed familiar.'

Inside, a chill shocked Martina. It was the man she'd spoken to on phone regarding the investigation. Something about his voice stayed with her; his uninspired, mechanical voice laced with anger. It was like a voice she had heard before, long before she had spoken to him on the phone, even before he'd dated Ingrid. She could not remember where. It was weird. It scared her. And she didn't know why.

'Where did you see the photo?' asked Lisa, her voice sounding nervous.

'I mean…it wasn't a photo. It was in a newspaper.' Martina had to lie so Lisa would not ask her for the photo.

'That animal,' said Lisa as she dropped the books she was carrying, and her face flushed pink.

'Why do you call him that? He was your mother's fiancé.'

'Thank God she never married him.'

'Why?'

'The mention of his name makes my skin crawl.'

'Lisa, you don't mean that,' said Martina, turning to face her, surprised by her diminished tone of voice.

'Drop it, Martina. Tord is a swine,' said Lisa, raising her voice. She stomped out of the room.

'What? The police inspector a swine?' asked Martina. She sensed something was gravely wrong. She followed Lisa to the kitchen, where she sat, her head buried in folded arms on the table. She was crying. Martina stood puzzled.

'What is wrong?' asked Martina. 'Why are you crying?' Lisa said nothing.

The repair crew packed up and left. The house felt secured for habitation, but it was freezing cold from the draught that slipped in through holes and gaps. Martina screwed up warmth on the central warming system and threw more logs in the fireplace. Neither of them had eaten since breakfast. She searched the kitchen cupboards and found a packet of chicken soup. She whipped it up on the stove and served it with frozen bread she defrosted in the microwave.

'Lisa, eat something. You'll feel better.'

Lisa sat upright, dried her tears, and started eating. She was hungry and tired. Though Martina was anxious to know about Tord, she pushed the issue back in her mind. Lisa might withdraw altogether and refuse to talk about it. They ate, listening to the spatter of rain on window glass.

Lisa remained silent at the table while Martina cleared dishes and started the dishwasher. She was preoccupied, pondering how to raise the question again, searching for the right words. She did not find any, so she just asked her.

'This Tord, what did he do that makes you call him a swine?'

'Don't ask me. You won't believe me even if I tell you.'

'I promise. I'll believe you.'

There was an ear-splitting silence. Martina held her breath, hoping Lisa would open up to her.

'It's the reason Mamma broke off the engagement,' said Lisa.

'What did he do?'

'He abused me. I mean sexually,' said Lisa, her eyes quickly shifting to the floor.

'Jesus, Lisa!' cried Martina as her hand flew to her gaping mouth. She hadn't known what to expect, but certainly it was not this. Her instincts confirmed the man was worse than weird. He was a paedophile.

'I was thirteen when he moved in with Mamma. At first he used to come and touch me in the night. Things escalated. Then he threatened to kill Mamma if I told. I used to scream and cry, but Mamma never came. I never understood why. I couldn't bear it anymore, so I told her. We found out he used to drug Mamma. Before bedtime he would make her a cup of tea. She always felt strange after drinking the tea. When I told her, she took the tea to a lab to be tested. They found traces of a powerful sleeping drug. She kicked him out of the house. We reported it to the police, but the case was closed for lack of evidence.'

'I'm so sorry. Why didn't you tell me?'

'I didn't want to dwell on it. Sometimes I think it is the reason why my relationships with men end up in failure. I don't seem to be able to reciprocate that kind of love.'

'One day you'll find someone to love.'

'But you're lucky,' said Lisa. 'You had Thomas and now Jonas. You're so much in love with Jonas. Do you plan on marrying him?'

'I don't know. He hasn't proposed.'

'But if he does. Will you marry him?

'It's too early to say.'

'Or you still have a thing for Thomas?'

'That's enough, Lisa. Let's go to bed.'

'Thomas is such a wonderful man. You were a lovely couple. Why did you divorce him?'

'Yes, he's a wonderful man. I don't dispute that.'

'But…?'

'Is this an interrogation or what?'

'No, I'm just curious. You never talk about it.'

'It's in the past and out of the way,' said Martina. 'It's done with. Gone.'

'Come on, Marty,' said Lisa. 'You can do better than that. Tell me.'

'Well, we developed in different directions. Call it conflict of interests.'

'I see,' said Lisa, her voice low as if taken aback by the answer.

'You seem surprised.'

'Oh no, I don't know much about such things,' said Lisa. 'I'm no expert on relationships.'

'I think we better turn in.'

'All right, if you say so. Good night,' said Lisa.

'Good night.'

What had happened to Lisa was outrageous, absurd and shocking, thought Martina as she got in bed. It confirmed her fears. Inspector Tord was a man lacking moral fibre – a child molester, a criminal, unfit for high office. There was a misleading falsity in his nature, almost as if he was scooped from the bottom of a barrel. By instinct she knew there was more to this man than met the eye. She didn't know what it was, but the certainty settled in her bones, gaining weight like a foul cancer.

Chapter 16

Life went on, seeming to disregard yesterday's wretchedness, inducing dreary hearts to plod on. For Martina, however, dark shadows clouded her mind with weariness and a nagging sensation of drowning in self-pity. Her apparent misery threatened to derail her out of control, but she trudged on, though robotically inattentive of her efforts. Whatever she did, wherever she turned, she seemed to command only tattered remnants of her former strength.

She worked on the second floor, in her parents' bedroom, picking up clothes from the cluttered floor, sorting things in paper bags to be sent either to dry cleaners or to charity. The Emmaus charity organization would be delighted to receive designer clothes and quality shoes. She dumped her mother's Valentino shoes in a separate paper box. The sound of a vacuum cleaner roared downstairs as cleaners set to work in the living room. Lisa supervised, anxious to get rid of the mess. It made her restless. Typical Lisa; she was the pedantic type.

A dog barked outside. Martina gazed through the window over the hedge to the Strand family compound towards the harsh sound. A man in black pants and sweatshirt was walking a big black dog. She narrowed her eyes and moved closer to the window, careful not to trip over sharp objects on the floor. Her forehead creased as she observed the man playing with the dog. The man turned his face, gazing up at Landegrind house.

Then she recognized him. Adrenaline surged through her body. 'What the heck is he…?'

She hit the stairway, taking two steps at a time and swishing past Lisa and the cleaning troop, charging towards the kitchen door.

'Where are you going?' asked Lisa.

Ignoring Lisa, Martina bolted out into the compound and charged towards the hedge, fuelled by anger. A crisp wind engulfed her, unprepared as she was in jeans and a T-shirt. Peering through the hedge, she confirmed her worst fears. The man on the other side of the hedge saw her and came closer, so that they were standing face to face on opposite sides of the hedge. The dog rummaged through the hedge to her side, growling and groaning. Martina disregarded it.

'Back here, Pagan,' roared the man. The dog stilled at his voice and then trotted back to him through the hedge.

What kind of name is that for a dog? Pagan! Martina silently pondered.

'What're you doing here?' asked Martina.

'Dr Edgren, what a pleasure,' said the man, a sinister grin on his face. He glared at her as if he was seeing her for the first time, dumbfounded by her extraordinary beauty.

The sound of his voice raised goosebumps on her skin, and she shuddered. 'I asked you a question,' said Martina.

'Calm down. You know better than that; such anger could land you in the emergency room.'

'Skip the crap. Answer me, Mister…'

'Doctor, it's Doctor Steven Rangor.'

A chill ran down her spine. Damn that name; it sounded like an old gong in her ear.

'What're you doing in Strand's compound,' said Martina, through gritted teeth.

'Wow, you roar like a lioness! I was considering inviting you to a house-warming party, but with that attitude, I'd have to reconsider.'

'What house-warming party? The last time I saw you, you were unemployed. Now you can afford a million-kroner property in an affluent area like this?'

'You don't do justice to your beauty. You should smile more often.'

'Don't patronize me.'

'You took the company global. And I understand that the cell antidote is causing a public stir, sending shock waves across the globe. Your company is grabbing market shares. You should be happy.'

Martina scowled at him. She saw right through his disguise: faked good manners, false pride, and superficial smiles that never touched his eyes.

'Lucky you recovered from the accident. It could have been fatal. Though it made me wonder what you're doing in Ribbyburg?'

'That's none of your business.'

'Oh yes, and I make it my business when I hear my neighbour's house was broken into.'

'Was it you who broke into my house?'

'Dr Edgren, you disappoint me. I'm no small-time thief.'

'Rather a big-time criminal, I would say,' said Martina, with a vicious stare.

Rangor looked at her unblinking, surprised by her malevolent disposition.

'We need to be civil to each other. I'm your neighbour, remember?'

'Was Patrick Strand coerced into selling you the house?'

'You really have a low opinion of me. Strand moved abroad. He wanted to liquidate his assets. I had the money, and I jumped at the opportunity.'

Patrick had moved abroad! That was news. 'Did you kill his wife?'

'What kind of question is that?' said Rangor, his eyes turning dark.

A bitter silence grew between them and animosity sparked heightening suspicion.

'In future, keep to your side of the hedge. If ever you stray to my compound, you'll never live to regret it. And that goes for the dog, too.'

'That's if you live long enough,' roared Rangor.

'Are you threatening me?' asked Martina, her high-pitched tone flaring up.

'You said I'll never live to regret it. Isn't that a threat, Doctor?'

'I wanted to make sure we understood each other,' said Martina, her voice as frosty as the wind that nudged her cheeks.

Lisa stood at the kitchen door watching them. 'Martina!' she hollered, her voice echoing like an oppressive crush of dread in the cold autumn air.

'Coming,' called Martina. She turned abruptly and sprinted back to the house, fear clutching at her heart like a giant hand tearing at it.

Rangor scowled furiously at her as she disappeared, a repugnant snarl on his lips. The words spoken like thunder charred his heart, and his soul cracked on every syllable. The dog scampered around him in circles, restless, sniffing hostility in his hand. He grabbed its collar, juggled it aggressively, and shoved it forward. It squeaked and ran, tail between legs.

Martina came into the warm kitchen where Lisa served tea and scones. She sat erect, pale as chalk. She grabbed a scone and munched it down. The turn of events jolted her: the insanity and audacity of a man who seemed to be following her around. Picking up the big mug, she filled it with hot water and submerged a teabag. She took a sip and winced as it scalded her tongue. She untangled her hands from her mug, sighed and lowered her forehead into them instead. The warmth still clinging to her hands was oddly soothing.

Lisa sat across the table, watching her, sipping her own tea. 'Why, you look terrible. Who was that man?'

Martina said nothing. She sipped her tea and winced again; still too hot. Finally, she spoke. 'We haven't been to the basement. Do you think those hunting rifles are still there?' she said softly, refusing to meet Lisa's gaze.

'They should be there, where your father kept them,' said Lisa. 'The basement door was untouched. Why do you ask?'

'Maybe we should go and get them.'

'It's because of that man, isn't it?'

'It's been a long time since we hunted,' said Martina, her voice glacial.

'What do you mean? I can tell you want to kill that man.'

Martina sipped her tea, cradling the cup in her hands, ignoring Lisa.

Lisa persisted. 'It wasn't a friendly conversation you had with him, was it? Is he a guest at the Strand house?'

Maybe she should tell Lisa about Rangor, the man who had lifted her father, Stellan, from the financial quagmire that had threatened to bury him. *Surely, Ribbyburg has been a valuable asset pulling Stellan out of bankruptcy – plus of course something else he stole.* But suppose Lisa regained the title deed of Ribbyburg; all hell would break loose. Could she stand up to her father and fight?

'No, he is not a guest of the Strand family. The Strands sold the house. He was the stranger at the funeral. The mysterious man in the grey suit?'

'Yes, I remember. He asked for you when I was serving refreshments. He didn't seem to know you in person. I believe he knew you only by name.'

'Well, he is the man your mother told us about, the American who helped your father out of financial difficulty. Turning Ribbyburg into a research Clinic was part of the settlement.'

'I'll be damned. Steven Rangor is your neighbour,' said Lisa. 'Martina, the man is father's friend. You must be careful. Maybe he broke in here.'

'There's more; Ribbyburg isn't purely a research Clinic. It's a camouflage for something sinister. Rangor worked for Pappa in America, but I don't think Pappa really knew the kind of man he was.'

'What kind of man is he?'

'The kind who will do anything for money. I think he only came to the funeral to confirm Pappa and Mamma were dead and buried.'

'That's chillingly evil. Why do you say that?'

'Instinct tells me he is after something,' said Martina. She paused and then said, 'Maybe he wants Althonat Global. I suppose he thinks that because I'm young, I'm naïve and easily manipulated.'

'That's a strange thing to say,' said Lisa. 'Why would he want Althonat Global?'

'To turn it around and use it for some sinister purpose, I suspect.'

'Well, that's not going to happen in a million years. You're fearless, Martina. You can handle him. And by that I don't mean you have to kill him.'

'I'm not going to kill him. I need to find out why he moved into the Strand house, in my neighbourhood, and what he is doing at Ribbyburg Clinic.'

'What do you think he is doing at Ribbyburg?'

'Illegal experiments.'

'That is what I mean, keep away from him.'

Martina simply stared at Lisa.

'But where did the Strands move?'

'He said Patrick moved abroad,' said Martina. 'I forgot to tell you, his wife died in car accident.'

'That fine woman is dead,' said Lisa. 'That is tragic, leaving her children.'

The sound of a barking dog was heard across the quiet neighbourhood. Pagan, Martina quietly deduced. Why was it barking continuously? She had noticed at the hedge that Pagan stilled when Rangor roared at it. *It seems the man has a temper.*

Martina got up and wandered to the living room, noticing cleanliness and order restored. 'The cleaners did a wonderful job.'

'Yes, it's as if nothing happened,' said Lisa, who stood right behind her.

'Lisa, you'd better run along,' said Martina. 'Tomorrow is Monday. I'll stay the night.'

'I can't leave you here alone with that man in your backyard.'

'I'll be fine. I'll call you tomorrow,' said Martina. 'And Lisa, thank you.'

Lisa hugged her and disappeared into the dark of night.

Martina secured the house, locking doors and windows, setting the alarm. For the first time she considered Torsten's offer of placing Althonat security guards outside the house. She called Thomas and told him she would be staying the night and to keep Joachim till tomorrow. The dog was barking again. She took a quick shower, changed into her silk pyjamas, and got into bed.

The dog kept barking and howling, disrupting her stream of thought, denying her tranquillity to conjure up sleep. Eventually, she started drifting in a limbo state when a thought struck her. She suddenly kicked away the bedding, sprang up, and peeled away her pyjamas. She opened closets and shuffled clothes as she looked for an appropriate outfit. She settled for dark blue jogging pants and a matching sweatshirt. In the hallway closet she found Sebastian's black wind jacket and his old baseball cap. She slid into the jacket. Holding up her hair, she tied it in a ponytail and then put on the cap. Going back to the bedroom she picked up her phone and pressed the on button. The monitor lit up, revealing three missed calls from Jonas. All evening she'd kept him at bay so she could focus on current problems. She pressed the off button and put the phone in her jacket pocket.

In the hallway, Martina slipped into black sneakers, set the alarm and went outside. The darkness blinded her at first while she adjusted to it, and the chilling temperatures froze her bones momentarily. In the small storehouse, she opened a toolbox and removed a screwdriver, flashlight, and utility knife.

She got in the black Volvo and pulled out of the garage onto the driveway. Turning onto the road she changed gears and accelerated. She checked her mirrors; no one was following her. A small car ahead turned right and disappeared. She was heading south. It was past midnight.

Near Ribbyburg Clinic, she left the gravel road and turned the Volvo at the local shopping centre. She parked in the deserted parking lot. She got out of the car, taking with her the phone and tools. She returned to the road and started jogging along the deserted path. Wind tugged at her cheeks, and the only sound she heard was the oscillating rhythm of her sneakers on gravel. Street lights lit her way. Most homes lay in murky darkness; the inhabitants had gone to sleep. Jogging was her favourite sport, but she rarely got time to do it. After a kilometre, Ribbyburg Clinic was just round the bend. She pushed on and then turned. She left the driveway and jogged behind hedges, approaching Ribbyburg Clinic. Sweat and stress reinforced the fear that lingered close to her throbbing heart. Light shone in a few windows. She headed for the old stables. The darkness, sense of loneliness, and eerie silence freaked her out and alerted her discernment. She heard the sound of galloping paws and barking dogs. When she turned, two black dogs leaped at her, gawking and growling with a menacing fury. She halted and stilled. Instinctively, though unnerved, she took a firm stance.

'Stay!' she said, as calmly and firmly as she could. The dogs stalled, confused momentarily, and then leaped again, charging viciously at her. She trotted backwards fast, putting space between her and the dogs. Her hand flew to her jacket pocket and pulled out a pepper spray can, adrenaline spiking high in her body. Her arm trembled, and she fumbled the can in her hand, but she held it and discharged the liquid into the dogs' eyes, emptying the can. The dogs stood motionless, blinded by the stinging sensation. With squinted eyes, they wobbled back to the house, squeaking, trotting in a crooked line. Somebody opened a door, peered outside, and hollered, 'Who's there?'

Martina lay low on the ground behind trees. The dogs went inside the house, and the door closed. She had only a few minutes. She must move fast. She darted to the stable door and retrieved the flashlight and screwdriver. Shining the light on the door lock, she realized it was unlocked. She pushed, and it creaked open. Still panting, she paused and nervously gazed around. Then she entered and flashed light inside the stable.

There used to be an underground passage through the stable to the house. She and Lisa used to play there. She hoped it was still there. There was another door. Opening it, she went down the rickety old wooden stairs, careful not to fall. She was now underground in a secret tunnel leading to the main house. She heard screeching and flapping sounds. She killed the light. Her heart leaped to her mouth, fear heavy in her bones. She listened and realized they were bats. Without light, it was pitch dark, and the smell of mould and old leather permeated the air. Flashing light again she saw dilapidated rusty horseshoes, saddles and old machinery discarded in the tunnel. It had functioned as storage before.

Coming to the end of the tunnel, she mounted broken steps to the back door. She took out her screwdriver and dislodged the lock. Then she pushed open the door and entered the house at the basement level. One more flight of stairs up brought her to another door. She dislodged the lock and entered the main building.

She stood in a corner against the wall, scanning the long hallway with her eyes. Ahead of her was the new extended patients' wing, built before the Clinic opened. A Nurse in white pants and top emerged from a room and headed towards her. Martina stepped back and waited. The Nurse disappeared into a room in the middle of the hallway.

Martina tiptoed to the first room and opened the door. She peeped inside. Young children lying still, sleeping, probably sedated. She went inside and closed the door. A chain was attached to the foot of each bed. She flipped up the cover on one of the beds, revealing the chained foot of a boy fastened to the metallic bed. He slept, seemingly calm.

In the next room another boy sat before a computer, playing video games. He saw her but did not react. Probably he was autistic – one of the new restless souls waiting to join the research program. Martina continued down the hallway, searching for a room with filing cabinets, computers, or an office. The Nurse came out of the room. Martina ducked into the nearest room and waited. It used to be the kitchen. Now it was a coffee room. She poked her head out of the door to survey the hallway. The Nurse disappeared into another room. Martina fell into a brisk soft walk and passed the room the Nurse was in. She paused, peered in the room and saw her injecting a child with a syringe. The child let out a brief screech.

The next room was the office. It was large but tacky and disorderly, furnished with a large desk, two old chairs and several dilapidated filing cabinets. Stellan must be holding a tight budget. The computer monitor on the table was still alive. Perfect; the Nurse did not lock it. Talk about security; leaving a computer unattended without an automatic lock. Martina sat and went to work on the keyboard, typing in Nicholas' name. She heard footsteps and rose from the chair, but they faded down the hallway. Nicholas' name popped up on the screen. Information on treatment, drugs and tests done was all here. Then she saw the diagnosis: schizophrenia. Jesus, that was not true. And the attending physician was listed as Dr Steven Rangor. Her jaw dropped. She was trembling and weak with shock.

Fumbling in her jacket pocket, she retrieved her smartphone and pressed the on button, awaking the monitor. She focused the camera and photographed documents on the computer screen. Footsteps returned, moving fast towards the room. She quickly closed the page on the screen and rapidly tiptoed to a closet in a corner. She ducked into the closet and squatted inside as the Nurse entered the room. She held her breath. A man's voice was heard talking to the Nurse.

'Have you seen any intruder in the building?' asked the man. Through a slight gap in the closet door, Martina saw a man in a dark uniform: a security guard.

'No one,' said the Nurse. 'Has anything happened?'

'The dogs were drenched in pepper spray.'

'Maybe the intruder is still outside,' said the Nurse.

The man left. The Nurse paused at the desk and then left the room. Martina heard her steps disappear along the hallway. She dashed out of the closet and into the hallway; then she headed up the stairs. Upstairs were living quarters. At the end of the hallway, a room was illuminated, and the door stood ajar. It used to be the study room. Hearing someone talk, Martina sauntered towards the door. She peered inside through the door crack. Stellan sat at the desk with computer on, forehead resting in his palm, holding a landline phone to his ear. Martina stood still and listened.

'I told you, and I'm telling you now. Forget it. Those are empty claims.'

There was a pause as Stellan listened to the voice at the end of the line. Then he surged to his feet, fury evident on his face. Martina took one step back and waited.

'Listen…no you listen, there's a lot of bad blood between us. You loved my wife behind my back, and when she divorced me, you tried to marry her. But all that I forgave you.'

Pause.

'I'm telling you, give it up. You've no right of entitlement.'

Martina wondered what he meant by empty claims, entitlement, and giving it up.

Silence fell again as Stellan listened. Martina slowly advanced closer to the door.

'Tord, you son of a bitch, you're not getting anything more out of me.' He slammed the phone down and exhaled. Martina trembled with the bang of the phone; clearly Tord had some kind of hold on Stellan. A sudden chill came over Martina, and she erupted in a subdued sneeze.

Stellan looked up. He walked to the door and peered around. Martina was gone.

She was in Lisa's old bedroom. The bed and reading table stood as they had before. She heard Stellan talking to someone in the hallway. The voices moved downstairs and faded. She dashed to the study. Stellan's computer monitor glared at her, still live. *Security sucks here.* He was writing an email. She pressed the downward arrow and scrolled the page, reading fast.

The email was addressed to CEO, Citaraph, Jacob Mattsson, and copied to Dr Steven Rangor:

> *I feel bad about my brother's death, but I'll try to do as you requested regarding the other half. I've given this much thought. It is not going to be easy, and I don't promise success. If all goes well, it will cost you a fortune.*
>
> *Yours,*
> *Stellan Strömstedt*

He feels bad about Pappa, does he? And the other half? It must mean one thing and one thing only. And he was grabbling for money again. His insatiable hunger for money was staggering.

Martina left the study and hurriedly walked downstairs and peeked furtively into the hallway. There was no one. She tiptoed along the hallway, eyes darting, watchful for any movement. At the end of the hallway, she heard footsteps behind her, and someone hollered,

'Hey, you there, stop!'

She turned and saw two security guards charging after her. In a burst of speed, she bolted for the stairs to the basement, ran down the creaking stairs, and ducked into the underground tunnel. She heard rapid footsteps closing in on her. Fumbling in the darkness, she relied on instinct to find the exit. Then the guards' flashlights spotlighted her. She dropped under an old wood table, raising dust. The dust suffocated her, and she suppressed a cough. Shaking, she felt her way round the tunnel with her hand moving along the cold stone wall. Boots treading on gravel and twigs sounded nearer. She stayed low in an effort to avoid flashlight beams. Bent over, she edged towards a secret exit she and Lisa used to use. Her heart pounded as if about to break in pieces. Her breathing was heavy. She was filthy and sweaty.

A voice howled, 'We know you're here. Come out.'

On reaching the secret exit, she saw faint moonlight streaming through cracks in the door. Flashlight beams spotted her again. She ducked, and the sound of gunfire deafened her. A bullet whizzed past her ear. She scrambled and dashed through the door, taking off at top speed. Bullets flew again. She threw herself into the bushes, bruising her arms, knees, and ribs. Her body ached. In darkness, among twigs and creepy creatures, she lay still, holding her breath, waiting for the blast of more shots.

No blast came. She heard muffled talk and boots sweeping shrubs. The guards turned and left. After a while, she got up and hobbled forward, panting like an overworked horse, moving like an indistinct black cat at twilight. Pain settled in her feet and knees. A confused mass of overgrown vegetation, trees as tall as lamp posts, with thick crowns like mushrooms, told her she was in forest land. It was charcoal dark, and the smell of damp earth combined with dead fallen leaves tickled her nose. She sneezed. Afraid of detection, she did not use her flashlight. She had no sense of bearing or direction. The silence was like walking in a graveyard.

A strange sound emanated from deep in the forest. It sounded like an old car engine. Trudging wearily over a carpet of moss and dense growth, she moved towards the sound. She saw headlights, forcing her to trek deeper in the wilderness. She heard spooky voices and huddled behind a tree observing a black van. Near the van, she saw a shallow hole freshly dug. She leaned against the tree watching, exhausted, benumbed.

Two men dressed in dark pants and jackets with hoods worked on the hole. The bulky one entered the van and killed the headlights. Everything plunged into darkness. Martina moved closer, felt for her phone in her jacket pocket, and pressed the on button to awaken the monitor. The two men moved to the rear of the van and opened the rear door. When they emerged, they carried something long in a black plastic bag. It looked like a body. She snapped her phone camera, taking photos without flashlight, hoping they would be good. Her heart throbbed. She couldn't breathe. Her knees buckled. She sank to the moist forest floor and curled up in a ball against a tree, scared and lonely. The men dumped the black bag in the hole and covered it quickly with soil. They looked around, collecting their tools and shovels, which they stashed in the rear of the van. Then they got in the van and sped away. Martina narrowed her eyes, trying to get a glimpse of the license number as the van vanished among silent trees, its lowlight beams blinking like ghost eyes in the dark.

Martina scrambled to her feet and wobbled to the grave, petrified. With the flashlight, she illuminated the area to take in the place in detail. Then she sank to her knees near the grave and started digging with bare hands. She shifted soil, shoving it aside till she felt the black plastic bag. She retrieved a utility knife from her pocket and flashed the light briefly. Her heart beat like a drum. She stuck the knife through the plastic and ripped it open. Taking a deep breath, she flashed the light again with a shaky hand.

The face of death glared at her; a young female, probably in her teens, lay cold and blue in the bag. Martina's head swam. Something welled up in her throat, and she reeled back, throwing up. Gasping for air, she collapsed at the graveside and lay flat on the cold forest floor, quivering. She recovered and returned to the grave. With paper tissue from her jacket pocket, she checked for ornaments on the body: rings, earrings, necklace, birthmarks or any identification marks. There were none. The body was naked. She photographed her dead face. A beautiful young woman dumped like trash in an unmarked grave. Grief washed over Martina. Gazing around rapidly, she closed the bag and covered the grave again with soil. Slowly she stood up, wondering if she was still alive. As she rose, she grasped her tools, looked at them, and wept.

Chapter 17

Grenzken awoke with a start, realizing he was late for work. With regret he departed from Birgit's intoxicating warmth, draped a bathrobe around his body, and sauntered to the bathroom.

Birgit opened her eyes and glanced at the clock on the bedside table. It was past eight. She closed her eyes again, thinking how embarrassing it was to neglect early morning duty. Everyone must have figured out what she and Grenzken were up to. She had forgotten to set the alarm clock because of that spicy drug Fritz had been giving her.

It stung like bees thrusting venom that propelled her onto a wild journey through shades and nuances of sensuality, vibrating mountains and surging valleys, clenches and shudders, till she was parched and breathless. In the beginning she hadn't liked it; it gave her shivers and chills, but once she got used to it, she yearned for it like a baby yearns for milk. She couldn't sleep without it.

She stretched in bed and swung her legs down to the fluffy woollen carpet. Her negligee flipped up, revealing corpulent, chunky thighs. She gazed at them as if seeing them for the first time. She knew she had become voluptuous since the onset of the spicy drug, but heavens, this was too much. She let out a laboured sigh, realizing she was hooked on something that had spun her weight out of control. And that carnal desire stayed with her all day like a raging fire, consuming her, keeping her thirsting for more, thirsting for Fritz.

Yet neither the weight nor the desire was her biggest worry; a red skin rash had sprouted on her belly and was spreading by the day. Sometimes it itched too. She hated to think about it, and yet she was mortified to tell Fritz for fear he might introduce another dubious drug. On the other hand, Fritz was her man, and the intimacy they shared was uncommon and unequalled by past experiences. Things were so good between them. They were sailing calm seas. She didn't want to rock the boat.

Fritz emerged from the bathroom and dressed in a black suit and white shirt with no tie. He smiled at Birgit, noticing her beautiful but clouded face.

'You look pensive. What is it?'

'I thought how nice we have it here, and yet we must go through the motions of the day before I see you again. Can't we just stay in today?'

A rare smile broke out on Grenzken's face. He sat on the edge of the bed and took her chubby hand in his, quizzically gazing into her green eyes.

'Very well then, let's stay.' A confused smile glinted on Birgit's face in wonderment. What had possessed Fritz to spend a day in bed just to tango with her?

Birgit eyed him and saw his muffled smile. They sprawled out in laughter.

'That was sweet, but aren't you behaving like a seventeen-year-old?'

'You're such a clown, Fritz,' Birgit said as she struggled up from the bed and wobbled to the bathroom. 'You'd better get going. What will they think?'

'As you wish,' said Fritz. He straightened up and went to Devilund Clinic.

When Birgit emerged from her quarters, she came face to face with fuming Helmut. His burning glare almost made her jump out of her skin. He opened his mouth to say something dirty but changed his mind. Finally, he said. 'Girls waiting long for you. What're you doing?'

Birgit sensed his exasperation, knowing that he knew about her and Fritz. Her face flushed as she passed him, heading to her office. His bad tempers worried her, but even worse was his unpredictability. His smoky greenish orange eyes and facial scars were enough to put her in line.

'Calm down, Helmut,' she reposted. 'I'm on my way.'

The Bottle Blonde and Brunette were sitting in her waiting room when she arrived. They leaned against each other, eyes closed, apparently trying to catch up on lost sleep. They startled as she entered the room, sobered by her presence. Terror was apparent in their eyes, as they slowly realized they were trapped. The night out with peculiar men had landed them in this outlandish place, and whatever their fate, it was too scary to even contemplate.

Birgit closed the door behind her, sat down, and activated her computer. She glared at the monitor, downloaded files, making a quick read. She addressed them by name. Gittel was the tall slinky one with bottle blonde hair, and Moa was the brunette. She showed them the shower room, and told them to shower. Perplexed, the girls did as they were told. After showering, she set about assessing them: listening to their hearts and lungs, checking blood pressure, double-checking for any medication or medical condition.

The girls, dressed in white Clinic shirts, returned to Devilund Clinic under the watchful eyes of Helmut. Birgit took a last lingering look at them as they descended the stairs and marvelled at how young and innocent they looked, yet naïve to the core. Her thoughts strayed, wondering if Fritz had slept with them. The notion lay heavy and sad in her heart. She blinked rapidly, dismissing the idea, feeling a carnal sensation build up below her belly. She sighed to numb the sensation. Fritz was her man. Small-time hookers were not to his taste.

She walked out of her office to the dining area. Ella, the housekeeper, had just brewed a fresh pot of coffee. 'Ella. How are you today?'

'I'm fine, Birgit, and you?'

'I'm a bit tired, but nothing a cup of coffee won't fix,' said Birgit as she fixed herself a cup of coffee.

'Can I make you a sandwich?' asked Ella.

'Coffee is fine. Thanks.' She remembered something and turned to Ella. 'How are arrangements for Friday coming along?'

'Christmas buffet plans are in order. You need not worry about anything.'

'That's good.'

Settling down at the table, Birgit grabbed the day's Frangipani, the last one, since Fritz had cancelled the subscription. She would have to buy her own copy at the shopping centre. Helmut appeared in the room, fury glowing on his face like a Halloween horror mask. He shot her a reprimanding glare and said, 'Grenzken don't like you reading that paper.'

Birgit shrugged, disregarding his outward display of anger. Frangipani was a good paper; alternative medicine and therapies were the future. However, it made sense to keep her loyalty to Fritz separate from her private interests. She must be discreet.

In Devilund Clinic, Grenzken looked in on the new boy. Nicholas was in his usual routine: repetitively rearranging furniture in circles, unconcerned about Grenzken's presence. His feet were bandaged up to prevent him from chewing on them.

Grenzken noted that his play was slowed. He could hardly keep a firm grip on the chair. His hands were rubbery. It must be the medication. Trying to figure out the cause of his ailment, Grenzken watched him intently, as he would observe a caged animal. He noticed the boy could rearrange the furniture in exactly the same way it was before and then start all over again. No doubt he was intelligent, this speechless boy devoid of eye contact. Some stupid scientists attributed the condition to vaccine damage. That was ridiculous. Vaccines never caused illness. The boy needed surgery to check what brain defects were causing his malingering. Then maybe any damage could be repaired. In a swift move, he grabbed the boy and strapped him onto the bed. His mad activities made too much noise.

Back in his office, Grenzken logged onto his mailbox and zapped through, searching for one email. There; a response from Citaraph on the final research report on the perfected version of Life-Vaccine. He clicked on it, eyes narrowing as he read the text. He grinned in approval.

He pushed his chair back and walked to Richard's room. 'Good morning, Fritz,' said Richard as he heard him come in.

'Morning, Richard,' said Grenzken. He stood hovering over him, his stocky figure irritating Richard. 'Our research report, on Anna, was approved. The new version of Life-Vaccine will go into the marketing phase. That calls for a celebration, wouldn't you say?' He stood, rocking back and forth on the balls of his feet.

Engrossed in paperwork, Richard said nothing. *Why is he asking me?*

'It will market under the same name, Life-Vaccine, but in reality it is a drug that will further our cause faster than we had anticipated. We shall save world resources and the earth will be in balance.'

'That's hardly good news,' murmured Richard, his voice cold and disengaged.

'What did you say?' asked Grenzken. Richard remained silent, focused on his paperwork.

'I want you to close Anna's file and make arrangements for her final procedure.'

Richard stirred and lifted his gaze to meet Grenzken's small, darting eyes. He'd expected to hear those words sooner or later, but hearing them now brought home a disturbing reality. 'But sir, did you read my report in your mail?' asked Richard.

'No. Is anything wrong?'

'Not really. I would rather you read it first,' said Richard.

'I will read it, but prepare Anna for surgery,' said Grenzken. 'The pain she's having, I need to check it out.' He left but hesitated and returned, 'And the boy, Nicholas. Prepare him for brain surgery tomorrow.'

Grenzken went to his room and clicked on Richards' mail. He stared at Richard's report in disbelief. How dare he ignore protocol, attempt to sabotage rules of implementation? He ran his fingers over his balding head, and his mouth curled in a vicious twist.

Richard knew he was in a quagmire and sinking fast unless he could come up with valid answers. He sat at his desk reading correspondence, unfocused, distracted, consumed by apprehension and the consequences of his actions. Suddenly he heard heavy footsteps approaching his room. He turned to meet Grenzken's furious glare.

Grenzken stood at the threshold, his serpentine eyes burning deep into Richard's wistful eyes. In his right hand, he held a hypodermic syringe filled with a colourless liquid. Richard slowly got up from his chair. His mind raced, and his muscles tensed, ready to fend him off.

'Take it easy. We can talk about this,' said Richard in a gentle voice.

A piercing cry from a distressed inmate echoed in the corridor. Grenzken flinched but maintained his aggressive advance towards Richard. He moved, narrowing the space between them.

'How could you send Anna's body away without an autopsy?'

Richard's eyes focused on the needle.

'The body was badly decomposed, and our facilities are unfit for storage,' said Richard, rapidly. 'It was my decision, and I stand by it.'

'How in hell am I supposed to make a final report without an autopsy?' asked Grenzken, moving closer, aiming the needle at Richard's neck.

'You don't want to do this, Fritz. Don't!' howled Richard. 'Put it down. Give it to me.'

An oddly unfamiliar sensation mixed with rage overcame Grenzken. He stared in bafflement at Richard, staggered backwards, and crashed to the floor. The syringe rolled out of his hand. He lay lifeless, his eyes fixed in an upward gaze. The cries of distress still echoed down the corridor.

Richard dropped to his knees and loosened Grenzken's shirt. He took his pulse. It was strong. Relieved, he picked up the syringe, examined it briefly, wondering about the content. He dropped it in his coat pocket and helped Grenzken to bed in a spare room.

The cries were coming from Nicholas' room. Richard went in and saw Nicholas strapped to the bed. He was struggling to free himself. He unstrapped the boy and pulled him up in a sitting position. The white Clinic shirt he wore hung loose on his emaciated body. He hardly ate anything. But something had changed; his reflexes were slower, with a visible loss of coordination. It must be the drugs Grenzken was giving him. Nicholas sat staring blankly, hardly noticing Richard.

A fleeting thought tormented Richard; he was torn between loyalty for Grenzken and compassion for the boy. He had already crossed Grenzken once and the thought of doing it again was unthinkable. Brain surgery seemed too drastic a procedure for the boy's condition. For Grenzken, the boy was just another research object. Whether he died, survived, or became incapacitated was of no consequence to him. He spun and twisted science data to fit his wretched schemes.

Richard ruffled Nicholas' sandy brown hair and left the room. He was beginning to feel the emotional stress and strain of the job, but perseverance was a habit he could not easily break.

Chapter 18

The bitter smell of pine mixed with the stench of death followed Martina to Slottsville house. She couldn't pin her thoughts down to grasp the dilemma of what she had seen, or define it in any way. It was mind-boggling and morbidly grisly. Those two ghastly characters had committed a gruesome crime and under the cover of murky darkness they had got rid of her body in the forest. The act had no form or shape of rationality. It was senseless and unthinkable, and it defied reason.

Standing in the bathroom, she took one look in the mirror and reeled away. Dried leaves and twigs festooned her matted hair; brown mud smeared her face, set off by purple bruises. She looked like a scarecrow and smelt like a skunk. She dragged herself through a quick shower, and winced at the sting of water against her bruises.

At length the warm water soothed her physical wounds but did nothing for her emotional trauma. Her body was both on edge and exhausted, as well as nauseated. She no longer cared about anything. Careful not to touch her sensitive wounds, she slipped into her silk negligee and crawled into bed. It was past five in the morning.

At midday she startled at the ringing phone. She stretched out and picked it up, still drowsy from deep sleep. She held the phone to her ear, saying nothing.

'Martina?' said Jonas' voice over the line.

No answer. Martina had drowsed back to sleep.

'Hello…? Martina, are you there?'

'I'm here,' murmured Martina, her voice slurred and weak.

'Darling, what's wrong? Are you ill?'

Silence again. Martina drifted back to sleep. The phone slipped from her hand to clatter against the floor. Jonas hung up.

In an hour he stood at Slottsville house, pressing the doorbell. There was no answer. Astrid must be off duty. He jiggled Martina's spare key in the lock and opened the door, letting himself in. He ran upstairs and knocked on Martina's bedroom door. There was no answer. Panic gripped his throat, choking him. He coughed and then turned the knob, opening the door. He was thinking she had sounded faint when he'd called. Was she all right?

Martina lay in bed motionless. The phone was on the floor. His heart jumped. He strode to the bedside and stuck his hand under her nose, feeling for her breath. She was alive, at least. He picked up the phone and cradled it.

'Martina.' He touched her forehead and caressed her cheek. She stirred and opened her eyes. A sudden mild shock registered on her face. Jonas saw it and quickly said, 'It's me.' He dropped to his knees at the bedside, so his face was level with hers.

'What are you doing here?' murmured Martina with half open eyes, her voice hardly audible.

'Darling, you scared the hell out of me. I was worried sick about you,' said Jonas. 'I've been calling you since yesterday without answer.'

'I'm okay.' She stretched out in bed and winced.

'Are you in pain?' asked Jonas. 'What happened? Was there more trouble in Väddö?'

'No, no trouble. We just cleaned the house.' She pulled her arm from under the covers and rubbed her sleepy eyes.

'Ooh, dear, what about these bruises on your arm and hand?' asked Jonas, bending, gently touching the purple blemishes on her hand and contusions on her arm. A worried look spread on his face.

'Ouch, that hurts,' cried Martina. She tensed, and her eyes opened wider.

'What's wrong with you?' asked Jonas. 'Why are you sleeping in the middle of the day?' Martina closed her eyes and drifted back to sleep.

'Get out of bed,' said Jonas, casting her bedclothes aside. The sight of her legs spooked him all over again. They were covered with lacerations.

'What's going on, Martina?' he said. 'You're all bruises.'

'Leave me alone,' she whispered, dragging the bedding back on top of her. 'Go back where you came from.'

'Martina, this is ridiculous,' said Jonas. 'Get out of bed, now.'

'I told you, go away.'

With a mixture of anger and confusion, Jonas went out of the room. He was disturbed by her condition, but there wasn't much he could do till she slept off that fatigue. What happened in Väddö? *Was she in a fight? Surely, the bruises can't be from cleaning, moving things and furniture?*

Putting his concerns aside, he went in the study and fired up Martina's computer. He must finish writing the *Operating Environment Analysis* for the new hospitals. Martina needed it tomorrow.

It was past three in the afternoon when Martina emerged in the kitchen. Jonas stood at the stove preparing lunch.

'It's good you're still here,' said Martina, standing at the threshold. 'I thought you had left.' She wore dark gym pants and matching sweatshirt.

'No, I didn't,' said Jonas. She came over and kissed him on the cheek.

'You look tired,' he said, gazing at her, unsmiling.

'You're cooking?'

'We have to eat.'

'What a bad host I am. Letting you cook in my house.'

'I let you cook in my place all the time. So what's the big deal?'

'So what are you cooking?'

'Spaghetti and chicken fillet with vegetables,' said Jonas. 'It's what I found.'

'It smells good,' said Martina. 'I'll get drinks. You want wine?'

'Yes, white wine will be fine.'

They ate in silence. Jonas was watching her, suspecting she was hiding something from him.

'It tastes great,' said Martina.

'Want more?'

'No, thank you. I'm done.'

'You've hardly eaten anything.'

'Jonas, don't start.'

'What is it?' asked Jonas. 'Why are you edgy?'

'I'm not edgy.'

Jonas lay his knife and folk on the plate and regarded her. She lowered her gaze, avoiding his glare.

'What was it with the wincing, the tensing, and the raw wounds on your body? What happened?'

'I told you, we cleaned the house.'

'Look, I'm not a child,' said Jonas, raising his voice, his tone serious. 'I can see something is wrong here.'

'Keep your voice down.'

'It worries me when you do outrageous things. You're fearless, courageous, and almost blind to danger. Now tell me, did you fight?'

'Is that how you perceive me?'

'Come on now,' said Jonas. 'You remember at the summer grill how you were up in arms against Patrick Strand. If not for Torsten and me, you'd have whacked him.'

'You think so?' asked Martina, amused.

'Oh, yes,' said Jonas as he burst out laughing.

Martina laughed too. Reaching out, she took his hand in both of hers and caressed his knuckles. She gazed into his anxious eyes, aching to tell him the truth, but no, she couldn't. The unsettling events of last night frightened her. The dead face of a young woman wouldn't leave her mind. She froze. She didn't want to talk about it, and yet still, he might not believe her.

'Darling, don't worry about me. I wasn't in a fight.'

'Promise me. You'll never fight anyone.'

'I can't promise that,' said Martina. 'I don't fight. I defend myself.'

'It's better to walk away,' said Jonas. 'Promise me you'll walk away or call security.'

Martina hesitated. Maybe he was right. She was too confrontational, too combative. 'I can only say I'll try but I can't promise.'

'Try by all means,' said Jonas. He paused and then said, 'You haven't answered my question. The bruises on your body, how did you get them?'

'I fell.'

'Really?' said Jonas, pinning her with a doubtful gaze.

'Yes,' said Martina. It pained her soul to lie to the man she loved, but she must.

Jonas thought her yes sounded more tentative than definite. What was she hiding? He sighed. 'Now that I know you're all right, I'd better get going.'

'So soon?'

'I've been here quite a while. Besides, I need to get the analysis document ready for my boss,' said Jonas as he winked one eye at her.

'Your boss, is she a tough woman?'

'Sometimes, but worse of all, she fights if she doesn't get what she wants.'

Martina kicked his feet under the table, and they both laughed. Then she walked him to the hallway. They kissed and she watched him walk out of the front door.

'Thanks for lunch.'

'Don't mention it.'

In the evening, Thomas brought Joachim back to Slottsville house. When he left, Martina spent an hour listening to Joachim's retelling of the cool Halloween bash: candy, funny costumes, and pranks played with friends. It was past eight when she tucked him in bed.

There was something she must do before turning in. The number kept spinning in her head, escaping, and coming back. She had better put it to rest. She went to the study and started her computer. She logged onto the home page of Swedish Transport Agency and put in a query for car license numbers. She fed the number in her head into the browser and punched the button. The search engine turned out no result available. Damn, the license number of the van was false. Dead end! She picked up her encrypted phone and dialled a number. A voice answered.

'Police House, Mats Malm.'

'I'm calling to report a homicide,' said Martina.

The officer responded, and she said, 'No, no names. I would rather remain anonymous.'

'Okay, then, go ahead.'

'There's a dead body of a girl, in a shallow grave, in a forested area near Ribbyburg Clinic.' And she hung up.

Chapter 19

Martina stood admiring the gift basket on her desk. Beautiful wrappings of pink and mauve muslin paper were gathered on top and held by a large golden yellow ribbon. Thanks to Pia's splendid taste. Martina put on her coat, picked up the gift basket, and walked out of the office.

Traffic was heavy, so cautious driving was in order. At Slussen she headed towards Värmdö Island, the middle of Stockholm's archipelago. A slight drizzle started as she arrived at the red-tiled villa. On the gate was engraved *Barbara Von Essen Nsamizi*.

Salty sea breeze mixed with rain washed over her as she pressed the doorbell. The door opened, and a lady in her mid-fifties stood at the door with a beaming smile. She wore a long, free-flowing African print dress and a matching headgear. Stray strands of her blonde hair swayed loosely at the nape of her neck.

'Well, Martina, it's been a long time.' Stepping forward, she gave Martina a tight hug. She took the gift basket from her, and they walked to the living room area.

'It's lovely to see you again, Barbara,' said Martina with a smile, her voice vibrant and excited.

'What a terrible thing to happen – the break-in at your country home. Did they take anything of value?'

'Not really. I think they were looking for something,' said Martina with a quiver in her voice.

'I see you shudder at the thought of it,' said Barbara, intuitively grasping her mood.

A crystal chandelier hung from the ceiling reflecting subtle beams of light on the white walls. The décor in antique furniture and satin drapes gave the room a bracing look. The centrepiece table in marble, standing on a leopard rug, blended well with works of African art adorning the walls. A snowshoe cat emerged from under the table, gazed up at Martina with a whine, and then meandered to the kitchen.

'We'll sit in the kitchen,' said Barbara. 'It is cosy and warmer this time of year. I'll make some tea. You come bearing gifts!' She placed the gift basket on the kitchen island, untied the golden yellow ribbon, and peeked inside at the contents. She enthused, 'Oh, my goodness – Dom Pérignon Rosé; my favourite champagne. And pinot noir, gourmet cheese, and – ah…chocolate truffle.'

She turned on her heels and regarded Martina, her eyes glittering with approval. 'You really shouldn't have.'

Martina gazed back in a moment of triumph, thinking, *Got you! You are always giving me gifts. Now it's my turn to reciprocate.* She gave her an open sweet smile. 'I wanted to, Barbara. It's a small token of thanks. Your donations to Althonat Global are well appreciated.'

'Take a seat, please.'

The kitchen island in radiant brown wood mirrored similar shades on cupboards and the sink area. Martina sat at the wood table adorned by four white chairs and two pendant lamps suspended from the ceiling. Through the large window she could see the gleaming sea in the lingering rain before dusk.

'The view is breathtaking.'

'Yes, even better when it starts snowing.'

'How is Phillip?' asked Martina.

'Phillip is fine, thanks to Althonat Global,' said Barbara. 'He's graduated from the Police academy. He is smart, intelligent, without a trace of past ailments. I'm glad your father started on him at an early age. Sometimes when I remember what Sam and I went through – not finding the right medical help, bouncing from one hospital to the next, even being blamed for our son's illness – I shed a tear in gratitude for your father. After we came to him, in six months Phillip started talking and developing along the same track as his age-mates. So when you talk about appreciation, I'm more than gratified giving back to help other children.' There were tears in her eyes.

'He didn't join the family business?'

'Today's youngsters prefer choosing their own path, though I hope one day he will change his mind.'

'I'm glad he's found his passion,' said Martina between sips of tea.

'His father would have been thrilled to see him grow into the strong, healthy young man he is today. That's why I want the donation to help vaccine-damaged children in Africa, where Sam spent his last years of work.'

'Africa, Asia and Latin America are strong pillars in our work. The bulk of our raw materials come from these regions. We are in environmental work too: for every herb we take, we replace it by planting a new one. We don't do plantations. We work with small local farmers, the rural population, and our partnership is fifty-fifty. It is all about creating wellness. And vaccine-damaged children remain our major priority.'

'Sam would be pleased,' said Barbara with a warm smile. 'I remember him, in the States, when he came to speak to your father about Phillip, just before he left for Africa. He was optimistic and excited about Phillip's detoxification regime and the individualized alternative therapies we were introduced to. Phillip must have been four then.'

Barbara's brow furrowed as she went on. 'Sam had just started his second term at the UN, and Africa was on the agenda. On that trip he caught malaria and died.'

It was an emotional moment for the two women, sharing a painful past; Martina realized she had a common bond here, a soothing oasis where she could draw strength from another woman.

Barbara restrained her tears and changed the subject. 'Martina, one thing bothers me.'

'What?'

'Your father turned his back on this country,' said Barbara. 'For heaven's sake, what possessed him to come back?'

'He wanted to follow up on certain somethings. He couldn't speak about it over the phone. He sounded anxious the last time I spoke to him. I left for Asia on business just before he and Mamma arrived. The day I returned is the day the accident happened.'

'Talk about bad timing,' said Barbara. 'And you haven't a clue what it was.'

'Nothing really,' said Martina with a heavy sigh. 'He told Sebastian it was urgent and must be dealt with immediately - something about an old quarrel in Hässelved and something else he didn't say.'

'You've to find out,' said Barbara. 'Let Torsten do some digging. It sounds important.'

'I've got a new neighbour in Väddö,' said Martina. 'You won't believe who.'

'Some dashing handsome bachelor, I'd guess,' said Barbara with a wink.

'Dr Rangor is no handsome bachelor,' said Martina with a tinge of contempt in her voice. 'He was at the funeral too.'

'You mean Dr Rangor, as in New York?'

'Yes.'

Barbara abruptly set down her teacup. 'You'd better be careful, my dear. Did you know his first wife died mysteriously? After her death he went underground, and now he's surfaced in Stockholm, at your father's funeral, and is your neighbour at Landegrind house,' said Barbara. 'That's more than a coincidence.'

'Father never talked much about him after what happened,' said Martina with a shrug.

'The question is, what is he doing in Stockholm – and why did he buy a house in your neighbourhood?' asked Barbara, her eyes darkening.

There was silence. Hearing Barbara's words reinforced Martina's suspicions, forcing her to face questions she had been trying to avoid. It was apparent the mystery surrounding the man was taking on a new unpredictable dimension.

Barbara broke the silence, sensing her words were too harsh and frightening for Martina. 'Don't make the same mistakes I made. People will see you're young and think you're naïve. They will pretend to be friends, offering help here and there. Don't trust them.'

'Barbara, I'm not naïve. It's just the unknown, what is lurking out there, that scares me.'

'Trust your instincts, and you'll be fine,' said Barbara with an encouraging smile. 'Enough about Dr Rangor! Now, how about your love life? Is Jonas stalling for time or are you? We need to hear wedding bells.'

Martina smiled, and her face flushed pink. 'You are funny, Barbara. No one is stalling for time.' Her blue eyes sparkled with unreadable emotion.

'I see your finger is unbranded, and yet you know he's a catch,' said Barbara, her eyes full of mischief.

'I don't want to rush into anything.'

'Or you're still harbouring tentative feelings for Thomas?' asked Barbara, peering at her closely.

'Oh, don't even go there. Thomas and I are history,' said Martina. She shifted in her chair and cupped her chin in her hand. She remembered that Lisa had said the same thing in Väddö. Had she given them reason to think so? Not that she knew of.

'You and Thomas were such a stunning couple when you were dating in the States, and when you got married, everybody knew you were the perfect match,' said Barbara, her bold gaze holding Martina's shy eyes.

A brief smile flitted across Martina's lips. She knew Barbara meant well. 'You will be the first to know when I decide on Prince Charming.' With that she pushed her chair back and got on her feet. 'I must be going.'

'I'll walk you out,' said Barbara. 'It was lovely to see you again. You should come more often.' She paused and then said, 'I'm impressed by your leadership qualities and stamina. Taking Althonat to global level was a great achievement. I read the Frangipani every day and savour every word. The letters stand out on the pages, and I know it's you speaking to the world. Your wisdom is unprecedented.' She hugged Martina as if to reassure her.

'Well, thank you, Barbara. That means a lot, coming from you.'

It was nine in the evening, and traffic was ebbing as Martina eased the Mercedes into the main road. The sky was shrouded by darkness, and as she drove on, a tear trailed down her cheek. She swiped it away and kept her eyes on the road. She got sentimental whenever she interacted with Barbara – maybe because she was like a sister she had never had or because there was a keen resemblance in their fated backgrounds.

Barbara's father worked in the timber industry. He had built a business empire equal to none. The Von Essen family was an old, noble family from northern Sweden, owners of forestland. When her father died, she inherited the business and took it global. Her work enabled her to travel. That was when she had met her husband, Sam Nsamizi, an African prince who excelled in diplomacy and rose to a high rank in the United Nations. When Phillip was born, he was a perfectly normal, chubby little boy but regressed after being vaccinated against childhood illnesses. By word of mouth they heard about Dr Peter Strömstedt and natural alternative medicine. Martina turned the car into the driveway at Slottsville house.

Thomas hadn't expected she would be so long. He'd been babysitting Joachim. Finally, he saw headlights flash. He was waiting at the door when Martina entered.

'What took you so long?' he queried.

'I'm sorry. You know how Barbara is. One thing leads to another, and before you know it, the evening is gone.'

'Joachim is sleeping. Tomorrow he has gymnastics. Remember to pack his gym clothes in his backpack.'

'That's fine.' Martina hesitated and then said, 'By the way, next weekend is my turn, but we can change so you take him instead. I have repairs at Landegrind house, in Väddö.'

Thomas paused, trying to recall his calendar. He tilted his head and said, 'Maybe I can help you with that. I really don't have any engagement over the weekend.'

'No, no, you can't. I'll manage.'

'Really, it's no problem.'

Martina gazed at him, reluctant to accept his offer, and then she said, 'If you insist.'

'That's settled then. See you on Saturday. I'll get Joachim to help me.'

As soon as she closed the door, her phone buzzed. She retrieved it from her bag and pressed the button. 'Martina,' she answered.

'It's Jonas, darling. How have you been?'

'I'm fine. How about you?'

'I miss you. Let's get away over the weekend,' he said. 'A cottage in the mountains would be relaxing.' There was a queasy silence as the seconds ticked past. 'Darling, are you there?'

'Yes, I'm here.'

'Did I catch you at a bad time?'

'Not really. Can't we do it some other time? I've got renovations in Väddö.'

'I can come and help with that.'
'Oh, no, I'll manage.'
'Sweet dreams, then.'
'Good night, darling.'
She turned to leave the great room and noticed a pile of mail on table. Thomas had picked it up from the postbox. A white glossy envelope with a golden Nobel logo stuck out. It looked familiar: an invitation to the Nobel Prize Awards Ceremony. She tore it open, and as usual they requested RSVP.

Chapter 20

At dawn Birgit woke and reached out for Grenzken in bed. He was not there. She sat up, perplexed. Where was he? He'd come in at eight, gave her a shot, and left, saying he had work to do. She had noted he was overly quiet and there was something about his mood. He seemed snappish and irritable, as if he was angry with her. She lay back in bed, bothered by where he might be. She wondered if he had spent the night with Miss Bottle Blonde, Gittel. She turned restlessly in bed, but tossed the idea out of her head.

At midday Grenzken appeared in her office with a shopping list. Birgit gazed at him, upset by his insensitivity. As he left, she gently grabbed his arm, pulled him back, and closed the door.

'Where were you last night?'

'I told you, I was busy. A situation came up demanding attention.' His voice was soft and persuasive. But his faint smile and tilted head brought no comfort to Birgit. Instead, her mind flickered, thinking...*a situation with the Bottle Blonde maybe.*

She glowered at him but then softened her eyes and dropped the subject. 'Will l see you tonight?'

'Of course, yes,' said Grenzken as he ran his finger over her pale cheek. She flushed crimson. 'What is wrong?' he said.

Trying to keep her emotions at bay, Birgit spoke softly: 'I'm burning up, Fritz. Your touch drives me wild.' She blushed madly, embarrassed yet utterly happy.

'Oh, that! I know,' said Grenzken as he held her chin in his hand, gazing in her amorous eyes. 'I'll come as soon as I can.' He disappeared as abruptly as he came.

Birgit scanned the shopping list in her hand: drugs and medical equipments.

A biting wind bent trees and kicked up snowflakes in the atmosphere. The wet slushy weather chilled quickly into a thick mantle of snow. Grenzken stood on his plush living room balcony, gazing down at Birgit as she edged the BMW out of the garage and accelerated into the maze of snow. He closed the doors and walked to the bedroom. Under the fluffy bedding a figure stirred, turning to face him. With a dazzling smile on her face, the Bottle Blonde stared back at him, her jaw hanging.

'Move over,' barked Grenzken. Gittel hitched the sheet around her naked body and made room for him. Directing his snaky gaze on her, he stripped naked, letting his pants and shirt cascade around him on the floor. He eased himself into bed beside her. Her eyes were a flinty lilac, blue and guarded. He took her in his awkward arms. Her nervous giggles spiked his arousal. He lunged into her, a squeak escaping her lips as they escalated into a bucking and arching of hips, colliding in loathsome serpentine rhythm.

That evening, The Group board members sat around a conference table listening to Grenzken's monotonous narration of success on perfecting Life-Vaccine to the point of making it an anti-fertility vaccine, which of course would market under the same name against a spectrum of female ailments. He then talked about his success story of Anna, who time and time again had miscarried due to the powerful Life-Vaccine. Though she was a mother of two prior to coming to the Devilund, she failed to carry any pregnancy to full term. The last trials proved she had become sterile. In a dull, overbearing tone he talked about her death which of course was inevitable, given the powerful drugs involved in the trials.

'Do you have the autopsy report?' asked Rangor. 'It's always good to assess, appraise, and evaluate cause of death. Also, of course, it helps ensure that no ghosts come haunting us.'

There was a panicked silence as Grenzken struggled to come up with the best excuse. His mouth dried, and a timid smile played across his face.

'I didn't think it was necessary,' he said.

The men around the table turned dark gazes on him, shifting and clearing throats, all wanting to speak at the same time. The air was thick with astonishment, disbelief and anger.

'It's standard procedure,' said Mattsson, CEO of Citaraph.

'Yes, it is,' said Grenzken, 'but the body was in a decomposed state after subjection to the noxious drugs. Though she was strong, almost like an ox. Most females don't last that long.' There was an air of arrogant indifference in his voice, and his sly eyes were evasive as a fox's.

'How do we know she died?' asked Tord.

'Of course, she died,' said Grenzken. He reached for a glass of sparkling water and poured it down his dry throat.

A palpable anxiety spread through the assemblage. The room heated up, prompting Stellan to peel off his grey sweater and discard it on the empty seat beside him. Grenzken pushed back his chair and strolled across the room, his steps shaky. He opened a window a crack, letting in a rush of chilled air. He inhaled deeply, hoping to relieve the strain on his mind.

When he returned to his seat, Mattsson was adamant. 'We can't pay,' he said and widened his eyes at Grenzken in undisguised anger.

'Wait a minute. We can still exhume the body and perform an autopsy,' said the silver-haired man in an exquisite pinstriped suit.

'What an undertaking!' breathed Stellan, his upper lip twitching.

The onus of the dilemma threatened to break up the conclave. It was evident to all that Grenzken had neglected procedure, and above all, security safeguards. For his part, Grenzken was partly blaming himself for trusting his subordinates too much and neglecting his duties. He reprimanded himself for overindulging in desires of the flesh, and in a biblical sense he was paying for his sins. He had allowed himself to lose focus, not paying enough attention to work. He must cut back on his outrageous intimate behaviour with research subjects.

Tord Stenbeck, Chief Inspector of police, breathed fire through his dragon nostrils. He didn't think it was funny. 'Lack of forensic evidence will land us all behind bars. Suppose Anna didn't die, and she is out there singing. What are our prospects? We are chanceless?'

Grenzken shifted in his seat again, his face pallid, his lips pressed in a hard-thin line. He made a gesture as if to speak but closed his mouth.

'If the worse comes to worst, we shall exhume the bodies for DNA testing,' said Mattsson.

'What are you saying?' asked Grenzken. 'The exhumation itself will attract attention.'

'Unless you produce Anna in person or her corpse, what alternatives do we have?' blared Tord, levelling a finger at him. Grenzken squirmed and glared out of the window.

'That is settled, then; Grenzken, find Anna,' said the silver-haired man. 'Next on, the dossier,' he announced, turning imperiously to Stellan. 'Any luck?'

Stellan took a deep breath and fumbled for words. He cleared his throat, and said, 'I haven't found it. It could be anywhere; here or in the States.'

'Focus on your niece, Dr Martina Strömstedt Edgren. She should know where it is,' said Rangor with a spitting emphasis on the middle name as if it was distasteful.

'It will take some stealthy digging. I can't go right out and ask her,' said Stellan, his voice wimpy and diffident.

'You're family. It shouldn't be difficult to access her house,' said the silver-haired man, with a tinge of haughtiness in his voice.

'In the business community, she is considered the most powerful woman in Sweden today. With the dossier in her hand, she would sink us like the Titanic,' said Mattsson.

'Stellan, find that dossier by all means,' said the silver-haired man.

Stellan wiped sweat beads off his forehead, thinking, *how am I going to accomplish that?* Rangor observed him with a sinister grin on his face. He leaned over and whispered in his ear, 'Once you've sold your soul, the rest is a piece of cake.' Stellan scowled at this, got up, and walked out of the room.

After the meeting, The Group had an early workplace Christmas celebration. Christmas dinner lay served in the dining room, and Grenzken humbly made the announcement. He sauntered out of the room in a sulky and shrunken demeanour, uninspired and feeling defeated. He alighted in the kitchen, coming under the scrutinizing gaze of Birgit.

'Why, Fritz, you look beaten. What happened?'

'Move, move...move it, Birgit. Get the drinks,' he said. 'Where's Helmut?'

'He's organizing the table,' said Birgit, hurt by his indignant riposte. She marched out of the kitchen and stood on the threshold to the dining room, ushering and sorting out sitting arrangements for guests.

She wore a red velvet full-length dress that hugged her voluptuous figure with sensuality. The sparkling diamond necklace accentuated her cleavage, and the matching earrings brought a shimmering glow to her complexion. In her cascading curly blonde hair, she wore a silver glittering band. Earlier she had soured because she wanted to invite her friend, Lena, but Grenzken put a stop to it.

'You look luscious in red, Birgit,' said Tord, eying her cleavage intently.

'Thank you, Tord,' said Birgit, a beguiling smile on her face. In the far corner of the room, Grenzken shot her a glare. The other guests smiled courteously as they glided past her to take their seats.

On the long table clusters of crystal glasses gleamed in chandelier light. Potted peach poinsettia and amaryllis adorned the windowsills. On the sideboard table, taking up the full length of the wall, a sumptuous meal of smorgasbord buffet was laid out. To the far right, the dining room extended into a bar area.

The chatter and tittle-tattle dominated the room as they ate to the soft humming of Christmas carols. A constant flow of drinks quenched dry throats. A view through the large double glazed windows revealed a rolling landscape shrouded in fluffy snow, and leafless trees crystallized in white flakes.

The conversation centred on winter activities, skiing, and winter travel holidays. The problems that had threatened them earlier were set aside for the moment, and they were happy.

'Cross country is my favourite. It conditions the body,' said Richard.

'For young people like you, perhaps,' said Grenzken as he regarded Richard munching a meatball. Birgit sat opposite watching him, thinking about those very lips curled around her nipples, sucking and kneading. She sighed. She wanted the guests to leave.

'Not really, I've been on the trail with seventy-year-olds,' said Richard.

Grenzken did not respond but continued to stare at Richard angrily, doubting his story that Anna had died.

To change her frame of mind, Birgit decided to focus on socializing and having a good time. 'Seventy years old, come on, Richard,' she said. Grenzken gazed at her, realizing for the first time she looked splendid in diamonds.

After dinner Rangor struck up a conversation with Richard about his research on new mind-altering drugs. He told him drugs would eradicate hyperactivity disorders, depression, and criminality in children.

Richard wanted to know how and where he was carrying out such trials. Rangor obliged, for he was among friends and sure that whatever transpired within these four walls was automatically confidential. He told him about trials he carried out on dogs and children at Ribbyburg Clinic, and the drugs he used.

'But these drugs cause impairment of thinking and memory loss,' said Richard. 'And they are addictive.'

'The addictive part is the best part because that is where we make money,' said Rangor with an ominous grin on his face.

A bolt from the blue came over Richard, but he tried to maintain a calm face. Rangor leaned in towards him so their faces were centimetres apart. This time he spoke in low undertones. 'Take Helmut, for example; he's a walking experiment – mind control drugs and steroids. We push limits here. We want to know how much the human mind can withstand before it cracks. But for him, we have to find a balance so he is functional too. He's still useful to us. Of course he feels much better than he did when he was destitute.'

'So when he ceases to be useful, you will crack him?'

'That will be for Grenzken to decide.'

'But Helmut is unpredictable and overly angry sometimes,' said Richard.

'Mood swings are a normal side effect but can be regulated with blood work and adjustment of medication.'

Richard regarded Rangor with alarm, thinking, *no wonder school children outrageously gun each other down in schools around the world.*

'That is not all,' continued Rangor. 'Medication can cause severe side effects too, like hallucinations, disruptive behaviour, creation of a zombie state or catatonia in the patient, and in extreme cases permanent insanity. With insanity we bind them up and restrain them with belts or chains. If need be, we put them in isolation cells for days.'

'You have isolation cells?'

'Yes, at Ribbyburg, in the basement.'

Richard faked a smile. 'What about the long-term effects of the drugs?' he said, watching Helmut leave the room.

'That's not a problem. Any side effects are countered by more drugs. That's the secret of continual growth of sales and profits,' said Rangor. 'That's what makes Citaraph one of the ten richest companies in the world. Our business is about money and shareholders. As long as we keep rolling in dough, shareholders are happy.'

Richard's insides shuddered. He gazed at the doctor, who reminded him of Josef Mengele in Nazi Germany.

'What about surgery? Does it improve hyperactivity disorders and behaviour disruptions in children?'

Rangor appeared taken aback by the question, but he answered it anyway: 'That's rather costly, and the results, unpredictable. I wouldn't go for surgery in such children. Drugs are more effective and give immediate results. That's where Grenzken and I differ in opinion. He's a strong believer in surgery.'

'And all this is legal…I mean making money on sick children?'

'It depends on what you mean by legal. It's a question of collaborating with powers that make laws to ensure the laws are supportive of business,' said Rangor as he took a gulp at his beer.

'You mean health authorities and the judiciary are in on this?'

'Richard, you ask too many questions.'

Richard gave Rangor a wan smile and decided he did not want to hear more. He nursed his drink, preferring to remain sober. He became apprehensive about Nicholas' surgery in the morning – about what Grenzken might do to him.

He glanced at Grenzken sitting at the bar, busy pouring himself another stiff drink. He had difficulty focusing; his hands were shaking and he kept spilling drink on the counter. *Tomorrow is surgery and the doctor is tanked. Has he forgotten his little song about rules and regulations?* Richard understood that in this shady business, everything was possible, justifiable as long as it hiked profits, even performing dubious surgery on small boys when one was drunk. He looked around for Helmut, anxious about surveillance cameras and doors in Devilund Clinic, wondering whether they were secured to hold back enemy forces should they choose a moment of weakness and strike tonight.

Throughout dinner Stellan sat eating quietly, saying nothing. His foreboding mind dreaded the skiing season. It brought memories of his brother's passing on that horrid road from a skiing resort. His falling out with his brother, Peter, was not something he had desired. It was unfortunate, but bad things happened sometimes. It was true that he had harboured jealous tendencies towards his brother. Peter excelled at whatever he touched, unlike him, who remained a mediocre person without direction. He shrank at his memory; even in death, Peter's shadow loomed larger in his life.

His brother's children hated him. He considered his life now, dark and shadowy, devoted to pursuing shady, unscrupulous deals. The forces that had brought him together with The Group had sealed his fate in their hands. He was no longer master of his destiny but rather slave to their ends, a tool for what they believed was a shared interest in the advancement of science. Together they must soar, and together they were ensnared in a twisted scheme of monetary gains. One wrong move or divergence, and he would be no more. He was like a trapped animal.

The night advanced, and the warm glow of flickering candlelight brought on a snuggling cosiness to the room. The babble of voices grew louder as levels of alcohol consumption escalated, fuelling a misguided sense of peace and serenity.

Helmut kept the drinks flowing, but for his part, he stuck to sodas. It was doctor's orders; medication was incompatible with alcohol. Once in a while, in his limited vocabulary, he shared a word or two with the guests and even managed a chuckle at some silly jokes. He appeared to be enjoying himself. Yet he remembered to keep a keen eye on inmates in Devilund. Inmates were not to be left unattended to for long hours.

Birgit, engrossed in animated talk with Tord, seemed taken in by his charm, laughing and gazing intently in his eyes. Grenzken sat at the bar, sipping whisky and watching them like a hawk, displeased by Birgit's openly flirtatious manner. He was still angry at the audacity of Mattsson's suggestion that he wouldn't be paid if he failed to produce Anna or her corpse. A reimbursement of thirty million kroner was not something to forfeit just like that. These days, overall costs had increased: maintenance of Devilund, outlays for research and development, overhead, repairs, and personnel. A new surveillance system too must be installed.

He wondered about Richard's honesty again. Had he been telling the truth about Anna's body being badly decomposed? He had never had reason to doubt him, but still he needed to probe him further for answers. He took another slug of whisky. His fierce eyes turned scarlet. His face flushed like a tomato. He was tanked to the brim.

Then a sudden frightful shrill emanated from behind the door. Heads turned in gasping horror; clearly many were not sure they had heard right. The door burst open, and in reeled Helmut, brandishing a rifle, anger seething like a wildfire in his eyes. Screams of terror rolled like thunder. Everyone took cover. Everyone sobered up. Bullets sprayed, and windows shattered from top to bottom.

Slurring inarticulately and raving like a disgruntled beast, Helmut moved around the room in a daze, pointing the barrel at anyone in his line of vision. He breathed hysteria among guests. Fear, like a giant hand, squeezed their hearts. Men and women scrambled on the floor, seeking cover under tables and chairs. The uncalculated momentum caused a crashing sound of breaking porcelain. The shatter of glass impacted the room in a whirlwind of chaos. The avalanche extinguished candles and plunged the room into darkness. Harsh high-pitched cries of despair echoed on walls. Then, everyone held their breath.

Chapter 21

In the dark basement of a dilapidated building, bats and rats milled around. A single flicker of green light at the end of the tunnel beckoned her. She wandered on unfamiliar ground, believing if she could only get to the light, she would be all right. She pushed on, afraid to attract attention, searching in circles for an exit. Trapped, helpless and hunted, she gasped in exasperation. The hunters were men in white coats, men with needles ready to take her out. She counted steps, paces. She was getting there.

Something stirred in the darkness. She stiffened, feeling her aching muscles, her eyes darting from side to side. Suddenly, a green light exploded, and a crowd of men in white coats rushed at her. She turned back, screeching, running for her life.

'Mamma, Mamma, stop screaming,' howled Joachim. 'Wake up. Your phone is ringing.'

Martina bolted up in bed, opened her eyes, and stared blankly at Joachim. She glanced at the clock on the bedside table. It was three in the morning.

She grabbed the phone from Joachim's hand. 'Martina,' she answered in a hoarse voice.

'It's Torsten. Sorry to wake you up so early.'

'That's okay. What's the problem?'

'There's an urgent distress signal from Scorpio.'

'Follow procedure. Go in with reinforcements,' said Martina. 'Do what you have to do, and get out. And Torsten, remember: no violence.'

'Will do,' said Torsten.

'Good luck,' Martina said and hung up.

Joachim stood watching his mother, wide-eyed. 'Mamma, why were you screaming? You frightened me.'

'I'm sorry, sweetheart. Come here,' said Martina, shifting in bed to make space for him. He clambered up, and snuggled up in her arms.

'I'm sorry I frightened you. I must have had a nightmare.'

'Like me?'

'Yes, like you,' said Martina, her thoughts flashing back to the dreadful dream she'd had.

'Were you scared too?' asked Joachim.

'Yes, I was,' she said, gazing blankly into dark space. 'I'm glad you came and woke me.'

She kissed his hair, and in minutes Joachim was asleep. Unlike him, sleep fled from her, evaporating into thin air. She lay in bed worrying about Scorpio, hoping Torsten and his security men would take care of the problem.

It was rare for Scorpio to use a distress signal. It had happened only once, when his companion was hit by a van and died instantly. The case had been written off as an accident, but it had still devastated Pappa.

On Saturday midday, the soft sunrays reflected a shimmer on white snow, blinding her vision as she drove with Joachim and Astrid to the family country home, Landegrind house, in Väddö. She adjusted the sunshield and accelerated though the white landscape. Lack of sleep and the constant worry about Scorpio and Torsten made her head throb. She hoped the problem could be resolved quickly without violence.

She parked in the driveway. Thomas arrived in his black BMW M6 Gran Coupé and parked beside her red Mercedes Coupé. He emerged from the car and walked to the storehouse where Martina was retrieving toolboxes. He stood at the entrance watching her.

When she turned, she startled. 'Oh, you scared me.'

'I didn't mean to. I'll take that and get started. Where's Joachim?'

'In the house.'

'You want a cup of coffee?'

'No, thanks, I already had some.'

He wandered to the house, stood in the hallway, and called for Joachim. Joachim scampered downstairs, shouting, 'Pappa!'

'Put on warm clothes, and come help me outside.'

Thomas removed his steamy eyeglasses and laid them on the low table in the living room.

Upstairs in her parents' room, Martina stood behind window drapes, peering down at Rangor's compound. Nothing moved; there was only dead silence, not even the barking of a dog. She wondered where he was. Still Torsten hadn't called. With a heavy heart she went to the kitchen to look for something to do with her hands – something to occupy her mind.

'What's for lunch?' she asked Astrid as she came into the kitchen.

'Chicken salad and fresh homemade bread.'

'I'll make the salad,' said Martina.

'Don't worry about it. I'll do it.'

Martina heard voices outside. Through the kitchen window she saw Thomas talking to a man in a dark blue police uniform. She hurried out to the veranda, where she saw a tall, handsome young man with super styled-short brown wavy hair. He looked like a model in a men's magazine. He held his flat cap in his hand.

Martina walked down the stairs and as she came nearer she narrowed her eyes and burst out, 'Phillip, what a pleasant surprise.' She smiled and Phillip Nsamizi smiled back, mirroring her warmth.

Thomas stood by gazing at them, understanding the outburst of joy. 'I'll leave you two to catch up,' he said as he returned to his chores. 'Phillip, nice seeing you.'

'Care for a coffee break?' asked Martina, gazing at Thomas.

'You two go ahead,' said Thomas. 'I would like to finish up here before it gets too cold.'

Martina turned to Phillip, and they walked into the living room and through to the kitchen, where they sat at the wooden table. 'How is your mother?' she said.

'She is fine, busy with business, travelling the world,' said Phillip. 'You know how she is – always active.'

Martina's fascinated gaze was all over him. 'Look at you, all handsome and grown up.' A shy smile crossed Phillip's face, and his eyes wandered to the window. 'I thought you would follow in your mother's footsteps.'

'We've the same passion for business. It's just that I directed mine to a different profession.'

'I'm glad you found your passion.' Astrid served tea and coffee with scones and withdrew discreetly. 'What brings you to Landegrind?'

'I'm head of the Police Investigative unit, and I would like to find out more about the break-in,' said Phillip, his face serious and business-like. 'The number of unsolved crimes in Stockholm has spiked, and our statistics are bad. We need to clear up these crimes.'

'I'm glad you're the one in charge.'

'So, was anything taken?'

'Nothing was taken. I think they were looking for something.'

'A footprint of shoe size forty-five was found on the veranda. Do you know anyone with that shoe size?'

'No, no one that comes to mind,' said Martina, wondering if Rangor's was size forty-five.

'Anyone?' insisted Phillip as he saw her hesitation.

'No, no one,' she said with a shake of her head.

'The damage done was extensive; I gather the culprit was angry. I know in your line of business you're bound to have enemies. Is there anyone in particular you can point to?'

'I've a new neighbour here,' said Martina as she turned her head towards Rangor's house. 'He just moved in. A Dr Steven Rangor?'

'The man who did consulting work for your father in the States?' asked Phillip as he sipped his coffee.

'Yes, he and Pappa parted on bad terms. A month ago he bought that house and moved in.'

Phillip paused, collecting his thoughts, and said, 'We have an eye on him, but this is between you and me. Keep it to yourself.' The surprise on Martina's face registered in Phillip's eyes, and he added, 'Things he did in the States.'

'Oh?' Martina wanted to know more but sensed Phillip's reluctance to delve into details.

'That will be all for now. Thank you.' He ate up his scones and emptied his coffee cup. 'I must run along.' Martina walked him outside, taking the opportunity to congratulate him on his rise in rank to Chief Investigative officer. He smiled and said, 'Thanks.'

The littel boy who had once been unfocused, devoid of speech, tormented by erratic hyperactive behaviour, was now healthy like anyone else. He had turned into a young charismatic man, strong, and pursuing a career in the police force. He was living proof of the exceptional work Althonat Global was doing.

The nagging discomfort in her chest returned. She had not heard from Torsten. The sound of loud talk drew her out of reverie as Thomas and Joachim emerged in the kitchen. Thomas remained standing at the threshold while Joachim rushed to his mother.

'Mamma, I repaired two railings all by myself,' said Joachim.

'Good boy. I'm proud of you and so is Pappa,' said Martina, gazing down at Joachim with a smile.

'The railing is done,' said Thomas, 'apart from painting, which you can do in summer.'

'Thanks,' said Martina. 'At least nothing will fall apart in the winter breeze.'

'Mamma, Mamma, I saw a squirrel under the bushes.'

'What was it doing?'

'It was eating something.'

Thomas gazed at mother and child, a sad expression on his face; he was wishing he still had his family intact. He regretted the pressures he'd put on Martina regarding his move to London. How could he have been so stupid, so short-sighted not to have foreseen the consequences of his foolish male ego? He observed her profile from the sidelines, admiring her exquisite beauty, calm disposition, and gorgeous figure. Her motherhood qualities were debatable, but those could be complemented by him. That was what marriage and parenthood were about: complementing each other. He got it now, but by the time he understood it, he had lost the most precious thing he'd ever had: his marriage.

'Lunch will be ready in five minutes,' said Martina.

Thomas snapped back from his daydreaming and said, 'I'll skip lunch if you don't mind.'

'Thomas, no, of course I mind. You can't drive back without eating. You want wine or a beer?'

'I'll have a beer,' he said as he sat at the table, relenting to her wish.

Joachim came scooting to the table, threatening to topple glasses as he crashed to a stop. 'Careful, Joachim,' said Thomas.

Martina poured a glass of beer and handed it to Thomas. She poured herself sparkling mineral water and milk for Joachim.

'You remember Dr Rangor?' she said as they fell to eating.

'The doctor who did consultant work for your father in the States?'

'Yes. He's my neighbour here. He bought the Strand house,' said Martina as she picked up her glass and took a sip of water.

'Has he moved to Sweden permanently?'

'I don't know.'

'Is he still doing consulting work for Althonat Global?'

'Not a chance,' said Martina. 'You know they parted on unfriendly terms, to put it mildly.'

Thomas gazed at her, clearly concerned. 'You have to be careful. It's possible he's after something. Let me know whenever you come out here.' He saw a nervous flicker in Martina's eyes and quickly added, 'Not that I want to keep tabs on you, but in case anything happens I need to know. And until the break-in issue is resolved, you can't relax.'

Without warning, at the same time they both reached for the table salt. Their hands touched accidentally, sending an electric charge to their emotions. Martina withdrew her hand as if scorched by his touch. 'You first.' Her face flushed pale pink, and a tingling sensation came over her.

It was apparent they had both just relived something old, something sensual – an attraction buried deep in their consciousness but nevertheless alive and present, ready to be rekindled and acted upon. They looked at each other. Martina lowered her gaze. Thomas took the salt.

She blinked and said, 'I'll let you know.'

'That's settled then,' said Thomas. 'And thanks for lunch.'

'You're welcome.'

'Joachim, say goodbye to your old man.'

'Can I come with you, Pappa?' Joachim asked.

'No, boy, stay here and take care of your mother,' said Thomas. 'Go get your books and read to her.'

'I'll read to her when I'm going to bed.'

Martina got up and cleared the table. Astrid appeared and took over from her.

In her bedroom, Martina sat on the bed, disturbed by the touch of Thomas' hand on hers. And the rush that braced her heart was astonishing to realize. Her rational mind told her something else, but her heart spoke loud and clear. Her sensual attraction to this man carried a sense of underlying oneness. In his warm, lingering gaze she saw a promise of love hanging, anticipating her power to take him back. It had been hard to let Thomas go, and it had taken her a long time to get over him, but was it possible she was still in love with him? Could she dump Jonas, and walk down the aisle with Thomas? *Get a leash on your thoughts, Martina,* something told her. She shook her head and discarded the idea.

She put the phone in her skirt pocket and said a silent prayer for Torsten and Scorpio.

She wanted to spend quality time with Joachim, so she went to the kitchen and made some yummy popcorn snack. In the TV-rum, they curled up on the sofa and watched the Pelle Svanslös movie while they ate popcorn.

After dinner, Joachim read to her and then she tucked him into bed.

As she walked downstairs, the phone vibrated. She retrieved it and run her finger on the screen. 'Martina.'

'It's Jonas.'

'Hi, darling.'

'Look, I am on my way to Landegrind,' said Jonas, his words clipped and abrupt. 'I need to speak to you; it's important.'

'What is it, you can't tell over the phone?'

'I can't.'

'Damn it, Jonas, you're scaring me.'

The line went dead. She remained holding the phone in her hand, a knot tightening in her stomach. She knew something was wrong.

At ten, the headlights of Jonas' Porsche flashed in the hallway. He got out of the car and strode to the house. Martina waited for him at the front door. The glum expression on his face told Martina his visit was other than social. At the door, their lips met in a brief kiss. Then he took her hand and led her to the living room.

'You look rattled, Jonas. What is wrong?' said Martina, desperation in her voice.

'Sit, Martina. Sit,' said Jonas as he ushered her to a sofa, his voice gentle but shaky.

'Don't ask me to sit. Tell me what's wrong.'

The torment in her eyes crushed his heart. He didn't know how to spare her the agony. He just had to tell it as it was. With his hand on her trembling shoulder, he gazed into her frightened eyes and said, 'I'm sorry, Martina. I'm so sorry, but Torsten is dead.' His voice cracked.

'Oh, my…my Lord!' she gasped. She went into a foetal position and collapsed on the floor. She remained there and let out a loud wail. Jonas went on his knees and hugged her quivering body. He slowly drew her to her feet and steered her to a sofa, where she flopped down and broke into inconsolable bawls, her body wrenching in spasms, tangled in grief.

Footsteps came pounding down the stairs. It was Joachim. He frowned at the stranger standing in his living room while his mother sobbed. His face flickered red with anger. 'Who're you?' he asked, moving to stand by his mother's side, his hand on her shoulder, his big eyes fixed on Jonas.

Getting a grip on herself, Martina lifted her teary eyes and gazed at Joachim. 'Joachim, this is my friend, Jonas,' she managed to say between sobs.

'Then why are you crying?'

'Something bad happened at work,' she stuttered, wiping away tears with her hand.

Joachim glared at Jonas again and said, 'I'll call Pappa.'

'No, darling, that won't be necessary,' said Martina. 'It's all right. Jonas is leaving soon.'

Jonas stood silent, watching mother and son, noting their strong resemblance: silky blond hair and piercing blue eyes. He was a very fine boy.

Joachim's stare surveyed the stranger and then went back to his mother. He glimpsed a pair of eyeglasses lying on the centrepiece table. 'Mamma, look. Pappa forgot his eyeglasses,' he blurted, picking them up.

'Keep them; we shall take them to him tomorrow,' said Martina as she raised her grieved eyes to meet Jonas' despairing glare.

A sinking feeling gripped Jonas' heart as dread, mistrust, and suspicion raged in his mind. He put his grief aside and tried rationalizing Thomas' visit to Landegrind house, but came up empty. He knew they had a child, but that was no reason, since Joachim wasn't sick or in urgent need of his father. The sound of Martina's voice pulled Jonas back.

'Joachim, go to bed,' she said. 'I'll come and tuck you in as soon as I'm finish with Jonas.'

Joachim scowled at Jonas but obeyed his mother and returned upstairs with a tentative step.

Then they heard soft steps padding the floor from Astrid's quarters. 'I couldn't help but hear the crying, Martina. Is everything all right?'

'No, Astrid. Everything is not all right. My Security Director has died.'

'I'm so sorry,' said Astrid. 'Indeed, very sorry.' She turned to Jonas and said, 'Good evening, sir.'

'Good evening, Astrid.'

'Martina, can I get you anything, perhaps a cup of tea?'

'No, I'm okay.' Then Martina cleared the hoarseness from her voice and said, 'Could you help Joachim to bed?'

'I'll see to that,' said Astrid, as she turned and headed upstairs.

Martina stretched out her hand to Jonas. Jonas grasped it and sat down beside her. She rested her head upon his chest. He gently caressed her back. They could hear the wind rustling against windows as it swept across the desolate landscape.

Martina tilted her head to look into his brooding eyes. 'Tell me, what happened?'

Jonas took a deep breath, sorrow eating at him for being the one to impart bad news to a woman already burdened by grief. 'The rescue mission went as planned. The place was deserted just as Scorpio had said it would be. But as they got into the jeep to leave, they were surprised by gunfire.'

'Gunfire?' asked Martina, raising her head to look at him. 'I told him, no violence.'

'No, they didn't fire a single shot. It was from the enemy camp. Torsten was last to reach the jeep after making sure his men were safe. He was hit in the chest. He collapsed, but they quickly got him into the jeep and sped away. He was unconscious when he arrived at the hospital.' Jonas sighed. 'The bullet had nicked his lung. He lost a lot of blood. He died on the operating table.'

Jonas felt Martina's body reverberate on his chest in a quiver, but she remained silent. He leaned over and gazed into her anguished eyes. Tears trailed her cheeks. He cradled her in his arms to quell her agony.

'Poor Torsten, he was the best,' she stuttered, breaking down in sobs. 'He and Pappa were old friends. He was the only person Pappa listened to.'

She broke out of Jonas' comforting arms and hastily wiped her tears with a tissue he gave her. She stopped sobbing and spoke, this time with resolve and determination. 'I'll contact his family and find out about funeral arrangements.'

But something bothered her still. Torsten was dead. What about Scorpio? She furrowed her brows and opened her mouth to say something but stopped.

'What is it?' asked Jonas.

She changed her mind and shook her head. 'Nothing.' She wanted to ask about Scorpio but remembered confidentiality must be maintained. Jonas wouldn't know about such things. She hoped Scorpio was all right; Jonas would have mentioned if another man had been injured or was dead.

'You know you can tell me anything.'

'No, it's nothing really.'

'All is well, my darling,' said Jonas. 'We have to be strong.'

It was past midnight when Jonas rose and asked, 'Will you be all right?' Martina replied in the affirmative and rose from the sofa. He kissed her hair tenderly, and she walked him to the door.

With a heavy heart Jonas drove back to Stockholm, hating every minute of it. He loathed leaving Martina traumatized. He wanted to stay but knew it was inappropriate with the boy in the house. Joachim would freak out if he woke up in the morning and found him in the house. He was protective of his mother, and that was understandable; it was harder for Jonas to shake the nipping pain that Thomas had been in Landegrind with Martina.

When the Porsche disappeared down the road, Martina rushed to the study and fired up her computer. Her sorrow and grief for Torsten put aside, she must find out if Scorpio was alive. When the main screen appeared, she clicked on her encrypted mailbox. To her relief there was mail from Scorpio. It was a report on the happenings at the rescue, with his condolences.

Torsten's death in the line of duty would stay with her for the rest of her life. Her mind jolted back to her parents. It was over a year ago that they had passed away. Now Torsten was dead. Her grief tripled. With effort she gathered herself and stumbled upstairs to her bedroom. She crawled into bed and cried her heart out.

Chapter 22

Vittaby Villa, Grenzken's residence, lay in darkness, amidst chaos and confusion with guests huddled under tables and chairs. The hour approached five in the morning. Helmut was still on the prowl in the inky dining room. His fingers tightened on the trigger and he fired. The deafening report ripped through the room, shattering windows. The room filled with smoke and the smell of gunpowder. Somebody found a light switch, illuminating Helmut's monstrous figure in motion. His pasty face twisted in grisly horror. His ferocious eyes shifted in colour like traffic lights – greenish yellow to ghastly orange and then dangerous red. His gaze was curiously morbid and empty. He wielded the rifle in his hands, ready for another blast.

From under the table, Tord eyed Rangor, Richard, and Bo in a silent signal. They heard another click as Helmut prepared to fire. The men burst from under the table and took him on in an avalanche, bringing him down. They pinned him to the floor, where he wailed and fought like a trapped wild pig. In the struggle, the rifle fell onto the floor under the table. Birgit grabbed it, scrambled to her feet, and ran out of the room with it.

Helmut kicked free from the men. He slipped out of their grip and sprang up to dart after Birgit. The men followed in hot pursuit. Rangor looked around for his medical bag. He found it flung against a wall. His hands trembled as he grabbed it and tore at it, retrieving a hypodermic needle. A brutal growling sound was heard down the hallway, then a scream, a loud struggle, and finally a thud. He quickly filled the needle with a liquid and ran to catch up with the men in a vicious brawl with a beast.

'Hold him down,' said Rangor, flashing the needle, inching in on Helmut. At the sight of the needle, a guttural roar escaped from Helmut's throat, and he lashed out with an iron fist, throwing men. He struggled up and galloped like a horse towards his quarters. Someone tripped him, bringing him down like Goliath. He yowled as he hit the hard floor. The men pinned him down on his belly. Tord sat on top of him and twisted his arms behind his back.

The menacing needle gleamed as Rangor spiked Helmut's thick neck. Helmut roared like a lion and then slackened. The men stood up, panting as they glared at his inert body and then at each other in utter terror. Deep in their minds loomed a mixture of horror and disbelief.

Rangor wiped the sweat off his brow with the back of his hand and asked, 'Where's Birgit?' Birgit emerged slowly from behind a door where she had watched the drama. In her hand she held the rifle. 'Birgit, we need to get him to bed. He will be out for some time.'

Birgit looked at Rangor in astonishment. 'Him?' she said. 'He can't stay here. What if he wakes up and starts attacking again? There is no knowing what he will do.'

Tord, Bo and Richard exchanged glances, appreciating Birgit's foresightedness. Rangor seemed at a loss. 'Where's Grenzken?' he asked with irritation in his voice.

Stellan and the silver-haired man joined them from wherever they had holed up. 'I don't think Grenzken is going to be of any use to you,' said the silver-haired man. 'He's passed out behind the bar.'

That was the understatement of the day. Rangor went over the edge.

'Wake him up, the bastard,' he said. 'He caused us all this trouble, and he's sleeping?'

'He's flat out on his back,' said Stellan.

As the men haggled over the pressing problem of Helmut, a lurking question emerged: what had sparked such rage in a man who had appeared to be having a good time? Tord surmised, 'Something must have happened in the Clinic.'

'You want to know what made him go bazooka?' said Stellan. 'It's the drugs Grenzken is pumping into him.'

'You know nothing about such things, Stellan,' said Rangor.

'You always minimize what I say,' said Stellan. 'But if you don't stop Grenzken's mad experiments, he will destroy Helmut.'

There were those in The Group who shared the same sentiment but dared not own up for fear of sounding disloyal.

'The Clinic will be a safe place for him to rest,' said Mattsson, who stood at a distance, listening.

Anxiety washed over Richard. Dread filled his heart. Helmut had been fine when he went down to the Clinic but had returned raving mad. Tord was right. Something terrible must have happened down there. He excused himself. 'I must see to things in Devilund,' he said.

Bo spoke up. 'I'll see about a place for Helmut in the Clinic. We can monitor him down there.' He left with an urgent step. Silence fell upon the room as Bo's steps disappeared into the distance.

The gaping glassless windows revealed the break of dawn and swirls of falling snow. Wind gusts filled the room, forcing guests to look for coats. They were tired and wanted to go home, but they still had many unanswered questions. 'Where did Helmut get the rifle?' asked the silver-haired man.

'It must be Grenzken's hunting rifle. He kept them in the lab,' said Birgit as she held her fingers over her mouth, suppressing a yawn.

'In the lab, without lock and key?' asked Tord. 'Keeping rifles and ammunition together is madness.'

'We can't solve these riddles now,' said Mattsson. 'We'd better go home, rest, and take it up later. We should be happy we are alive.'

Then they heard faint footsteps coming from the dining room. It was Grenzken, barefooted, his hair standing on end. He rubbed his sleepy eyes with his fingers. His blue shirt was crinkled and hung over his black pants. A brown rug hung loosely around his shoulders. Everybody turned to stare at him. He looked flustered and kept his gaze on the floor, avoiding everyone's eyes.

'Slept well, doctor?' smirked Mattsson.

Grenzken blinked, trying to adjust to the hostile atmosphere. 'I was tired.' He glared down at Helmut and flinched. 'What is wrong with Helmut?' He sunk to his knees and touched him. 'Helmut, Helmut.' He tried to wake him up. Helmut snored loudly like a rhinoceros.

'Leave him alone,' said Tord. 'If you weren't such a drunk, all this wouldn't have happened.'

Rangor asked, 'You were too tired to hear what was going on?'

'I heard, but I was too tired to get up,' said Grenzken.

His words sparked animosities all around. Tord made an aggressive move towards him.

Birgit scowled at Tord, freezing him in place. She thought she'd better defuse the situation. 'That's it. Let me get you to bed, Fritz,' she said. 'You'll talk sense when you've rested.' She held him by the arm and led him upstairs to his quarters. Grenzken fell into step with her without a word.

Richard and Bo came from the elevator with a wheelchair. They hoisted Helmut up with his arms on their shoulders, feet dragging on the floor, and fumbled him into the chair, almost buckling under his weight.

Rangor adjusted the wheelchair behind him and they eased him down. He gave instructions on what to do when Helmut came to, and hoped Grenzken would be fully functional by then to take care of the situation.

The guests left Vittaby Villa with a dose of confusion that might have served as an eye-opener in normal people. But these were soulless creatures, men of darkness, without conscience or moral compass.

The first shock registered when Richard came down to the Clinic and found doors open ajar. Even the heavy steel security doors to the courtyard gaped wide open. Wind gusted in, and inmates screeched from chilling cold. Bo went to the rifle cabinet and saw the key hanging in the lock. It wasn't there before. Helmut must have taken Grenzken's key from somewhere. They went through a check of all inmates, making sure everyone was there. Nicholas was missing.

'How could this happen?' Bo quizzed. With all the security in this place – surveillance cameras, alarm system, coded doors. What had Helmut done with the boy?

'That we deliberately neglected to lock up? Planned this? That's ridiculous,' said Richard. 'The surveillance system has been failing for months, ever since his contract with the security company lapsed. Grenzken needed to renew it, but he's been stalling. The system is dilapidated and worthless. He can't pin this on us.'

'We can handle Grenzken, but The Group is a bunch of thugs. They will pressure him for answers, and he'll be forced to pin it on us.'

'Let them try. The man is a fucking drunkard,' thundered Richard. 'That alone aggravated security. Maybe he did it himself.'

Richard lunged out of the room and strode down the hallway to the steel doors, now secured. He pressed the security code, opening the door with a click. He emerged in the courtyard, examining the grounds for anything unusual. He opened the gate. A cold wind caught him as he stepped outside. He scanned the gravel grounds, snowflakes blinding his eyes. Suddenly, in the empty parking lot, he saw fresh tire tracks, almost erased by snow. Beside the tires was a large crimson coloured stain seeping through the snow. His heart skipped a beat. Was it blood? Could Helmut have shot someone? He was alarmed at the size of the stain, thinking if it was blood, the person might not survive. He stood scanning the white landscape for any movement, feeling the chill in his cheeks and a nervous tremor down his spine.

In the afternoon, the dining room windows were replaced. Birgit was grateful that Emergency Glass Repair Services came immediately. She called in the cleaning lady and asked her to put in overtime. Then she alighted at Grenzken's quarters and knocked on the door, but there was no answer. She entered the apartment and went to the bedroom. Grenzken was still sleeping. She walked to the bathroom and ran up a hot bath. The sound of running water awakened Grenzken. He came and stood at the bathroom door as Birgit switched off the tap. When she turned, he was gazing at her, an embarrassed grin on his pasty face. He was still wearing clothes he'd had on at the party.

'Feeling better?' asked Birgit.

'What time is it?' asked Grenzken, his voice husky.

'It's nearly six, why?'

'Has anybody said anything about Helmut?'

Birgit looked at the man, not comprehending his outlook on life. Would he ever learn to relax, to enjoy life? Despite all the money he had, it was always work and more work. Then, it was Helmut, Helmut all the time. At party time, he drank too much, taking the joy out of life.

'Fritz, it's Saturday,' she said. 'You should relax. Richard and Bo are taking care of things. Take a bath, and I'll bring you something to eat.' She walked to the closet, looking for fresh towels.

Grenzken glared at her. She was right about taking a bath and eating, but relaxing was out of question. How could he relax after what had happened last night? Inside, his soul was broken. Last night's brawl, Helmut's major freak-out, the mystery of what had sparked it, and the piercing eyes of The Group. Even the glaring task of finding Anna's corpse put him in a bad spot. How could he have slept through last night's turmoil? He should have maintained professional dignity and self-respect. His depression daunted him. He wanted to crawl back in bed and stay there. After bathing, he must see Helmut, regardless of what Birgit said.

'I'll have a bath and eat, but I must go to Helmut,' he said.

Birgit came out of the closet, holding towels, with a heavy frown creasing her brow. 'Richard and Bo are down there,' she asserted. 'You and I need to talk.'

'Talk about what?'

'About what happened last night.' Birgit raised her voice. 'You and your wretched drinking!'

'Wretched drinking?'

'Yes, Fritz, you drank till you blacked out! It's disgusting and embarrassing. It must stop.'

'Birgit, I didn't black out,' he said. 'I just took some whisky, that's all.'

'Just took some whisky? You don't get it, do you? What about Helmut? Was he just playing with the rifle?'

'His medication must have worn off.'

'It's always medication; one shot here, another pill there, a few more doses, and everything will be all right,' said Birgit. 'What're you giving him anyway?'

'Shut up.'

'Don't you dare shut me up! Have you seen his eyes lately? They gleam like traffic lights. I'm sick and tired of his unpredictable nature. It scares me. He almost killed us last night.'

'Helmut is not dangerous.'

'The man is a walking weapon,' said Birgit. 'If he doesn't leave, I'll leave. Take your pick.' She turned a threatening glare to him.

Stars blinded Grenzken's eyes. His hangover cleared up, and his attention centred on Birgit. 'Stop talking like that. It's not that bad.'

'You're always in the lab, buried in piles of paper,' said Birgit. 'What do you know about Helmut? I'm the one who is always in the house with the beast.'

'Birgit, stop it. Don't do this. I can handle Helmut.'

'I suggest you move him to his parents' old house near the woods.'

'That's out of the question.'

'Then you've made your choice. I'll leave in the morning,' said Birgit, throwing the towels in his face and storming from the room.

'Birgit…Birgit, don't you walk out on me!' said Grenzken. 'Come back here!' He ran after her, but when he came to the stairs, she was gone. He hurried back to the bedroom, put on his in-house sandals, and ran to the west wing. He knocked on the door. There was silence. He turned the knob. It was locked.

'Birgit, open the door!' He said. 'Open, or I'll break it down.'

'Break it then,' she hollered from inside.

'Open,' said Grenzken, softening his voice. 'You're right. We need to talk.'

There was no answer. Grenzken leaned his throbbing head on the door, wondering how it had come to this. He waited outside for nearly an hour prompting her to open, but Birgit did not open the door. He took a heavy breath and sauntered back to his quarters, a tight cramp in his chest.

Chapter 23

Still numbed by Torsten's death, Martina sat in her office at Althonat Hospital. It was Sunday but she wanted to catch up on certain things. She read mail. One mail from Africa caught her attention.

To: CEO, Althonat Global,

Cell antidote for Africa contaminated.

Situation teeters on the brink of disaster.

Urgent help needed.

Sincerely,

Dr Christine Obo

CEO, Althonat Global, Africa

Martina closed her eyes and shook her head to clear her disordered mind. How could this happen? She took a minute, and decided she needed a change of scenery. She picked up the phone.

'Hi, Mikael, it's Martina.' There was a pause as she listened to the voice at the other end of line. 'Yes, it's been a while,' she said. 'Look, I need reservations for two. Seven in the evening.'

Another pause.

'The Chambre Separé will be fine. Thank you, Mikael,' she said and hung up. She heard footsteps in the hallway.

'There you are. I didn't expect you so soon,' said Jonas, standing in the doorway. Martina gazed at him; he looked great in a dark suit with pink shirt and no tie.

'Let's go,' she said, as she rose from her seat.

'You look lovely in that pink dress,' said Jonas. 'It seems we decided on wearing the same colours.'

'Oh, that pink shirt dresses well with your dark suit.'

Suddenly, a dizzy spell come over her as she walked towards him. She stumbled. He grabbed her just in time before she fell. 'Darling, are you all right?'

She stopped and held her forehead a moment. 'I'm okay,' she said. 'I didn't get much sleep last night.'

'Let me take you home.'

'No, I'm all right. Let's go. We don't want to keep Dr Nasiro waiting.'

Jonas released her, noticing her pale complexion. 'I wasn't sure you would come after what happened last night.'

'We lost Torsten, but his work must continue in us.'

'I hated leaving you like that.'

'Don't worry about it. I had Joachim.'

'He's an adorable boy, and very protective of you.'

'He's very special to me.'

'I could see that.'

At the children's ward, Dr George Nasiro, a man of African ancestry with soft facial features and a friendly smile, sat in a patient's room, waiting. He got up as Martina and Jonas came through the door.

'Martina, Jonas, come in,' he said. He offered them seats by the bed. The white curtains brightened the room, making it look larger than it was. In bed lay a boy, sleeping. Martina leaned over and gently touched his forehead and warm cheek. He breathed softly and looked peaceful.

'Nicholas,' she whispered.

'Let him sleep,' said Jonas. 'He's been in such an ordeal.'

The joy Martina felt for his return equalled the grief she felt for losing Torsten. The two opposite emotions clashed inside her, torturing her like fire and ice. She buckled in and out of grief, teetering on the verge of despair, feeling a double-edged sword slash through her. Remembering Nicholas' mother, Ebba, Martina abruptly rose and walked to the window, blinking back her tears. Poor boy. He had no mother, only a drunken witless father who had sold him.

'Martina, are you all right?' asked Jonas as he came to her side. He saw her moist eyes.

'I'm fine,' she replied quickly, trying to get a grip on herself, not wanting to lose control in front of George. She remembered her father had once told her that a leader must put up a brave front even in the midst of great adversity, especially in the presence of subordinates.

Discreetly, she dried her eyes with her fingers and turned to George. 'How long has he been sleeping?'

'An hour or so. He was in bad shape when he came in – elevated hyperactivity and panic attacks. I wonder what they were giving him. He had bruises on his wrists and ankles. They must have restrained him.'

'I know what they were giving him,' said Martina. 'It's pretty strong stuff – antipsychotic drugs including benzodiazepine, which was banned years ago. It is highly addictive and could have driven him insane.'

'We have started the cleansing process,' said George.

'You'll use deep detoxification to rid his system of harmful substances,' said Martina. 'He has blocked energy that needs to be stimulated to bring about self-healing. The therapist should able to resolve that.'

Then she turned to Jonas. 'Will you get in touch with the curator and see about contacting Social Services? We need to find a home for Nicholas.'

'We shouldn't rush things,' said Jonas. 'It's best to restore him to full health first without interruptions. We've already lost ample time.'

'You're right,' said Martina as she shifted her gaze to George. 'Thank you, George.'

They left the ward, and Jonas asked, 'How did you know about the medication they gave him?'

'Our surveillance network,' said Martina, omitting the fact that she'd been in Ribbyburg Clinic.

Of course, thought Jonas. How stupid of him.

'Torsten did a marvellous job saving Nicholas' life,' said Martina. 'It's regrettable he lost his. We had to act immediately. Still, I should have been cautious sending him on such a mission without proper planning.'

'You couldn't have known …'

'That they had guns?' replied Martina. 'It's no excuse.'

Jonas kept quiet, not wanting to aggravate her fragile disposition. After a while, he said, 'I thought Nicholas was in Ribbyburg Clinic.'

'Yes, he was. It's a long sad story,' said Martina. 'Patrick Strand sold his son, Nicholas, to a research program at Ribbyburg Clinic for a million kroner. But Ebba caused havoc, so they transferred the boy to the wicked doctor Grenzken, at Devilund Clinic. Apparently, Grenzken decided to do brain surgery on him. We had to go in and rescue the boy.'

'Selling a sick child is the sickest thing I've ever heard.'

'That was not all. Ebba was charged with denying her child proper medical care because she didn't want Nicholas treated by Dr Rangor. She was due in court when she was killed in a car accident.'

'Nicholas' mother died?'

'Yes, I'm sure they killed her to cover up whatever is going on at Ribbyburg Clinic.'

'She was a dedicated mother.'

They walked in silence, disturbed by the words spoken. Jonas looked at Martina, noticing that melancholic gloom on her face.

'How are you feeling now?' he said.

'I'm fine.'

'Tell me if you need something to help you cope,' he said. 'Our herbal relaxer is highly recommended for anxiety.'

'Jonas, don't fuss. I told you I'm fine.'

'I'm not fussing. I can see that near-to-tears expression in your eyes, your tight jaw, and tensed muscles.'

'Okay, I heard you,' she retorted. 'When I need help I'll ask for it.'

'I know you: always in control. It's human to profess vulnerability and accept help, Martina.'

'Will you stop it? You've made your point.'

Jonas relented as they entered her office. They got down to business, discussing findings of his report on Life-Vaccine. A controlled study of vaccinated versus unvaccinated women, implicit and other cultural factors neutralized, showed that vaccinated women faced difficulties conceiving. He briefed her on the rising incidence of infertility and the rise in cervical cancer among vaccinated women.

'Husbands are disgruntled that wives aren't getting pregnant, but then the reverse is also true; vaccinated men aren't getting women pregnant.'

'What is the success rate at the fertility Clinic?'

'Three in ten.'

'It seems like our efforts are futile.'

'True, it's a lost cause for a whole generation,' said Jonas. 'I wish we could do more.'

'We must focus on educating the younger generation. Even mainstream paediatricians and other medical doctors are ignorant when it comes to the dangers of Life-Vaccine. Whether wilfully or blindly, they are ignorant. They need to be taught how to dissect 'studies' claiming Life-Vaccine safety. They need to follow the money, as people who have concerns about the dangers of Life-Vaccine. They need to read Frangipani.'

It was six in the evening by the time the doctors wrapped up their discussions and decided on a plan of action. They locked up and left. Martina hooked her arm under Jonas' and curiously regarded him.

'I have a proposal.'

'Ooh, a marriage proposal?' asked Jonas, his voice curious.

'Ah, ah, not yet,' said Martina. 'You need to be drilled and tested to prove yourself before you gain that valuable prize.'

'It sounds like military training.'

'It is military training, and I'm your commander in chief.'

'You've got my attention. Who do I kill?'

'You don't have to kill anybody. You just have to obey.'

'That sounds easy. Tell me more.'

'Come with me.'

'To your house or my place?'

'No, this is a surprise. My treat. I told you, you just need to obey.'

'I'm tempted to obey, Commander.'

'Good, you're an ardent follower,' said Martina, as she studied him again and laughed.

'It's nice to hear you laugh.'

Jonas' silver Porsche was left in executive parking at the hospital while they took Martina's Mercedes towards central Stockholm. They arrived at Gondolen, a restaurant suspended between sky and sea at an altitude of thirty-three metres. At the entrance they paused, waiting for the attendant. The owner arrived, ready to usher them to their table.

'Good evening, Martina,' said Mikael with an open smile, shaking her hand. 'It has been a while.'

'Yes, it has,' said Martina, mirroring his warmth.

He grasped Jonas' hand. 'Dr Eneroth, welcome.'

'Thank you, Mikael,' said Jonas.

'If you follow me, I'll show you to your table.'

They followed him through the chattering guests. Through the window, they gasped at the breathtaking view of Lake Mälaren and Salt Lake.

He led them to the Chambre Separé in the King's Room with a panoramic scenery over City Hall, Old Town, and Maria Magdalena Church. The environment was sober and elegant, and the interior décor serene and appeasing. Crisp white linen covered the table, crystal glasses gleamed and red chairs brightened the room. A single crimson rose in a crystal vase added glamour to the evening.

'Meticulous planning, Commander. Reservations and all, I'm impressed,' teased Jonas as they took seats at the table.

'I told you it was easy,' whispered Martina, a luscious smile on her face.

A white-suited waiter took their orders. Martina opted for shellfish rolls and vegetables with hash browns and horseradish butter sauce. Jonas went for beef tenderloin medallions with porcini, marsala wine gravy, and potatoes au gratin with parmesan cheese. For drinks, they ordered a bottle of red wine. The waiter disappeared and returned shortly with their drinks, his movements elegant and fluid. He served and left.

They clinked glasses in a toast, and took a sip as they held each other's gaze. 'It tastes lovely – crisp and nippy,' said Martina.

Jonas gazed into her fathomless eyes, relishing their piercing blue that sparkled brighter than the sea. He was happy his Martina was back, joyous and funny. The atmosphere was idyllic and utopian; it made him starry-eyed.

The waiter appeared again with their food, served it, and disappeared.

'You look fabulous tonight.'

'I've been in the dumps since yesterday. I needed a change of scene. I'm glad you could join me.'

'Let's go to Paris.' said Jonas. 'Take a short vacation – a break from what has happened. We could fly out Thursday and return Sunday. What do you think?'

Martina tasted her fish. 'It tastes heavenly. How is your beef?'

'The flavour is lovely,' he said as he munched beef with gravy. 'You didn't answer my question.'

'I can't go to Paris,' said Martina, 'I'm going to Africa.'

Jonas lay his cutlery on the plate, thrown by her answer. 'You never cease to amaze me. What's happened in Africa?' he said, trying to contain his disappointment. She explained the problem of the contaminated shipment of cell antidote and that urgent help was needed.

'You need a break, Martina,' said Jonas. 'Send Diana. She was your CEO in Africa. She knows the continent like the back of her hand.'

Martina regarded him, surprised he could suggest such a thing. Of course Diana was competent and well versed with the continent, but he missed the point. A leader must align herself with her staff in the face of adversity. It was good public relations. However, she did not want to get into an argument with him, preferring to maintain a delightful ambience.

'I'll think about it, but Paris in winter?'

'It's the city of lights, and besides, I want to romance you. Lights and romance hold true for Paris regardless of time. Paris is timeless, darling.' He grasped her hand across the table and squeezed it, adding, 'If you only knew what you mean to me, and how much I love you, you would stop being stubborn.'

'How're you spending Christmas?'

'I'll be with family on the west coast, my parents, sister, brothers and their families. What about you?'

'Sebastian and family are coming. We shall be at our country home, Landegrind house, in Väddö. It will be nice for Joachim to meet his cousins.'

Jonas regarded her for a long moment, still holding her hand, gliding his thumb over her knuckles, feeling her warmth. Finally, he asked something he'd always wanted to ask her. 'Do you ever want to have more children?'

Surprised by the question, Martina stared at him, wondering where his inquiry was leading. To be on the safe side, she reciprocated with a question: 'You mean you and I?'

'We have been together for over a year,' said Jonas. 'We need to cement our relationship. Give it a definite direction.'

Oh, here came the question she'd dreaded for months. Jonas meant the world to her, but the prospect of becoming his wife unsettled her. How could she cope with combining work, family and wifely duties? It was a daunting exercise. She'd done it before with Thomas and failed miserably, and even then, Pappa had managed the company workload. She was unsure about her capacity in the role of a wife. Astrid was her rock and a great resource, tending the house and looking after Joachim, but marriage was not on her priority list. Besides, managing Althonat Global was proving to be a challenge, with so many problems to deal with.

'Martina, you heard what I said.'

'Are you proposing to me?'

'When I propose, I want to do it properly,' said Jonas. 'I'm trying to get my bearings on where we stand in our relationship.'

He was moving too fast for her. She didn't like it. She needed time with Althonat Global. She must stall him. She cleared her throat and said, 'You know you mean the world to me, and it's very sweet of you asking, but can't we wait till things are stabilized with the business?'

'I can wait,' said Jonas. 'Take all the time you need, but we aren't getting any younger. Don't wait too long. Nothing would please me more than you becoming my wife.'

The waiter appeared, cleared away the plates, and returned later with dessert: passion fruit and dark chocolate mousse with brownie, compliments of Gondolen Restaurant. Jonas asked him for two glasses of cognac and he promptly brought them.

Jonas picked up his wine glass, and took a long sip as he regarded Martina, tantalized by her beauty. She sank into his gaze and sighed. She could marry him today if not for the business.

'Yes, I would be honoured to have your children, if that's what you wanted to know.'

Jonas' face lit up in a surprised smile as her words dissolved his worst fears. 'I'm delighted to hear that,' he said, with a broad smile.

They caught up on recent events. Martina told him she'd talked to Torsten's wife, and the funeral would be in three weeks' time.

They finished their drinks, and Martina summoned the waiter and directed him to charge the bill to her account. Jonas fumbled for his wallet, pulled out a green note, and placed it in the waiter's palm as a tip. He thanked him for the luscious meal and impeccable service.

'We'd better get going,' said Martina. 'I have got to work on my speech for tomorrow.'

They returned to Slottsville house, Martina's residence in Lidingö, on the outskirts of Stockholm. Tonight was their night. The good food, excellent wine, and enticing environment stirred their passion into flames. The dim glow from the art deco table lamp threw pale shades of a golden gleam on the glossy satin beddings. A faint whiff of Martina's favourite scent teased the air. The overall ambience of the room was distinctively cosy and inviting.

Martina finished writing her speech and snuggled up in bed waiting for Jonas, who was still brushing his teeth. Her eyes brightened with anticipation. At last a moment alone with the man of her dreams. Given her busy schedule, these moments were rare and when it happened she relished the minutes, savouring the magical experience.

Jonas appeared in the doorway, half naked in pyjama pants hanging sexy on his hips. His hairy chest, masculine shoulders, and jumbled hair bumped Martina's hormones into high gear. He glided into bed next to her, and smiled down at her. He took her in his arms, cuddled and kissed her.

Soon they were moving, surging and ebbing into a tidal wave of enormous power. It engulfed them as they rocketed through the universe. She gasped, and her moaning became high pitched. He groaned deep in his throat as his release spilled into her, dissolving the knots in her tense body with an ocean of peace.

Chapter 24

After the hassle with Birgit, Grenzken lost his appetite. He neither wanted to eat or to see Helmut. Things came to a head when Birgit threatened to leave if Helmut did not move out of Vittaby Villa. Grenzken was in a dilemma. He could not send Helmut away to that horrible dilapidated, half burnt down house. Its memories would haunt him. Yet losing Birgit was unthinkable. She was the only woman who overlooked his diabolical schemes and insatiable appetite for testing the boundaries of science. She loved him for what he was.

At a loss for what to do, he sauntered down to Devilund. What had pushed Helmut over the edge, sending him raving out of control, was still a mystery to him. Maybe the new drug he'd brought from Germany was too strong for him.

The Clinic seemed deserted. He was greeted by an eerie silence. He went through his usual routine of pacing the corridor, gazing through viewports, taking inventory on inmates. He noted room number six was empty. 'What?' he breathed. The room was neat and orderly as if the inmate had expired. He jangled keys in the lock, and the sound rattled his nerves. He entered the room, disturbed; where was Nicholas? He hoped he was with Richard and Bo in the examination room.

He heard footsteps in the corridor. It was Richard. He came in the room, meeting Grenzken's smouldering gaze. 'Where is the boy?' he asked.

'I don't know. When we came down last night, he was gone. The doors were gaping open, and wind was gushing in.'

'Gone? Are you crazy? Gone where?' asked Grenzken, his tone high-pitched and annoyed. His head throbbed like a hammer, and his blood ran hot. He paced the small room, ranting about security procedures, rules and regulations. 'What happened?'

Richard jumped, startled by his rage.

'No one escapes from Devilund,' continued Grenzken. 'Unless…' He paused and then spun around to face Richard, his glare vicious. 'Unless you planned this.'

Richard stood paralyzed by Grenzken's blazing words, reflecting on the rules and regulation and the dilapidated security system. What was he thinking? *Gadgets are machinery. They depreciate and need updating, replacing every now and again.* And when he had enemies, as he did, he needed to triple the budget for investment in a reliable security system.

'Did you or did you not neglect security? Is this an inside job? Tell me,' asked Grenzken, levelling a finger at Richard.

'I can't tell you anything,' said Richard. 'I don't know what happened. Ask Helmut.'

'Don't you tell me to ask Helmut. You and Bo are responsible for this!'

Richard saw no reason in arguing with him. He said nothing.

Grenzken continued in a flat spin, asking for answers, howling, and threatening Richard with an avalanche of repercussions if he didn't come up with a reasonable explanation.

Bo heard the squabbling and entered the room. Grenzken crackled on again with the bizarre scenario of an inside job, with him and Richard as prime suspects.

Bo did not spare him. He shot back with a bigger blaze of fire. 'What about you, you dirty drunkard?' said Bo as he stormed towards him. 'You were flat out on your back while the rest of us made the best of the situation.' They stood face to face, their noses almost touching.

Grenzken stepped aside, staggered by Bo's furious advance. He scowled at the irate pair, realizing he couldn't grapple with their youth and physical strength in the isolated basement Clinic. He relented and walked away. 'Get back to work,' he said. Halfway out, he hesitated and returned. 'Where's Helmut?'

'He went upstairs to his room,' said Richard.

To the house, thought Grenzken. Oh no. Birgit will be furious if she sees him there. Grenzken strolled to his office. There was a pile of mail on his desk. He shuffled through reports and bills. A white glossy envelope with a golden Nobel logo caught his attention – an invitation to the Nobel Prize Award Ceremony.

He gazed at the letter, remembering how he had soured, in October, when the Nobel Prize winners were announced, and his name did not make the list. According to Citaraph, he was among the top scientists nominated for outstanding achievement in medicine. He stroked his he-goat beard, hoping for better luck next time. He pocketed the letter in his jacket pocket, unsure whether he wanted to go, doubting Birgit would go with him.

He was tired, drained. Maybe Birgit was right. He should take time off and relax. He went to the medicine cabinet, picked up a few packages, and left. He must find Helmut. He walked into the east wing and knocked on Helmut's door. Helmut opened, looking panicked and petrified.

Grenzken saw there was something depressive about him.

The room looked simple but comfortable. There was a sofa, a red carpet, and a TV in the corner, a table with a computer and a chair. On the glass centre table were video games and bodybuilding magazines.

'Sit,' said Grenzken. 'Sit down and tell me what happened last night.'

Helmut sank his bulky body in the sofa, making it look like miniature furniture. Grenzken grabbed a chair by the computer table and sat down facing him.

'What happened in the Clinic last night? Where's Nicholas?'

Helmut clenched his thick hand in a fist, and gnashed his teeth. The gnawing sound unnerved Grenzken. 'Stop that sound, stop it,' said Grenzken. Helmut stopped, and slowly raised his gaze to make eye contact. His multicoloured eyes gleamed like a peacock's feathers. He did not like it when Master turned dark like thunder.

'Okay, tell me, tell me now,' prompted Grenzken.

Helmut opened his mouth and stuttered, 'Cold, verry…cold. Door open.' He swallowed and then continued, 'Ca…aar, car, men in car come.' He suddenly looked away, agitated. A deep frown grew on his thick-hairy brow.

'Calm down. What did the men do?' asked Grenzken.

Helmut started shaking like a branch ready to fall off a tree. He shifted on the sofa, and stammered, 'Toook, took Niiicholas. I…I heard gu…uun…shots.'

'Did you get the car number?'

'No…no nummer. Dark…outside.'

'How many men?'

He did not answer. Instead a wail of misery escaped his dry lips. He heaved his massive body up and headed for the door, bawling like a sick monkey. Giant tears rolled down his cheeks.

Grenzken went after him, grabbed him by his well-knit muscular wrist and dragged him back to the room. 'Sit down!'

With his hand, Grenzken dabbed Helmut's fat cheeks, wiping his tears. Startled, he paused and gazed at the clammy, shiny substance on his fingers. He felt it with his other hand and gasped. It was oil! Helmut was shedding tears of oil! Grenzken dropped his head, fascinated, pondering if it was the medication or if he was overfeeding Helmut. Certainly, the phenomenon would make another research project.

He dug into his jacket pocket and retrieved a hypodermic needle. He filled it with a liquid from a small bottle and injected Helmut in the upper arm. Helmut trumpeted like an agitated elephant, a sad expression on his face.

'Come,' said Grenzken. Helmut got up and followed him to the bedroom, where he told him to get in bed. Helmut glided under the covers. 'Sleep,' said Grenzken. He stood over him, captivated that at thirty-two years of age, Helmut was such a toddler. He switched off the lights and left.

Who were those men who had taken Nicholas, and how had they got in? The question lingered as he came to the west wing. He hoped Birgit would let him in. He knocked on the door and waited. Nothing happened. He knocked again.

'Who is it?' hollered Birgit.

'Open the door, Birgit.' said Grenzken, in a soft voice. 'I want to talk.'

'Go away.'

'Please, I've a solution to our problems. I want to you to hear me out.'

'Has Helmut moved to his parents' house?' Birgit asked through the door.

'Just open the door and hear me out.'

The door flew open, and Grenzken shrank back.

Birgit stood staring at him. 'What do you want?'

'Birgit, we can talk. May I come in?'

'You've one minute, and if you talk nonsense, you're out.'

In the hallway to the living room were packed suitcases and bags. Piles of old newspapers and magazines covered the floor. The sight was depressing. Grenzken realized Birgit had made up her mind to leave him. He stood in the middle of the room, wondering where to start.

He breathed and turned to her. 'Birgit, you…you don't have to leave,' he stammered. 'I'll move Helmut to the Clinic. There is plenty of room there. I can refurnish and make a decent living space for him.'

'Grenzken, is that –?'

'No, hear me out…listen, you don't have to see him if you don't want,' said Grenzken. 'I'll see to it he doesn't come to the house. And about my drinking, you're right. I'll cut down on drinking.'

Birgit glared at him, surprised by the humbleness in his voice. She thought he looked pathetic. In just hours, since their row, he seemed to have shrunk in size.

'What do you say?'

'When is he moving?'

'I need one week to organize, if that is okay with you.'

'One week it is,' said Birgit. 'But if you don't hold true to your promise, I'll be out of here so fast you won't get a chance to stop me.'

Grenzken breathed a silent sigh of victory. His face lit up in a faint smile. 'I'll not disappoint you. Can I help you unpack?'

'No, I'll do it myself. And if you don't mind, I would like to be alone.'

'Of course, take all the time you need.' He made a move to leave but hesitated. 'There's one more thing I wanted to ask you.'

'What?' asked Birgit as she set about sorting papers and magazines on the floor.

'I've an invitation here,' said Grenzken, taking the envelope from his jacket pocket. 'I want you to come with me to the Nobel festivities.'

Birgit dropped the magazine she was holding. Her face lit up like the moon around Jupiter. Her cold exterior warmed up in disbelief, her dispute with Grenzken forgotten. 'Why, Fritz, you must be joking,' she said, with a smile that abruptly faded. 'But what shall I wear?'

Grenzken grinned, amused by the flicker of joy in her eyes. 'The designer gown I bought you in Paris and the diamond necklace set. Or if you don't like it, you can go shopping.'

He returned to his quarters, satisfied Birgit had agreed to stay and happy that she'd accepted his invitation to the Nobel festivities.

Chapter 25

On the tenth of December, trees glistened as if the snow possessed a light of its own. The silver grey sky reflected an unearthly pallor reminiscent of a day unlike any other. Cascades of soft snowflakes floated to the ground like flocks of lost butterflies. In the Swedish capital, fever-pitched sensation gripped the city in anticipation of the most prestigious event that captivated world attention. The world turned its face to Sweden as Nobel laureates made headlines in international media.

The limousines glided to a halt outside the Stockholm Concert Hall, marking the beginning of a well-rehearsed ritual where every minute had been planned by the Nobel Foundation, the host of the event. The place was swarming with security, as men in white ties and black tailcoats, looking like penguins, filed into the hall, with ladies in floor-length gowns. The gowns rustled and swished, the jewellery glistened, and the air crackled with academic triumph, royalty, culture, great inventions, wondrous prose, and remarkable feats of human nature from both the Swedish and the international community. It was a melting pot of nationalities, a spectrum of cultures in a common gesture of reconciliation and hope. It was commonplace to hear about athletic Olympics, but these were academic Olympics – time to honour men and women who had advanced science and the arts on earth. It was the Nobel Prize Award Ceremony.

Flowers adorned the hall's interior, in bright primary and pastel colours: carnations, gerbera, pink roses, orchids and silver fir branches of juniper provided a contrasting Swedish winter feel by the stage and walls of the balcony.

One thousand three hundred guests were seated in the stalls waiting for the festivities to begin. Martina sat on the stage with ninety other members: the Nobel Foundation's Board of directors, the Royal Swedish Academy of Science, and previous laureates. Her eyes scanned the concert hall with its massive pillars, high ceiling, and huge chandeliers lending a gentle glow to the enormous hall. Among the guests were the laureates' families, the Riksdag, government officials, and members of the business community and the diplomatic corps. The grand twenty-five-man Royal Philharmonic Orchestra was perched on the balcony.

Martina wore a strapless, floor-length silver and turquoise satin gown. It fitted and flattered her curves. A matching wrap draped her shoulders. Her golden hair was held back in a ball revealing her slender neck, adorned by her mother's scintillating diamond necklace with matching drop earrings. Her heels were Christian Louboutin. She kept her makeup to a minimum: eyeliner and mascara, a touch of pink blush, and pale pink lipstick giving her a natural glow. In her hand she held a satin and silver clutch purse in which she had tucked her speech. She scanned the stalls where family and friends of Nobel laureates and other dignitaries sat. In the middle row she glimpsed Jonas, sitting with an amiable expression on his face. He seemed to be enjoying the quiet ambience of the occasion.

The orchestra came alive, and the audience rose. The Royal Anthem Kungsången played as the royal family made a palatial entrance. They took their seats on the stage.

The orchestra began a piece by Mozart. The audience rose again, and the stars of the ceremony, the nine Nobel Prize winners, emerged to take their seats, opposite the royal family. Their chairs were different – antique, crimson in colour.

The music swelled, and the Nobel laureate in Medicine stepped forward to receive his diploma and a medal from HM the King of Sweden. The King shook his hand. The laureate took the Prize from the King's hand and then stepped back and bowed to the King, to fellow laureates, and to the audience in the stalls. Applause echoed through the hall as the audience expressed admiration.

Martina shuddered, feeling a sudden discomfort wash over her as if she were being observed, as if a penetrating glare burrowed through her. She looked around and saw a silver-haired man at the end of the row glowering at her. The face was familiar and fresh in her memory. Their eyes locked and she looked away. The orchestra played again as the Physics laureate concluded his speech. Martina rose mechanically, clapping hands with everyone else, but her mind reeled back, recalling the man who had taunted, tormented and harassed her father, finally forcing him to resign from his job: the director of the National Board of Health and Welfare, Fabian Franzen. He had aged remarkably; his silver hair used to be brown. The creases around his eyes had deepened.

The trumpets resounded, and the Nobel laureate in Economics stepped down from the stage. Martina rose in a wave of standing ovation with the audience, clapping robotically, and then sat, unfocused and disturbed. From the corner of her eye, she saw Fabian's steady, sinister glare at her. It chilled her bones. She became oblivious to the proceedings, preoccupied by the bitter past.

The speeches and standing ovations faded into a distance till she was startled from her fears by the sound of her name: 'To conclude the ceremony, our next speaker is the Chairman of the Nobel Foundation, Dr Martina Strömstedt Edgren.' Martina fumbled to her feet, her heart frantic, almost stumbling in her heels. Fighting her panic, she retrieved her speech from the purse, dropped the purse and wrap on her seat, and majestically walked to the stage. She stood there taking in the magnitude of the task, the nonpareil audience, and the unnerving silence. She could almost have heard a pin drop.

She took a deep breath, steadied her nerves, and said in clipped, cool tones, 'Academics, business, science, and the arts have long been the cornerstones of civilization. In many places we have eradicated illiteracy, poverty and disease, but as we move into the twenty-first century, these remain the biggest challenges for humanity. We need to consolidate further with laser-beam focus our efforts on academics, business, science, and the arts for a better world. As you return to your homes, businesses and work, I would like you to take back a few words with you.'

She paused before concluding, 'We have more medicine but less wellness. Wealth has never been about money but about well-being. Ladies and gentlemen, thank you.'

A resonating applause rocked the hall, erupting into a standing ovation.

As she walked back to her seat, the Swedish national anthem brought the ceremony to a close. She looked around. Fabian was gone. Dignitaries came out to the podium, and she joined them in congratulating the laureates. She conferred briefly with other Board members, exchanging pleasantries, pride shining in their eyes for a job well done. On the floor she spotted Jonas talking to Barbara and Philip. She crossed to them and exchanged warm hugs, kisses, laughter and gratitude for a short but powerful speech.

'I sensed the feminine touch in the ceremony, thanks to you, Martina,' said Barbara. 'Even the music took on a more youthful tone.'

Martina smiled.

'We'd better get going,' said Philip. 'Everybody is leaving.'

On arrival at the Stockholm City Hall, the guests saw the building illuminated against the December twilight. The process of entry to the Blue Hall moved in a synchronized human chain, as gowns rustled, jewellery glistened, and champagne bubbles fizzed. The whole city hall was fragrant with candles, torches and perfumes, and draped with thousands of green trimmings, pillars, wreaths, medallions and pyramids of flowers on the staircase and balcony.

Once inside the Blue Hall, a twenty-five-metre-long table of honour was laid out with golden Nobel tableware in harmonizing style. Sixty-six tables were covered with four hundred metres of linen cloth, and the meticulous table setting used seven thousand porcelain pieces, five thousand crystal glasses, and ten thousand items of silverware.

At seven the procession began its entrance down the sweeping staircase, led by HM the King and his allocated dinner partner. The rest of the guests of honour followed in procession with their table partners, accompanied by organ music. The banquet program began, and dinner was served.

THE NOBEL BANQUET
MENU
CURED REINDEER FILLET AND SMOKED DUCK

ASPARAGUS SALAD WITH TRUFFLE
FILLET OF COD FROM THE COAST OF MÖRE
JERUSALEM ARTICHOKE PURÉE

JUNIPER BERRY AND THYME MARINATED
ELK WITH BERNY AND GLAZED TURNIP
CARAMEL AND CHOCOLATE GLAZED BANANA
MOUSSE WITH PEANUT MERINGUE

CHAMPAGNE JACQUESSON CUVÉE NO 733
RIESLING CUVÉE FRÉDÉRIC ÉMILE 2004 TRIMBACK
POUIL FUMÉ 2008 ANDRÉ DEZAT ET FILS
NAPA VALLEY CABERNET SAUVIGNON
2005 – ROBERT MONDAVI

COFFEE AND LIQUEURS

After the coffee and liqueurs, a student parade appeared on the grand staircase, representing colleges and universities in the province. Their attire – black gowns, black shoes, white gloves, and student hats – gave the ceremony an academic touch.

At ten the Ambassadeur Orchestra struck up the dance in the Golden Hall. Jonas took Martina into his embrace and started moving. She graciously moved in accord to his step, lost in the music. She could dance anything with Jonas. They whirled around, sweeping across the dance floor as they smiled to each other.

'I love this song,' murmured Martina, gazing up at him.

'I know.' He was no longer smiling but serious, moving with the music, taking her with him. 'You were sensational tonight. That speech carried a powerful message.'

'I couldn't have done it without you. Your love and support mean a lot to me.'

Jonas beamed down at her and then grew serious again. It was just the two of them and the band. They were in their own private place, their own bubble. As the song finished, they both applauded with the audience. The orchestra bowed graciously.

'May I cut in?' said a raspy voice.

Martina turned towards the irritable voice. It was the silver-haired man, Fabian. Jonas grudgingly let her go, wondering who the man was. Martina's blood froze, but she maintained her calm. The band began another song, and Fabian pulled her into his arms. He was shorter than her, about sixty years of age, and he danced out of sync to the rhythm.

'I guess you remember me,' said Fabian.

'How could I forget?' Martina kept her voice careful and deliberate.

Jonas grinned and wandered away to the other side of the dance hall.

Martina's conversation with Fabian was stilted and jumbled. She listened distractedly to his grating voice, trying to get to the bottom of the resentment he'd directed towards her earlier, at the ceremony.

'Power is intoxicating, wouldn't you say?' asked Fabian.

'How would I know?'

'That little speech you made gave you power. Didn't it?' The sarcasm in his voice was livid.

'I haven't the slightest clue.'

'Enjoy the limelight while you can. Some things are a passing illusion.'

He swirled her across the floor as the band drifted into another song. Martina tried to let go, but he held her, taking her with him, stepping on her shoes.

'Are you playing games with me?' said Martina. 'If you have something to say, say it.'

'All right then, if you insist. It has come to my knowledge that Althonat Global is engaging in subversive activities: kidnapping children and treating them against parents' consent.'

Martina banked her emotion, refusing to be intimidated. 'The laws are clear, and we follow them diligently.'

Her calm disposition and indifference unsettled him. He fidgeted under a surge of animosity. 'You know I can whip up a storm and shut you down. After all, the man who founded Althonat Global, your father, was a disgraced medical professional.'

'Watch your foul mouth, you hypocrite,' said Martina. 'Althonat Global is an international company. No one shuts us down. You may try, but you'll never succeed.' She jerked out of his nasty grip and walked away, leaving him gaping on the dance floor. Fabian grimaced, humiliated by her audacity to ditch him publicly.

Jonas alighted at her side and said, 'There you are.' Martina knew she was visibly flustered. 'Was he bothering you?'

'Fabian is a spiteful old man. I can handle him.'

'Who is he?'

'The director of the National Board of Health and Welfare – the man who had hounded Pappa and forced him to resign from the Institute.'

'Come, there is someone I want you to meet,' said Jonas as he took her hand, and they pushed through the dancing crowd to a young lady in student attire, talking with fellow students. She saw them and started towards them, a smile on her face.

'Martina, this is Charlotte, my niece,' said Jonas. 'Charlotte, this is Martina.'

'My, I'm delighted to make your acquaintance,' said Charlotte, her face beaming with admiration.

'I love your attire,' said Martina, smiling and shaking her hand.

'Charlotte's a big fan of you and your work,' said Jonas. 'She's studying complementary medicine at Gothenburg University.'

'I'm happy you introduced the program at my university,' said Charlotte, staring at Martina.

'I'm glad it's of interest to you,' said Martina.

As they talked, a man with a balding head and a beard on his chin stood gazing at Martina, waiting to catch her attention. Martina continued talking to Charlotte and finally said, 'Well then, good luck with your studies. And remember, we have an internship program at the hospital.'

'I'll remember that,' said Charlotte. She returned to join her friends.

The balding man approached Martina and Jonas. 'I'm Dr Grenzken, and this is my friend, Birgit,' he said, grasping Martina's hand, and then Jonas' hand. Martina recognized him from Scorpio's videotapes – the master of the universe, himself, as she'd nicknamed him. He looked better on tape. Gazing into his small dark darting eyes at close range, Martina knew Grenzken was untrustworthy.

Birgit was beside herself, as if she were meeting royalty, curtseying with a radiant smile, dazzled by Martina's presence. 'You look even more beautiful in reality than in newspapers,' said Birgit.

'Thank you,' said Martina, noting Birgit's well-fitted sky-blue gown. A bit on the overweight side, but she had the most gorgeous smile and in fact was a beautiful woman.

'I read the Frangipani every day,' said Birgit. Grenzken flinched.

'You'll benefit in the long run,' said Martina. 'Keep it up.'

Grenzken cleared his throat. 'The festivities had a genuine sparkle to them, but your speech… I must say, I choose to differ. Wealth is all about money and not well-being. Otherwise, why do we do anything at all?'

Martina tried to detach herself from what he was saying and resisted being upset by his insidious narrow-mindedness. 'Well, we're all entitled to our own opinions, but think about this. In the economic system of the world, corporations are greedy entities that compete with the sole aim of profits. They pursue that aim relentlessly and with absolute ruthlessness. Nature, animals, even their employees are no more than lifeless objects on a spreadsheet, meaningless slaves to be used and then discarded without a care for their health or wellness. Tell me, is that the world you want?'

Jonas stood by, listening. He enjoyed seeing Martina in full flow.

Grenzken smiled smugly and said, 'You put it so crudely, it almost sounds vulgar.'

'Exactly, your concept is vulgar,' thundered Martina. She gazed at him intently and added, 'Let me tell you something. The likes of you feed on the system the way a parasite feeds on its host. You and your kind are traitors from inside out.'

Grenzken felt a lump grow in his throat. His tongue twisted into a knot. His emotional sensors arrested, he scowled at Martina, feeling diminished as if someone had pulled a humiliating stunt on him. Except it wasn't a stunt, but an insult from a woman he regarded with scorn.

The musicians struck up their favourite song, and Jonas took the chance to forestall further dialogue. Taking Martina's hand, he hastily said, 'Let's dance,' and then, 'Nice meeting you, Birgit, Dr Grenzken.'

They swayed away to float across the floor to the exhilarating sounds of Lorna Lindberg's 'Such Is Life'.

Birgit remained standing with Grenzken, reprimanding him for his tactless remarks.

As the song drew to a close, Martina moved to interact with dignitaries while Jonas went to dance with Barbara. She caught up with the Ethiopian ambassador. 'How delightful to see you again, Mr Gebresaye,' she said. He told her that the partnership project in Ethiopia was yielding results, giving locals opportunities to better lives. Martina couldn't have been happier at the news.

Moving on, she spotted Leif Swanson standing with a group of industrialists and went to say hello.

'Martina, you were sensational tonight,' said Leif as he gave her a kiss on both cheeks. He was a major supplier of medical equipment to Althonat Global.

Throughout the evening, a steady stream of men and women came to shake her hand and exchange pleasantries. Some even told her Althonat Global had changed the way they viewed medicine. Others tipped her as the perfect candidate for next year's Nobel Prize in medicine.

She went in search of Jonas. On her way, she spotted Fabian in a dark corner talking to a woman in skyscraper heels and a black mini-dress that clung to her body. They stood intimately close to each other. Curious to see who she was, Martina walked by and recognized Leila, her senior researcher. The pair, engrossed in each other, did not see her. That Leila was acquainted with Fabian jolted Martina.

Phillip came and asked Martina to dance. He noticed her angry eyes and less than enthusiastic mood. 'What is it, Martina? You look like you've seen a ghost.'

'No, Phillip,' said Martina. 'No ghost, just traitors.'

'Traitors?' asked Phillip. He put his arm around her and swung her onto the dance floor.

'How is the investigation going?' asked Martina, changing the subject.

'We're making progress, though slow. I'll come by and brief you.'

A waltz began and Jonas returned to take Martina in his arms. They gave it another swing, but the mood had shifted to a negative note.

'I want to go home,' said Martina.

Jonas gave her a quizzical look. 'Did Phillip say anything to upset you?'

'No, I'm tired. Take me home.'

'Of course, darling, I'll take you home.'

Chapter 26

Joachim stormed in at Slottsville house and hugged his mother. Thomas watched as Martina showered him with kisses and carried him to the grand room, where they sank into a sofa.

'Mamma, you were great on television,' said Joachim.

'You watched me on television?'

'Even Pappa said you're beautiful.'

Thomas smiled. 'You were brilliant,' he said.

'Well, thank you,' said Martina, surprised by Thomas' compliment. He'd been short on compliments when they were married.

'Go wash up, Joachim,' said Martina. 'Dinner will be ready in a minute.' She turned to Thomas. 'You're eating with us, I hope?'

Thomas hesitated, prompting her to add quickly, 'Please, we'd love to have your company.'

'Since you put it that way, I'll join you,' said Thomas with a smile.

Soon they sat at the dining table, eating. Thomas studied Martina, understanding from what he'd seen on television that she and Jonas might be more than friends. The way she leaned on him was something beyond casual. He knew they'd had a passing interest in dancing, but that was in the States. He suspected anything could happen. He was her Chief Medical Officer, and they worked together.

'It must have been a magnificent ceremony,' said Thomas as he picked his glass of wine and took a sip.

'Yes, it was, and so many people.'

'And the banquet?'

'It was sensational, meticulously planned and coordinated. One wonders how they manage it, given the massive numbers of guests.'

'They say it's the banquet of banquets. There is none other like it in the world.'

'Yes, it is grand,' said Martina forking a piece of grilled salmon.

'What are your plans after Christmas?' he said. 'I would like Joachim to spend the first week of the New Year with me. His grandparents would like to see him.'

'No, two days are enough,' she replied.

'He doesn't start school till mid-January.'

'His cousins will be here for only two weeks.'

Thomas paused, careful not to spark a conflict, yet he wanted to do what was right for his son. 'Two days is too little.'

'I don't want to seem unreasonable, but he doesn't get to see his cousins often.'

'What about my parents? He hasn't seen them since I moved back from London.'

'And that's my fault?' asked Martina, her tone growing angry.

Suddenly Joachim pushed his chair back, sprang up, and left the table.

Martina felt a sense of guilt come over her. She remembered how uncomfortable Joachim was when they argued. She took a deep breath. Thomas gazed at her, not understanding the cause of her outrage.

'Look,' she said, 'I hate it when we argue, and it breaks my heart to see what it does to Joachim.'

'I wasn't arguing. I wanted Joachim to spend valuable time with his grandparents. I must have expressed myself ineptly.'

'Three days would be appropriate,' she said, 'and then you can have him for midterm holidays in February.'

'I wanted a week, but that will be fine,' said Thomas. 'I'd better get going. Thanks for dinner.'

He got up, and Martina walked him to the hallway. He grabbed his winter jacket from the railing and slid it on. His eyes wandered to the sleek black shoes on the shoe-stand. *They must be Berluti*, he thought. He could not help but ask, 'Those can't be Joachim's shoes, are they?'

Martina looked at him with a sly grin and said, 'They're mine.'

Thomas chuckled. 'Since when do you wear men's shoes? Besides, they're not your size.'

Martina remembered Jonas changing his shoes when they were dressing for the Nobel festivities. He'd left the extra pair on the shoe-stand. She knew exactly where Thomas was leading with that question.

'What is it, Thomas?' asked Martina. The grin on her face was gone.

'I don't know. Maybe a friend of yours left them here?'

'Maybe, maybe not. What's it to you?'

'Nothing. It's your life, Martina.'

'That's right. Then back off.'

Thomas fell silent.

Martina paused, remembering something, and said, 'By the way, Joachim has your eyeglasses somewhere here. You forgot them at Landegrind house. I'll get them.' She left the hallway and returned with a small burgundy leather case which she handed to him.

Thomas took it, paused and said, 'It reminds me… I don't know how to say this, and I don't mean to pry. It's just that Joachim was unhappy when you dropped him off on Saturday. What happened?'

'What did he say?' asked Martina, a look of concern spreading on her face.

'Not much, just that you were very upset for some reason.'

'Yes, I was. My Security Director, Torsten Widstam, was gunned down. He was on a business mission. It was all very unfortunate and unexpected. The funeral will be in January.'

'Yes, I remember reading about it in the papers. I'm sorry,' said Thomas, relieved she was in no danger from that mysterious Jonas, as Joachim had indicated. He must have been there to deliver the sad news or, even worse, to comfort her. Damn, whichever way he twisted it, all signs indicated that Martina had moved on with this guy.

Chapter 27

Tord, the Chief Inspector of police, looked taller and better groomed than usual in his crisp dark blue uniform. Even his beak nose appeared less prominent, subdued by his bedecked exterior. He evoked a sense of authority, power, security and comfort. On the surface, he was an orderly law enforcement officer, a nationalist but able to adopt a political elite rhetoric to advance his career. He was a policing role model and the national spokesman on gender equality in the police force, utterly opposed to sexism. He was known as politically correct and so sensitive to women's issues that he was nicknamed 'Captain Skirt'. In spite of the joke, he had quickly risen to the rank of dean of the police training academy and eventually Chief Police Inspector.

On this afternoon, he delivered his eloquent lecture on women's rights to a group of young police aspirants.

'Your assignment this week,' he announced, 'is to find the root cause of the growing incidence of prostitution among young women. Hand it in by next week.'

In the evening, he discarded his role as a women's liberationist for a more shrouded role. He stood on an apartment balcony, in a salubrious Stockholm suburb, speaking to the Weasel. He had peeled off his respectable dark blue uniform, and replaced it with comfortable jeans, a matching denim shirt and black sports jacket.

The man with the weather-beaten face briefed him on the illicit merchandise that had just arrived from across the Baltic Sea. In quiet undertones they were haggling over financial remuneration. 'It's too expensive,' said Tord.

'They are fresh and supple,' said Weasel. 'You won't be disappointed.'

'They are minors, aren't they?'

'That's how the market is these days. They get younger every day.'

Tord held a leather briefcase stashed with cash, leather whips, handcuffs, and blindfolds. He opened the case, took out a thick envelope, and handed it to Weasel. 'Prepare them to leave immediately.' His tone was urgent.

Inside the apartment two girls sat drinking liquor. They must have been sixteen or seventeen. Their English was mediocre, and they spoke no Swedish. On the dining table were empty dishes of food. They had just eaten their evening meal.

'Get your stuff, you're leaving,' said Weasel.

The girls panicked, surprised to be leaving so soon. They'd just arrived, and the agreement had been to acquire decent work in Sweden. At least, that was what their agent in Tallinn had promised. 'Where are you taking us?' asked one of the girls in Russian. Weasel did not answer her.

Tord saw fright in their eyes and wanted to quell their suspicions. 'Take it easy. There's no cause for alarm. You're coming with me. You need not fear. I'll fix the jobs.' They glared at him, registering nothing. Weasel stepped in, translating quickly into Russian along with more lies to convince them all was well. He called them Dasha and Natalia.

On arriving at a five-star hotel in central Stockholm, Tord and the girls were joined from the shadows by the silver-haired man, Fabian Franzen. Tord picked up the key from the front desk, and in minutes the four were riding up in the elevator. The company grew later on in the evening when two men in tailored suits joined them.

*****

Grenzken in his office went over yearly account reports. Devilund's profit margins had shrunk by six percent. He shook his head in disappointment, sure it had gone to Althonat Global. Althonat's market share grew like mushrooms on anthills. He compiled next year's investment budget, sceptical there would be sufficient funds. The new security system was a priority and must be installed by the first quarter. No matter how much he earned, he still worried about money. He decided to speak to the accountant to see where he might cut costs.

His irritation grew when he saw the amount swallowed up by taxes, eating into profit margins again. He must speak to his lawyer and do something about it. Money and its accumulation gave Grenzken a feeling of importance and superiority. It diminished his sense of self when someone else made more money than he did. It was like losing a prized possession.

He paused to think about what Martina had insinuated at the Nobel Prize Award Ceremony: wealth is never about money, but about well-being. What a silly notion. She must have gotten it the other way round. Wealth was about money, things, possessions, and nothing else. Such was her twisted mind, talking about greedy corporations sucking out the poor masses. Those were the innuendos and whispers by the underprivileged, sowing seeds of hatred between the rich and poor. A shudder racked his body when he recalled her calling him a parasite, a traitor from inside out – him and his kind. How dare she call him that?

He let out a laboured breath and sat motionless, staring into open space. He tilted his head, his eyes darkening like those of a snake about to strike an unknowing victim. *Wait till I get that other half of Rensblad formula from her. We shall take one hundred per cent market shares. She will squirm and beg. Althonat Global will wither and perish like herbs grown on barren soil. Then I will take her silly head, open her brain, and find out what made her say those demeaning words.*

He picked up the telephone and dialled a number. A voice answered. He asked, 'What's taking so long?' There was silence as he listened to the voice at the other end. 'See you then,' he said, and hung up.

It was past midnight and lights were out in Devilund Clinic, apart from a dim glow in the hallway. Indistinct sounds of distress were heard through the walls from restless inmates, which was not unusual. Richard was on night duty but somewhere in the personnel room. Grenzken converged on room six, jangled the keys, and turned the doorknob. He entered and shut the door behind him. A dull light emanated from a table lamp. Also on the table was a plate of untouched food. In the bed lay Miss Bottle Blonde, Gittel. She glanced at Grenzken and softly hitched the bedclothes over her head. She felt as if she'd been stricken by a tropical illness that left her feverish and vulnerable.

Grenzken pulled a chair near the bed, sat, and glared down at her. Gittel remained still. 'I know you're awake,' he said. 'Take the covers off your head.'

Silence prevailed. Grenzken was losing patience. For days Gittel had been on a hunger strike, resisting Clinical procedures, demanding to be released. His dilemma was that food and medication went hand in hand; otherwise results were inconclusive. He agreed he'd enjoyed a brief fling in the hay with her, but business must go on.

Gittel had been disillusioned when Grenzken turned on her with gynaecological procedures and regular injections that sapped her body. She turned rebellious, refusing to eat. Grenzken knew what he wanted, and he pursued it with grim ruthlessness and a determination bordering on obsession. He was not used to being disobeyed.

He got up and tore the covers off her body, flinging them to the floor. She lay in a foetal position, her white cotton shirt drawn up, exposing her slim youthful thighs. She did not move a muscle. He grabbed her shoulders and shook her violently.

'I say, get up. Sit up and eat,' said Grenzken, pulling her up into sitting position.

Gittel opened her eyes and gave him a daggers glare. She slackened back on the bed. He grabbed the plate from the table and shoved it under her nose on the pillow. She did not move. Grenzken sat down abruptly, and his face softened – maybe because of her beautiful body that had once brought pleasure to him.

'Gittel, eat something.' His voice was subdued and gentler. 'You have to eat. You can't win this one.'

Gittel said nothing. Her breath was shallow and her face pale. Grenzken's eyes glinted amber in the dim glow of the lamp. She knew her stance: she would rather die than succumb to his wicked schemes.

There was a faint knock at the door. 'Come in,' hollered Grenzken.

It was Helmut. Grenzken got up and left the room with the plate of food. He handed it to Helmut and told him to throw it away.

'Tord, waiting outside,' said Helmut. Grenzken jangled keys again and locked the door. Gittel broke down in tears.

Outside, the cold wind nipped Tord's aging grey skin, aggravating the wrinkles around his face. 'Delivery, new merchandise,' he announced as Grenzken stepped out of the door. Grenzken noted there was something cold about Tord.

Tord opened the rear door of the van and waved his hand at the girls.

'Out,' he said. Two timid girls, Dasha and Natalia, emerged from the car. They clung on to each other, shoulders hunched, and moved slowly with an uncertain step.

Tord, irritated by their slow pace, shoved them by the shoulders as if they were cattle. 'Quickly, hurry up,' he said, pointing a finger to the door. 'In there, go in there.'

Helmut opened the doors, and the girls trotted inside, hugging themselves, freezing in tiny miniskirts and short leather jackets.

In the office, Grenzken asked Helmut to tell Richard to take care of the girls. Helmut gestured for the girls to follow him down the corridor.

Sitting at Grenzken's conference table, Tord opened his briefcase and retrieved a paper. He shoved it across to Grenzken. 'Invoice for delivered merchandise,' he said.

Grenzken picked it up and looked at it. His brows furrowed. 'You've doubled the price.'

'They're young and strong. I've tasted them,' said Tord, a devilish grin on his face. 'You'll achieve best results. Besides, it's very risky business dealing in minors.'

Grenzken swallowed and said, 'I'll ask the accountant to transfer payment.'

'Good,' said Tord as the creases around his eyes relaxed. He cleared his throat and let out a small cough. He started, 'The night we had the Christmas buffet, the night everything went wrong, was there a shooting outside Vittaby Villa?'

Grenzken's eyes widened. He had been sitting on these facts, trying to come up with a way to relay them to The Group. Now he'd been cornered as if he was hiding something. He stroked his beard, thinking what to say.

'I can only tell you what Helmut told me. He said he saw men in a car. He took my hunting rifle and shot in the air. But he killed no one.'

"Where did he find your rifle?'

'In my office. I keep it under lock and key but I don't know how he got hold of the key.'

'Right now I have a homicide case on my desk. The Security Director of Althonat Global, Torsten Widstam, was murdered outside your Villa.'

'It...it wasn't Helmut,' Grenzken stuttered.

'The murder was reported by Martina,' boomed Tord. 'I guess she's coming after us, and she's coming strong.'

There was a knock on the door. Grenzken turned toward it with an angry face. 'Yes?' he hollered. Helmut poked his head around the door and announced that there were guests.

'In the middle of the night?' said Grenzken, raising to his feet.

He was still speaking when the door flung open, and in marched Jacob Mattsson, Steven Rangor, Stellan Strömstedt, and the silver-haired man, Fabian Franzen.

Grenzken furrowed his brow. 'What's going on?' The gentlemen spread around the table and grabbed seats.

'Tord called and said we're having an ad hoc meeting,' said Fabian.

'Couldn't it wait till tomorrow?' asked Grenzken, scowling at Tord.

Tord waved a hand. 'Sit down, Grenzken.'

A strangled sensation came over him. He felt the confines of being in a small room with five men. How dare they move on him without warning, catching him off guard and unprepared? He deflated and lowered himself into a chair. 'Very well, then, let's hear it.'

'As I was saying, Martina reported a homicide to the police. It's a disturbing development. What was her Security Director doing outside Vittaby Villa? You've all read Grenzken's report that Nicholas went missing. I'm convinced Torsten and his men took him. But something went wrong, and he got killed.'

Fabian shifted in his chair. 'This homicide report – can't you kill it?'

Tord took a moment, surprised at Fabian's words. 'No, not when it involves Martina. She's a persistent woman and won't let up till she gets answers. Killing the report might jeopardize my position. Another thing, there is a young officer who has risen in the ranks in the Police Investigative Unit. He is ambitious and diligent, leaves no stone unturned. Phillip Nsamizi, Barbara Von Essen Nsamizi's son, is a man with a mission to reach the height of his ambition.' He said the name with strong emphasis on Von Essen, a noble family, considered close to royalty.

Tord fidgeted in his chair and crossed his legs but got no relief from his fears. 'Phillip's detectives may be here any time,' he thundered. 'Trust me. He works like a dog, and he does it by the book.'

There was a long silence as the implications sank in. Grenzken did not know where to look, realizing angry eyes were upon him. He stroked his whiskers, but even that did not give him comfort or consolation. 'We have to find a way to stop the murder investigation,' he blurted, even knowing it was nonsense. Then he abruptly added, 'Helmut did not kill anyone.'

Tord gave him a frustrated look, wondering what it would feel like to wring his neck.

'If Helmut did it,' said Fabian, 'let's hand him over to the police, and everything will stop there.'

'We can get him a good lawyer,' said Rangor, 'and he could plead insanity. He'll be out in no time. That's how the system works these days.'

Grenzken frowned at Rangor, and the lump in his throat threatened to choke him. He let out a loud cough to mask his anger. 'Don't...don't even consider that,' he managed to say. 'No one touches Helmut.'

'Cut the crap!' roared Fabian. 'This is no joke. You messed him up, and all you say is 'No one touches Helmut?'

With a quick movement Fabian was up, clenched fist raised high, closing in on Grenzken. Before anyone could stop him, he struck Grenzken's jaw soundly. Grenzken yowled, and his chair tipped over backwards bringing him down. He writhed and wriggled like a beaten snake as he struggled to get loose from the chair. Seething in rage, Fabian moved in on him, flexing his muscles, clenching his fist again, ready to punch him.

'Enough!' said Mattsson as he quickly grabbed Fabian's arm and pushed him away. Tord bent over and helped Grenzken up. Shaken and unsteady, Grenzken scrambled to his feet and wiped his mouth with the back of his hand. It was oozing with blood. He licked his lips, tasting metallic iron. He cowered and sauntered out of the room without a word. Fabian kicked the chair, tumbling it into a corner.

Ack, such savages, thought Stellan, who stood watching, benumbed by Fabian's barbaric behaviour. How had he gotten involved with such a bunch? If it weren't for the money, he wouldn't be here.

Outside, dawn was breaking, speeding up the day, spinning events. Fabian knew something had to be done, and quickly, to stop the police investigation, but what? The Group grappled for answers, trapped and strangled in each other's destiny. Things were falling apart at the seams. All this wrangling and squabbling took valuable time away from quality research. Instead, focus shifted to self-inflicted problems

— the careless mistakes of Anna, Nicholas and Helmut, and now a murder investigation. At this crazy pace, work was jargonized and goals unfulfilled. Althonat Global gained an advantage on the market stage, while Citaraph struggled with bad publicity. The furore bolstered Martina's propaganda machinery. How would he explain these fiascos to his superiors? It might cost him his job. He let out a heavy breath.

Chapter 28

Martina could hear Jonas on the phone from outside the door, where she stood waiting to come in.

'She awakened from the coma?'

Long pause.

'That is wonderful news indeed.'

Short pause.

'No, she hasn't arrived, but she should be here anytime.'

He listened again, and said, 'All right then, see you.' He hung up and turned to his computer.

Martina pushed the door open, came in, and closed it behind her.

'Just on time,' said Jonas, as he lifted his gaze. He got up, met her halfway across the room, and planted a kiss on her lips. 'That was Dr Nasiro. He is expecting us,' said Jonas. 'But sit down first. I need to speak to you.'

'It sounds serious,' said Martina as she lowered herself on a sofa.

'Patrick Strand has sued the hospital for kidnapping his son and treating him without parental consent. His lawyer sent the letter.' Jonas handed her the letter.

Martina was not surprised. A quick perusal through the letter confirmed her suspicion. 'Fabian Franzen is behind this,' she said. 'He threatened me with the same issue at the Nobel banquet.'

'You mean the short, stout, silver-haired man?'

'Yes, the director of National Board of Health and Welfare. He is full of revenge and bitterness. It bothers him that Althonat Global is up and running despite his efforts to stop us. He taunted Pappa and made a mockery of him, turning him into an object of ridicule. He persistently rejected our applications when we tried to open Althonat in Sweden. But when the political winds changed, his arm was twisted by higher powers forcing him to approve our claim. Ever since, he's been on a mission to destroy us.'

'I remember it made headlines in the media,' said Jonas. 'Politicians were involved.'

'People knew of our success in the States and wanted the same benefits of Complementary medicine. The Social Democrats risked losing the election that year if they refused another application. Fabian was forced to back down. He never forgave Pappa for that. He wears animosity on his face like a mask.'

'It sounds more like an obsession,' said Jonas. 'It's best to be vigilant.'

'Patrick Strand sold his son. He has no claim on Nicholas,' said Martina. 'How can he be so stupid as to sue us? With the evidence I have, he'll definitely do jail time. He doesn't understand that Fabian is using him to get at me.'

'You have evidence?'

'Yes, his wife, Ebba, gave me an envelope before she died. That is why she came to Landegrind house on the night we had the summer grill.'

'No wonder she looked rattled.'

'Send the letter to our Corporate Lawyers,' said Martina. 'They'll take care of it. And should Fabian try any more tricks, I'll bury him.'

'What do you have on him?'

'I have a lot of stuff on Fabian and I suspect he's spreading his tentacles into Althonat Global. He is spying on us.' Her memory flashed back to Fabian and Leila, in a dark corner, at the Nobel banquet.

'Be careful, Martina. I want you in one piece,' said Jonas. 'You and I have great plans. I don't want them jeopardized for any reason.'

'What plans?' asked Martina, snapping out of her reverie.

'Marriage, children – I want it all and very soon.' He winked at her and smiled.

Martina was not amused by the very soon. 'Are you always so sure about what you want?'

'I can feel it in my bones, and when I do, I'm never wrong,' said Jonas. 'You're right for me, Martina.'

'Stop your romantic gibbering,' said Martina as she got to her feet. 'Did you speak to the curator about Nicholas?'

'Yes, she's going to contact Social Services.'

They walked down the stairs from the eighth floor to the sixth floor, to Dr Nasiro's office.

'How wonderful that she's regained consciousness,' said Martina, coming to the point.

'Yes, it's excellent news,' said Dr Nasiro. 'Her immune system was shutting down when she arrived. A toxic vaccine in her body was causing violent seizures. Her system was infested with viruses and heavy metals. We flushed all that out and restored her body to self-healing. Her skin, too, cleared of the rash and acne. But still one thing bothers me.'

'What is that?' asked Martina.

'I found genetically engineered DNA in her blood. There is a risk it can begin reproducing in her cells. The contamination might initiate mutations and lead to cancer.'

'She was used as an unknowing, unwilling research subject in engineering Life-Vaccine,' said Martina, a worried look on her face. 'This confirms my worst fears. Life-Vaccine is a toxic biological weapon, purposely made for mass destruction.'

'Whoever injected her with that stuff must be an evil person,' said Dr Nasiro. 'I wonder what kind of science he studied.'

'He studied the same science as you and me,' said Martina. 'But he misuses it and distorts it, because someone with money and power told him to do so.'

Dr Nasiro blinked as if he had never heard of medical corruption.

'What are her chances of having children?' asked Jonas.

'Nil. Whatever they gave her reduced her uterus to the size of a pea.'

'Keep monitoring her DNA status,' said Martina. 'Good work, doctor. Shall we?'

'Yes. This way, please,' said Dr Nasiro. He led them out to room number sixty-six down the corridor. He knocked on the door, and a soft voice answered, 'Come in.'

In bed lay a young woman in her late teens holding a book. She glanced up as the doctors came in and shifted into a sitting position. Dr Nasiro introduced the doctors to her. Her face lit up in a broad smile.

'I'm Anna Forsman,' she said, extending her hand to Martina and then to Jonas.

'How are you feeling, Anna?' asked Martina with a tender voice.

'I feel wonderful.'

'I'm glad to hear that,' said Martina. 'What are you reading?'

'It's a book on nutrition. Dr Nasiro said I should follow good nutrition even when I leave the hospital.' Suddenly, she narrowed her brows and looked at the picture on the book cover and then back at Martina. 'You're the famous doctor who wrote this book,' she burst out. 'Oh my, I'm glad to meet you, Dr Edgren.'

'I'm honoured to meet you too, Anna,' said Martina as she sat on the chair beside the bed, and took her hand. 'What you went through was brutal, but you're lucky you came out alive. We're pleased with your progress.'

'That crazy man, Grenzken, wanted to kill me. He was a cold, insensitive man, a barbaric psychopath whose only pleasure was to inflict pain. Whatever he injected me with, gave me excruciating stomach pains; it drove me up the wall. The headaches made me pass out several times a day.'

'Were there other patients?' asked Martina.

'Patients?' said Anna with anger in her voice. 'He called us inmates. The facility was built like a prison. I never saw anyone, but I am sure there were others. I used to hear them wailing and crying.' She paused, tears flooding her eyes. 'I was desperate to live.'

Martina cuddled her and said, 'Hush now, you're safe.'

'I think we should leave you to rest,' said Dr Nasiro. 'I'll check on you later.'

Martina and Jonas went to lunch in the hospital restaurant. 'She is a brilliant young woman,' said Martina as they ate.

'And a brave one too. Though I'm worried about her safety here at the hospital.'

'You're right. She knows too much. They may try to finish her off.'

'And after her treatment she has no place to go,' said Jonas. 'She is an orphan. Her parents were drug addicts and died of HIV. She never fared well in foster homes. A troubled child, she was. She refused help from Social Service and doesn't trust people. She ended up on the street, in bad company. That's where a pimp found her and hooked her up with a man who took her to the mad scientist, Grenzken. She's been through a lot.'

'There is a lot to deal with here,' said Martina. 'Talk to our new Security director, Christer Sorenson. Have him post guards outside Anna's ward.'

'I'll get on it as soon as we're finished here,' said Jonas after he drained his glass of beer.

Martina paused a moment and then said, 'Don't you see?'

'See what?'

'The connection. The fact that her uterus atrophied means Life-Vaccine was engineered for a sinister purpose. Think about the findings of your research study. You said men were disgruntled their wives were not getting pregnant. The wives who were not getting pregnant had been injected with Life-Vaccine. Those who were not injected are having babies.'

'You're right. That, along with the fact that it is a toxic biological weapon…the consequences of Life-Vaccine could be devastating for humanity.'

There was an uneasy silence, but Martina did not want to quibble about the problem, at least not now. 'When are you leaving for Gothenburg?' she said, changing the subject.

'Tonight; my flight is at eight.'

'I won't be seeing you for two weeks. I'll miss you,' she said, and then, took a sip at her sparkling water.

'You can come with me,' said Jonas, cocking his head on one side, smiling. 'I can book you on the same flight if you want.'

'No, I can't. Sebastian is arriving today with family. He will kill me if I'm not here. We've business to discuss.'

'I can explain to him that we're madly in love and inseparable.'

'It's more complicated than that. I have to think of Joachim. I'm not an irresponsible teenager who just takes off with a cupid-stricken lover.'

'That is rather disastrous; cupid-struck indeed, like Romeo. I want you to spend Christmas with my family next year.' His greenish brown eyes pulled her in, reminding her of the strong attraction she felt for him.

They had been friends first, but she had never dreamt she would fall helplessly in love with him. She recalled the evening she walked into Stockholm Salsa dance club with an open mind, expecting nothing. She had waved a hand at Sanchez, the owner, and scanned the room for an empty table. The club was filled with people drinking and chatting. Others were shaking it out on the dance floor.

At the far end, in a corner, a man with brown hair caught her attention. The dim spotlights from the ceiling gleamed in his face. He seemed familiar. He sat alone, his head buried in a magazine, a glass of wine on the table in front of him. He raised his face momentarily, and she saw it was Jonas.

With her usual graceful stride, she approached his table. 'Hi, stranger,' she said.

Jonas lifted his gaze from the magazine, and their eyes locked. His face lit up in a gorgeous smile, and he said, 'Martina Strömstedt Edgren.'

Martina smiled to herself, remembering the sudden joy of wonder in his eyes.

'What are you smiling at?' asked Jonas, startling her back from daydreaming.

'I'm glad I came to the Salsa dance club that evening.'

'What're you talking about?'

'Do you remember when we met at the Salsa club?'

'Oh, that. Me too, I'm glad you came,' he said, and then munched Caesar salad. He reached across the table, took her hand, and caressed her knuckles.

'I thought you were on the west coast, settled in with wife and kids,' said Martina.

Jonas chuckled. 'Not a chance. I was waiting for you,' he said jokingly. 'But I knew about you, your divorce, and Althonat's success. You were a celebrity, even then.'

'It seems you were keeping tabs on me,' said Martina as she forked her last bit of cheese pie.

'I was interested. Even in the States, you knew I loved you.'

'Why didn't you call me?'

Jonas' face fell as he realized that at the time he'd had unhappy circumstances of his own. 'I wasn't sure you wanted me.'

'Two years after the divorce and it was just Joachim and me,' said Martina. 'I got tired of baby talk. I wanted to come out, meet people, get my social life back on track.'

'I used to come to the club hoping you would turn up.'

'Dr Eneroth, are you a psychic?' asked Martina, bursting out in a loud laugh.

'Yes, I am, you naughty girl!' said Jonas. 'I knew you loved dancing salsa. That was my bait.' He kissed her knuckles.

Martina gently withdrew her hand, looking around. Other employees sat eating and chitchatting at surrounding tables. 'Jonas, staff may be watching,' she whispered.

'Then let's go to your penthouse.'

'Darling, the penthouse is out of bounds for you during office hours.'

'It's just ten floors up,' said Jonas. 'You said you'll miss me.'

'I know what I said.'

'I can't help it when you turn me on like this.'

'You're distracting me,' said Martina as she hastily glanced at her watch, and rose. 'I'd better get going. I have a meeting. I wish you a safe journey and a merry Christmas, lover boy.'

'I'll miss you,' said Jonas. 'Have a merry Christmas.'

He watched her walk away and felt an impulse to cancel his flight. But he knew it would be useless. She had her own family to take care of during the holidays. The thought made him realize how he hated these separations. One of these days, he would propose to her.

Chapter 29

The Christmas season had arrived and the sunlight hours had grown very few. Flakes of snow tumbled down like ground corn, forming a foggy cloud and reducing visibility to zero. The Mercedes swayed and ambled on the last kilometre of country road headed for Landegrind house. Martina turned into the driveway and parked besides Sebastian's Lexus GX 460.

Joachim helped his mother with a sack full of wrapped gifts. He took it into the living room and put it under the Christmas tree. A log fire blazed in the cosy room.

Sebastian appeared on the staircase landing. 'How lovely to see you,' he said. 'We were beginning to worry. The weather is terrible.'

'We drove slowly,' said Martina. 'The roads were slippery and unattended to.'

'Joachim, my boy, how are you?' said Sebastian as he walked up to Joachim and patted his shoulder.

'Did you bring my posters, Uncle Sebastian?' asked Joachim.

'Yes, I did. Go upstairs and ask the girls.' Joachim dashed upstairs.

Henrietta, Sebastian's wife, emerged from the kitchen with a beaming smile and walked graciously towards Martina. She was a woman whose well-formed body was of average height. She and Sebastian had met when she was an exchange student at Lund University. From her amiable and vibrant nature, you could tell she was American.

'Martina, my dear, it's been a long time,' she said, as she opened her arms and gave her a huge hug.

'Did you have a safe journey?' asked Martina with a smile.

'There were strong winds in London, but we managed a safe take-off,' said Henrietta. 'And that terrible accident that took your parents – I'm so sorry. How is Joachim?'

'He is a vibrant boy, thank God,' said Martina.

'Come sit, and let's catch up on things,' said Henrietta.

They sank into the deep, comfortable sofas, joining Sebastian, who was reading the Frangipani. Stephanie and Pamela came downstairs, exhibiting good manners and grace. They greeted Martina and disappeared upstairs again.

In the background, the stereo hummed 'Silent Night.' Astrid came and announced dinner was ready.

The family gathered around the large wooden table in the dining room and ate dinner. Later, sated and sleepy after the long journeys, they made it an early night.

The house could accommodate four families at a go. Martina's father had built it for the future, anticipating grandchildren. During better days, Stellan and his family had spent Christmas at Landegrind house.

On Christmas Day Lisa arrived around noon. She was the only guest invited. A lavish feast of Christmas smorgasbord was served in the dining room. After the sumptuous meal, sacks of gifts were opened, to the children's cries of glee. There was excitement and animated chatter as gifts were exchanged. The sounds of ripping and tearing filled the room as the children frantically saw their wishes fulfilled. With their newfound toys, they clambered upstairs to play. Sebastian and the ladies sat sipping coffee and cognac, talking about events and happenings. Soft music played in the background.

The light was dim yet welcoming, glowing invitingly from spotlights in the ceiling, but overwhelmingly from the log fire burning in the huge open grate. Its light danced over the walls and furniture, amber and warming, punctuated by crackling and popping as the oak logs slowly burned to ashes. It gave a relaxed ambience to the room.

Tranquillity prevailed. The joy and laughter of children relaxed Martina's mind. She leaned back on the sofa, and lost herself in the simple delight of being.

Outside, in the cold breeze, a man parked his car on the side road and walked up to Landegrind house. He wore a hooded black winter jacket. He pressed the doorbell.

Sebastian raised a speculative eyebrow at Martina. 'Expecting company?'

'No,' she said.

He got up and walked to the front door. As he talked, Martina heard another male voice. After a while, Sebastian returned. Behind him was a tall man with a weak nerveless step as if he was unsure of where he was. Martina thought it was someone who lost his way in the blizzard and needed help. In his hand, he clutched a large paper bag. When she lifted her eyes, a sudden ghastly chill swept over her. It was Stellan.

She closed her eyes and prayed that she might be civil under the shocking, utterly unexpected circumstances. This audacious creature coming and barging in on her family unannounced was a lot to take in. She knew that sitting in the same room with Stellan would be like waiting for a ticking time bomb to explode.

When the shock had eased, she summoned her good manners. 'Please, take a seat,' she said, standing to offer him her place on the sofa.

Lisa hardly looked at her father, fighting the urge to rise and leave the room. She could not breathe, feeling suffocated by his dark shadow.

'Merry Christmas and good evening to everyone,' said Stellan as he took a seat. He handed the paper bag to Martina and said, 'Gifts for the children.'

Martina said, 'Thank you.'

The warmth from the log fire thawed Stellan's frozen body, bringing on a jittery ache in his legs. The display of miniature lights in the Christmas tree blinded his eyes. The smell of homemade food, alcohol and the playful sound of children upstairs amplified his loneliness, bringing home the sad reality of what he missed in life; family. The large paintings that adorned the walls were missing. He wondered if they'd been stolen during the break-in. Then he saw Peter's empty rocking chair by the fireplace, and bitter memories flooded his feeble mind. He wanted to bolt up and leave, but something kept him in place.

In an entertaining spirit, Henrietta offered to get Stellan something to eat.

'Can I bring you something to eat, or perhaps would you like to come and pick what you prefer from the smorgasbord?'

'Thank you, I think I'll come with you,' said Stellan, getting up to follow her to the dining room.

Martina leaned towards Sebastian and murmured, 'What does he want?'

'Search me! I thought you invited him,' said Sebastian.

'I didn't invite him.'

'Watch it,' whispered Lisa, 'he's after something.'

Stellan's arrival contaminated the peaceful ambience of the evening, and seeds of anger, suspicion and disgust grew like a cancer in the now gloomy room. There was no knowing when the fermented brew of his poisoned mind would froth over and blow the lid off whatever sizzled beneath. There was even a possibility that, rather than sizzle, the brew might under great pressure erupt like a violent volcano.

Henrietta returned with a tray of food: sherry herrings, cold salmon, pickled cod and egg halves with caviar as starters. She placed the tray on a side table and filled Stellan's glass with beer. Stellan sat down and started eating. The situation was awkward, but he put up a brave face.

Everyone was tongue-tied apart from the music on the stereo. Lisa watched her father from the sidelines, noting that he had not looked at her since he came in.

Sebastian broke the silence. 'It's been a long time, Uncle Stellan,' he said.

'It has,' said Stellan. 'I knew you'd be here this time of year. I wanted to see the children and wish you all a merry Christmas.'

'You'll see them,' said Sebastian. 'They're playing upstairs.'

Martina engaged in conversation with Henrietta, sipping cognac but keeping her ears pricked. She half listened to Henrietta and half to Stellan's talk with Sebastian. Lisa picked up a magazine from the centrepiece table and paged through it, pretending to read. It was not the Christmas she had anticipated.

'So what's new in Stockholm?' asked Sebastian, trying to make conversation.

'Nothing really,' replied Stellan. 'It's just the cold and the darkness.'

'I understand Ribbyburg is a Clinic for disabled children.' The talk sounded stilted and strained, but Martina knew Sebastian, the accomplished diplomat, could handle it.

'Yes, I leased it out so as to…to help pay my debts.'

Lisa rose and wandered upstairs, thinking it was better to play with children than tango with this disoriented old man.

Martina sat looking at Stellan, her thoughts bouncing wildly in her head, hardly hearing what Henrietta was saying. She heard the dog bark and wondered if Rangor had put him up to it, to spy on them.

Stellan felt Martina's penetrating glare to the bone. He decided to keep a steady gaze on Sebastian, the only place he could look without being intimidated.

Astrid appeared and took away Stellan's empty plate. She returned with another tray, the main course. With a gluttonous appetite, Stellan ate Jansson's temptation, smoked ribs with honey, boiled potatoes, baked ham, red cabbage and sour cream.

'Martina, this is delicious,' said Stellan, trying to sound friendly.

'Mamma's old recipes,' said Martina. 'Taste the meatballs too. You'll like them.' He's enjoying the food, she thought. Maybe he will tell us what he wants. She recalled the email she had seen on his computer screen, in Ribbyburg Clinic, about the other half of Rensblad. Was that why he was here? Or was it because of the dossier? Maybe it was loneliness that brought him here.

Sebastian talked on about life in the States and the new administration in Washington. He went on about New York, the 9/11 catastrophe, and its long-term effects on people's health. He told him about Wall Street – the hardening economic climate, unemployment, corruption, and rising criminality. Stellan listened intently, throwing in a word or two, seeming to enjoy the attention from his nephew.

Martina and Henrietta wandered to the kitchen to brew more coffee and tea.

The sound of playing children escalated from soft sounds to noisy banging. Henrietta went to the landing and hollered for them to come down and eat rice pudding. They scooted down in a row and swept through the living room to the kitchen.

As Martina came in with a tray of cheese and fruit, she overheard Stellan ask Sebastian if he could speak to him in private. Sebastian glanced at Martina and said, 'If it concerns family or business, Martina and I have no secrets.'

'Whatever you want to say, you can speak here,' said Martina.

That was a nasty snag Stellan had not anticipated. He decided to try another angle; maybe he could find something in the attic.

'It was noth…nothing, really. I wanted to access the attic to look for documents. I suspect there was a mix up of Peter's things and mine during the move from Hässelved farm.'

'Well –' said Sebastian, but Martina cut him short.

'What documents?' she said, her eyes pinning him, her voice suspicious. Her mind spun off again in swirls of growing anger, wondering why he didn't just leave.

Stellan scowled at her, angered by her overbearing manner. A silence elapsed as Stellan searched his mind for a credible response, a plausible motive to get into the attic. He swallowed and stared at Martina.

She stood hovering over him with a tray in her hands. She wanted to dump it on his thick head, but instead she leaned forward and placed it on the low central table. She continued to glare at him in silent fury.

'I'm selling my share of antique furniture from Hässelved. I need receipts and specifications. They must be in your attic.'

'There are no such documents in the attic,' Martina replied, as calmly as she could. 'I was there recently, cleaning out.'

Feeling the confining discomfort of Martina's imposing figure, Stellan got on his feet and stood facing her, determined to force his will on her. He knew it was no easy task, but try he must. He must get in the attic, at least to check if there was anything incriminating against him and the Group. 'I just want to check. You can come with me if you don't trust me.'

'No,' said Martina. 'There's nothing of yours in there.'

Stellan turned to Sebastian, who sat gazing up at him with an impassive face. Henrietta was in the kitchen with the children.

'Sebastian, get me the key,' said Stellan.

'Actually, that's Martina's territory,' said Sebastian. 'She's in charge here. Talk to her nicely; perhaps she will get you the key.'

'Martina, you heard Sebastian,' said Stellan, suppressing his anger.

Sebastian the diplomat, silently thought Martina – what could he say. *Doesn't Stellan get it that Sebastian and I stick together?* 'You heard me. I said no.'

Stellan lost it. He sidestepped her and with an unsteady tread marched to the stairway. 'Then I'll break in the door,' he declared.

'Stop, where are you going?' said Martina, following him and going around him to block his way.

'Get out of my way,' he said.

Sebastian sprang to his feet. Henrietta, hearing the scuffle, emerged from the kitchen and stood beside her husband, clinging to his arm.

Martina's eyes smouldered like embers ready to burst into flame. Everything came back to her as she touched base with the rising pain in her back. It set her off, spitting venom. 'How dare you come here after what you did to Pappa?' she asked.

Henrietta did not want to be a part of the family feud. She eased back to the kitchen, even though Sebastian squeezed her hand to stay. She returned briefly with the children and sent them upstairs, getting them out of the volatile minefield.

'I said get out of my way,' repeated Stellan.

Martina did not move. 'You get out of my house, you thief.'

'Thief?' asked Stellan. 'What are you talking about?'

'I'm talking about Rensblad.' Martina's voice was rising. 'The half formula you sold to Citaraph.'

Her anger was palpable. Tears welled in her eyes, suddenly overwhelmed by sadness, but she must not cry; she must be strong – strong to make her point. Her face paled, and her nerves were taut as guitar strings.

'Rensblad half belonged to me,' said Stellan, his breath ailing and raspy. 'It was joint ownership. Everything we did in Hässelved, Peter and I shared.'

'What joint ownership? Then, you should have known that Rensblad mixed with foreign ingredients turned lethal. Do you know how many lives you've destroyed? How much suffering you've caused? Come to the hospital and see. You've brought the world to its knees. But of course all that means nothing to you, so long as you roll in money.'

Time seemed suspended as Sebastian took a deep breath and moved towards Martina.

Lisa came running down the stairs, having heard the altercation. She scowled at her father, who paled beneath his designer wool-and-mohair blend grey suit.

'What joint ownership? Everything you have, you've stolen,' interjected Lisa. 'Like Ribbyburg. You stole it from under my nose, dear father.'

'Get out of my house,' said Martina. Her implacable voice startled Sebastian and Henrietta. Her blazing eyes never once left Stellan as she stepped up and slapped him hard across the face. The sound of the impact echoed in the room.

Stellan's eyes went wide in alarm and then dimmed as he clutched his reddened cheek, staring in horror at Martina. For a moment he stood immobilized as the shock registered on his face.

Martina moved closer, invading his space, her fierce eyes conveying a clear threat.

Sebastian decisively stepped in, grabbed Martina's arm, and gently pushed her aside. 'That's enough, Martina. Stop it.'

Resisting his push, Martina continued to blare, 'Take your filthy lies, you conniving old man. Take your treachery, and feed it to your traitor friends.'

'Martina, that's enough,' said Sebastian.

Something kept Stellan rooted in the middle of the room as if he were paralyzed. With a heavy frown hanging over his ageing brows, his weary frosty eyes appeared unfocused.

In a trice, Lisa came to Martina's side and told her father through gritted teeth, 'Get out. You've done enough damage.'

The children heard the rumble and began to charge downstairs, but Henrietta sent them back. She then turned to Sebastian and gave him a reprimanding frown, rebuking him into arresting the situation.

Sebastian responded by raising his arms in the air. He snapped his fingers, 'Enough, everybody quiet.' His tone shifted from regular civilian to military command. He turned to Stellan and emphatically said, 'I'm sorry, Stellan, you heard the ladies. Please leave.'

Stellan hurriedly walked to the foyer, not bothered about Sebastian's offer to walk him to the door. He grabbed his winter jacket, pulled it on, and trotted out into the freezing cold, cursing.

A tense silence settled like a wet blanket over the Strömstedt home. The four family members sank into seats and stared blankly at each other.

Martina furrowed her brow and slowly turned to Sebastian. 'Can you believe it? He claims Rensblad half belonged to him,' she said, her voice gentle and husky but strong. 'We all know that when the medical community turned their backs on Pappa, he planned to move to the States but did not know what to expect. For safekeeping he divided the formula into two documents. Stellan kept one half and Pappa kept the other half. His plan was, when he settled in the States, he would bring the two halves together and start production. But Stellan got into financial difficulty and sold the half in his custody. What a scoundrel.'

Sebastian paused, gazed at his sister as if gathering his thoughts to process what had transpired, just then and in the past. He thought his sister had handled the situation well. 'What can he say?' Sebastian asked. 'All thieves come up with excuses to avoid shame and embarrassment.'

'I can't stand him,' said Martina. 'He's changed.'

'He kept shifting on the sofa as if he was sitting on pins,' said Henrietta as she munched a gingerbread cookie with cheese. 'He didn't come on his own accord. Someone put him to it.'

'He's an idiot,' said Lisa, 'dealing with the likes of Tord and Rangor. He's bound to change for the worse.' She popped a grape into her mouth.

'Stellan made some bad choices,' said Sebastian. 'I'm sure he's learnt his lessons. It's sad to see him lonely though.'

'You seem sympathetic, Sebastian,' said Martina. 'The man doesn't deserve sympathy. His actions have brought humanity to the brink of disaster. I can't sleep at night thinking about those young girls lapsing into infertility before their time. We're fumbling in darkness for answers to stop the nightmare, and you're feeling sorry for him?'

'Martina, don't get me wrong,' said Sebastian. 'That's not what I meant. I mean as a human being to another human being. We all make mistakes, but should he be hanged for it? Of course what he did staggers me, but mostly it was bad company that misled him. I don't think he understood the consequences of what he was getting himself into.'

Henrietta looked at her husband adoringly and offered him a piece of her gingerbread cookie and cheese. Sebastian took it and ate it, holding her gaze with a smile.

'I'm sure he wanted the dossier,' said Lisa. 'He's desperate to get his hands on it. He's afraid you'll sue him. My father is a loser. He's lost his moral compass. He has nothing to offer but grief.'

Sebastian looked at his cousin wearily and said, 'That's harsh.'

'You don't know him, Sebastian. You haven't lived with him.'

'He wants the dossier and the other half of Rensblad,' said Martina.

Temperatures dropped further as Stellan left Landegrind house and strolled along the dark street illuminated by a dim glow of street lights. The gusting wind howled, tugging and pulling at his jacket. With shoulders hunched, he walked in a confused daze, his eyes fixed on the dull muddy snow on the ground. His mind dwelt painfully on the past – the loss of his company, the debts that almost buried him, the falling out with his brother, his estranged daughter, and on the other side of the scale, the nefarious Group; his so-called friends, but friends he'd never learnt to understand.

Peter's legacy continued to haunt him through his children. They wanted nothing of him and yet he must build a relationship with them to come to grips with his past, to repair the damage in his life and move on to whatever future he had left. He wanted to speak to Sebastian, to negotiate and retrieve the dossier. He was always able to talk to Sebastian. Martina was strong-headed like her father, never allowing him so much as the time of day.

He remembered how he had been taken in by Rangor, a relationship that had led him on a dark path he never imagined was possible. True, money was a motive, and so far, his financial standing had improved remarkably, but at what price? Ingrid had divorced him, and his relationship with his daughter was irreparable. As long as that dossier was out there, he would never be at peace. There was no knowing what could happen if Martina decided to sue him and the Group. He suspected the dossier was already in her possession. His reputation could be marred for good if contents of the dossier were revealed in a lawsuit. His future dangled uncertain. He could go to jail.

He recalled the bitter row he'd had with his brother, Peter, when he accused him of stealing the formula. Peter had threatened him with a dossier he had compiled, on him and the Group. He had promised to use it against him to obtain justice.

Stellan walked into Rangor's driveway but kept close to the hedge and continued to the rear part of the house, out of view from Landegrind house. He saw the light on in Rangor's living room and hoped he was alone. He sauntered to the kitchen door and pressed the bell.

Rangor startled. He hated to be interrupted. 'I wonder who it is,' he said to his guest. 'I'm not expecting company.'

The bell sounded again. Rangor rose from the sofa and stalked to the kitchen. Looking through the viewport he saw Stellan. He quickly opened the door. It was past midnight.

Stellan read the frown on his face and apologized instantly for coming unannounced and at such a late hour. Pagan tottered into the kitchen and yapped at him, wagging its tail. He touched the dog briefly, and it meandered to the living room.

'What happened? I thought you were at Martina's.'

'The situation got out of hand. I can't get to Sebastian as long as Martina is there.'

'What do you mean you can't get to Sebastian?' asked Rangor as he looked at him with utter disdain.

Stellan stared back at him with tired blank eyes and said, 'Martina watches my every move like a hawk. She dismissed every word I said, and worse, my daughter was there too. I can't do it, Steven. You have to find another way!'

There was silence, and then a female voice from the living room called, 'Steven?'

'I'm coming, dear, just a moment,' Rangor said and then turned to Stellan.

'I've a guest, we can talk about that later,' he said.

'Look,' said Stellan, 'I don't want to hold you up, but I need something to get me through the night.'

'Did you take your evening dose?'

Stellan blinked, a desperate look spreading on his aged face. 'Yes, but I need the needle. It goes straight to the bloodstream.'

'That stuff is habit-forming,' said Rangor. 'It's no joke.'

'I think I'm already addicted,' said Stellan, despair in his voice. 'Please, Steven.'

Rangor regarded him hesitantly. Stellan placed a trembling hand on his shoulder. 'Please.'

Not being able to dissuade him, seeing the agitated discomposure in his eyes, Rangor relented. Besides, he did not like keeping his guest waiting.

'Okay, let's go to the study.' They went to a room at the end of the hallway. He told him to sit in a chair by the desk as he retrieved a hypodermic needle from a medicine cabinet. He filled it with a liquid.

Stellan took off his coat and rolled up his shirtsleeve. Rangor injected his upper arm. Stellan closed his eyes and exhaled.

'It's late,' said Rangor. 'You can sleep here if you like.'

'No, I don't want to impose,' said Stellan, clutching his injected arm. 'I'll be all right.'

With a scattered mind and feelings of humiliation, he rose slowly from the chair and sauntered to the hallway. As he came out from the study, a woman in skinny jeans and a white top appeared from the kitchen with a glass of water in her hand. It was Rangor's guest – Leila.

'Oh, hi, Stellan,' she said. 'Care to join us?'

'Hello,' said Stellan. 'I'm leaving. I just came to pick up something.'

'I'll be with you in a moment, Leila,' said Rangor, as Leila entered the living room.

Stellan walked to his car, two blocks away, and drove to Ribbyburg.

'Now, where were we?' asked Rangor as he took a seat on a sofa opposite Leila.

The room had minimal furniture: two ordinary sofas, a brown wood centrepiece table and simple cotton curtains hung in the windows.

'He looked terrible,' said Leila. 'What is ailing him?'

'He takes life too seriously,' said Rangor. 'If only he could relax, he would be fine.'

'It must be eating at him, ditching his family the way he did.'

'It was a choice he made. We all make choices in life. And whether they are good or bad choices, it doesn't matter. What matters is having the guts to live with them.'

Leila smiled wanly, thinking, *what a heartless man.*

'Now back to our discussion,' said Rangor. 'The Botanik Herbier project…what engineering process are you using?'

'It's complicated. It's not something I have at my fingertips.'

Rangor became serious, dissatisfied by her curt answer. 'Let me put it this way. How much is enough?'

'Steven, this is not about money,' she said. 'This is about my work. I can't go around revealing corporate secrets. I'll lose my job. Not only that, but I could end up in jail for industrial espionage.'

'Is that what you're worried about? I can get you another job just like that,' said Rangor, snapping his fingers. 'And as for industrial espionage, I can get you the best lawyers in the world.'

'Then you don't know me very well. I love my job.'

Rangor burst out in cynical laughter, ignoring her look of contempt. 'Lies. I know you well enough to know you're not being truthful about the money issue. You like fine things, exotic holidays, designer clothes, fast cars…need I say more?'

'I've done a lot of things for you in the past that I'm not proud of.'

'How much does Queen Strömstedt Edgren pay you anyway?'

'She pays me well enough to maintain my lavish lifestyle,' said Leila, and then, 'End of conversation. I'm going home.'

'You can spend the night here.'

'No, I must sleep in my bed.'

'Since when?'

'What do you mean by that?'

'You think I don't know who you're shaking it up with these days.'

'It's none of your business,' said Leila. 'Will you see me out?'

'You can find your own way out. You don't need me to help you with that.'

'You've never changed. You're always mean, rude, and arrogant.'

Rangor shrugged and watched as Leila stormed out of the room. He heard the front door slam. A sardonic grin materialized on his face. Next time he must make her talk.

*****

Deep in the night, Martina stood at the window in her parents' dark bedroom, looking down at Rangor's compound. The lights in the living room were on. She wondered if Stellan was there. Suddenly, she saw the figure of a woman emerge from the main door of the house. At that distance, it was too foggy to see who she was. The woman walked to the road and disappeared in the dark. Martina guessed she must have parked her car in the visitors' parking lot, three blocks away, not wanting her car to be seen in Rangor's compound. So Rangor had female company. Martina wondered who she was.

Chapter 30

On the weekend, Henrietta and the children travelled to Lund to visit a friend. Martina and Sebastian stayed at Landegrind house to catch up on business, and family matters.

At a market square in Gullmarsplan stood a man in dark coat and hat, clutching a Saddleback leather bag over his shoulder. A black Volvo pulled up, and he got in the rear seat. He exchanged greetings with the chauffeur, who quickly checked his mirrors and rolled the car into traffic.

The street lights shone like beads on a string as the car gained speed. The chauffeur, a young man with dark crew-cut hair, tightened his hold on the steering wheel. He glanced in the rear-view mirror, checking if he was being followed.

The passenger in the back seat sat radiating a deadly brooding silence. There was a nervous glare in his eyes as he occasionally glanced through the rear window screen. The Volvo roared through the southern tunnel linking up with Stockholm Central. It stopped at traffic lights, and then drove up, swerving into Master Samuelsgatan street. It slowed down, and turned swiftly into an underground parking garage. It parked, and halted besides a waiting black BMW. In the BMW sat another crew-cut chauffeur.

A black Dodge van entered the garage and parked opposite the Volvo.

The passenger made a move to get out of the Volvo. 'Wait,' said the chauffeur, his eyes roving left to right and back to the mirrors. Finally, they settled on the Dodge van. A woman emerged from the van and walked briskly to the elevators.

The chauffeur turned to the passenger and nodded. In a swift move, the passenger got out of the Volvo and transferred to the BMW.

'Good evening, sir,' said the chauffeur in the BMW.

'Good evening,' said the passenger.

The chauffeur ignited the engine, and the BMW glided towards the exit. It left the garage and emerged on route four. The driver cut through the traffic, crossing two lanes to pass slower cars, and merged into the fast lane headed north.

At Kungshamra, he swung the BMW onto route eighteen. The sudden swerve rocked the passenger in the back seat, throwing him back, a grim expression on his face as he clutched his Saddleback bag under his arm.

*****

Martina sat in the library, reading. The room flashed in shadows of shifting lights. She glanced out of the window and saw the BMW parking in the driveway. The passenger adjusted his hat, opened the door, and stepped out of the car. The chauffeur backed the BMW into the road and sped off, disappearing into the cloak of night. With long strides, the passenger walked to the front door. He waved a friendly hand at the two security guards standing in the compound and pressed the front doorbell. They knew he was expected.

Sebastian opened the door. Animated talk and laughter rang through the hallway. Martina perceived the muffled sounds from the library as Sebastian and the visitor chattered, exchanging pleasantries and sharing jokes. Now and then Sebastian fell into uncontrollable laughter at whatever the visitor had imparted to him. They had been friends for a long time, and Martina was used to their bluster.

'You still…remember it all?' stammered Sebastian as his body rocked with laughter.

'How could I forget?' said the visitor. 'It was the best training I've ever had.'

Martina appeared at Sebastian's side, and the mood shifted from light to dark, martial to civilian, comical to respectable; for the visitor now stood before his boss. There was mystery about his bright grey eyes that came across as stand-offish, yet seemed fascinating, drawing one in to discover him. He was well groomed and had a great sense of humour.

Suddenly his body went upright, erect, and his eyes serious. This time his tone was formal, and orderly. 'Birth name Daniel Lindahl reporting, professional name Richard, code name Scorpio.'

'I'm glad you could make it, Daniel,' said Martina, grasping his hand.

'It's my pleasure, Dr Edgren,' he said with an amiable smile, his body shifting at ease.

'This way, Daniel,' said Martina as she led the way. 'We shall sit in the study.' Sebastian and Daniel sat at the round glass conference table, in a corner, talking and laughing. Martina left and soon returned with a pile of papers. Astrid came in with a tray of coffee, tea and blueberry pie with vanilla cream.

Daniel's eyes wandered randomly across the room, a habit dating from military academy. The décor was in balmy shades, a dark wood desk and matching leather chair occupied half of the room, flanked by a red wood bookcase filled with books. The window drapes were a rich golden brown.

Martina saw Daniel's concerned eyes and said, 'We are safe here. Our security team has swept for eavesdropping devices.' She handed him a cup of coffee and asked, 'Did you have a good trip?'

'Yes, I was well taken care of,' said Daniel. 'Your men are professionals. Very impressive.'

'Simon and Tobias are our best bodyguards and security personnel at Althonat Securitos,' said Martina.

'All ex-military men,' said Sebastian with a lopsided grin, his gaze on Daniel. Another shared joke. Daniel laughed back at him. Martina, not understanding the joke, shrugged it off as one of those moments when boys will be boys.

On a serious note, Daniel turned to his briefing. He reported on his findings at Devilund Clinic: the inmates, the goings-on at Vittaby Villa, secret meetings, and recent developments about Anna and Nicholas. Then he concluded, 'The goal is to maintain humanity at one billion in perpetual balance with natural resources.' Daniel handed the report to Martina.

Sebastian almost spilled his coffee. He lowered his cup to the table and asked, 'Why?'

'They believe people are consuming too many resources,' said Daniel.

'That's insane,' said Sebastian.

'The numbers are staggering,' said Martina, reading from Daniel's report. 'You mean Ninety-five percent of world population will be eliminated using Life-Vaccine?'

'Yes, that's the plan according to the Group,' said Daniel.

'What is it with these people anyway?' breathed Sebastian.

'I suspect there are more powerful people behind the Group. I'm still investigating,' said Daniel.

'We must sharpen our strategy to combat this menace,' said Martina in an imperious voice.

Sebastian glared at her, surprised by her calm disposition. 'Martina, this is bigger than we thought.'

'It can't be bigger than seven billion people! These criminals thrive on concealment. All we need to do is reveal their secrets to the masses.'

'Knowledge is power,' said Daniel, in agreement.

'We must be careful not to take on more than we can handle,' said Sebastian trying to rein in his sister's enthusiasm.

'You're right, Sebastian. We will be careful,' said Martina. 'This is a gigantic fraud by a powerful company.'

Daniel concurred with a nod.

Martina changed the subject. 'How's security at Devilund?'

'It's the one thing that has been to my advantage,' said Daniel. 'Grenzken is consumed by his research. He is ignorant about security and technology. He uses an inexpensive security company for his surveillance solutions. It's an aging system and easy to manipulate.'

'You did a brilliant job getting Anna out,' said Martina.

'I had to get her out. She had suffered too long. It was early morning, and I was alone. I saw the laundry man and got an idea. I froze all surveillance cameras, making it appear like a malfunction. For a small fee the laundry man agreed to take Anna to Althonat Hospital. She was too sick; he almost refused but I persuaded him. I told him to ask for Dr Jonas Eneroth.'

'She was comatose for weeks,' said Martina. 'We didn't think she would make it. She is doing well.'

'Nicholas became my next challenge,' said Daniel. 'Grenzken put him on a cocktail of drugs recommended by Rangor. At first he lapsed into a zombie state as if he'd succumbed to some lethal poison. Then he became hyperactive; for days he never slept a wink. Grenzken talked about intervening with brain surgery. I became desperate. That was when I sent a distress signal.'

'You did well,' said Martina. 'Though sadly we lost Torsten in the process.'

'Unfortunate circumstances played against us at the eleventh hour,' said Daniel.

'That was tragic,' said Sebastian. 'He was a great resource and a good friend. Having been there from the onset of the company, he knew everything about Althonat Global.'

'We don't know who did it, but I think it was Helmut. He is Grenzken's henchman,' said Daniel as he took another bite of pie. 'He does all kinds of odd jobs. Grenzken has him hooked on medication. He can be volatile one minute and depressive the next. He does the most bizarre things at times. He can be out all night only to return dirty and sweaty.'

'Dirty and sweaty,' said Martina, lifting her brow in a worrisome expression.

'He is the one who put a brick through your windscreen at Ribbyburg and disabled your brakes. He works as a watchman at Ribbyburg Clinic sometimes. His job is to clear any vehicle parked within the vicinity of the Clinic. And he has a photographic memory. He never forgets a license number.'

'It's disturbing to exploit a mentally unstable creature like Helmut,' said Sebastian.

'How many inmates are in Devilund Clinic?' asked Martina.

'At any one time, it could be fifteen to twenty,' said Daniel. 'The sad thing is inmates are dying. No one leaves Devilund alive.' His voice broke on the last words.

'I know,' said Martina. 'But we must build a watertight case. Highly placed officials are involved in this insane project.'

'And don't forget,' said Daniel, 'the toxic biological elements in Life-Vaccine are causing widespread genetic mutations in growing numbers of people, causing illness, chronic diseases and cancer. We must act fast. This might be the beginning of the extinction of humankind.'

'It is a sterilizing agent too,' said Martina, with a shudder in her body.

Sebastian ran his fingers through his hair, unsettled by what he heard.

The trio gazed at one another. A despairing silence felling upon the room. Martina froze inside.

'What about Fabian Franzen, the witch hunter?' asked Sebastian. 'What is he up to?'

'He's angered by Althonal's success,' Daniel said. 'grabbing market shares from Citaraph, causing a pharmaceutical war, opening a rift in the medical community, turning the masses against Life-Vaccine, stirring public unrest, making his job difficult. In fact, it's not only him. To be clear, the Group are enraged.'

'This Group seems to have grown since you started your assignment,' said Sebastian.

'Yes, it has, but it's still a small covert Group of people working under Citaraph with a secret motive against humanity. Tord, the police inspector, and Lilian, the permanent secretary joined after I started there. But as I said, I think the Group is backed by powerful insidious wealthy investors.'

'Shadowy elitists!' said Martina. 'together with corrupt politicians and greed-driven Citaraph, are using subverted science to control the population.'

'Let's not jump to conclusions,' said Sebastian. 'Let's wait until Daniel gets more facts.'

Martina thought a lot of things but decided to follow her brother's advice.

'I understand Fabian bought a house here, in Väddö,' said Daniel, 'to keep a keen eye on you, Dr Edgren.'

A flicker of rage crossed Martina's face. 'What house?' she asked.

'The house Rangor is living in,' said Daniel. 'Fabian leases it to him.'

'Rangor told me he bought it,' said Martina.

'No, he can't buy property here,' said Daniel. 'He's a man who needs to move at short notice.'

'So, the house belongs to Fabian?' said Martina, for emphasis, disbelief in her voice.

'Yes,' said Daniel.

The things Daniel said were distressful but nevertheless must be heard. He was their surveillance guru, their eyes and ears. His words were pure gold.

Sebastian sighed and cupped his chin in his hand, frowning. 'The son of a bitch,' he said. 'How long is he going to hunt us down?'

'These people are obsessed, Sebastian,' said Martina. 'Fabian especially. He is beset, and he will die trying to derail us, but he will never succeed. He forgets Althonat Global is doing a great job – curing disease, educating lots of people about well-being, setting them free from lifelong medication, from bogus medication that condemns them to a slow death. Today people are aware of good medical delivery, and they're able to make good choices about their health.'

'No one can compete with that,' said Sebastian. 'Even Fabian can understand that, but it's his ego. His ego has been hurt.'

Daniel opened his Saddleback bag, retrieved a large brown envelope, and handed it to Martina. 'I've got more stuff on Fabian, the kind we need to wreck him. He's an arrogant, tenacious, vicious man, and you'll need high-velocity artillery to bring him down.'

'What could that be?' asked Martina. The surprise in her voice was total. She took the envelope from Daniel and clutched it carefully as if it was a valued prize.

'You don't have to open it now,' cautioned Daniel.

Sebastian shifted in his chair, trying to muffle his amusement without success. At last he erupted in laughter.

'Sebastian, it's not funny,' said Martina, scolding him.

'Maybe we should bring in tanks, too,' said Sebastian, ignoring Martina's stern gaze. In the end, it struck her as funny too, and she burst out laughing. They were all amused by the military jargon.

The laughter died down instantly as voices were heard from outside the house. The sounds grew louder and became agitated, as if in an ongoing wrangle.

Sebastian sprang to his feet. 'I'll go check,' he said, but Martina was already out of the door.

Daniel stayed, his military mind pondering his next manoeuvre. He got up, walked to the window, and carefully peeked from behind the drapes. He saw two security guards, as well as Martina and Sebastian, talking to Rangor, their faces glum and stony, snowflakes dripping on them. He could not hear what they were saying but Martina looked frantic. Her lips moved fast, and her hands flew in wild gestures. She suddenly moved towards Rangor, invading his personal space. Rangor raised a clenched fist at her. The guards stepped in, grabbed him, and escorted him off the property.

In a disturbed state, Sebastian and Martina returned to the study. Without doubt, the relationship with their alien neighbour was deteriorating, and pressure was building up. The battle could get uglier.

As Martina entered the study, she gazed at Daniel standing in the middle of the room. Her memory strayed to the past when things had got bad between Pappa and Stellan. Daniel had visited with Sebastian from the military academy. His background as a biochemist and later a military intelligence and security officer, in the Swedish Army, appealed to Pappa. He admired his intelligence, calm poise and articulate manner – qualities valued for undercover work – and offered him the job. Daniel was aware of the challenges and risks involved, but the prospects of the job excited him, and the financial end was staggering. He left the military and took a clandestine position at Devilund Clinic. The position fitted well with what Grenzken had advertised, an assistant researcher with biochemistry background.

'Is everything okay?' asked Daniel, drawing Martina from her reverie.

'It was Rangor, looking for his dog,' said Martina.

'At this hour?' asked Daniel. 'I hope he didn't see me come.'

'Ah, no, he couldn't have,' said Sebastian. 'He can't see the front of our house from his place, and the guards have been patrolling the grounds.'

'Watch out for him,' said Daniel. 'He's under investigation in the States, as you know. He prefers to keep a low profile, away from authority, and uses affluent Swedes to get by. But under the surface he's ruthless.'

'That's true,' said Martina, nodding slowly. 'The reports you sent me about his work on the children in Ribbyburg are atrocious. He is committing crimes against humanity.'

'It seems he is the head of operations at Ribbyburg and Devilund,' said Daniel. 'He is very knowledgeable about whatever goes on there.'

Martina wondered if that was the reason why he'd been so interested in Botanik Herbier the first time he came to her office, after the funeral. Maybe he wanted to use it for some sinister purpose on the sick children.

'One more thing,' said Daniel. 'I saved the best for last.'

'What?' asked Martina.

Daniel dipped his hand in the Saddleback bag and retrieved a document sealed in a plastic bag. It looked worn out and was written on special company paper with the Althonat Global logo, the frangipani flower, embossed in the top left-hand corner.

Sebastian leaned forward in his seat to get a closer look at the document. Martina moved to sit next to Daniel. Her heart throbbed erratically and her mouth went dry as she tried to understand what it was.

Daniel held the document in his hand and said, 'The other half of Rensblad formula. The half Stellan stole from your father and sold to Citaraph.'

Martina gasped. Sebastian's mouth moved wordlessly.

'Dear Lord, Daniel, it can't be,' cried Martina. 'It can't be.'

'It's a true original,' said Daniel.

Sebastian's shaking hand snatched the document from Daniel's hand and studied it long and hard. At last he breathed, 'I'll be damned.'

He looked at it again, recognizing ingredients in the formula: names of herbs, roots, and plants, with the requisite quantities. Even the logo, the stamp, and Pappa's signature looked genuine, just as they did the last time he saw them in Hässelved.

'It's an original, all right,' he finally said. 'With the two halves in our custody, we can manufacture Rensblad, the natural wonder drug.' He lifted the paper and put it close to his nose, and then added, 'It even smells like Hässelved.'

'What a miracle,' shrieked Martina as she got up and danced, humming a victory song. 'Pappa would have been ecstatic.'

Sebastian regarded his lyrical little sister and then, stared back at Daniel. They both beamed, amused by Martina's enthralled excitement. Martina leaned over, clasped her hands around Daniel's cheeks, gazed into his soul, and kissed his lips. Daniel smiled.

'Well, Martina, we are set for bigger business,' said Sebastian, exhilaration in his voice.

'I'm delirious,' said Martina.

'Daniel, I…I don't know what to say,' said Sebastian. He got to his feet, extended his hand to Daniel, and pulled him up into a hug.

'May I ask how you got it?' asked Sebastian.

'It was easy. It was luck,' said Daniel. 'Grenzken drinks. One day he came in drunk and upset about something but determined to wrap up a vaccine that night. He shifted the medicine cabinet, in the lab, and opened the safety box in the wall. Funny he could remember the combination in the state he was in. Earlier on, surveillance transmitters had activated when he entered the lab. I watched everything on my computer monitor, in my room. When he was done, he locked the safety box, replaced the cabinet, and forgot the formula on his desk. He must have been very tired. I went and took it. To this day I don't think he knows it's gone. If he does, then he hasn't told Citaraph for fear of repercussions.'

'Stellan made a bundle of money on that formula,' said Martina, recollecting the dossier holding copies of wire transfer slips showing millions of dollars funnelled to Stellan's secret offshore bank account from Citaraph.

'Well, now we have it back,' said Sebastian. 'He can't make any more money on it.'

'Before I forget, Daniel,' said Martina. 'The contents of the hypodermic needle Grenzken tried to inject you with when he discovered Anna missing – analysis showed it was a lethal biochemical weapon.'

'What was in it?' asked Daniel, startled.

'It is a vaccine, similar to Life-Vaccine but more deadly; a silent killer that causes immune system malfunction, bringing on an arsenal of diseases that could have gradually killed you in no time. It is untraceable in the body.' She retrieved a paper from her pile and handed it to him.

Daniel took it and gazed at it intently. 'It is a covert murder weapon,' he said.

'With a gruesome twist of cannibalism,' added Martina. 'Aborted human foetal tissues were one of the ingredients.'

'If that vaccine was used on the population, humanity would be wiped out immediately, and no one would know the cause,' said Daniel.

Sebastian heaved a sigh and turned to Daniel. 'Daniel, you have to be watchful of the mad scientist, and I'm not talking about surveillance but about your safety. Hopefully, it won't be long before we move against Citaraph. What do you say, Martina?'

'We have ample information,' said Martina. 'But we lack witnesses. The inmates subjected to these Gestapo-style trials could be witnesses, but they don't survive the ordeal. We have Anna but we need more inmates who can testify in a lawsuit.'

'My surveillance team is looking into that,' said Daniel. 'We plan on saving more victims.'

Talking about the deceased 'inmates' jolted Martina's memory back to the dark forest and the dead girl in a shallow grave. 'Daniel, what happens to bodies of expired inmates?'

'When inmates die, the bodies are kept in a cold room. Whoever disposes of them comes in through a secret entrance. I'm yet to confirm who it is, but my colleague, Bo, told me the bodies are dumped in a nearby forest.'

Martina cupped her mouth with her hand, shocked but not surprised, and on second thought was happy she had reported the dead girl to the police. 'Police are investigating that forest,' she said.

Daniel stared at Martina lost for words.

'You've got a hell of a job ahead of you, Daniel,' said Sebastian. 'You'll have to set up cameras in that cold room.'

'It will be rewarding to rid the world of these murderers,' said Daniel.

At past midnight Daniel rose to leave. He reminded Martina to keep an eye on Anna. 'They're searching for her corpse. If they don't find it, they will figure out where she is and come looking.'

'What about you?' asked Martina, with a worried expression on her face.

'I'll be all right. There's much to do,' said Daniel, then he hesitated a moment. 'I almost forgot,' he said. 'You must scan Anna for a tracking microchip. It might be embedded in her arm or hand. Remove it as soon as possible.'

'A tracking microchip?' Martina said with a gasp.

'That's a gross invasion of personal integrity,' said Sebastian.

'Yes, inmates are tracked like cattle in case they escape,' said Daniel. 'That's the extent of those twisted minds.'

Sebastian picked up his phone from the table and dialled a number. In minutes the black BMW arrived in the driveway.

'Take care, Daniel, and thank you,' said Martina shaking his hand.

'Thank you, Dr Edgren,' said Daniel, and then turning to Sebastian, 'It was good seeing you, buddy.' Sebastian nudged his shoulder and smiled.

Grabbing his Saddleback bag, Daniel walked out to the BMW. It was snowing heavily. The chauffeur started the engine and accelerated, quickly disappearing into darkness.

'I think I'd better turn in,' said Sebastian.

'No, let's check the high-velocity artillery he said would bring Fabian down,' said Martina. 'I'm dying to know what it is. Aren't you?'

She ripped open the envelope and pulled out photos, a DVD, and Daniel's report.

In the first photo were Fabian, Tord, and two young girls. They stood outside a five-star hotel. That man again, with a hawkish nose, the Police Inspector, thought Martina as she remembered what he had done to Lisa. Martina quivered. Another photo showed the inside of a hotel suite with four men and the two girls. They were drinking, and the girls were half naked.

She handed the photo to Sebastian and paged through the report. She threw it on the table, disgusted by what she read.

'What is it?' asked Sebastian.

'Dasha and Natalia. Human trafficking,' said Martina. 'Fabian and Tord are trafficking young girls for prostitution. After that they sell them into research to the unhinged scientist, Grenzken.' It did not surprise her that Fabian, the director of National Board of Health and Welfare, and Police Inspector, Tord Stenbeck, were acquainted and that their interests were bizarre. What a freakish combination.

'How about the DVD?' asked Sebastian.

'You don't want to watch that, Sebastian,' said Martina. 'To judge from these photos, it must be some kind of orgy or sex party.'

'I'll watch it tomorrow,' said Sebastian, a distraught look on his face. 'I want to see how low our highly placed officials can sink.'

'I'll stay a while,' said Martina. 'This material is more than high-velocity artillery. It is self-propelled anti-aircraft missiles. It will bring Fabian and Tord crawling out of the dense canopies where they are hiding.'

'It's deeply incriminating material,' said Sebastian, and then, 'You're certainly catching up on military jargon.' He laughed and walked out of the room. Martina laughed too.

They did not often indulge in laughter, but when they did, it helped relieve the pressure.

Chapter 31

Two days later the Strömstedts awoke to a snow-capped landscape and clear skies. Henrietta and the children brought luggage to the staircase landing. Martina and Sebastian sat in the study, wrapping up last-minute touches about business.

'Talk about miraculous luck,' said Martina. 'Rensblad was a huge surprise.'

'You'd better get to Switzerland if you are going to make anything of Rensblad,' said Sebastian.

'I'll be speaking at the World Economic Forum in Davos next week,' said Martina. 'I'll fly to Zurich and visit the bank vault at Credit Suisse.'

'Remember Friends of Peter, father's network of friends,' said Sebastian, 'in case you need their expertise or resources. There are there to help you. And Martina' – he fixed her with a serious look – 'stop stepping up to men threatening combat. You did it with Stellan and then Rangor. It's detrimental. Leave it to Security.'

'I know,' said Martina 'It's just that I get so mad.'

'You can't do that,' said Sebastian. 'Let the guards do their job. That's why you pay them so well.'

Martina's phone vibrated on the table. She picked it up and pressed the button. 'Martina.' she answered and listened. 'Hi, Diana, how are you doing?'

A pause.

'Is everything under control?'

A longer pause.

'That's great. Well done. Okay, see you next week.' Martina hung up.

'That was Diana in Uganda. The contaminated cell antidote affected many people, and there were a few deaths, but the problem is under control.'

'That's one hell of a lady. You should give her a salary raise,' said Sebastian, getting to his feet. 'I don't want to keep Henrietta and the kids waiting.'

The north wind started blowing as Martina and Joachim said goodbye to Sebastian and family. 'Take care now,' said Sebastian, as he relaxed his hug on his sister. 'Use the security measures Daniel devised for you, and remember I'm just a phone call away.' He turned to Joachim, ruffled his hair, and said, 'Joachim, come and visit us sometime.' Joachim smiled.

The Lexus roared into motion. Henrietta and the girls waved. The car picked speed and disappeared in the early morning mist, heading towards Arlanda Airport.

'Mamma, I'll miss Stephanie and Pamela.'

'Me too, but you'll go visit them.'

'Can I?' asked Joachim in excitement.

'Of course you can.' She looked down at Joachim, sadly realizing how lonely he would be without the girls. She yearned for another child, a sibling for Joachim. Jonas was right about taking their relationship to the next level.

In the evening, Thomas arrived at Slottsville house to pick up Joachim, only to be accosted by security demanding identification. When he got into the house, he fumed.

'What is it with security?' he asked Martina, his tone cold and accusatory.

'We've tightened security around Althonat Global facilities.'

'Why?'

'It's complicated. I can't talk about it,' said Martina. 'Company policy.'

'Company policy…who cares about company policy!' said Thomas. 'I only care about my son's safety. You put my son in the midst of a security siege, and you give me crap about company policy?'

'What's going on with you, Thomas?'

'Why is the house besieged by security?'

'I said, I can't talk about it.'

'You can't tell me? Then, I'll file for full custody.'

That got Martina's full attention. She straightened up and regarded him. 'Wait, what do you mean, file for full custody? I told you it was a company issue.'

'I want you to tell me why, or I'll drag you to court and get full custody of Joachim.'

'You can't do that,' said Martina, her words trailing off in desperation.

'Of course, I can,' he said staring at her.

'Joachim is safe with me, I promise. If his life was in any danger, I would freely give him to you.'

They stood facing each other in the kitchen, Martina leaning back against the kitchen sink. Thomas gazed into her fathomless blue eyes and sank into them. He took her warm hand, and caressed it. Martina stilled and drew in a soft sharp breath. She lowered her gaze to the floor, avoiding the sting in his eye that drew her in. He spread out his fingers, entwining them with hers. She tried to pull away her hand, but he held it. The mood changed.

'You feel it – the electric charge, the titillating sensation,' said Thomas, pulling her chin up, drinking in her luscious eyes. He inched closer to her. She could smell him, that familiar whiff of Thomas she had once been used to.

'Stop it, Thomas.' She tried to resist his unwelcome advances, to block the enticing sensation spreading through her body, but it persisted and slowly grew.

Thomas ignored her protests, He wrapped his arms around her waist so their bodies touched, and their faces were a breath apart.

'Why do you deny us? My love for you, your love for me?' asked Thomas. 'It's there. You feel it as much as I do. And it was there in Landegrind, when we touched accidentally. You felt it then, and you feel it now.'

A sense of shame and guilt washed over Martina. She would rather not hear those words, but the way he said them made her wish they were not true. Fragmented thoughts ran through her mind. She questioned how he could evoke such feelings in her. She thought she had gotten over him.

She stepped sideways, away from him, and he let her go. 'Promise you'll leave as soon as I tell you about the security issue.'

Thomas gazed at her in a daze. He did not hear what she said. He was thinking, *God, she is beautiful.* 'Martina, I asked you once to remarry me. I'm asking you again.'

Why is he doing this? Why can't he leave? 'The security issue stemmed partly from Althonat's problems with competitors and partly from people who hated Pappa's work. Joachim will be safe here.'

Thomas shook his head to clear his clouded mind, wondering what she was talking about. He lost track of his thoughts, overwhelmed by the silken touch of her hand, her body against his. Ripples of anger, rejection, and affection ripped through his body as he tried to make sense of his feelings.

'Why can't you accept my love?' he asked again, his voice ragged and breathless, his eyes ablaze, tempting her.

'I think you should leave.'

'Martina, you keep changing the subject, but that won't help. I love you.'

Joachim barged into the kitchen, declared he was finished packing, and asked would they please leave because he wanted to play ice hockey with Leo at the net. Thomas hurriedly stepped out of the kitchen and told Joachim to get his backpack; moments later they left.

In her bedroom Martina lay on the bed, disturbed by Thomas' relentless proposal of remarriage. He was right: she still felt something for him. But was it possible to feel two different kinds of love for two different men at the same time? One strong and beguiling; the other simmering, persistent, and unobserved, like an undercurrent.

She startled at the ringing of her phone. She picked it up from the bedside table and answered, 'Martina.'

It was Jonas' captivating voice. 'Darling, how was your holiday?'

'Jonas, you are back!'

'Yes, I am.'

'Oh, darling, it was wonderful to spend time with Sebastian and family. How about yours?'

'It was great to see family and friends,' said Jonas. 'Listen, can we have dinner at my place tomorrow?'

'That's a brilliant idea. I'll check my schedule, and call you back?'

'Please, do that. I've missed you.'

'I missed you too, darling.'

'Call me.'

'I will.'

'Good night, darling.'

'Good night, sweetheart.' She hung up.

She slumped on the bed, her mind musing again on Jonas and on what she felt for Thomas tonight. She wondered if that was cheating on Jonas. Partly, she was angry with Thomas for pressuring her into remarrying him, reviving feelings she thought were long gone; still, she also understood that it was harder for him to let go. She sighed. Her heart was taken by Jonas, but she did not know how to tell Thomas. What they'd had was special, but it was over and done with. Why couldn't he accept that, marry someone else and get on with his life?

Her life, in any case, was complicated and heaped with misery, and her future with Althonat Global was hidden by dark clouds. She hoped Thomas would not become another thorn in her side. She yawned, jumped off the bed, and got into her pink flannel pyjamas. She slid under the warm satin covers and drifted into unsettled sleep.

*****

In the morning Martina went through the piles of correspondence stacked on her office desk. Diana, her finance director, sat across from her, filling her in on her work in Uganda.

'It was good I got there in time,' said Diana with a smile, revealing beautiful, even teeth. 'The authorities were beginning to panic, and the local media were digging deep into the scandal. I managed to reassure the authorities, restore confidence in our products, and quiet public unrest. The arrival of the new batch of cell antidote helped. The sick got better, and we were back on top of things.'

'You did an amazing job, Diana,' said Martina. She studied her for a moment and continued, 'Regarding the position you applied for, Deputy CEO at Althonat Global: I see you as the leading candidate. Are you still interested?'

Diana's face lit up. 'Yes, I'm very interested. I'd be delighted to serve you at that level.'

'The job is yours, then. But keep it to yourself until the paperwork is completed.'

Diana left and Pia, Martina's personal secretary, popped her head around the door. 'Your flight for Davos leaves at four tomorrow afternoon,' she said. 'Security will be here to pick you up at two.'

'Thank you, Pia,' said Martina.

As Pia returned to her office, senior researcher Leila Eklund came in, saying she wanted time with Martina.

'Just hold on, I'll check,' said Pia. She left the room and returned almost immediately. 'Go in, she will see you.'

Leila smiled and hurried to Martina's office, where she knocked on the door.

'Come in,' said Martina.

Leila marched in, wrapped in a tight black miniskirt, a suggestive low-necked top, skyscraper heels and crimson lipstick.

'Take a seat,' said Martina.

Leila sat, flapped her mascared eyelashes, and crossed her legs, exposing thick thighs.

'Yes,' said Martina, giving her full attention, but rather disappointed in her dress code.

'It's regarding the position of Deputy CEO at Althonat Global. I applied, but I hear rumours you're considering Diana for the position. I would like to get your feedback.'

'You believe in rumours, Leila?'

'Not really, but I'm very interested in this position, and if I don't get it…'

'Then what?' quizzed Martina, irritated by her presumptive threat.

'Then I…I don't know what I'll do,' said Leila, a nervous smile on her face; she felt intimidated by Martina's angry voice.

Martina regarded the little tart sitting before her and wanted to fire her on the spot. Images of her standing in a dark corner with creepy Fabian, at the Nobel banquet, came to mind. She understood she must act fast and deal with her.

'Yes, it's true. I'm considering Diana for the position.'

'What?' Leila sprang up, her face twisted in rage. 'I'm more qualified than she is.'

'Will you please sit down?' said Martina. Leila sank back into her seat. 'I understand your disappointment, but we need you in the research department. Besides, Diana is better qualified for the position, considering her background and experience.'

'What background and experience?' said Leila settling in her seat again.

'She was CEO in Althonat Africa, and she's my finance director now. Also she speaks Chinese and Russian. China and Russia are major markets we plan to focus on in the future.'

Leila rolled her eyes, feeling diminished, having to concede that competition was tough. 'At least you could raise my salary,' she said softly.

'I can't do that,' said Martina. 'In fact I wanted to speak to you about your work. Your performance on Botanik Herbier is falling behind schedule. Why?'

'It's the working conditions…Sten, my Chief in the Research department, keeps asking me to help with other projects.'

'Sten told me he hired two assistants to help with your backlog.'

'Yes, that may be true, but there's so much to do, and there's never enough time.'

'You're busy doing other things, aren't you? You're not focusing on your work.'

'I'm not doing anything else. I work, but no one appreciates what I do.'

'Leila, we can't have it like this. Goals have to be met, and projects completed on time.'

Leila became silent. Her angry eyes fixed on Martina.

'You understand what I'm saying?'

'No, I don't. I think it's time I considered other options.'

'What other options?' asked Martina.

'It's none of your business,' said Leila as she sprang up and stormed out of the room.

Martina exhaled. She picked up the phone and dialled. A voice answered. 'Sten.'

'Sten, can you come in here a minute?' said Martina.

In minutes Sten Lindholm, Chief of Research department, came in and took a seat.

'I'm moving Leila to administration,' said Martina.

'You can't do that,' said Sten. 'She's one of the best I have. What am I going to do with Botanik Herbier?'

'You'll find a replacement.'

'That will stall the project further,' said Sten. 'Why, what happened?'

'She's a security risk,' said Martina. 'We can't have her working on Botanik Herbier.'

'What will she do in administration?'

'Talk to HR; they will find something for her.'

'It will devastate her. She loves her work, and she's good when she's attentive. But recently she has been unfocused and difficult to deal with.'

'Fix it, as soon as possible.'

'As you wish,' said Sten, 'but I can't promise we'll launch Botanik Herbier as scheduled.'

'We'll see about that,' said Martina.

Sten left.

*****

It was past six when Martina arrived at Strandvägen, in Jonas' penthouse. Jonas met her in the foyer and walked her into the penthouse. In the hallway he removed her coat and draped it over a hanger on the railing. He hadn't seen her since the Christmas holidays.

Martina set her bag down and smoothed her red Dior square-necked dress with her hands.

'You look stunning in red,' said Jonas.

Martina said nothing but put her arms around his neck and delicately kissed his jaw, stubble, and lips. He pulled her in and tightened his grip on her, deepening the kiss. She teased his tongue with hers and sucked his lower lip.

'Hmm, that was steamy,' said Jonas. 'To what do I owe this sensuous display of passion? It can't be that you missed me that much.'

'Deliriously happy,' she said with a twinkle in her eyes. 'Of course I missed you tons, and I'm glad you're back.' She dipped her hand in her bag and flashed a bottle of Bollinger. 'It's celebration time!' she announced, a ravishing smile on her face.

Jonas furrowed his brow but smiled, though not understanding her good spirits. 'What's the occasion?'

'Fix me a drink, and I'll tell you.'

He took her hand and walked her to the kitchen area. There he popped open the champagne without spilling a molecule. He pulled two glasses from the cupboard and filled them. He handed her a glass, clinked his glass with hers, and they took a sip.

'Wow…lovely, it tastes like stars,' said Martina.

'How do you know how stars taste?'

'I know, because they sparkle like champagne.'

Jonas smiled. 'That rhymes like beautiful poetry.'

'Shall we eat? I'm famished,' said Martina. 'You cooked?'

'Of course I cooked,' said Jonas. 'You're teasing me.'

'Ah, ah! I know you're a good cook,' said Martina. She took another sip at her champagne.

They talked while they ate. Martina told him about Torsten's funeral.

'How was it?

'It was beautiful, though sad,' she said. 'We opened an education trust fund for his grandchildren. Greta, his wife, was touched.'

'She should be.'

'And she will receive Torsten's salary plus pension for the rest of her life.'

'That was generous.'

'Ah, I love this,' gasped Martina munching cod and spinach. 'It all tastes splendid.' She took another sip at the champagne. The crisp flavour swamped her mouth. She smiled.

'What?' asked Jonas.

'The food and the Bollinger, what else?' said Martina. 'It's superb.'

Jonas regarded her, still mystified by her youthful intonations and excitable mood.

'Now, will you tell me what we're celebrating, so I can catch up with your high spirits?'

Martina laughed and gazed into his amorous brownish eyes turning green. She sighed. 'You're right, my darling. It's Rensblad.'

'What about Rensblad?'

'The other half of the formula stolen by Stellan. We got it back.'

Jonas dropped the cutlery on his plate. He leaned back in his chair, and his brow lifted in wonder. 'What!' he said.

'Yes, I know. That's what I thought too.'

'That is incredible. You're right. This does call for a celebration.' He took her hand and kissed it. They drank some more champagne, savouring the moment.

'I called yesterday,' said Jonas, 'but your phone was deactivated till late evening.'

'I was with Joachim. Thomas came to pick him up.'

A flicker of annoyance tempered Jonas' mood with disappointment. He suddenly remembered the eyeglasses Thomas had forgotten in Landegrind house. What was Martina up to with the man?

Suddenly he felt a sense of suffocation and wanted air. 'How about taking a walk with me?' He pushed his chair back and got up.

'Now?' asked Martina. 'It's snowing!'

'Yes, now, we need fresh air.'

'Okay.' She got to her feet, surprised by his sudden change in disposition. Then she hesitated as if recalling something.

'What is it?' asked Jonas. 'Are you coming?'

'I didn't tell you about the security situation.'

'What about it?'

'Security has been tightened around Althonat Global facilities, and I'm afraid that includes me.'

'You mean because of the break-in at Landegrind house?'

'Yes, that and other things,' said Martina. 'Christer, the new Security Director, thinks the threat is real.'

'Hell,' said Jonas as he stalked to the hallway.

He held out her mink coat for her. She slid into it and buttoned up. 'It's you I care about,' he said as he planted a kiss on her forehead. 'They can beef up all the security they want as long as they don't stop me from seeing you.'

'I don't think it will come to that,' said Martina.

'If it comes to that, we'll have to get married,' said Jonas. 'I want you to make an honest man of me.'

'Marry?'

'Yes, Martina, you marry me. I want you to be my wife.'

Oh my, he's talking marriage again.

The two security guards, Simon and Tobias, waited in the Volvo outside. When they saw Martina, they quickly scrambled out to fall in step behind her and Jonas, keeping a safe distance. Temperatures were bone freezing, but the air was clear and crisp. They crossed the street over to Djurgården Bridge and walked along the waterfront hand in hand to Skansen. They came to Sisters' Helin Voltaire Café and went inside. A number of people sat drinking coffee and talking.

Jonas ordered herbal tea for Martina, coffee for himself, and two fresh fruit tartlets. The café was small but warm and cosy. Simon and Tobias sat to one side in full view of Martina's table, as if they were not in the same company.

'I'm going to Davos tomorrow,' said Martina as she ate her fruit tartlet.

'Switzerland?'

'Yes, I'm going to speak on health at the World Economic Forum.'

'When will you be back?'

'On Friday.'

'I think I can survive a few days without you,' said Jonas, as he regarded her, thinking how strikingly beautiful she looked with that pinkish glow on her cool cheeks.

Martina sipped her tea and suddenly furrowed her brows. She leaned forward across table so their heads almost touched. 'I almost forget. You need to scan Anna for a tracking microchip,' she whispered.

'Tracking microchip?' said Jonas, his eyes turning black. 'You mean like a microchip implant with GPS tracking capabilities, locating latitude, longitude, speed, and direction of movement?'

'Yes. Check her hands or upper arms,' said Martina. 'Call Dr Nasiro, and ask him do it tonight.'

'What a barbaric thing to do,' said Jonas. 'It's distasteful and unethical.'

'Shh…shh,' said Martina. Glancing around, she reassured herself that no one had overheard them, but in a far corner sat a broad-shouldered man in dark leather jacket with spikes of metal on the shoulders and front. He studied at Martina from beneath the black broad-brimmed hat that covered half his face. His evil glare seemed to hint at an obscure, sinister purpose. She wondered why he kept the hat on in the warm café. A dusky blush rose in her cheeks, and she shuddered.

Curious to see what agitated her, Jonas started to turn for a look, but she quickly reprimanded him not to look.

'Don't turn. Continue talking,' whispered Martina. 'It seems we've been followed.'

A frozen stare registered on Jonas' face, and his lips tightened. 'Signal Simon that we're leaving.'

'No, we don't want to make it obvious,' said Martina. 'Keep talking.'

'Martina –'

'Please, Jonas, talk to me,' she said, her voice nervous and faint.

'You want to talk? Then let's talk.' There was a deep melancholic sound to his tone. She knew he was angry. 'What was Thomas doing in Landegrind?' he smirked. 'The day he forgot his eyeglasses there.'

'That's unfair,' thundered Martina.

'No…you tell me,' said Jonas, raising his voice. 'The man is your ex-husband. Why were you socializing with him?'

'Keep your voice down,' Martina murmured, sneaking another furtive glare at the man in the hat. He still glowered at her. He shifted in his chair and then sprang up to walk past their table with a twisted sneer on his lips. He headed for the door. Between the dim lights and his brimmed hat, Martina could not see who he was.

'I asked you a question.'

Martina said nothing but rose and deliberately pushed her chair back so it squeaked on the tile floor, to the irritation of other guests. Faces twisted and turned, angered by her rudeness. 'I'm going home,' she said and walked out into the chilling mix of snow and rain.

Jonas followed her, angry and perplexed. Simon and Tobias fell in step behind them.

They were no sooner out in the blinding snow than they heard a rumbling sound behind them. An explosion of gunfire sprayed bullets, splintering trees metres away from Martina.

A desperate cry from Simon cut the air: 'Martina, down…take cover! Down, get down!'

The confusion made Martina turn her head in time to see a black Dodge van roaring down the sidewalk, bearing down on her at high speed. Gunfire was spitting from the muzzle of a silenced weapon. Jonas grabbed her hand, and they took off in a burst of speed, behind clusters of trees. They flung themselves into a clammy blanket of snow.

The Dodge roared and hovered near the trees, a gun muzzle sticking out through the window, letting off random shots in their direction. They lay still under the chilling snow.

Simon and Tobias raced after the van, spraying gun bullets on its metallic façade, smashing windscreens, unfortunately missing the tires. The van reached an intersection, where it wriggled back on the road, stabilized, and thundered away south on screeching tires.

Simon ran to Martina and Jonas. 'Are you all right?' he asked, anxiously.

They slowly got to their feet, looking like disoriented snowmen. They trudged through thick snow back to the sidewalk. Martina leaned heavily on Jonas, limping from a pain in her ankle.

'Can you walk?' asked Simon as he came to her and took her trembling hand. She gazed at him, terror in her eyes, her face contorted in pain. She opened her mouth to say something but her tongue stayed glued to her dry palate. Tears of fear subsided into silent horror.

'Gunfire,' she finally whimpered and collapsed in Jonas' arms.

'Let's get her to the penthouse, quick,' said Jonas, panting. 'They might come back.'

'Attempted assassination,' breathed Simon. 'We're lucky it was misty with the falling snow.'

'Assassination?' startled Jonas, alarm in his eyes.

Back in the penthouse, Simon was on the telephone reporting to Security Director, Christer Sorenson.

Christer told him reinforcements were on the way to secure the penthouse. He asked if Martina needed medical attention, prompting Simon to hand the phone to Jonas. Martina was in his bedroom, resting.

'How is Martina doing?' asked Christer.

'She's shaken but fine, apart from a mild sprained ankle and a few bruises,' said Jonas.

'Do you think she needs hospitalization?'

'I prefer to keep her here for observation. I've applied ice packs to her ankle and bandaged it up. That should reduce the swelling and stabilize the joint. With herbal anti-inflammatory medication for pain, she should be all right.'

'I'm sending another security team to take over,' said Christer. 'Tell the boys to get back to headquarters as soon as the other team arrives.'

'I will,' said Jonas and hung up. He stalked to the bedroom, anxiety on his face, unsure if Martina would be well enough to travel to Davos. She was asleep. He sat on the side bed, listening to her soft breathing, touching base with his own fearful nerves. He gently smoothed her hair. Someone had tried to assassinate her tonight. *They could have murdered us all.* How was he going to protect the woman he loved? If anything happened to her, it would kill him.

Chapter 32

At Devilund Clinic, Richard immersed himself in morning duties with inmates. He noted the new surveillance system was in place; dome security cameras in inmates' rooms and on hallway walls, including his room and Bo's room. They covered every aspect of space in the Clinic.

Outside were weatherproof outdoor cameras. Richard scratched his head as he marvelled over the concentration of equipment in proportion to area. Could the system be manipulated? The door buzzed, and from the CCTV monitor in his room he saw Tord and Fabian outside.

In the next room, Grenzken startled at their images on camera. He creased his brows, displeased by another one of their sporadic visits. He touched his jaw and winced. It was sore, and he was still angry at Fabian. Nevertheless, he pressed the button on the keypad, and the door opened. Tord and Fabian soon entered his room, leaving the door ajar.

Richard wedged himself outside the door, out of sight, and heard Grenzken ask, 'What is it this time? You want to fight?' Fabian said nothing.

'Anna has been located,' said Tord.

Richard's heart skipped a beat. His instructions to Martina had been specific: to remove the microchip from Anna's body immediately.

There was a deadly silence, and then Grenzken said, 'Oh?'

'Is that all you can say, oh?' asked Fabian, his tone pitched.

'Don't use that tone with me,' said Grenzken. 'I'm just as stunned as you are.'

'Anna was dead, you said; thanks to your reliable staff,' said Tord. 'The bloody idiots lied. You can't trust them. Do you know where we found her?'

Grenzken simply stared at Tord.

'Althonat Hospital.'

'We must go after her,' said Fabian, levelling a fat finger at Grenzken, 'before she breathes a word to that Strömstedt woman. After that we shall deal with you, Grenzken.'

Grenzken tightened his lips, fighting the urge to grab that sausage of a finger and break it in two.

Tord moved and slammed the door shut, curtailing Richard's eavesdropping.

Richard returned to his computer, logged in to his secured mail, and wrote a message. He stabbed the button, hoping Martina was online.

The next morning detectives from Phillip Nsamizi's office arrived at Vittaby Villa. Birgit opened the door and let them in. She offered them seats while she went to get Grenzken.

Grenzken led them to the study. 'We can talk in here,' he said. Confusion and anxiety loomed large in his mind as he struggled to come up with a plan.

'The night of December fifth, there was a shooting and a murder here,' said the first officer. 'Do you remember what happened that night?'

Grenzken paused, sweat beads forming on his forehead. 'I have a diffused memory of that night,' he said. 'What I know is that we had a Christmas party, and there were about ten of us here. In the beginning nothing unusual happened. But then, that's all I remember.'

'We would like to search the house,' said the second officer.

'No,' said Grenzken.

'No? Why not?' asked the first officer.

'Because you've no right.'

'Then we shall return with a search warrant,' said the first officer, and they left.

Grenzken strolled to Birgit's office and slumped into one of her chairs, sweat running down his face as if someone had doused him with a bucket of water.

'Fritz, you're smelly,' said Birgit. 'Go get a shower.'

Grenzken grimaced and remained silent.

'What did the detectives say?' asked Birgit, as she offered him a Kleenex paper tissue.

He took the tissue and dabbed his face. 'They said they will return with a search warrant.'

'That definitely is bad news,' said Birgit. 'You must stop them.' Her tone was nonchalant.

'How, Birgit? How the hell am I supposed to do that?'

'You must find a way,' said Birgit. 'You and *the Group* always do.'

Grenzken rose to his feet and strode off to the Clinic, disappointed with Birgit's unsympathetic tone. More often than not she denied him the comfort and empathy he craved when things went wrong. Ever since that night when he'd drunk himself silly, Birgit's attitude had changed towards him; now she treated him as worthless and undeserving of her affection.

In the Clinic, Richard and Bo were discussing the examination results of Gittel and Moa. 'Gittel miscarried twice,' said Bo. 'Moa had not conceived at all. But nonetheless, the new Life-Vaccine had caused their reproductive organs to grow.'

'Holy cow, what a gross disgusting thing,' cried Richard.

A door opened and slammed shut in the corridor. A sharp clatter of shoes on the concrete was heard coming towards them. Grenzken entered the room and closed the door behind him. Richard noticed his soured saturnine mood. Fear seized his bones.

'What're you gaping at?' Grenzken asked.

Silence persisted as Richard and Bo scowled at him, unsure of what ailed him.

'Are you in the habit of lying?' he asked Richard.

Richard knew where he was heading, and he was prepared. 'What do you mean?'

'Anna – you knew she was alive, yet you told me she was dead and buried. Why?'

'That's what I thought at the time,' said Richard. 'Sometimes we make mistakes, but when we need your expert help, you're busy nursing your hangovers.'

'Richard,' scolded Bo.

'I'm talking about your lies,' said Grenzken. 'Do you understand? Lies!'

'Anything could have happened between here and the burial grounds,' Richard said. 'Maybe she came to and escaped. At least she was dead when I put her in the cool room. Have you asked the undertaker who collects the corpses?'

'Or have you asked Helmut?' said Bo.

'It can't be Helmut,' growled Grenzken. 'Everything is Helmut, Helmut. I'm sick and tired of everybody picking on Helmut. I don't want to hear it.'

'Don't bet on it, Fritz,' said Richard. 'He could have done it under sleep-induced hypnosis. You hypnotize him all the time, making him do things, don't you?'

Grenzken stopped in his tracks as he considered what Richard said. He rubbed his chin whiskers and took a deep breath. 'I don't know,' he said, shaking his head.

'Especially if you hypnotize him when you're under the influence of alcohol; it creates a nightmare,' continued Richard.

'If Helmut took Anna, you two would have seen him,' said Grenzken.

'Not if we're busy with inmates,' said Bo. 'And the surveillance cameras have been out of order for some time.'

'All these problems stemmed from a dilapidated security system,' said Richard.

'But the new system will capture all goings and comings,' said Grenzken.

All in all, the conversation raised more questions than answers for Grenzken, casting a morbid shadow over his dealings, a lack of insight in what was going on in the Clinic. The hypnosis scenario scared him. It was true, he hypnotized Helmut sometimes, but only for research purposes. He did not want to venture down that road for fear of what he might find. Everything was fuzzy. He had difficulty remembering things in the past.

Two days later, three detectives returned with a search warrant. They started upstairs in Grenzken's quarters, turning things upside down – opening closets and drawers, searching under beds and carpets, looking for anything suspicious, anything to do with firearms.

In the dining room they found gunpowder residue on furniture surfaces and doorknobs, as well as two bullets imbedded in a wall. Multiple fingerprints were found and lifted, including several larger-than-life prints from many surfaces.

'These huge fingerprints can't be human,' said the technician.

'I think they're Helmut's, my employee,' said Grenzken. 'He's quite huge.'

The detectives went downstairs to Devilund Clinic. The steel door was locked. 'Open it,' said the first detective.

'There is nothing there,' said Grenzken.

'Open, I say.'

Hesitantly Grenzken retrieved keys from his pocket and opened the door. The Clinic was pitch dark, like a black hole. Grenzken fumbled for a light switch on the wall. A dilapidated lamp dangled from the ceiling, dimly lighting the hallway. As he led the way in, a damp clammy smell of mould and decay revolted them. The rooms were empty and dusty and looked unoccupied. Faded, dirty curtains hung up in the small windows. Cobwebs gauzed the corners, and spiders crawled on walls. The detectives searched through all the rooms, finding the same neglect. The gynaecological chair in the examination room and medicine cabinets were gone, replaced by gaping tarnished walls.

'What was this basement used for before?' asked the second detective.

Grenzken's mouth dried up. He swallowed, cleared his throat, and said, 'It was a warehouse. My father used it for storage. He was in the business of exporting medical equipment.'

'And the rooms, what were they used for?' asked the first detective.

'Wor…workers,' stuttered Grenzken, 'my father's workers…stayed here sometimes, mainly immigrants who stayed short periods of time.' He caressed his beard but quickly withdrew his hand when he noticed it was shaking. He clasped his hands behind his back.

'How long ago?' asked the first detective, his cold gaze pinning him.

'Twenty, twenty-five years ago.'

The detective eyed him as if surprised by his answer. 'That long ago?'

'Yes,' said Grenzken, his forehead beginning to glisten with sweat. 'I've been thinking of using the space for business purposes, but nothing has come of it.'

The party continued back to the hallway towards the courtyard. On the courtyard floor the first detective found a bullet. He picked it up, looked at it and put it in a plastic bag.

'You've got guns?' asked the first detective.

'No, I have no guns,' said Grenzken.

'Then where did this bullet come from?'

'I don't know.'

In the parking lot, the third detective searched the ground and saw a shiny piece of metal protruding from muddy snow. He kicked it with his boot. It was a fountain pen. He picked it up, cleaned off the mud, and examined it. It was a golden pen, engraved with the words, *Torsten Widstam, Althonat Global.* 'Here's something,' he hollered.

The other detectives converged on him at a run. 'This pen puts Torsten at the scene of crime,' said the detective. 'We know for sure he was murdered here.'

The first detective turned and just where they stood he noticed a patch of red colour in the snow. 'This could be blood,' he said. 'Take a sample for DNA testing.' The second detective scooped up a sample of red coloured snow and put it in a plastic bag.

On hearing those words, Grenzken felt an irresistible urge to drink. When the detectives left, he retired to his quarters and poured himself a glass of vodka. He stayed there all day, drinking.

Chapter 33

In the Scandinavian sky the difference between day and night was obscured as daylight broke later than usual. In the dark bedroom, Jonas awoke and groped beside him for Martina. She was not there. He got on the phone.

'Martina,' she answered.

'Darling, why didn't you wake me?'

'It was too early,' she said. 'I didn't want to disturb you. I came home to do some work before I leave for Davos.'

'Are you okay?' he said sensing her voice sounded dispirited with a resigned intonation.

'I'm all right. I'll see you on Friday.'

'Martina, you know it was an attempt on your life?'

'I know, darling, but I can't talk right now.'

'How is your sprained ankle?'

'It's still sore but compressed,' said Martina. 'I'll use low heels.'

'Safe journey, darling, and be careful.'

'Bye, honey,' She hung up.

Yesterday's barbarous attack had inflicted languid emotions ranging from mild discontentment to deep grief. It had reawakened a sense of self-searching in her veins, and the doubt that coursed through her blood made her question the path she had chosen. A tear trailed her cheek. The desire to save humanity was well grounded in her heart, but when weighed upon her motherly role to Joachim, it brought on a new dimension of clarity prompting her to redefine her priorities. The dilemma glared at her, and she desperately prayed she could live to master both priorities.

*****

At Althonat Hospital, patients slept, and staff prepared for the morning shifts. A figure in a doctor's white gown emerged from the elevator and walked with a purposeful stride to the entrance of a ward. Two security guards approached her at the entrance and demanded ID. They matched her name against a roster of personnel on duty. Her name was not on the roster.

'Why is your name not on the roster?' asked one guard.

'I'm replacing someone who called in sick,' came the reply. 'An updated list will be sent.'

'Who is sick?'

'Elin Johansson.' Sure enough, the name was on that roster.

'What is that?' asked the other guard, pointing to a device in her gown pocket.

'It's a combination of pen and pager,' came the polite answer.

The guards cleared her for passage. As she walked farther down the corridor she quickened her pace. One of the guards followed her with his gaze, sensing a nervousness to her gait.

The room was dark, but a glint of light gleamed through the bathroom door that was open a crack. Suddenly, Anna awoke to the soft click of a door closing. She looked at the clock on the wall and relaxed, thinking it was too early for her medication, and her Nurse wasn't due for another hour. Maybe it was a doctor who had mistakenly come to the wrong room.

The silhouette of a figure in white gown, dimly visible, silently approached her bed. Anna could not decipher any facial features but guessed from the fluid movement that she was female. She followed the shadow with her eyes. Her heart pounded inside her chest like a drum. The shadow stopped at the foot of the bed, dipped a hand in her gown pocket, and retrieved something that glistened in the faint light.

Anna sat up in the bed. With a frightened tremor in her voice, she said, 'Is it time for medication?'

The elusive figure did not answer but moved alongside the bed towards her. Anna saw the woman's face contorted in rage. Suddenly, the woman grabbed Anna's neck and flashed a hypodermic needle. A high-pitched shrill escaped Anna's mouth. She hitched herself free and bolted out of bed, landing with a thud on the hard floor. She cried in agony and quickly clambered to her feet. The strenuous effort made her every nerve twitch as she visibly shook with fear.

The woman rapidly bridged the gap between them and yanked Anna's upper arm, ready to strike the needle. Memories of Devilund came alive before Anna's eyes, turning her fright into fury. She yanked her arm free, and with a storm of anger snatched the needle and turned it on the woman. With a swift move, she took a tight grip on the collar of the woman's gown and drove her back, pinning her to a wall. The woman screeched in horror, begging for mercy. Her hysterical screams crescendoed through the hallway.

Anna was about to spike the woman's neck with the needle when doors flew open. Medical staff and security guards swarmed the room. Anna dropped the needle and fell into the arms of a Nurse, who whisked her out of the room. The mysterious attacker sprang up with a vicious attack on the guards. A doctor recognized the woman and yelled, 'Leila, what are you doing?' The guards bundled up Leila and took her away.

A medical team arrived to take Anna for scanning.

In late afternoon Diana, the Deputy CEO, appeared in Jonas' office. It was clear from her unsmiling face that this was not a social call. He'd expected her arrival ever since he mailed her a report informing her of the attack on Anna.

Jonas rose to his feet as Diana came in. They were the same age. She was a woman known for her brilliance, well-bred manner, and, as some held, workaholic habits. She was Martina's right hand.

'Diana,' said Jonas amicably.

'Sit down, Jonas.'

Jonas did as he was told. With Martina gone, he knew he was answerable to Diana.

Her manner was as meticulous as her dark brown designer trouser suit, which accentuated her flawless African anthill colour complexion. A streak of light from the table lamp made her dark curly hair gleam like ebony. Like a figure out of central casting with distinguished bearing, she crossed her legs, and sat erect with her hands clasped on one knee.

'Your report made unpleasant reading,' she said. 'I understand Anna was supposed to be scanned last evening. How come it was done this morning?'

Jonas reflected on the dinner with Martina, the late evening walk, and the unforeseen precarious circumstances of last night. He'd simply had no time to arrange the scan. But he knew better than to blabber about his private affairs with Martina, to Diana or anyone else. He knew she was aware of the attempt on Martina's life but unaware he'd spent all night attending to her medical needs.

'It was my miss. I relayed information to Dr Nasiro early this morning.'

'It almost cost Anna her life.'

Jonas did not know what to say.

'Well, see that it doesn't happen again,' said Diana.

'No, of course not,' said Jonas. 'Leila is in police custody pending investigation. According to analysis of the syringe's content, the injection could have killed Anna instantly. It's nothing we've ever seen before. I wonder where Leila got such a lethal drug.'

'We need to move Anna to a safer place,' said Diana. 'Christer will contact you about details of moving her.'

'The security guards that let Leila through have been taken off duty,' said Jonas. 'We've a new team in place.'

'The medical war is escalating,' said Diana as she rose to her feet. 'People will do bizarre things for the most outlandish reasons. We have to be on alert.'

'It won't happen again,' said Jonas as he walked her to the door. He took a moment listening to her high heels click away into the distance. A drench of failure washed over him, anguished by what Martina would say about his fiasco.

The phone rang, interrupting his accusatory thoughts. 'Jonas,' he answered.

'Hi, Jonas. It's me, Viviane.'

The sound of the voice stifled nerves in his spine. It brought back deplorable memories he had long thought were gone and done with.

'Jonas, are you there?' said the voice. 'It's me, Viviane Thos. Remember me?'

'Where did you get my number?'

'Oh boy, that's some enthusiastic answer! I would like to see you.'

'That's a bad idea,' said Jonas.

'Jonas, please. I understand how you feel, but we must talk.'

'I've nothing to say to you.'

'There are circumstances I want to explain. Where can we meet?'

'Never call me again… You hear me?' said Jonas, barely managing to articulate the words. He hung up.

A few minutes later the phone rang again. He knew it was Viviane. He let it ring.

He leaned back in the chair, and clasped his hands behind his head.

'Oh my, what a day!' he murmured to himself.

Chapter 34

At night Grenzken tossed and turned in bed, blinded by a shimmer of light from a hole in the roof of Devilund Clinic. In the middle of the light was a hand dangling a document. He must get the document, but it was too high, just out of reach. He set up a ladder and climbed to get to the document. But the hand kept sliding farther up into the hole, towards the inky sky, taking the document with it.

He was grasping for life itself. He got to the top of the ladder, near the hole. The hand dangled the document in his face, teasing him, and then moved farther up. He took one desperate leap to grasp the document. The hand whisked the document away, spiralling it into the fathomless sky. Grenzken lost his balance and fell on the stony floor.

He startled and sat upright in bed, dripping with sweat. His mouth felt dry. In a daze, he fumbled for the light switch and flipped on a bedside lamp. He looked at the clock next to it: four in the morning. He dragged himself out of bed and went to the kitchen for a glass of water.

He crawled back in bed and lay awake in the dark, unsettled by the dream. It was an important document, something he owned but had lost. From the deep creases of his soaked mind, something troubling came to memory. He kicked the bedding aside and jumped out of bed, showered, and went to the Clinic. It had been restored after the detectives left. Inmates were back, surveillance cameras in place, the rooms looking exactly as they always did. In reality nothing had changed, for he had misled the detectives by showing them another part of the basement which was not in use.

Richard and Bo heard Grenzken open and close his office door. Then they heard a continual banging of bureau doors and cabinet drawers and furniture being shoved aside. After a while, a haunting yowl echoed through the building, bouncing off the walls of Devilund, sparking fear and alarm among inmates and staff. Richard and Bo rushed to Grenzken's door. This time it sounded like a desperate cry from a broken man.

Without warning, the door was flung open. Richard and Bo stepped back, confronted by a rampaging Grenzken. He charged out of the room and paced the corridor, his face twisted in pain.

'Who took the Rensblad formula?' he howled. 'This is sabotage, theft of trade secrets, a crime.'

The two men watched him, saying nothing.

'Did you take it, Richard? Bo, where is it? Tell me…tell me now,' he wailed.

He traversed the corridor again, his hands clasped over his head, roaring and squabbling.

'Stop gaping at me like idiots,' he said. 'Where is the formula?'

'Stop making a fool of yourself,' thundered Bo.

'If you took it, Bo, tell me?' Grenzken said, shaking his open hands, his voice desperate.

Bo scowled at him, wondering what possessed the old man. Richard feigned ignorance.

'You should take better care of your stuff,' said Richard. 'Stop drinking. It's that simple.'

In vivid contrast to the terrible discovery of losing the formula, in sheer despair of attacking Richard and Bo, Grenzken forgot he was a thief himself. Frantically, raving and panting, he wished the floor could open and swallow him.

'Calm down,' said Richard. 'Stop ranting about like a sissy.'

'How dare you call me a sissy?' said Grenzken, turning on Richard and striking him across the face.

Richard snatched his arm, twisted it back and pinned him to a wall. Quickly, he spiked his neck with a hypodermic needle. Grenzken growled and sprawled to the floor, where he lay still, his eyes closed.

Bo shook his head in amazement.

'We'd better get him to bed,' said Richard.

They carried Grenzken's awkward body to an empty room and put him in bed. Richard locked the door. 'He'll have to holler to get out,' said Richard. 'I don't want him waking up and surprising us.'

Some hours later, Grenzken turned in bed and opened his eyes. Confused, he tried to find his bearings. He noticed the confined dark room with a small window near the ceiling and realized he was in an inmate's room. He raised his head and winced, feeling a sharp pain in his neck. His head was throbbing. He glanced at his watch – past five in the afternoon. He must have slept twelve hours. What had Richard injected into him?

Then it all came back to him: the missing formula and the fight with staff. He slumped back in the bed and gazed up the ceiling, distraught over the missing formula. He was the only person with access to the safety box. How had it happened? He dragged himself out of bed, weak and tired as if he'd been working the graveyard shift. He sauntered to the door and turned the knob. It was locked. He squalled in panic, frantic that the boys might have locked him in, to turn him into an inmate.

'Open, open up!' he shouted, banging on the door. He heard a key turn in the lock, and the door opened. Richard stood, frowning down at him. In haste, Grenzken pushed him aside and stormed out of the room, cursing, 'How dare you lock me up like an animal!'

His mind was spinning. He must remember where he'd put the formula; he must find it. He went to his room and turned it upside down, leaving no space or hole unexamined. His face was turning blue when his phone buzzed.

'Grenzken,' he answered.

'Do you know what time it is?' asked Birgit. 'What are you doing in the lab so late?'

'What is it, Birgit?'

'It's Helmut. You must come up.'

Grenzken rushed to the house and found Helmut in a frenzy, pacing the hallway, tearing at his greasy hair, hooting like an owl.

Birgit stood watching him as he seethed in fits of psychotic despair, certain that the raucous noise was a cry for help.

'Calm down, Helmut!' said Grenzken. 'Go to your room, and stay there till I come.' Grenzken went into his study and almost immediately emerged with a medical bag.

'What're you giving him?' asked Birgit.

'It's none of your business.'

'Stop clogging his system with toxic drugs,' said Birgit. 'You should cleanse his system instead of aggravating it with more drugs. Read the Frangipani.'

'You mean unscientific detoxification and quack medicine?'

'No, natural herbal detoxification,' said Birgit. 'It's more scientific than poisonous drugs. It's more aligned with nature and the body.'

'I told you to stop reading silly books and that trash propaganda newspaper,' said Grenzken. 'You're brainwashed, Birgit.'

'Brainwashed?' asked Birgit. 'You'll destroy him just as you've destroyed me.'

Grenzken stopped and eyed her with surprise. 'What do you mean I've destroyed you?'

Birgit ignored him and walked to her quarters.

Hurriedly, Grenzken went after Helmut, who was on his way out to the main entrance. He caught up with him at the door and dragged him back to the east wing.

Arguing with Birgit depressed Grenzken. They never saw eye to eyes on things anymore. He feared they were gliding apart, but he did not understand why Birgit was always angry with him. However, he had his suspicions. It must be Helmut's presence in the house. He must see about moving him to the Clinic.

Grenzken gave Helmut an injection and put him to bed, where he fell asleep immediately.

In her room, Birgit sat in bed reading Martina's book on Wellness. Grenzken came in and sat down on her bedside.

'What did you mean by saying I've destroyed you?' asked Grenzken.

'Don't disturb me.'

'Birgit, I didn't come here to argue with you,' said Grenzken. 'I came to talk.'

'Talk about what?'

'Why are you always angry with me?'

'Leave, I want to be alone.'

'I have something for you,' said Grenzken, as he took a syringe from his jacket pocket. 'You've been miserable all these days. This will help with your depression.'

'You silly rat,' said Birgit. 'I told you, you've destroyed me, and all you offer is more drugs?' She flung the bedclothes aside and pulled up her lace-trimmed negligee, revealing her fat thighs. 'Look...look how big I've become since you started me on that spicy stuff, and that is nothing compared to... that carnal sensation, and itchy rash I have to endure every day.'

'Yes, I know you're needy,' said Grenzken, cunning in his voice. 'That animal lust is good for you, because then I know you are thinking about me. The rash and the weight gain I can help you with. I love you, Birgit.'

'Take your sick love, and get out.'

'This will take away your rash and slim you down,' said Grenzken, flashing the needle again, his eyes dripping with evil.

Suddenly, he lurched onto her and stabbed her arm.

Birgit screeched and kicked him off the bed. He landed on the hard floor with a groan. She threw the book at him, and it landed on his balding head.

'Why did you do that?' she wailed.

'I…I hate to see you depressed,' stuttered Grenzken as he rose from the floor, clutching his head and bottom.

'You're a sick, perverted old man,' said Birgit. 'Get out, and if you come back, I'll kill you.'

Grenzken stood rooted, glowering at Birgit, not quite believing she could kill him.

'I'll be in my quarters if you need me,' he said and sauntered out of the room.

Birgit picked up the syringe from the floor where he'd dropped it and looked at the residue of colourless liquid inside. She put it in her bag and then locked her door.

Benumbed by fear, she realized Grenzken tended towards threatening behaviour. She turned off the light switch and lay in darkness, weighing her options, to stay or to leave him. The situation was getting ugly. She suspected he wanted to control her with drugs.

Without warning, the carnal desire returned stronger than ever before. It must be the injection he had given her. She tried to suppress her bodily need, to avoid him, but in the end she relented, clambered out of bed, and walked to his quarters. The light was still on. She knocked on the door.

Grenzken opened. The ominous smile on his face, as if he had been expecting her, scared her. His dark heart had concocted yet another black deed. She hesitated and then whimpered, 'Fritz, I need you.'

'Come in, Birgit.'

He engulfed her in his arms and swept her off her feet. He carried her to the bedroom and switched off the light.

Chapter 35

The earth tilted, directing the most sunlight on the southern balcony of the penthouse. It was midwinter, and branches swung under a load of heavy snow. Depressing dark clouds coursed the skies, predicting yet another snowfall.

Jonas stood slumped on the balcony taking in the white desolate landscape over Djurgården. The cold wind drained all warmth from his blood. He closed the balcony door and headed to the kitchen area to make tea.

He was expecting Martina's arrival anytime. He had not seen her since she had returned from Davos. They were going cross-country skiing out of town. A warm cup of tea would be nice before they set off.

The doorbell buzzed. There she is, he thought. Without speaking in the intercom to ask who it was, he pressed the button in the keypad and opened the door. He went to the foyer and waited for her at the elevator landing. The grinding sound of the elevator stopped as it lurched to a halt on the top floor.

The doors glided open, and his face lit up in a wide smile, expecting to see the love of his life emerge. But his smile froze when he saw the woman with black hair. He was thunderstruck, not because she was beautiful, but because he wanted nothing to do with her.

'What the fucking shit are you doing here?' boomed Jonas. 'Who gave you my address?'

'What kind of welcome is that?' asked Viviane.

Anger bubbled within as Jonas contemplated the fastest way to get rid of her. He stood transfixed. Martina would be here any time. Before he could say anything, Viviane bypassed him and moved farther into the apartment.

'Don't go in there,' he said. He followed her into the apartment, leaving the door ajar. 'You can't barge in here and expect to be welcome.'

'Darling Jonas, it's the twenty-first century, remember? I Googled your name on Eniro, and there you are: address, phone numbers, even where you work.' She talked as she peeled off her coat and hung it on the railing with her bag. She kicked off her leather boots and then spun around to face him. Jonas turned pale as a sheet.

'Darling, stop looking like you've seen a ghost,' said Viviane. 'Be courteous; give me a grand tour of this marvellous place.'

'Stop calling me darling.'

Viviane ignoring him and moved to the living room with easy grace in her silk stockings. She opened the sliding glass doors to the main balcony and stood taking in the view. In the distance, she saw the frozen lake and shimmering snow lighting up a gloomy sky.

'What a stunning view,' she gasped. She closed the doors and moved on in the apartment. Jonas followed her, imploring her to leave. But Viviane wandered to the bathroom. She heaved. 'Wow, a Jacuzzi too!'

'What are you doing?' He seized her arm, and shoved her to the front door. She shrugged him off and rushed to the next door – the bedroom.

'What a large bed,' she said. 'Do you sleep in it alone? Those glossy antique ebony lampshades must have cost a fortune. Everything in this apartment breathes money. You've done well for yourself, Jonas. Compared to that little apartment we had when we first met.'

'Stop talking nonsense, and get out.'

'I mean it,' said Viviane, 'with such a spacious penthouse on the most exclusive street in Stockholm, you should be celebrating.'

'Leave!' said Jonas. 'I'm not interested in anything you have to say.'

Viviane returned to the living room and stood admiring him: his furious, sexy eyes, well-built body, and deep masculine voice. How could she have been so stupid as to leave him?

'Please don't be angry with me,' she pleaded. 'I was such a fool to listen to my parents. Carlos was their choice for a husband. I didn't love him, but I had to please my parents. The marriage failed and I divorced him, much to the disgrace of my family. But you...you and I can try again.'

'Are you crazy?' said Jonas. 'You broke our engagement, walked out on me without a word, and now you expect me to take you back. Why am I even discussing this? I said get out!'

The sound of his voice grated in her ears, and she winced. She must defuse his anger. She must change tactics. She moved closer to him, touched his arm, and said, 'Jonas, I still love you. You remember –'

He cut her off. 'I remember nothing of your past with me.' He stepped firmly away from her.

Viviane scowled at him in annoyance that quickly turned to sadness. 'You don't mean that. What a horrible thing to say. You loved me once.' Tears pooled in her eyes, but she blinked rapidly, pushing them back, not wanting to appear weak in front of him.

'Get out,' said Jonas, pointing her to the door. 'I'm expecting company.' Viviane tentatively reached up and touched his cheek. He brushed her hand away. 'Stop fooling around, and leave!' said Jonas. He snatched her coat off the railing and dropped it over her shoulders, picked up her bag and handed it to her. She let the coat glide to the floor and ignored the bag, leaving it hanging on his hand. Finally, he collected all her things and dumped them in the foyer.

The doorbell buzzed, startling them both. Jonas' mind froze. Unable to think, he took a deep breath, and this time rushed to the intercom. 'Who is it?' he said.

'Open, Jonas. It's me, Martina.' He pressed the button and opened the door.

'Martina? Who is she?' asked Viviane. A chill went through her body at the prospect of Jonas having a girlfriend.

In a desperate effort, Jonas grabbed her arm and propelled her towards the door, out in the foyer. 'Pick up your stuff, now, and use the stairs.'

'No, I'm not leaving,' said Viviane, shrugging him off. 'I want to meet Martina.'

'What? No, you can't meet her. You must leave.'

The elevator ground to a halt, and out came Martina. She carried a big golden bag with packages in wrappings.

Jonas quickly came to the foyer, took her hand, and kissed it. 'Welcome back, darling,' he said.

Darling? Viviane's heart shattered to pieces. He was taken, she realized.

Martina stopped, her eyes fixed on the woman in a grey dress, noting her manicured nails and long dark eyelashes. Time stood still as her memory conjured up a photograph she had once seen in Jonas' album, when they had started dating. It had since disappeared without a trace. Instantly, she knew this was Viviane.

'Come in,' said Jonas, masking his dilemma. Martina didn't move; neither did Viviane. It seemed like the trio stood transfixed, immobilized by shock, fear, disappointment and betrayal. The air crackled with suppressed emotions.

Martina couldn't breathe. She tried to make sense of the awkward situation, focusing on Viviane – her feet in silk stockings, the clutter of her coat, bag, and boots on the floor in the foyer. What was going on? Was she moving in or out?

An unsettling frown glazed Viviane's brows. She glared at the well-groomed, tall, blue-eyed blonde standing before her. Her lilac silk-jersey wrap dress, underneath her unbuttoned woollen coat in matching colour, emphasized her sense of style. Her face seemed familiar. Then it dawned on her. Jesus, she was the most celebrated woman in the world – the natural therapist guru. Even in Spain she was a household name. Her mind took a deep spin as she recalled Jonas calling her *Darling* and kissing her hand. *Jonas and Martina Strömstedt Edgren are a couple.* My, that was some competition to contend with…the money, the big houses and flashy cars. How was she going to win Jonas back?

Martina scowled at Jonas, noticing his tight jaw and thin curled lips. Without warning, she swung the golden bag, landing it on his head. 'You two-timing bastard, how dare you cheat on me!'

Jonas cringed and clutched his painful head.

The bag dropped to the floor and its contents welled out and scattered everywhere.

In two steps Martina lunged at Viviane who darted for a side balcony door, and out into the freezing weather. She turned and flung her full weight on the door, stopping Martina from opening it. Nonetheless, Martina shouldered the unbreakable glass door with a mighty force, causing a momentum that threw Viviane flat on her back onto the snowy balcony. Viviane yowled.

'You cheap slut!' thundered Martina as she bridged the space between them. She made to kick her side but changed her mind, and said, 'Get up!'

Viviane froze, petrified by Martina's burning rage.

Jonas grabbed Martina's arm and yanked her to him.

Martina slapped him hard across the face.

Jonas winced. 'Stop it,' her said, restraining her.

'Don't touch me. You disgust me.' She pushed at him, stalked from the balcony and out of the apartment. She snatched the elevator door, sprang in, and pressed the button. Jonas, consumed by panic and confusion, quickly followed her. The descent passed without a word. In minutes the elevator halted, and the doors glided open. Martina stepped out and walked with a brisk pace to the car, her face smudged in tears. Jonas trotted alongside her, his body shaking like a feather. He was in a T-shirt, jeans and house slippers.

'Stop crying,' said Jonas, 'and hear me out. It's not what you think.'

Martina ignored his pleas. She approached the Mercedes, and Simon opened the door. As she got in the rear seat, she cried to Simon, 'Keep him away from me.'

Jonas grabbed the rear door, trying to get in, but Simon accosted him. 'Dr Eneroth, please don't do that.'

Jonas reluctantly let go of the door, frustration and pain evident in his eyes. He wanted to kneel down on the frozen pavement and beg her to stay.

Simon jumped into the driver's seat, punched the ignition and hauled the car out of its parking space. It took off at high speed. Jonas watched in dismay as it disappeared in the busy Saturday traffic. A drizzle of snow blinded his eyes, washing his tears. A dizzy spell surged through his body, leaving him emotionally drained and disillusioned. He hung his head and walked back to the apartment, feeling a sense of loss.

When he alighted on the top floor, the door to the apartment stood ajar. Viviane was gone. He picked up the golden bag and the packages and took them in with him. He grabbed his phone and rang Martina. After several rings, he hung up.

In the living room he noticed the Kosta Boda crystal sculpture of *Dancing Man Ruby*, which had stood on the piano, was gone. It had been a birthday present from Martina. Viviane must have taken it.

Chapter 36

On Sunday morning Martina sat in her study, at Slottsville house, working at her laptop. There was mail from Jonas – a report on Anna's attack. She read quickly, ascertaining he had not acted as instructed.

There was a report from Diana on the contaminated cell antidote and who was responsible. She clicked on the attached file with film footage. On film, a broad-shouldered man was sneaking around in the manufacturing plant, the Althonat Plant. Standing beside a production line, he poured a substance into the ready-to-pack cell antidote. He abruptly stopped when he saw another employee pass by, then continued. On instructions from Diana, the man was fired, prosecuted, and jailed. His name was Anton Lundel, and his problems supposedly stemmed from difficult working relationships with co-workers. Martina zoomed in the footage and observed there was something about his snarled lips that reminded her of the man at Sisters' Helin Voltaire Café.

The next mail – a report from Christer, the Security Director: the five million dollars that were transferred yearly from Athonat's New York account to a Shell company in the Caribbean was a cloaked identity transaction. From the Shell Company the funds were deposited into a Lawyer's account in Cayman Island. Eventually, they found their way to a business account in southern Sweden. Investigation continues, said the report. *Jesus, why was Pappa transferring hooded funds to Sweden?* she stopped to think. It didn't make sense to her.

Scorpio's mail caught her eye. She opened it and went straight on to the attachment: more footage. It was hazy and poorly lit. She zoomed to enlarge it. In a sleazy hotel room two figures lay in bed, exchanging illicit sexual favours. A man with silver hair turned and lay on top of the woman, unknowingly enhancing their images on camera. It was Fabian and Leila.

'Ojojo!' startled Martina, repulsed by the footage. For what seemed like hours, she glared at the footage in disbelief. She knew Leila to be a difficult employee of questionable moral reputation, but she did not expect conspiracy from her. Yet, even when she had seen her with Fabian Franzen at the Nobel Banquet, she had not expected her to go this far with that animal. Martina was not in the habit of judging people, but for reasons unknown to her, she felt debased by Leila's lack of moral virtue as if her behaviour reflected on Althonat's reputation. Leila's association with Fabian spelled disaster for Althonat Global.

As she looked at the footage again, a wave of nausea came over her. A deep intake of breath stifled the repugnant sensation. She logged out.

The phone startled her out of her shock. She picked it up and answered, 'Martina.'

'It's Christer. Listen, Leila is still in police custody pending investigation but may be released any time.'

'Why is that?'

'It will depend on police findings,' said Christer. 'If they don't find a strong case, they can't hold her any longer.'

'She tried to murder Anna, for God's sake,' cried Martina. 'What're the Lawyers doing?'

'They are working on it.'

'Tell them to work harder,' said Martina. 'Leila belongs behind bars.'

There was a pause.

'Christer, how could this happen? How did Leila get through security, without detection?'

'I've reprimanded my staff, and we're reorganizing teams. It won't happen again.'

Martina heard voices. A squabble was going on outside. 'Christer, I'll get back to you,' she said and hung up.

She pushed her chair back, and moved to the window. A man in a camel coloured coat stood outside the gate engaging in an altercation with security. It was Jonas. She strode out of the study onto the balcony. Jonas saw her and called, 'Martina, please ask them to let me in. We must talk.'

Martina stared at him as if she had not heard a thing he'd said. Inside, her pain returned, along with anger at his audacity – turning up at her home, picking a quarrel with staff. How dare he disturb her tranquillity on Sunday morning? She shot him another glare and returned to the study.

'Martina … Martina, please!' hollered Jonas. His voice echoed through the neighbourhood. Martina heard one of the guards say, 'Sorry, Dr Eneroth, you must leave. She won't see you.'

That evening, Thomas brought Joachim home. In the hallway, Joachim jumped up and hugged his mother, babbling on about his skiing holiday and his improved skill on the slopes, taking sharp curves, and getting on and off slopes unaided.

'You're a smart boy,' said Martina as she softly pinched his cheek.

'Mamma… Mamma, I –'

'That's enough, Joachim,' said Thomas cutting him short. 'You'd better go to bed. It's late.'

'No, Pappa. Can't I stay a little longer and talk to Mamma?'

'No, you can't.'

'Go on, Joachim. You heard your father,' said Martina; and then, 'Have you eaten?'

'We ate at my parents' place,' said Thomas.

Joachim kissed Mamma and Pappa goodnight and ran upstairs.

Martina shifted her gaze to Thomas. 'Coffee?'

'No thanks, I want to go home and catch up with work.'

'Stay for a while and talk to me.' Thomas raised a brow and smiled.

'Don't get ideas. I just want company,' said Martina, realizing her words might be misunderstood.

'It wasn't so long ago you threw me out of this house, and now you're asking me to stay?' His reproach was laced with humour.

'We can sit in the kitchen. Are you sure you don't want coffee?'

'No. What is it you want to talk about?' asked Thomas as he joined her at the kitchen table. On impulse he leaned over and kissed her lips.

'That is not why I asked you to stay.'

'Maybe I can get you to accommodate my feelings.'

'Stop it, Thomas.'

'What is it anyway?' asked Thomas, getting angry. 'Is it Jonas?'

'Why do you say that?'

'I know it's Jonas,' said Thomas. 'I've long suspected since I saw you two, in the media, at the Nobel banquet.'

Martina silently sighed but said nothing.

'Did he tell you about Viviane?' asked Thomas.

'What about Viviane?' asked Martina, straightening up.

On second thought, Thomas remained tight lipped. He leaned in to kiss her again, but she turned her face away. Her curiosity awakened, she asked again, 'What about Viviane?'

'Let's drop it. It's nothing.'

'No, we can't drop it. You started to say something; you might as well spit it out.'

Thomas glanced at his watch and rose to his feet. 'I'd better get going.'

The frustration in Martina's eyes was palpable. She wanted to beg him to tell her, but he appeared adamant. His unwillingness to tell her only increased her suspicion of Jonas. She let it go, though it rattled her mind. She gazed at the intricate mosaic in the table linen, hardly noticing it, lost in thought. In a dispirited voice she said, 'I'll see you out.'

Thomas gazed at her and noticed tears pooling in her eyes. 'Why are you crying?' he said, sitting down again.

'Oh, Thomas, everything is so hard.'

'What's hard? Your personal life or business?'

'Everything is a mess.'

'I heard about the attempt on your life,' said Thomas. 'Is that it?'

'The Dodge van, yes. That was frightening,' said Martina. 'There are people trying to get rid of me. I think it's the same people who hated Pappa.'

'Althonat Global has done well since you took over,' he said. 'It's had tremendous growth. You've taken business away from other pharmaceutical companies. You have them worried.'

'Yes, Citaraph is our major competitor. But they have government backing and media support. Highly placed government people and editors of major newspapers sit on their Board. Althonat Global has no such backing, but we tell people the truth, and people are beginning to listen and understand that they can make enlightened choices about their health.'

'I see demonstrations in town, people protesting that their tax money is wasted on drugs and vaccines that don't cure disease.'

'There're more drugs out there than people getting cured. People are looking for better alternatives, for cures to illness, and Althonat Global has offered them that.'

'But the medical community by and large remains sceptical of alternative medicine,' said Thomas.

'They will come around when we launch Rensblad.'

'Oh, yeah, did you recover the other half of the recipe?'

'Yes, luckily we did,' said Martina with a smile.

'So are you going to manufacture the wonder drug?'

'I think we should,' said Martina with a sparkle in her eyes. 'The Board has yet to decide. I'm excited about it. You know, it's an herbal cleanser and a drug, in one, all ingredients from nature. It will cure a wide range of diseases, from childhood illnesses to Alzheimer's. No side effects. One dose will cleanse, repair, restore cell damage, and heal the body for all time. The immune system will be restored and strengthened. No patient will be hooked on lifelong drugs.'

'Aren't you being too optimistic?'

'No, Thomas, listen,' said Martina. 'this was researched by Pappa for many years. It's scientifically proven and tested. And it's not going to cost a fortune. Availability will be to all nations, at reasonable cost. If a nation is too poor to afford, we shall provide it free of charge. Rensblad will render other drugs and vaccines obsolete.'

Thomas leaned back in his chair, surprised by her confidence. 'You sound like a prophet.'

'No, I'm no prophet. It's just me, Martina.'

'But that will make Althonat Global a monopoly. Competition will be curtailed. You'll take all profits.'

'Profit has never been a driving force in our business. But wellness for the greatest majority is our trademark. As for monopoly, it will be a good monopoly since we don't intend to exploit or dominate the population. Our patients know we don't treat them as a commodity for profits.'

'You seem sure of yourself.'

'No, I'm not,' said Martina. 'I know Citaraph will never sell another drug once we launch Rensblad, and this is going to cause a medical war, a pharmaceutical war, and even a political war for that matter.'

'Then why do it, why put your life in danger?'

'Somebody has to do it. If we don't, humanity will cease to exist.'

'Now you've lost me.'

'I know it's complicated, but trust me, this is the right way.'

'If it's going to cause a war,' said Thomas, 'maybe I should move in with you.'

'No, you can't protect me. I've got to do this on my own.'

'You must be careful though. My son needs a mother…remember.'

'Don't you think I know that?' said Martina. 'I intend to see Joachim grow up.'

Thomas got to his feet. 'I must go,' he said.

In the hallway he put on his coat. When he turned, Martina's eyes were teary again. 'What is making you so emotional? What is wrong?'

'It's nothing,' said Martina, gauging him, reading his mood. Then she asked, 'What is it you're not telling me about Jonas and Viviane? I want to know.' She wiped her tears with her hand.

A flicker of disappointment crossed Thomas' face as he noted with displeasure her deep interest in Jonas' affairs.

'Are you worried Viviane will patch things up with Jonas?' said Thomas blatantly. 'Is that what the tears are about?'

'Tell me, please.'

'It's nothing, just everyday gossip,' said Thomas.

'Just tell me.'

'Well then, it's something I overheard at a business conference. Viviane attended, and I heard her ask a colleague about raising business capital. She then mentioned Jonas' name, saying she was moving back to Stockholm to join her fiancé.'

Martina's face remained impassive, giving nothing away, but her blood boiled.

'You're right, it's gossip – nothing to do with me,' said Martina. 'I hardly know Viviane.'

'Neither do I, but when I heard her mention Jonas' name, I asked my colleague. He told me her name was Viviane Thos.'

'Go on, Thomas. It's getting late.'

Thomas left, and Martina retired upstairs to check on Joachim. He was fast asleep. As she entered the bedroom, her phone rang. She picked it and checked the monitor. It was Jonas. She ignored it, put the phone down, and went to brush her teeth.

She got in bed and became overwhelmed with emotion. Torrents of tears welled up in her eyes. She sobbed inconsolably, feeling sick at heart. Her body heaved and shuddered. Fiery gouts of anger, fear, resentment and disappointment ripped through her. The sharp ache in her heart was like a gash, a wound that would never heal; the scab kept peeling off, bringing back an unending stream of grief. It sapped her energy. She could not get on top of it. Her world was falling apart.

Chapter 37

The police station reception area was cold and a strange place to be for Martina. She sat and waited for the officer. Finally, the doors opened, and a female officer emerged. She ushered her into a long corridor. Dim bulbs in the ceiling illuminated empty space, plain walls without ornaments of art. They came to a huge steel door, and the officer swept her card in the magnetic door lock and the door clicked open. They came to another reception area.

'Take a seat,' the officer said, pointing to a bench against a wall. Martina sat down facing a glass wall. On the other side of the wall she saw Leila emerge in a striped prison cotton dress. She looked pale and appeared to have lost weight. She picked up the phone. Martina advanced and picked up too, mirroring her. They each placed the phone to their ear.

'How have you been, Leila?'

'What do you expect?' asked Leila.

'Why did you try to murder Anna?'

Leila opened her trembling lips but closed them again.

'Tell me. Who put you up to it?'

Leila rolled her big eyes and breathed. 'I'm sick and tired of people using me.'

'Who is using you?'

'You…you used me, and then you passed me over for promotion. You've never showed me any appreciation.'

'Wait a minute. What promotion?'

'The position you gave to Diana. You rejected me just like that.'

'I already explained to you: Diana was the best qualified candidate for the position. Is that why you tried to murder Anna?'

Leila sat hunched over with an icy glare in her eyes. The air in the room was stagnant and stale. Something about Leila told Martina there was more to this than just promotion.

'What is it, Leila?'

Leila lowered her gaze to the desk, and when she looked up again there was bitter hostility in her eyes. She bit her lower lip, chewing on it as if to stifle rage or fear.

'Who told you to do it?' asked Martina. 'You didn't do it on your own, did you?'

'I'm not answering any questions.'

'What about Fabian Franzen?' asked Martina. 'What is your connection with him?'

There was shock in Leila's eyes. She looked away evasively and said, 'I don't know what you're talking about.'

'Haven't you been intimate with him?' asked Martina in a low voice.

'What kind of question is that?' asked Leila. 'You think because you own Althonat Global, you own my life. Well, let me tell you something, Doctor Herbal Weed, my private life is none of your business.' She abruptly stood, sending the stool tumbling like a drum across the floor, but she remained holding the phone.

'You'll rot in jail,' said Martina. 'Fabian will never help you get out of here.'

'You think you're high and mighty,' said Leila. 'Wait till they come after you. You'll be dead like your father.'

'Is that a threat?' asked Martina.

'Take it any way you like.'

It became clear the conversation was leading nowhere. Leila had reached a point of no return. There was no hope of imparting reason to her soggy mind, no chance of swaying her back to sound judgement, no point in redeeming her.

'Guards!' hollered Martina. A woman officer appeared and ushered Leila out. Leila scowled at Martina as she followed the officer.

'You are a lot of things, Leila, but I never thought you would turn treacherous,' said Martina, her voice breaking. She disliked people threatening her, but worse, she hated it when they devalued her father. Another guard opened the door for Martina to pass. She rose and walked right into the door. It cut her eyebrow, which started bleeding. The guard plastered her up.

Panic-stricken and wound up, Martina returned to the office. It was as if she was tearing at her hair in a maze of questions without answers.

She fumbled in a dark tunnel, oblivious of light, of hope. She couldn't understand how and when her best researcher had turned treacherous. Sebastian had spoken about being vigilant. Had she missed something, neglected Leila in any way or taken her for granted, pushing her into the enemy camp?

*****

In the afternoon, the Board meeting was short. Martina came out later with a consensus for production of Rensblad. It was a moment she normally would have celebrated, but a lot weighed on her depressive heart. The triumphant milestone was blurred by problems.

She logged onto her computer and wrote mails to the communications director and the PR people to see about the launch for Rensblad. Proposals for campaign plans, strategy and analytics were to be delivered for her viewing before end of month.

The phone rang. She picked it up. 'Martina,' she answered.

It was her secretary, Pia. 'Dr Eneroth is here to see you.'

A faint tremor preyed on her heart, reminding her of the dull pain in her chest. She wasn't sure she wanted to see Jonas; she had avoided him at the Board meeting but she might as well hear his version of the story and see if their relationship was worth saving. 'Send him in.'

Soon Jonas stood before her desk gazing down at her, his greenish brown eyes tinged with shadows of grey. She glanced up at him, briefly, and knew he harboured resentment.

'Hi,' he said, trying to sound casual.

'Sit down, Jonas,' said Martina, focusing on her computer. Jonas sat in a chair across from her desk, quietly waiting for her attention. Martina continued clicking away at the computer, ignoring him. After a while, she lifted her gaze to meet his. He looked fatigued and deflated, as if he hadn't eaten for days.

In a cheerless manner, he observed her in composed silence.

'You wanted to see me,' said Martina, adopting a formal tone.

'You've been avoiding me,' said Jonas. 'You never answer my calls. You ignore me when you see me. I've been to Slottsville house twice, and the guards turned me away, saying those were your orders. You stopped coming to our weekly meetings at the hospital. Instead you adopted video conferencing. Damn it, Martina, why?'

'You ask me why? You really want to know?'

'I didn't do anything,' said Jonas.

'I need time and space away from you,' said Martina.

'Time and space for what?'

'Time and space to reflect on our relationship, to consider whether it's really you I want in my life.'

Jonas leaned forward in the chair and faced her squarely, his eyes more serious than ever. The prospect of losing Martina daunted him. 'What happened was a huge misunderstanding. Viviane found my address on the net, at Eniro. I was stunned myself to see her at Strandvägen. I asked her to leave immediately, and she was leaving when you arrived.'

'I leave town for a few days, and your fiancée moves in?' said Martina. 'That was a sleazy, gross and unprecedented betrayal. How could you do that to me?'

Jonas' eyes flickered in disappointment. He hadn't expected her to say that. He came to his feet and moved to her side of the desk, standing over her.

'I resent that,' he said. 'I have never cheated on you.'

'Sure, Jonas?' asked Martina, her voice pitched. 'Viviane! With her standing barefooted and cosy in your apartment, her stuff spread all over your floor, like she owned the place. Was she moving in or out?'

'Stop talking like that,' said Jonas. 'She didn't spend a night there.'

'I don't believe you.'

'Believe what you like. I didn't invite her,' said Jonas. 'I was waiting for you. How could I be so stupid?'

'Don't you think I know she's planning to move in with you? She's looking for capital to start a business?' Martina paused, pinned him with a frosty glare and persisted. 'So when were you planning on telling me it was over between us?'

Jonas was thrown by her words. The creases in his forehead screamed confusion. He abruptly sank to a squat beside her and gazed up into her icy eyes. 'What are you talking about? Who told you that?'

'Don't ask me who told me. I found out.'

'You know that it's not true, and whoever told you is jealous or envious of our relationship,' said Jonas. 'I have no plans with that woman.'

'What did she want, then?'

'It's immaterial what she wanted.'

'She wanted you back, didn't she?'

'I said it's immaterial what she wanted.'

'Do you still love her?'

'Look, darling, please don't do this,' pleaded Jonas. 'Viviane was a part of my past. I've long since moved on, and it's you I love.'

The gnawing pain in Martina's heart returned. His words were just words without substance. In her mind she knew Viviane wanted him back in her arms. The way she had stood ogling him that afternoon spoke volumes on the seduction scale. Was he strong enough to resist her advances? Even worse: was she prepared for a perpetual wrangle with Miss Spain over him? The prospects aggravated her mind. She lashed at him again.

'How dare you flaunt your fiancée in front of me?'

'Stop calling her my fiancée,' said Jonas. 'And snap out of it, Martina.'

'Then what the hell was she doing in your apartment?' said Martina her voice rising.

'Why are you shouting?' whispered Jonas, struggling to contain his anger. 'Look, I didn't sleep with her, if that's what you're getting at.' He got to his feet and perched on her desk so he was gazing down at her. 'What do I have to do to convince you nothing happened between me and that woman?'

Martina stared up in his desperate eyes, thinking she knew him but she wouldn't trust Viviane.

'Tell me, what if that little twerp persists in pursuing you, what will you do?'

'I'm not a child, Martina. It's you I love.'

A moment passed, and Martina temporarily returned to her computer, clicking away. She retrieved Jonas' mail and spent a few more minutes reading his report. She raised her unhappy gaze and said, 'I wanted to speak to you.'

'About what?'

'Anna; she almost got killed. You ignored instructions to scan her immediately.'

'I didn't ignore instructions. It was the night they made an attempt on your life. Everything was chaotic, and I couldn't get Dr Nasiro on the phone.'

'You could have done it yourself.'

'I couldn't leave you in that horrid condition. You were traumatized.'

'Instructions are instructions, and immediate means immediate. Althonat Global is always teeming with doctors. You could have asked any doctor to do it.'

Jonas kept his cool. He knew she was right. 'I take full responsibility for what happened. It was my failure, my mistake. It won't happen again.'

Martina paused, surprised by the remorse in his voice. She had expected him to be up in arms about this. She knew he was a good doctor, but mistakes should be avoided.

'The patient's security is paramount,' said Martina. 'Make sure it doesn't happen again. Now, if you'll excuse me, I would like to get on with my work.'

'Are we friends again?'

'I still need some distance to think things over.'

'Martina, there's nothing to think over,' said Jonas. 'Please, drop it.' Something caught his eye. He leaned down and looked at her sore eyebrow. 'That's a nasty cut. What happened?'

'Leila. I visited her in prison.'

'And she turned violent on you?'

'No, I bumped into a door when I was leaving.'

'You should put something on it,' said Jonas. 'What made her do it?'

'Leila is a disturbed woman,' said Martina. 'She is involved with people who are bent on using her to get at Althonat Global. I get a strong feeling money wasn't her motive. It was something else, but I don't know what. She seemed frightened.'

'Her work on Botanik Herbier could have made her a target for our competitors.'

'Leila used to work with Pappa in New York. Before Pappa died she suddenly asked to be transferred to Stockholm. I don't know why.'

'Well, maybe she knows Rangor,' said Jonas.

Martina hadn't thought about that. 'But Leila is not a stupid woman,' said Martina. 'To do what she did, could be someone has a hold on her…maybe Rangor or Fabian.'

'Blackmail?'

'Perhaps,' said Martina.

'Ask Christer to look into it,' said Jonas. Then, he changed the subject. 'Have dinner with me?'

'Not today. I've a lot of work to do.'

'What about tomorrow?'

'I can't promise.'

'You're still angry with me?'

'I didn't say that,' said Martina. 'Now, vamoose!'

Jonas strolled out of the room with a smile on his face.

Chapter 38

Cameras clicked and flashed, lighting up her face to reveal a sparkling smile. Martina stood at the central stage in the large conference hall at Althonat Towers, flanked by members of her Board. Her heart raced, the air crackled with enthusiasm and sizzled in excitement. Anticipation was the order of the day. The hall brimmed with world press, journalists, business people, scientists, shareholders, friends and well-wishers.

The launching of Rensblad, the ground-breaking medical discovery, was in the making. The world turned its face to Stockholm to honour the woman who had made it happen. In her mind, one thing was missing: her father, the man who had had the courage to follow his passion. It was his vision, his battles that had brought her to stand on this platform. She wore a metallic black and silver grey skirt suit, a peach blouse and impressive heels.

Martina's voice cut through the air like a sickle. Her message was loud and clear.

'It is a great pleasure to be here today with my Board, staff, colleagues, and friends to launch the wonder drug, Rensblad. I would like to thank those involved in this exciting challenge of supplying the first holistic wonder drug to the world. The way people work, play, and live has been transformed. Globalization and advancement in knowledge have impacted patterns of health and ways of thinking. We're now facing a different kind of marketplace, and we need to adapt treatments and cures of illnesses to natural therapies that are well tailored to the body, nature, and patients' needs. Ladies and gentlemen of the press, I believe Rensblad will be a more effective way to promote wellness and health among populations. I'm delighted for the opportunity I've been given to collaborate on this groundbreaking project. Thank you, and I wish you all a lovely evening.'

A wave of applause reverberated through the hall, amplified by walls and ceiling. Cameras and light bulbs flickered and blinked, blinding Martina's eyes as she waved to the audience. She revelled in the limelight, shaking hands, congratulating her Board and staff. Champagne flowed, and the celebration started. Leaving the stage, she gracefully descended to the floor where she mingled and interacted with the press and audience, constantly skirted by men in black suits and white shirts, her security guards.

Richard and Bo were watching in Devilund's TV room. Richard beamed, clapping his hands enthusiastically, applauding with the audience on television as Martina concluded her speech.

Bo watched him, thinking he was overzealous about the whole thing. 'You know her?' he said.

'Sort of…through friends,' said Richard, smiling. 'She's sensational.'

'Yes, she is,' said Bo. 'She's changed the entire outlook on the medical profession. The pharmaceutical companies are cursing.'

'Citaraph will fade in prominence,' said Richard. 'Althonat Global is the future.'

'It's too early to tell. Pharmaceuticals are always waging wars against each other,' said Bo. 'Who knows what Citaraph has up its sleeve?'

'Citaraph has no vision. It is devoid of ideas.'

'Yeah, thanks to Grenzken!' said Bo, breaking out into a laugh.

'I wonder what is going on up there?' asked Richard, pointing upstairs.

'They're probably grilling Grenzken. Citaraph's loss is largely due to outsourcing research to Grenzken Consulting.'

'They outsourced to accommodate a clandestine agenda – to avoid detection.'

'What clandestine agenda?' Bo asked.

'I'll get coffee. Want some?' asked Richard, changing the subject.

'Yes, thanks, I will have some.'

Richard disappeared to the kitchen area.

*****

The Group sat with stupefied faces in Grenzken's living room, watching Martina's launch on television. When Martina stepped down from the stage, Fabian pressed the remote, switching off the television.

The mood in the room resembled a funeral parlour, as if someone had died without leaving a comfortable inheritance. In silence, long faces stared angrily at each other. Each one harboured a secret grudge on whom to blame, condemn, or take to task. But that would give no comfort or consolation, for the inflicted wound was deep, and no pain relief could be had.

Grenzken sat on the sofa, hanging his head and rubbing his temple. He felt mortified and humiliated beyond measure. The void in his heart outweighed his guilt, and yet with all things put together, it was the loss of Rensblad formula that staggered him most. The mystery of how and when he'd lost it defied perception; answers simply weren't there. He was a shell of a man, without regard or respect from his fellows. He had fallen hard and low like Lucifer. From under his eyelids he peeked, catching movements, whispers, heated glares, shaking of heads in disbelief, anger, cynicism, and even hatred from the gloomy, disgruntled faces around him. It was early March, and the central heating system was still on, but the room felt cold.

Mattsson, Tord and Rangor sat talking in undertones, disappointment harsh on their faces. Mattsson talked about legal proceedings against Grenzken, forgetting he was a thief himself. How could Grenzken lose half the Rensblad formula to Althonat Global? Or had he conspired with the Strömstedt woman, Mattsson silently pondered. Tord and Rangor wanted nothing more than to chop him into pieces and leave his remains to the vultures in the hills. He was a lackadaisical fool casting a shadow over business and future financial gains.

Fabian focused his nervous interest on following movements in the market. He sat with his gaze on his smartphone touch screen, peeling away at it, surfing on the stock exchange website, updating himself on developments. His lips were compressed in a thin line; he was hoping and praying it all was a huge mistake and that Althonat Global shares could plummet anytime.

He sighed, raised his contorted face in a glare at Grenzken. 'Damn, Citaraph shares have plunged ten percent since the Rensblad launch.'

'That's only an hour ago,' said Mattsson.

'This is scandalous,' said Rangor, eyeing Grenzken. 'We had half the formula in hand. We only needed the other half.'

Grenzken hunched his shoulders, his gaze fixed on the floor, avoiding eye contact with the others. He wanted to get up and leave, find Helmut and play video games. Helmut was uncomplicated, undemanding and easier to deal with than these transgressors in his living room. Maybe he should make a scene and throw them out. But that could cause more problems.

'We're foolish to trust Grenzken,' said Tord, shooting him another cold stare.

Grenzken cringed further, wishing the floor could unlatch and swallow him. He remained silent, as remorse and shame submerged him. Where could he hide?

'We can't just sit and let Queen Strömstedt Edgren proceed unhindered,' said Rangor.

'What do you suggest we do?' said Fabian.

'We negotiate,' interjected Stellan Strömstedt, quickly and timidly.

'Negotiate what, with your niece?' said Tord. 'You're family; your vote doesn't count here.'

The sound of subdued laughter was heard in the room but no one thought it was funny.

Suddenly, voices were heard from outside the room, followed by a knock. The door opened, and Helmut poked his head, announcing, 'Lilian Linsjö.'

Rustling noises spread through the room as men straightened up, adjusted ties, and cleared throats. A middle-aged woman in a blue blazer and black trouser entered the room. Her jade green eyes drank in the occupants of the room as she nodded and grinned in greeting. Mattsson offered her a seat. She sat down with her hands clasped in her lap. She was the executive chairman of Citaraph Board and permanent secretary to the Ministry of Health and Welfare.

'Lillian, it's a pleasure to have you here today,' said Mattsson. 'It's tough times, and it's encouraging to know we have your full support.'

'Thank you, Mattsson. I'll get to the point. Althonat Global shares are up twenty percent as we speak. However, we urgently need to finish projects in the pipeline. All girls and boys above age four must receive Life-Vaccine as soon as possible. We're targeting schools.' She looked at Mattsson. 'We shall buy whatever you have, but we may need more to complete the task.'

The men paid attention, for now it was the long arm of the government speaking.

'Public opinion is shifting; people are rejecting Life-Vaccine,' said Tord. 'How are you going to accomplish the task?'

'I used the word *urgently,* if you heard me,' said Lillian. 'And mark this, a law has been passed…it is now mandatory to vaccinate all children. Any parent resisting vaccination of their child will be prosecuted.'

Stellan took a deep, laboured breath and dropped his head.

Rangor glared at him, and said, 'That's a great move. It will certainly help further our cause.'

'Caution,' said Fabian. 'If you push too hard, people will reject our party in the next election. Demonstrations against Life-Vaccine are rampant countrywide now.'

'Of course, re-election of our party is a major milestone. Nothing can be allowed to jeopardize that. Democracy must prevail,' said Lillian. 'Now if you'll excuse me, I'll leave you to it, gentlemen.'

Mattsson rose and walked her to the door. When he returned, a heated discussion had broken out as men interpreted a deeper meaning to her words.

'It sounded like Citaraph is a sinking ship,' said Tord. 'Complete programs urgently, she said, but what she didn't say was more important. What will happen if people riot and storm Parliament and defy the law – defy Life-Vaccine? That will be the end of Citaraph. The government will be forced to retreat.'

'But she also said, anyone resisting the law will be prosecuted,' said Rangor. 'Government vaccine programmes must continue despite the will of the people.'

Stellan yawned and thought about the consequences of doing time in jail if Citaraph went under. Fabian's eyes turned black, and anxiety ripped through his bones as he feared things might escalate and government could be forced by the masses to retreat, dumping the blame on The Group. They could become scapegoats. He thought about Leila in prison; he had been brooding about her and what she had done but dared not show his face in prison to visit her. He worried about her fiasco, another nightmare she had created. And Anna was still at large.

Chapter 39

At six in the evening, the banquet hall at Slottsville house bustled with people. Available seats were filled, and guests mingled, talked, smiled, drank and ate. Conversation throbbed and pulsated with vibrant energy.

The celebrations had moved from Althonat Towers to Slottsville house. The atmosphere surged and crackled with feverish animation. A sense of success, accomplishment and triumph hung in the air. Barbara Von Essen spotted Martina at the bar and quickly manoeuvred through the crowd to get to her.

Martina stood sipping champagne, flanked by Olausson and Sten, talking to a small group of doctors and researchers. She laughed, amused by something Olausson said. She had changed into a sapphire blue cocktail dress with a black belt. Jonas sat on the sofa, in the great room, engrossed in conversation with Diana. He told her Anna had been moved to a safe house owned by Friends of Peter. Diana told him Anna's student visa had come through, and she would be travelling to the States to study. Althonat Global had granted her a scholarship. Thomas was in the dining room helping Joachim sort out his favourite snack.

'Martina,' said Barbara. 'You're the toast of Sweden.'

'Hi, Barbara,' said Martina with a warm smile. She excused herself and turned to Barbara. Olausson greeted Barbara with a soft nod and said, 'Nice to see you, Barbara.'

The two women embraced each other in a friendly hug and laughed. 'Brilliant! You did it again, you little rascal,' said Barbara with a teasing glimmer in her eyes.

'Did I?' asked Martina, smiling mischievously.

When the laughter ebbed, Barbara inched in on her and whispered, 'How is your love life?'

'What about it?' said Martina.

'I heard Viviane is back in town and determined to patch it up with her ex-fiancé.'

'You mean that little twit,' said Martina. 'She doesn't stand a chance with Jonas.'

'Oh my, such confidence you have,' said Barbara, wide-eyed. 'Viviane is a stubborn little bitch. Don't underestimate her.'

'Jonas is mine,' whispered Martina. 'Wait until I kick her back into that sinkhole where she came from.'

Barbara giggled, and then turned serious.

'Martina, dear, Thomas is still madly in love with you,' she said in a hushed tone. 'Give him a chance.'

'Barbara, you never change. Now, let me get you something to eat.'

They weaved through the crowd, to the dining area that opened into a banquet hall. A superb quality long birch dining table covered in white linen and twenty chairs stood in the centre of the hall. Eight matching white chromed ceiling lights hung like pendulums over the table, spreading a celebrative light glow over the room.

The caterers, in white-suited attires, held trays of glasses brimming with champagne. Martina gracefully picked two glasses, offering one to Barbara. At the table were served buffet-style snacks. It was self-service. People sat eating at the table, others mingled, talking and eating from small plates balanced in their hands. Martina secured two empty seats at the table from a couple who just finished their meal. Astrid handed Barbara a plate. Barbara's eyes feasted on the magnificent meal, tempted by everything, unsure what to pick. She opted for turkey breast wrap, asparagus, and celery stalks with guacamole.

'Taste the black beans too, with salsa,' said Martina. 'They're my favourite.'

Barbara noticed Lisa, Mona and her husband Roland sitting at the far end of the table and waved. They smiled and waved back.

Barbara ate, and Martina sipped champagne, enjoying the savour of victory. She told Barbara she was going to Gothenburg University the next day to visit her projects.

'The science department?' said Barbara.

'Yes, they need publicity to attract additional funding to match the grants I offered them.'

Thomas joined them at the table with a glass of champagne and a plate of dessert. He took a seat beside Martina. 'Hi, Barbara. How're you doing?'

'Fine,' said Barbara. 'How is the move to Stockholm treating you?'

'Things are much better than I expected,' said Thomas.

Talking about Gothenburg, Martina remembered she hadn't made arrangements for Joachim.

'Thomas, sorry to interrupt,' said Martina. 'I'm going to Gothenburg tomorrow. I'll be back in two days. Could you take care of Joachim?'

'Sure I will,' said Thomas.

A sympathetic smile lit Barbara's face, and she gazed first at Martina and then Thomas. 'It's a challenge juggling work and child.'

'With planning, it's manageable,' said Martina.

In the doorway, Jonas appeared, taking in the trio sitting at one end of the table: Barbara with her back towards him and Martina and Thomas side by side in full view of the door. Martina smiled at him as he came further into the room, but Jonas was no longer in a happy mood. Instead he shot Thomas an angry glare, animosity evident in his face. *What is the moron doing sitting next to her with a smug smile on his face?*

As he came within earshot, Barbara, unaware, talked on. 'You two should get married again. You're such a perfect couple, and we need a wedding.'

Unable to warn Barbara, Martina dropped her jittery gaze to her knotted fingers. The slight smile on her face froze, and she discerned the pain on Jonas' face.

Jonas stopped right behind Barbara's chair, freezing in place when he heard those words. He clenched his fist in a struggle against the urge to smash Barbara's head.

Thomas saw Jonas and the knot of anger in his jaw. He perceived he was jealous of seeing him sitting next to Martina.

Minutes of anxiety ticked away as everyone held their breath. Jonas regained control over his rage, remembering his good manners. He stayed where he was but said, 'Good evening, Mrs Nsamizi.' His steady voice masked the knot in his throat.

Barbara startled and turned around, meeting Jonas' subdued gaze. 'Oh, Dr Eneroth, good evening,' she said, a bit flustered. 'What a pleasant surprise.' She glanced at Martina and raised an eyebrow, half in embarrassment, half in apology.

'Thomas,' said Jonas, greeting him with a cold nod.

'Jonas,' reciprocated Thomas, with great civility.

An awkward silence filled the air. Martina took a deep breath and lifted her gaze, meeting Jonas' disapproving glare. Despite his feigned polite manners, tension was palpable.

'Did I miss something?' asked Jonas. 'I thought I heard some matchmaking game going on.'

'Jonas, drop it,' said Martina.

'No, Martina…let me speak. Appearances can be misleading to outsiders. Truly, only those involved in a couple can judge the compatibility or non-compatibility of a relationship. A relationship once trashed can never live up to expectations, even when forcefully revived. The rest is just a farce.'

'That's a farce coming from an amateur like you,' rebutted Thomas. 'What do you know about relationships?'

'Speak to the point,' Jonas retorted. 'What're you doing here anyway?'

Thomas leaped from his chair and moved to confront him. 'Keep your mouth shut,' he said, banging a fist on the table.

Barbara squeaked.

Jonas stepped up and shook a fist at him, his rage taking on a life of its own.

Martina sprang to her feet. 'Stop it, both of you.'

Jonas stilled at her voice and lowered his fist, but kept his angry glare on Thomas.

'Dr Eneroth, please, I meant no offence,' pleaded Barbara. 'It was just a senseless personal observation.'

'Sit down, Thomas,' said Martina. It was a command. Thomas scowled at her and remained where he was, weighing Jonas' next move.

The air tensed, and the men were still ready to tear each other to pieces. The argument had attracted attention, and guests gathered in the hall, nervous at what might erupt.

'Gentlemen, keep your differences at bay,' thundered Phillip. 'Or go settle it outside in the yard.'

One glance at Phillip, and the men cowered, retreating to their corners. Phillip, in police uniform, had defused the brawl instantaneously, to everyone's relief.

'Hell,' snorted Jonas as he stormed out of the room and left the house. The door slammed, and Martina shuddered. Thomas regained his composure and resumed his seat, ignoring Martina's reprimanding stare.

Phillip cleared his throat and turned to his mother, Barbara. 'Mother, how're you doing?' He then shook Martina's and Thomas' hands.

'It's nice to see you, Phillip,' said Barbara, a soft smile on her face.

'What was that all about?' Phillip asked.

'Please, Phillip, sit down,' said Martina, changing the subject. 'I'll get you something to eat.'

'Phillip, dear, in uniform, at such a grand occasion?' said Barbara.

'I just dropped by, Mother,' said Phillip. 'I'm still on duty.'

'Oh, you should come and see me sometime. We never get to visit.'

Phillip smiled at his mother and shook his head, recalling he'd just been there over the weekend.

Astrid came with a plate of food for Phillip and a glass of champagne.

'Thank you, Astrid,' he said.

'Barbara, you should be proud of Phillip. He's the best,' said Thomas.

Phillip smiled and nudged Thomas' arm as he ate.

'Oh yes, I'm,' said Barbara, smiling back at Thomas.

After coffee and dessert, Phillip turned to Martina. 'Martina, may I have a word with you?' Martina rose from the table, and they went to the Library.

'I want to place police guards around Slottsville house and Althonat Towers.'

'No, Phillip, that won't be necessary.'

'There's a real threat to your life,' said Phillip. 'With due respect, you can't pull this off with your security guards.'

'Why, what happened?'

'Forensic results from the scene of the accident revealed another car was involved. Your parents' Volvo was white in colour. We found traces of black paint in the dent of the wreckage. And in the snow, we got tyre impressions consistent with a big car, possibly a van.'

Martina leaned on the table to anchor her trembling body. She had the sudden thought that Joachim's nightmares about a van were true.

'Murdered,' she managed to say, tears pooling in her eyes.

'Yes, I'm afraid so,' continued Phillip. 'A shoe imprint in the snow was cast at the scene. We're still investigating.'

'Do you have any idea who did it?'

'No, but we intend to find out.'

'Who would do such a vicious thing?' She wiped a tear from her cheek with her hand.

'These are unscrupulous psychopaths with no moral compass – people driven by the delusion of deranged minds. I see them all the time in this longitudinal country. It's full of them.'

'An accident, yes, I could live with that. But murdered?'

'I'm sorry, Martina,' said Phillip. He let a moment elapse as she dealt with her shock and grief. 'Now, how about my suggestion, police guards outside your home and office?'

'No, I don't need police protection.'

'Martina, why are you fighting me on this?' asked Phillip. 'This is a question of national security.'

'National security?' asked Martina, her voice registering surprise.

'I told you, there's a serious threat to your life,' said Phillip. 'Besides, an attempt has already been made on your life. You're a prominent business leader in this country. We can't allow anything to happen to you.'

Martina looked at him but said nothing.

In her hesitant eyes, he sensed there was something more to her resistance. 'Martina, forget the uniform,' said Phillip. 'Look, I'm telling you this as a family friend.'

'Let me think about it.'

'I would rather you didn't.'

Martina slowly paced the room, convinced it was not police protection she needed.

'Is there anything in your family history that could have brought this senseless killing on? Are there enemies or people you know hated your father?'

'My father, by the time of his death, had many enemies due to his work. Citaraph is our foremost contender.' Uncomfortable under his penetrating gaze, Martina turned away. His persistent sternness intimidated her.

Phillip regarded at her intently, thwarted by her unyielding attitude, lost in her shifting moods, crumbling emotional façade, and outright lack of cooperation. What was she hiding?

'Martina…'

'I'm going to Gothenburg tomorrow. I will speak to you when I return.'

'I'm sorry for imparting this horrible news to you,' said Phillip. 'I'll wait. But call me when you return.' He paused. 'And let me congratulate you on your major accomplishment with Rensblad.' With that, Phillip walked out of the room.

'Thank you,' she said, and then called his name.

'Yes,' said Phillip returning to the room.

She wanted to tell him everything about Citaraph and the Group, and that she had an idea of who had broken into her house, and who had tried to kill her, but she remembered, she must wait for Scorpio to come up with more witnesses. A lump grew in her throat. She coughed, and said, "I appreciate your concern.'

'Safe journey then,' said Phillip as he stepped out of the room.

Though it had been a lovely day that exceeded expectations, it ended for her with feverish shivers. The confirmation of her parents' murder opened a new dimension in her life. The buffet she had eaten had vanished from her system, and she felt famished. The launch and celebrations earlier in the day were no consolation, wiped from her mind by the dire news. She racked her brain for answers. Questions of who and why afflicted her weary mind like a plague of hornets, and she felt as if her head was swelling from internal pressure. Her eyes darted across the room as her mind cast about on how and where to proceed.

At last she emerged from the Library to receive the farewells of her guests and their gratitude for a historic day. It was past eleven when the last finally left.

Alone in the kitchen, she leaned against the kitchen sink, exhausted by the debilitating effects of the day. Her limbs ached. It seemed whenever she tried to rise above her depression, an evil force clamped her down, dragging her deeper into the vast abyss of despair.

'Care for a cup of tea?' asked Jonas, standing at the threshold.

Martina startled. 'I thought you'd left.'

'Not without kissing you good night,' said Jonas. 'Now, will you have tea?'

'Yes, I'll have some,' said Martina. 'Where did you go?'

Jonas said nothing but noticed turbulent emotions in her eyes. He knew something was wrong, but for now he quietly brewed two cups of tea.

Martina uttered a sigh that was almost a sob and sank into a dining chair at the table. They sat sipping tea. Conversation was stilted.

'What's up?' asked Jonas. 'What took you so long with the detective?'

'Can't we talk about something else?'

'Then let's drink up and go to bed.'

His words were loaded with expectation. Yet all Martina wanted was a good night's sleep. 'Then I suggest you use the guest room, because I'm sleeping alone.'

'What's wrong, darling?'

The compassion in his voice did it for her. Her barriers were breached, and she disintegrated into an avalanche of inconsolable sobs. Her body convulsed, raging in spasms of anger, pain, and grief.

Jonas was staggered, confused and even disturbed by the sudden gust of sorrow. What was aggravating her? He took her in his arms. She leaned against him; her body racked by violent sobs. He caressed her back, reassuring her.

'Did the detective upset you?' asked Jonas.

'I…I'm just overwhelmed by everything,' she stammered between sobs, wiping tears with the back of her hand.

'Use my shirt,' said Jonas. 'And you're freezing cold. Let me get you something to eat.'

'No…no food,' said Martina, between hitches of sobs.

'Tell me,' said Jonas. 'What did the detective say?'

'You keep asking about the detective,' she said, and stopped crying. 'What was that about you and Thomas?'

'Martina, I don't want to fight about that.'

'You shouldn't have taken it out on Thomas.'

'And you think what Barbara said was polite?' said Jonas, shifting her so he could look in her eyes.

'She didn't mean it that way,' said Martina as she straightened up and glared at him.

'Oh yes, you sat there with your blockheaded ex-husband, and Barbara blubbered on about your reunion, and you expected me to smile?'

'You're crazy,' said Martina, scowling at him through moist eyes. 'Barbara has a way with words. She never meant any harm. Thomas was calm, but you attacked him.'

'Tell me, tell me now, Martina,' said Jonas. 'Are you still in love with Thomas?'

'Don't be ridiculous.'

'You call this ridiculous?' said Jonas. 'I know you still have a thing for him. Why were his eyeglasses in Landegrind? What was he doing there that weekend? Tell me you love him. Tell me now, and I'll walk out that door and never come back. Then you can go marry him.'

'Keep your voice down,' said Martina. 'Joachim is sleeping. Why are you so angry? Thomas helped me with repairs in Landegrind, and he forgot his glasses. That's all. There's nothing going on between me and him.'

'I wanted to help with those repairs, and you turned me down. Why? You wanted to be with him, didn't you?'

'For God's sake, stop it,' she said in a hushed tone. 'I don't need this. I'm going to bed.'

'This is not over yet.'

'I'm not discussing this anymore.' Martina rose to her feet. 'It's childish, Jonas. Grow up.'

Jonas stood up and gazed at her, a questioning frown over his brow. He breathed, 'You didn't mean that about sleeping alone. Did you?'

'Of course not, but you're to behave. Joachim is sleeping upstairs.'

Martina walked to her bedroom. Jonas changed his mind. He did not follow her. He went to the guest room instead. He wanted to be alone. Also, should Joachim wander around unexpectedly, he could still keep a straight face if the boy discovered him in the guest room rather than in his mother's bed.

Jonas was familiar with the guest room and quickly settled in. It was an ensuite, and a double bed dominated the room. He opened the chest of drawers and found a T-shirt and cotton pants. He changed, went to the bathroom, brushed his teeth, and got into bed.

He lay awake, disturbed by Martina's lack of understanding for his rage at blockheaded Thomas. He had taken it out on Thomas because he was the source of their problems. It showed in his lustful eyes – the way he looked at Martina – that he still loved her. Mrs Nsamizi may have articulated what she saw as love between them, but it was unpalatable of her to encourage his offensive hunger for Martina. If Thomas did not cloud Martina's mind, they would have been married by now. He drifted into uneasy sleep.

*****

In the night, the moonlight shimmered through the curtains, bathing the guest room in a dim yellow glow. Martina wandered into the room and gazed at Jonas asleep. He lay on his back, eyes closed, looking peaceful, a far cry from his earlier state. She loved him but hated how he spiralled into insecurity whenever Thomas came to mind. How could she make him understand her love, her commitment to him? She went on her knees by the bedside, and leaned over him, feeling his soft breath on her face. Bending closer, she gently kissed his warm lips. He stirred and opened his eyes.

'Martina,' he said and stretched out in bed.

'You look peaceful when you're sleeping.'

'What time is it?'

'Past two,' she said. 'I want to talk.'

'Creep in here,' said Jonas as he pushed the duvet to one side and moved to accommodate her. 'I'm glad you want to talk. It's a healthy sign.'

She got in bed and rested her head on his arm. She wanted to lay close to him to soothe her disrupted nerves. Her mind was still reeling from her encounter with Phillip. He pulled the cover over her and rested his other arm on her waist.

She cleared her throat and said, 'They were murdered.'

'Who were murdered?' said Jonas. 'Be specific. You're not making sense.'

'My parents. They were run off the road by a van. That's what Phillip said.'

'Jesus, Martina, I'm so sorry,' said Jonas. 'Darling, that's a horrendous thing to happen to one's parents. Did he say who did it?' He moved his hand, caressing her back.

'No,' said Martina and then, added after a pause, 'Inspector Tord tried to pass it off as an accident.'

'I wonder why.'

'It could be coincidence or malice – or he's hiding something.'

'What do you mean he's hiding something?'

'I called him about the investigation some time back. His voice sounded familiar, like someone I'd met before.'

'Where could you have met him?' said Jonas. 'You think he was involved in the murder?'

'I don't know, but I intend to find out who murdered my parents.'

'You can't do that,' said Jonas. 'Let the police do their job.'

'You don't understand. This is personal.'

'It's a police case. Phillip must have told you they're investigating.'

'I know, but I need to do my own investigation.'

'Forgive me, darling, but you're an intelligent woman, and you know better. That's a precarious undertaking.'

'I have to. Phillip is a good detective but there are things I'd rather investigate myself.'

She wanted to tell Jonas about the threat Phillip had spoken about and about police protection, but decided against it. She did not want to burden him with her problems. Grief overwhelmed her again, and tears rolled down her face. She sniffled.

'Please, darling, don't start with tears again,' said Jonas. 'I can't bear to see you cry. Stop talking about digging up old stuff. It will only aggravate your health. Let's take a vacation, get away from these pressures, and have a change of scene. You'll gain a new perspective and feel better. All this madness will…will…clear up.'

Martina muffled his words with a kiss on the lips. He reciprocated, kissing her and drawing her onto him, kissing her again till she gasped for air. His hand caressed her back, gliding under her silk pyjamas. His touch was magic. It soothed her wounded mind, softened her rigid muscles, and tantalized her inner longing, reawakening her sensual desire. And his smell, that Jonas scent, intoxicated her senses. She warmed to him, welcoming his advances, mirroring his hands, dragging his pants down. In one swift move, she was straddling him. She stilled a second, gasped, and then started moving, taking him with her, riding him, throwing off all restraint. She rode on wild waves of sheer ecstasy. Something burst inside her, and an uninhibited cry of satisfaction engulfed her. She collapsed on his chest. He groaned deep in his throat.

After several hours of sleep, she opened her eyes. At first she was disoriented, confused, and then she saw Jonas. They were entangled in each other – their legs entwined, his arm around her and hers around his neck. She stirred free, careful not to wake him, but Jonas moved and opened his eyes. He gazed at her and smiled.

'Go back to sleep,' she whispered.

'Now, where were we?' asked Jonas as he rubbed his drowsy eyes and gazed into her sleepy baby blue eyes.

'What?'

'That little romantic escapade you indulged me in, what was it about?' he said, drawing her closer.

'Take it as a declaration of my undying love for you,' she said. 'I do love you, Jonas.'

'Ah, Martina, you never cease to fascinate me. You entice me and beguile me. No day is like the other,' said Jonas. 'I love you, and I love waking up in the same bed with you.' He smiled, and he then added, 'Let's make it official. Let's tell the whole world.' He trailed a finger over her cheek and kissed her lips.

Thick, sultry air in the room somehow changed the words, and they disturbed her mood. She said nothing but glanced at the clock on the wall.

'Ooh, it's dawn,' she said, and scrambled out of bed. 'I've work to do before I leave for Gothenburg.'

He grasped her wrist and pulled her back in bed.

'Jonas!'

'Get back here,' said Jonas. 'Why is it that whenever I talk about tying the knot, you freak out? What're you afraid of?'

'That's pretty heavy stuff to discuss early in the morning.'

'I want you to be my wife.'

'I know, darling,' said Martina. 'But can't you just move in with me, and we can live happily ever after?'

'Live in sin?'

'It's good enough for me.'

Jonas rose abruptly on his elbow and furrowed his brows, seriously gazing down at her. He looked for that little smile on her face. It wasn't there.

'Ah, ah, Martina, no,' he said. 'That's not good enough for me. I want us to be married.' His disturbed gaze held her wavering eyes.

She broke eye contact and buried her face in the pillow. She couldn't bear the hurt in his eyes.

'Martina?'

'Can't we talk about this when I return from Gothenburg?'

Jonas flopped back on the pillow, exhaled, and gazed up at the ceiling.

'Okay, we'll talk when you return, but please, moving in with you is out of the question.' Then an outrageous thought came to mind, and he added, 'If it's your wealth you're worried about, I'll sign any prenuptial papers your lawyers put before me.'

Martina abruptly lifted her head off the pillow and gave him an icy stare.

'That's a preposterous, absurd cockeyed idea,' she blurted, 'and you know it. I've never thought of you as a gold-digger in our relationship, never.' She cast aside the bedclothes and headed upstairs to take a shower.

'Then what is it?' yelled Jonas.

He sprang up from bed, frustration eating at him. He strolled to the bathroom and took a quick shower. In a special closet reserved for him he found a spanking new suit, a present from Martina, which he had forgotten to take with him some time back. Beside it, hung a white shirt and silver-gray tie. He dressed and went upstairs.

He knocked on her bedroom door. She opened, still in her bathrobe. The sweet scent of her body wash swamped him. He stood on the threshold, mesmerized by her unexpected warm smile, and the graciousness with which she tilted her head made him want to undress and get back in bed.

The shower had shifted her mood, lightening it up as she realized she would not be seeing him for two days. Yet, deep inside she maintained there would be no signing of prenuptials if she was to marry him. Whatever she owned would be theirs.

'You're ready to leave?' she said. 'It's still early.'

'I have to be in the theatre by six, supervising students in non-surgical therapy.'

'I wanted to make you breakfast.'

'I'll grab a sandwich at the canteen,' said Jonas. 'I wanted to wish you a safe journey, and please think about what I said.'

'I'll be back the day after tomorrow.'

'Thanks for the suit,' said Jonas. 'It fits perfectly.'

'You look gorgeous,' said Martina as she reached up and gave him a quick kiss on lips. He pulled her into a passionate embrace and kissed her long and hard. 'Bye, darling,' he said, walking away. He already missed her.

Chapter 40

On the final day of the seminar, University hall was seated to full capacity with medical students, university personnel and business people. Martina made her closing remarks.

'Malaria is becoming resistant to chloroquine, and Althonat Global is on the brink of formulating a new natural antimalarial therapy, Botanik Herbier,' she said. 'With that remark we come to the end of this seminar. Thank you all for attending. And for those interested in our medical exchange programs in Africa and Asia, check out our website. You may make out applications online.'

Resounding applause startled her as the audience rose in a standing ovation. The head student came forward, thanked her, and handed her a gorgeous bouquet of flowers. The cheers blended into animated talk as the students gathered up front to thank her.

Charlotte, Jonas' niece, appeared at her side. 'Thank you for such a wonderful seminar,' she said, her face beaming.

'So, are you inspired to come and work for me?' asked Martina with a smile.

'I would like to go on the exchange program first before I make up my mind.'

'Just call me when you are ready.'

'I will,' said Charlotte; then, 'Let me help you with that,' she said as she took the flowers.

Grabbing her briefcase and laptop, Martina looked around for Evert, her bodyguard. He was supposed to be somewhere in the room, keeping an eye on her.

'Are you looking for someone?' asked Charlotte.

'Yes, my security man. I came in with him.'

'Maybe he is waiting downstairs,' said the head student.

That was highly unlikely, thought Martina. 'Anyway, I'll go down and look,' she said.

Charlotte and the head student escorted her to the elevators. The head student pressed the button, and the elevator jolted to a stop. The doors glided open. Charlotte handed her the flowers, and the head student thanked her again. Martina stepped into the elevator.

Moving to the back of the elevator, she retrieved her smartphone from her jacket pocket and pressed the on button to check for missed calls. As the elevator doors were gliding shut, a man in a slick dark suit rushed in just in time. He stood on one side of the elevator, observing her. An odd sensation came over Martina as she realised that, whoever he was, he had his penetrating eyes fixed on her. She looked up from the phone and gazed at the man. Her jaw dropped, her hand went limp, and the phone dropped to the elevator floor.

She scrambled to pick it up, but he was faster. He picked it up and glared at it, noting it was the flashy latest solid model with multiple functions. 'Splendid gadget,' he said as he handed it to her. 'You should be more careful with it.'

Martina took the phone without a word. Her heart was racing. What was he doing here?

Finally, she found her tongue. 'Are you stalking me, Dr Rangor?'

'Why would I do that?' said Rangor. 'I happened to be in the vicinity, and I heard about your seminar. I came to attend.'

'You shouldn't have come,' said Martina, her tone abrupt and terse.

'Brilliant performance, Doctor,' he said. 'I wouldn't have missed it for the world. So you're ready to stun the world again with another wonder drug, Botanik Herbier.'

Martina said nothing.

The elevator doors opened on the ground floor, and Martina walked out with Rangor at her heels.

She paused outside the elevator, scanning the huge hall and reception area for Evert and Ludwig. They were not there. She checked at the cafeteria at the far end of the corridor, hoping they were having coffee. Rangor followed her and continued to bore her with his nonsensical gabble.

The cafeteria was closed. 'Looking for something?' asked Rangor. Martina ignored him. He regarded her; her delicate skin, sleek golden hair and designer skirt suit that shaped her perfect body. She was extravagantly beautiful. He felt a powerful attraction, and wanted to act on it. But not today. Today he had other plans and depending on her reaction, he would decide.

People shuffled around them, passing and talking.

'You live in a fortress these days,' said Rangor. 'Are you protecting yourself from danger or isolating yourself from the world?'

'Skip the crap, and stop following me around,' she said. 'I can sue you for stalking.'

Surprisingly, Rangor remained silent. From the corner of her eye, Martina glanced at the odd creature walking beside her and noticed his cynically contorted smile; it was an expression of perhaps pain and rage, but she couldn't be sure. She wished he would speak his mind and leave her alone. She liked him better when he spoke. That way she knew where she had him.

'You made a fatal mistake launching Rensblad,' said Rangor abruptly. 'You've angered the medical establishment and even the government. And you've started a pharmaceutical war.'

Her mind strayed for a second to a disturbing phone call she'd received, in her hotel room, last night. A disguised frosty voice had threatened her to withdraw Rensblad from the market or live to regret it. It even spoke about a legal claim on Rensblad. Was it Rangor, she wondered?

Suddenly, she turned on her heel, and faced him. Realizing she stood too close, she backed one step away but maintained her scorching eyes on him. 'I do what I do for the wellness of my patients,' she declared. 'The medical establishment and government have duped the people of this country. Instead of protecting them, they've collaborated with Citaraph to destroy lives.'

'You've got in over your head now,' said Rangor. 'With that mentality you're treading on dangerous ground, risking everything you've worked for. You're breaking the law when you criticize medical authorities and government.'

'And what is the law? That the privileged should band together to exploit and dominate the underprivileged for the sake of profits?'

'Listen, your father was a friend of mine, and I want to help you out of this mess you've created for yourself.'

Martina's ears scorched at the sound of his diabolical words, the insinuations, the empty talk offered as bait to ensnare her into his manipulative schemes.

'Excuse me?' said Martina. 'You were never Father's friend. You don't even know the meaning of the word. You and Stellan conspired against him. You stole the Rensblad formula and sold it to Citaraph.'

'Hey, it was his portion. Stellan owned it, and he had a right to do as he pleased with it.'

'It's all lies,' said Martina. 'That's the name of your trade. You two will end up in jail for industrial espionage. And that is a promise.'

'You have no proof,' said Rangor, observing her face intently for any giveaway sign that she might have evidence against him.

Martina remained impassive, giving nothing away, understanding he was an arrogant psychopath with no sense of remorse or guilt. Anger flared up in her voice. 'Get out of my sight, you, conniving parasite,' she said, biting off each word. 'Go cheat someone else.'

In a rage, Rangor yanked her arm. She jerked out of his grip and staggered backwards out of his reach. She tottered on her heels but recovered balance. 'Ouch, that hurt!' she screamed.

'Don't ever call me a parasite,' said Rangor.

The reception clerk, who had observed the whole thing, approached Martina. People all around glared. Rangor took off and headed for the exit.

'Did he hurt you, miss?' asked the clerk. 'I can call security.'

'No, I'm all right, thank you,' she answered as she put down her bags and flowers and rubbed her bruised arm.

The clerk stood by, noticing she was shaken. 'Are you sure you're okay?'

'Yes, I'm fine,' said Martina. 'I'd better get going.'

'Do you want me to escort you to the parking lot?'

'No, I'll manage,' said Martina. 'Thanks anyway.' She picked up her stuff, and then as an afterthought she asked, 'Would you like these flowers?'

The clerk's face lit up in a surprised smile. 'Yes, I would like them. Thank you,' he said as he took the flowers with a wide grin on his face.

'By the way, have you seen two security guards in black suits and white shirts?'

'No, I haven't seen them. I just started the night shift,' said the clerk. 'I'm sorry.'

'Well then, I'd better get going.'

The clerk wandered back to his desk with the flowers.

As Martina walked towards the exit, she called Evert's number. There was no answer. She called Ludwig's number. No answer. Her heart sank.

It was past seven in the evening when she emerged from the reception area. She stood at the top of the stairs, gazing into the dark parking lot, unnerved. Rangor might be out there. Panic-stricken, and upset, she carefully went down the stairs, watching her surroundings. Her focus returned when she saw the black Volvo in the parking lot.

Her tweed skirt suit no longer provided enough warmth in the evening chill. The gabardine trench coat fluttered and flapped in the wind like the trepidation in her stomach. The air was crisp and frosty. She was hungry and cold.

She came to the Volvo. It stood empty; no Evert, no Ludwig. It dawned on her she must deal with the issue of her missing staff immediately. But something blocked her mind – nervousness maybe. She must think. Surely Christer, the Security Director, had not changed plans and forgotten to inform her. Or had Rangor hurt them, kidnapped them? Jesus, she hoped they were all right.

A broad-shouldered man in a dark leather jacket with metallic spikes passed by. He wore a broad-brimmed black hat. Martina's mind flashed back to the day of the attempted assassination. He resembled the man she'd seen in the café. Her heart flipped. Quickly she retrieved her spare keys from her handbag and opened the Volvo door. She got in the driver's seat and, with shaking hands, dug for her encrypted phone again and made a call.

The Security Director answered, 'Christer.'

'It's Martina. Have you heard from Evert and Ludwig?'

'No, they're supposed to be with you.'

'They're not, and I can't find them.'

'Where are you?'

'I'm still at the University campus.'

'When did you last see them?'

'In the afternoon. Ludwig stayed outside in the car, and Evert came with me into the conference hall, but when the seminar ended, he wasn't there. Neither is Ludwig in the car.'

'I'll find out. In the meantime, I'll call Securitos in Gothenburg and get you a replacement detail.'

'I can't wait here, Christer,' said Martina. 'It's spooky. I'll drive to Securitos and pick up replacements myself. Let them know I'm coming.'

'Keep your phone on so I have your bearings,' said Christer. 'And as soon as you get to Securitos, switch it off.'

'Okay,' said Martina. 'And Christer, I want you to know Rangor was here.'

'What? How?' asked Christer, clearly surprised. 'What did he want?'

'I don't know, but he was angry we'd launched Rensblad.'

'Martina, get out of there, and get out fast,' said Christer. 'It might be a trap. I'll call Securitos.'

Martina hung up, cradled the phone and put it on loudspeaker.

Two parking spaces away from the Volvo, she noticed a black Dodge van with tinted windows. She couldn't see inside. She took a deep breath and started the car engine. The Volvo eased out of its space and accelerated to the driveway. As she left the university area, she saw the Dodge leaving the parking lot. She stopped at Vasagatan for the bus to pass, and then accelerated towards Vasaplatsen. At the crossing of Västra Hamngatan and Nya Allén, she stopped at a red light, and in the rear-view mirror she spotted the Dodge behind her.

When the traffic light turned green, she signalled and turned onto Nya Allén and accelerated with surprising speed across lanes, passing other cars. She was heading west. The tram followed behind, coming between her and the Dodge. She floored the gas pedal, the momentum throwing her back in the seat as she pressed on to Norra Allégatan, speeding through a red light. She tightened her grip on the steering wheel, her heart pounding.

The phone vibrated. She pressed the button and answered, 'Martina.'

'It's Christer. Securitos have been alerted. They're expecting you.'

'Christer, I'm being tailed by a black Dodge van,' said Martina. 'Take this number down.' She read the number to him.

'I got it. Keep driving, don't stop,' said Christer. 'I'll deploy the chopper. We may need it.'

Martina hung up and checked her mirrors again. The Dodge was not there. She breathed a sigh of relief, hoping it was just her nerves getting the better of her. Still, the whereabouts of Evert and Ludwig were a mystery.

Traffic thinned out as she left the city centre. Keeping her eyes on the road, she knew she was almost there. Her hands were clammy and sweaty and ached from gripping the steering wheel tightly.

At Järntorgsmötet, she stopped for a red light and then merged onto Masthamnsbro. The fading shimmer of light revealed the gleaming sea to her left. It was covered by crystal ice. In combination with the marina, the boats and the silver-grey skyline, it was a stunning view. A few pedestrians strolled along the Waterfront promenade. As she approached the intersection of Masthamnsbro and Esperantoplatsen, she saw chopper lights twinkling above the horizon like jewels in the sky.

Her phone buzzed. She answered, 'Martina.'

'It's Captain John. I'm coming in with the chopper. I can see you. Keep going. You're almost there.'

'Thank you, John,' said Martina as she hauled the Volvo towards Skeppsbron.

When she looked to the right, her heart fell. The Dodge emerged from Esperantoplatsen, plunged across the street without warning, aiming straight for the Volvo. Its steel front bumpers glared like weapons, ready to kill.

Amidst the horror, her reactions were impulsive. Desperate, she swerved the Volvo in a U-turn, but not quickly enough to avoid impact. The Dodge slammed into the Volvo, propelling it into a vicious spin in the air. It tumbled over the guardrail and into the icy sea. A despairing scream escaped from inside the Volvo, but no one heard it. The sky flipped upside down and went dark, cold shock seeped through her body. Her life became like a light switch – first on, and then off.

Screeching and chaos erupted among the people on the promenade walk as they took cover from flying metal and breaking glass.

The blast of cracking ice sounded like a giant glass breaking; shards spattered in the air like flying drones with projectiles. The impact of the collision and scraping of metal on asphalted road, struck sparks in the atmosphere. The smell of burning tyres and petrol fumes fouled the air. Then there was silence, as if whatever the sea had swallowed belonged to it.

In the chopper, Captain John was appalled, not believing his eyes. 'Lord, no, nooo… Martina, Martina!' he shrieked into the phone.

The Dodge taxied down Masthamnsbron towards Olof Palmes Plats. John tore the skies asunder as he revved the chopper's rotor blades, chasing the Dodge down the road. He hovered over the Dodge and fired artillery. Gunshots ripped through the metallic roof of the van. The Dodge surged and swayed but managed to zigzag into underground parking beneath the Stenaline building.

Captain John, numb, fired up the helicopter. As he headed back to base, he relayed the shocking news to Christer and then to Securitos.

That night, the world press converged on Gothenburg and broke the shocking news. The world's most renowned natural healer had disappeared under the icy sea in a fatal car accident. Given frosty temperatures in the sea and blowing glacial winds, Martina's survival hung on a thread. Newspapers speculated wildly on who might succeed her at Althonat Global.

High above the clustered houses and the grey harbour skies of Gothenburg, the loving spirit hovered and is free.

Note From The Author

I have been delighted and thrilled that you picked this book for your reading experience.

I would like to invite you to review, Traitors From Inside Out, and post your views at Amazon.com, Barnesandnoble.com, and at Goodreads.com.
Much appreciated.

Connect with me on social media:

https://www.facebook.com/mmjustine/
https://twitter.com/mmjustineAuthor

Join my mailing list by visiting my website:

https://www.mmjustine.com/